Near Dracula's Castle

Near Dracula's Castle

Patrick Vaitus

iUniverse, Inc.
Bloomington

Near Dracula's Castle

iUniverse books may be ordered through booksellers or by contacting:

iUniverse
1663 Liberty Drive
Bloomington, IN 47403
www.iuniverse.com
1-800-Authors (1-800-288-4677)

ISBN: 978-1 4620 3433 8 (sc)
ISBN: 978-1-4620-3435-2 (hc)
ISBN: 978-1-4620-3434-5 (ebk)

Printed in the United States of America

iUniverse rev. date: 07/20/2011

For thousands of years until now we have been here. For thousand of years ago until now we have been living **near Dracula's castle***.*

We are Romanian witches.

. . . . .And we are strong.

Chapter 1

Even the people would say it is rough
Even the people would say it is witches stuff
The people can say what they want.
But I will always believe in the power of Magic.
-Romanian folk song

Reluctantly, I walked on the street for almost half of the day. I walked around the city with no destination in mind. I walked, unable to focus on anything in particular. It is like I am not myself. It is hard to describe how I feel at this moment. I am sure I have never felt like this before. Never . . . This is all very strange.

Allow me to introduce myself, my name is Laura Williams. You might know me, I am a very famous pop singer. You may have heard some of my songs. It is normal for me to walk in the streets and be recognized. I cannot walk in this city without being approached or accosted. I can hear people around me asking themselves. Is that really her?"

I really like that feeling.

I finally have finished my latest album, and I became a worldwide success. Combining the harmony of the songs, and the passion of my music with its lyrics, it has made my music clearer, more vibrant, and stronger. This kind of success can make your life complete. It's unique melody fills you with all these wonderful feelings. Surrender to my music, and it can do wonderful things to you. It is like a drug that makes you fly in a different world, in your own world, and your own paradise. My pop music is as strong as a drug. It gives you a high, as you have never had before. It is a world where you like to be, and want to be again. As result of this euphoric feeling you set the melody on repeat. The melody will continue to bring you into this wonderful world again, and again. You will discover new thoughts and feelings each time. You will listen to it again and again until you become elated. When you are sad, alone, and bored by your life, go to your room and light a candle. Put my music on and let the melody start flowing over you. Focus on the words, and really live the music. If you can do that my music will lift you out of this physical life, and into your own world. Realize the blessings of your life and it's happiness, and you will want these feelings forever. Listen repeatedly to my music and let it fill your life with vibrant colors.

I have had many shows, always-full to capacity. I have seen people enjoying my music, being filled with ecstasy watching me, and listening to my music so intently. Everyone excitedly is singing with me, never missing a beat. It is like being together in a trance, going into a wonderful world. It is like touching a superior stage of meditation. It is very unique, every time something new and every time something undoubtedly different.

It is hard to believe that was only a year ago . . .

And now, reluctantly I am walking with no destination in mind for almost half of the day, feeling the vibrancy of the city around me. I find myself in the middle of Calgary's downtown. I have always found this city to have a human face. I am thirty-five years old and I have been around the world. I have observed cities and towns, and explored the countryside. I have watched people at work, at play, at happiness and madness. My comparisons come not from movies or books, but from what I have personally experienced in both my memories and my current life.

This Plaza is perfect for me right now with its fountain right in the middle and at the same level of the street. I can touch the water, hear it, and feel it. It is as if a friendly artist designed it just now, and just for you. His only task was to be closer to you using his skills. I walked down the street, aware of all the reflections in the shop windows. I come to my favorite metal horse standing in the street. It is large and in-congruent in stature. It respects the proportions of a horse but on a much bigger scale. It always reminds me of the legend of the conquest of Troy, a simple horse trick to destroy the central gate and then to conquer the entire city.

I walked in the city without a plan of where to go or what to do. The world is in different colors as I walk and observe. This world changes every day. I stop and gaze into the windows of a travel agency. Maybe I need a vacation. It might work out for me, as I need a break. But where do I want to go? My success makes me . . . somehow alone. I have no close friends that I can think of to travel with to a destination. Though a vacation would definitely be welcome right now. At least if nothing else it might help me to pass this stage, this undecided feeling that I have been carrying with me as of late. Maybe I have to go to a place where I can be close with my passion, which is magic.

I have always been attracted to magic, to the paranormal, and such things, but I have never become proficient in any way. I wish it so much, maybe even more than my music.

The posters look so inviting, especially the one with the dark castle . . . Romania. A sensation of dizziness comes over me. This one castle in particular might be Dracula's castle. I am so attracted to the history of Dracula's legend. I think there is an unclear line between history and legend, between real things and imaginative things. I want to know so much more. I am attracted to Dracula and all its tales both fact and fiction. I reach out to steady myself against the window frame and see an agent inside start to rise out of his chair.

It is getting cold very quickly. We have learned in Calgary to accept the way the weather can change so dramatically in such a short period of time, sometimes hours. But I still shiver and sweat with every turn. Perhaps I'll hurry along to the Bankers towers.

*   *   *

There is a man at the upper level of the Commercial Center of the Bankers Hall. He is just sitting there alone on a big chair. His feet are bare; he sits in a lotus position. He appears to be focusing on something, but for the people who pass close to him, he appears just a strange man. As it is a free country here the people don't pay to much attention.

"Where are you? Where are you? I know you are close by."

*   *   *

Banker Hall is twin towers. From the outside you may be impressed by their grandness, and you forget to notice their slight detail, that their colors are slightly different. You may pass by this detail as this is the only thing that differentiates each tower from the other. I will go by the West Tower entrance. I stand here taking in my surroundings. Two huge and modern towers stand here, and at the entrance of the West Tower a couple of statues are suggesting to us that homo sapiens are rising right now from the animal kingdom. The first statue is just here where I can touch it. I am touching this naked man statue. I hug it. Two handsome men who pass by smile; they recognize me but they don't intrude. I continue into the vastness of the West Tower. There are more statues like outside. It is like an extension of the outside genesis. When it is minus thirty-five or more in the winter the dichotomy of inside is striking the snow covering outdoors and the vibrant lush indoors. Through the glass corridors, called +15's because they are raised 15 feet above the street, I can go from here to almost every part of the downtown core. It is a blessing in the winter. I think we Canadians could be the first who are able to send colonies to moon or to the planet Mars. We know how to live indoors. We know how to manage and to live in the arctic weather. Sometimes I think that even though the planet Mars may be just a little bit colder, I think we could manage this issue.

I very much like this building. Three years ago I had a lover who worked in these towers and I came here every day. I still recognize some of the people. For example, one of the security guards, he is still here. I find him handsome with his muscular body and shaved head. Many of the men in this building seem to work out, and they seem to all have very nice bodies. There must be a gym in the building they can use. My lover . . . . he was gorgeous, with an exceptional body, from swimming, working out and eating very carefully every day. I was so much in love with him, until I came to understand that loving him was like dealing with an iceberg. The love was weak and not reciprocated. You can try to convince yourself you love someone, but if the emotion is not strong the love cannot last very long. I was always asking myself why a good looking man such him had such a bad personality. No other answer came to mind than he just is what he is. End of story.

My thoughts of where she was came back to haunt me. I haven't felt this strange since recording the album. I say 'the album' even though there had been previous ones. But they didn't connect and they didn't sell. I was noticed and some people listened to it, but those albums didn't take my listeners or me to that other place. That other place for my fans was what I wanted. I searched and prayed for that, but the inspiration was elusive. Until I dreamed of her and my life turned to celebrity overnight.

I dreamed about her. I dreamed of this tiny lovely girl. I need to be clear about this, as I take dreams very seriously. I believe that the spirits speak to us through our dreams. They give us guidance and advice. She started to play with me. We played together all night. Yes, I think that was all we did the first night. She did not even mention her name. And I . . . being afraid of destroying our fragile friendship, did not ask her. For me she was like a fragile China doll. I always played with her with immense care. So when this little girl said "I want to be your friend", I listened. And I enjoyed her friendship.

When I awoke the next morning it felt so real, but by noon I felt like it was a dream. I feel like she may be my 'inner child' and perhaps she is. The inner game can be abstract. But she was so real and by evening I felt like crying over a friend who I would never see again. But then . . . I dreamed her again! I laughed and she laughed with me with a crystal laugh. She had a wisdom that exceeded her appearance, and her talent and understanding of the world was beyond her age. It excited and stimulated me. Yet she was the one who asked me questions, questions that took me deep inside, and opened places within me. I knew it was a dream. Don't ask me how but I knew, and I didn't want it to end. I began to feel an anxiety and fear that it would be over, and I would forget. Or even worse, never see her again! There was still so much to discover. I begged her to meet me again. She said to go to my cabin in the woods. It was deep winter by that time. My property is almost sixty acres of the boreal forest and in the middle is my cabin and I have always loved going there alone, even in the winter. This cabin is a piece of me; a piece of my personality. I can stand there alone in the middle of the boreal forest.

After my delicious black morning coffee, and my breakfast comprised of just one banana, I started to figure out things. I needed to be there at the cabin.

I packed my backpack with the essentials and dressed in layers to deal with the cold snap we were experiencing. I regret now not cutting more wood in the fall. Even though I have an efficient fireplace and a cook stove and the fireplace can hold huge logs; making the atmosphere in my cabin warm and cozy. I might not have enough wood to last my visit.

Driving my Jeep I reached the outskirts of the city, and though the temperature was a frightening minus twenty-five the sun was still bright. I always thought this is very normal for Alberta, so cold but a nice shiny sun. I stopped at the small general store on the way to pick up groceries and a bottle of Canadian rye whiskey.

The roads were now snow packed but clear and I pulled off the highway at the trail to the cabin. The old road was drifted over completely with snow and as I expected closed. I started to dig through the snow beneath the tree where I left the sled in the fall. I piled all of the stuff that I brought with me into the sled. I locked the Jeep and started on the long trek to the cabin. It was going to take me more than an hour in this bad weather. It was hard going but I was excited to get to the cabin and when I turned the last bend and saw the picture postcard cabin I stopped. I just sat on the sled and breathed the fresh crisp air and listened to the wind shift through the branches, causing the snow to swirl in beautiful sparkling patterns.

I opened the door to the cabin and it felt almost colder inside than out. It would be a chilly few hours before the cabin would be warm.

As usual when I arrived I touched my dream catcher in the big window. It is hand made by a wizard, my friend the North Indian wizard. He told me this is the first thing that I should always do when I come into the cabin because, in the woods there are so many evil spirits and the dream catcher will catch them for me. As a result they would be unable to penetrate my cabin. I can sleep well here through the night and they will stay outside unable to catch me, unable to badly influence my dreams.

My old friend, he is a North Indian. He is wizard North Indian or . . . so he pretends to be a wizard. I admire him so very much. We have spent many long summer evenings together here, or at his place. We have stayed watching the sunset, having a nice fire in the fire pit, smoking and discussing magic. I am so fascinated about everything magic entails. He has never proved his abilities in spectacular magic to me. Even without proof magic will remain my first fascination, even beyond my music.

Only needing one match for both fires, the fireplace and stove very quickly sent out welcome waves of heat. I immediately pulled back the quilts on the bed so the sheets could find the warmth as well. I wondered how soon I could crawl in between them and dream of my sweet friend and what she would tell me. I opened a can of stew and put it on the stove to heat. To warm myself up I chose to have a big glass of whiskey. I also lit a couple of candles. I feel like candles warm the cold air and create a warm atmosphere of the cabin much more quickly than just a fire.

Still in my parka and boots I sat in front of the fireplace and gazed at the fire as it turned the kindling to coals. "You can get hypnotized watching the patterns of the flames," my friend the North Indian wizard once told me. Before I realized it the stew was bubbling on the stove. I took off my coat and the bowl of the stew warmed my hands. The last of the sun's rays scattered the light through the window, adding at least the illusion of warmth. The crackling of the fire was the only sound I heard until a low yet piercing howl came from the ravine close to the cabin. Wolves . . . . it was sound of my distant enemies.

They are always disturbing me over the winter; sometimes in the summer too. Then I heard a repeating howl closer to the cabin. I looked out of the window but the shadows of the evening were not going to reveal a wolf unless he so chose. I checked the rifle and bullets just to be sure. I also repeated to myself the location of the hunting knives. On the fireplace wall I also have two curved Chinese swords nicely sharpened, I am quite good at using them.

I was tired and wanted to go to bed. I needed to bring in a couple more logs from outside. Cautiously I opened the front door. It was dead quiet, and the darkness fell upon me with the moon behind the shifting clouds on the top of the old pine trees. Instead of going out I decided that I wanted to be in bed and dreaming. So I filled the stove and put the logs on the fire and went to crawl under the covers.

I woke suddenly in the middle of the night. It was quiet yet the cabin was freezing. I had to get the fire going on again. I worried that I wouldn't have enough wood inside, and I didn't want to go out again even though the howling had stopped. I hadn't dreamed of my friend. At least I didn't think I had. I started crying, thinking I had lost her or made her up. My sobs became louder and the anger I felt turned my sobs into angry hysterical screams. I didn't care, I was in the middle of the woods and no one could hear.

Finally I slept; this time she came to me. Something . . . was terribly wrong. Her young face looked very tired. She looked as if she had been crying, and told me that it was a mistake to ask me to come to the cabin. I did not understand but saw her anxiety. I felt her confusion. She said that I should leave as soon as possible. The dream was as if the TV reception was bad and her image faded and dissolved a couple times. With each effort she appeared more tired and anxious as she tried to sustain her image. I felt the need to calm her. I pledged I would leave at first light and return to Calgary. With one last effort her image became clear and warned me to take the rifle and plenty of bullets and then I heard the faded whispering the wolves. I don't know how, but I was sure she heard the howling of the wolves outside to the cabin also. I awoke with a start and though it was very early and still dark I prepared to leave.

I was breaking all the rules by not setting up the fires for the next visit and I wasn't going to be burdened by the sled. I tried to focus on the way back, and on my journey to make it through the snow back to my Jeep. I put the bullets for the rifle where I could grab them in the pocket of my coat, and opened the door of the cabin. Instantly I heard the scrape of bushes against the shed and saw the snow had covered my footprints. I closed the door and leaned against it.

I have to do this. There is no choice.

I am by myself, alone, in the middle of the woods, with hungry wolves all around. I can't stay here. I am good with a gun. I am very strong and I know what I'm doing. I opened the door again to silence.

It had snowed during the night and the trail from the sled I had made the day before was not of much use although the snow was packed. I followed the faint trail and started to run. I adjusted my breath to an even rhythm and kept my moves economical. I felt the wolves close by and focused my mind. I felt their hunger and knew an attack is close. I pulled a handful of bullets from my pocket to have ready. I couldn't see how many wolves there were and really it didn't matter. I would make no mistakes. I couldn't, simply because that would be deadly.

I thought about firing a warning shot but remembered how fierce they were when they killed my dog last year, and thought that I shouldn't waste my few bullets.

Wolves don't play. They are deadly and hungry.

The first one charged directly into my rifle and dropped instantly from my careful aim. In quick succession three others came at me, and calmly I shot two dead, and the other wolf was badly hit. I kept my cool. I had great training from my grandfather, and I focused my mind. I decided not to shoot the wounded wolf for now, as he is not able to attack me because I hurt him already. Quickly, I reloaded the rifle and took careful aim at another wolf ready to attack. It dropped in its tracks and I quickly scanned the trees for others.

There were more gathering but I was close to my Jeep now and pressed the remote starter, which startled the approaching wolves. I felt her with me, urging me quickly to my vehicle. The new snow filled in the tracks I had made and I couldn't move the Jeep. I spun the wheels trying to back out, watching the pack of wolves approaching from all sides out. I tried to calm down and proceeded to rock the car forward and then back. I hit the pavement and braced the traction I needed, as one of the wolves leaped against my window. It was too late for them now. I was gone and drove straight to the city without a second thought.

When I got home I ran a hot bath and the chill of the morning finally left me. I got out of the bath. Wrapped myself in a towel and lay down on my bed. I was exhausted, both mentally and physically, and fell asleep quickly. She came to me, shyly, hesitantly, avoiding my eyes.

"I feel so guilty," she said, "about asking you to go to the cabin."

I told her, "I do want to know what happened but it's okay right now. I just need you to stay with me now."

"Now I can, but not forever," she replied.

There were a thousand questions going though my head. We chose to just remain silent for a long time.

Then she started to giggle. She took me by the hand, suddenly we were playing in the woods, laughing, and hiding in the trees. I felt free and young, and loved the energy of this wonderful child. We finally sat beneath a large tree in the warm sun and she asked me to sing for her. I hesitated and said I didn't know what to sing for her although I knew many songs.

"Maybe you need a new song, a new style, and . . . some inspiration" she said. Softly she began to hum a melody. It drew me in and I listened intently to the simple but compelling tune. She began to sing louder, her voice surprisingly strong and clear for one so young. Though maybe just a little bit too crystalline. My voice would work better for this song, I thought in that moment. I felt the inspiration of the song and began to join with her in the melody. This was it! This was the song I was aching for, and I knew immediately. It would be the success I needed. She smiled to me and as she reached out to touch my lips. She faded and I woke with the song still on them. I immediately began to write out the melody and it would become my international success that brought me the worldwide attention I was seeking. It was a busy year with touring gigs. It was good and I grew, as I didn't dream. I just did.

*   *   *

Now I am so sad and standing here in the vastness of the corridor between the two towers. I miss her now. I feel so small and lonely. The corridor is bright from the sun through the skylights and so many people are rushing about. They range from fashionable women, good-looking businessmen, and trendy young people. Sometimes we are so alone, even when surrounded by so many people. I take the escalator to the top mezzanine watching the people on the main level below. Maybe my ex will pass by and we could go for a coffee. Then . . .

I see a little girl. She is standing there alone. It was like she was looking for someone. A strange thought was coming into my mind. *She is looking for me.* Children are unusual in the tower at this time, so I watch her. I catch my breath and think, *no she can't be.* I rush to the escalator going down and push past people just standing on the steps. I reach the main level, yet I can't see her. I turn, and there she is standing looking directly at me. I feel my legs give away, and reach for her saying:

"You cannot be here. You are only in my mind!"

And that is the moment I lost my consciousness.

Chapter 2

Sometimes I watch you from your window,
Sometimes I stay close to you, or . . .
I am sleeping in the bed with you.
Good evening,
I am the ghost of your house.

-Raluka – Ghost mediation

I think I was lying down unconscious for a couple minutes. When I came back to life I saw a lot of people around me wondering what's going on. Maybe they recognized me, and they all started to wonder. It is for sure very unusual to see someone lying down in the middle of the Bankers Hall's floor. Some of them were just at the point they wanted to reach out and rescue me. I also saw the little girl with her tiny body bent towards me. She was standing near me. With her tiny hands she touched my face. I saw the tears in her eyes. I felt one tear from her eye coming down and touched my face. It was a very hot tear. I had in that moment a strong protective feeling for this little girl. I caught her in my arms and using all my power I pulled myself up.

"It's okay . . . it's okay." I tried to calm down the people around me. "It was just a headache. Please relax. Everything is under control."

With the little girl in my arms I was running toward the escalator, to escape from the people's eyes. I ran with the girl in my arms, and finally I found a silent corner. In the terrible rush I heard the girl laughing. Her laugh was so crystalline . . . .

I felt like I have known this little girl for a very long time. I felt like she was a very good friend of mine. In fact this is the truth. Because of her, I am rich now.

"How are you?" I asked the girl.

"I am very good," she replied.

With her black eyes the little girl was gazing at me. There was a silent moment. To break it, I felt like it is a good idea to introduce myself.

"I am . . ."

"I know who you are," the little girl interrupted me. "You are Laura."

"How?" I was surprised, and almost speechless.

The little girl was laughing again with her crystalline laugh.

"Everyone in the world knows you. I know you too. I very much like your songs."

I felt embarrassed. Yes it is normal that all the people know me. It was kind of a stupid question from my side.

"I am Christina," she introduced herself.

"Nice to meet you Christina." I was really fascinated finally to know the name of the enigmatic little girl.

Suddenly, a small cell phone started to ring in her pocket. Polite, or too polite for her age, she asked me, " May I?" Then she started talking in a foreign language I have never heard. I noticed it sounded close to Italian or Spanish or maybe even French. It is normal here in Canada, in the streets, when I am getting my groceries, when I am getting my hair cut and so on, I her people speaking in lots of strange languages. Sometimes I am embarrassed that I can speak only English. The language of this little girl sounded very strange to me too. I deduced that she was giving information to someone regarding where she is. In her conversation she mentioned my name a couple times. Somehow I feel very guilty now. I took her with me, and she was there with someone else. It is like I kidnapped her. Yet she looks so familiar to me. It is like I have known her for a long time. It is like she is an old friend of mine. I am sure that when I explain to the person who she is, they will understand.

Finally she was done with her conversation. She looked up at me smiling.

"This was Romanian that I was speaking. I was talking with my Uncle. He is so upset that I did not wait in the same place. I calmed him down. I told him that I met with you and we went away from the crowd together. He will be here very shortly."

15

Her English was very good. There was almost no foreign accent, only her voice was so crystalline and with a childish sound. She is already a bilingual child. By nature she is able perfectly to use two languages and very correct.

She had not yet finished speaking and a man just showed up near us. He was touching the shoulder of the little girl and he addressed to me in caring tone.

"Hello Laura. Are you okay?"

"Yes, yes," I said, "Why would I not be?"

I was looking at him. He was an attractive man. At first look I thought he was thirty or so. Upon looking further I saw a couple of wrinkles, and I could tell he was closer to forty. His body was very well maintained. I could see that he completed a regular fitness program. Also he was very well dressed. His clothes were tight to his nice body. I found him attractive.

"Well . . . my niece just told me that you lost consciousness, and that there were lots of people around you." He paused, and he studied me to make sure I was okay.

"Look, lets go to this Chinese restaurant. We can have a nice lunch together and we can easily chat over lunch. What do you think? By the way, my name is Paul Negru."

"Paul? Are you Paul Negru? The Romanian guy?" I was so excited to meet him. "I know you. I mean, I have heard about you."

Now he was looking at me very confused.

"You know me? How?" He asked curiously.

I was very matter of fact in my reply to him. "My best friend regularly attends your Romanian parties. She told me about the gorgeous roasts, cabbage rolls, the amazing homemade cakes, and the red wine called 'Vampire'. I have been so jealous. I've always intended to go to one of these wonderful parties. She told me about a nice Romanian lady who taught her to dance a couple of the Romanian dances. She has always had a lot of fun at your parties."

A nice smile was rising upon his face. "Dear Laura, you are always welcome to attend my parties. For now though, I have just invited you to lunch. Are you going to accept my invitation? As I said, we can chat more over lunch."

"Yes, yes," I said in a hurry. "In fact I have nothing to do. I've had an . . . abnormal day. I feel very confused. It is like I needed something exciting to come up in my life to save me from all the confusion."

He was smiling again, his nice smile. "Okay, we can talk about your strange, and confusing day. But I know for sure we will have much more interesting stuff to discuss. What do you think?"

It was my turn to smile to him. "I think you are right Paul."

*   *   *

We are able to get a table near the window. From the restaurant table, I can see Ninth Avenue from my window. It is my new passion, watching through the windows at everything and everyone. I love to watch the elegant people who are walking on the street. I also was checking for the next signs of spring. I love the spring.

"I recommend the Seafood in the Nest," Paul suggested to me.

"The what?" I didn't understand what he meant.

"Oh dear are you not hungry at all? I suggested to you number twenty three in the menu. I know they have something very good called Seafood in the Nest. He seemed very confident about his suggestion.

"Okay, I will have Seafood in the Nest." I decided immediately, and without hesitation.

"Seafood in the Nest is delicious," said little Christina. She appeared to be very excited about this idea.

" It is my favourite," she beamed.

Shortly the waiter took our order. We asked for green tea and a soft drink for Christina too.

This little girl is so nice. I am still a little confused about it all. If she exists how can I dream her without knowing her before? How has she inspired me with my famous songs? How can I ask this? Maybe she just looks like the girl from my dreams. No, it is her. The same face, the same body, the same gestures, the same everything.

"We are from Romania. Do you know Romania? It is known as Dracula's country. Lots of people visit Bran's castle believing that it is the real Dracula's castle. Have you seen it?" Paul asked me with a hopeful look on his face.

"No . . ." I said little bit embarrassed. "Though I intend to go soon if I can."

"Come with us," said the little girl as she became excited. "We are going back next week."

"Oh dear. I don't know." I tried to calm down the excitement of this wonderful little girl. To be honest though I started to become very excited myself. They looked like very nice people. I have the money, and the time, yet I was just complaining I have no one to travel with. It looks like it might be a nice arrangement for me, a fantastic opportunity in fact.

"Well my niece is right. Please come with us. I would like to be your guide there if you would allow me this privilege." Paul was being very sincere in his request.

I was very surprised, and even taken aback a little by this unexpected invitation.

No matter what I felt, I must extend my gratitude.

"I would like to go, though I am not sure. However I would like to say that no matter my decision, I thank you for inviting me."

"Yes, I'm sure this trip will be welcome. You won't regret it. Romania is an exciting country. It is a very beautiful country. A friend of mine lives in Malta. As I know that he very much likes to ski, I invited him to Calgary to ski. He told me that he wants to ski only in one place and that place is Romania." Paul sounded very sure of himself about how much I would enjoy my time there.

"Really? It is that nice there?" I had to ask for affirmation of this before I made any decision.

"You have to come and then you will see. The mountains are exquisite, and the nature is just gorgeous there."

I was unsure. "What are you doing there Paul?"

"Well, I live in Canada the most of the year, but a couple times of the year I have to go to Romania. I am a . . ." Paul pauses briefly.

"He is a wizard." Christina interupts in our discussion.

I started laughing.

"A what?" I asked.

He looked very seriously at me. "Yes, I am. I consider that our universe is not a complete and constant universe without magic."

And he was deeply looking at me, almost as if he was looking into my very soul.

"You said we have Claudia as a common friend. She attends my parties. I know she has my book."

"I have your book too, 'The Spatial Magic', It is an amazing book. After I read it, I felt like I was a witch. It was like I gained some miraculous powers."

"But you are a witch," Christina said.

"Yes, seriously," he completed the little girl's sentence. "Actually I can feel a strong energy from you."

He made me think a little bit. Could it be true? Does he really have extra sensory powers? Could he really use his powers to feel something hidden in me?

"However, how are you a wizard?" I asked bluntly.

"How would I be able to write my book 'The Spatial Magic' if I was not a wizard? Or without having solid knowledge about magic?"

"To be honest I asked myself that question when I was reading your book. I found it astonishing. I was tempted to do some of the stuff by myself as you had written it in the book."

He interrupted me.

"I have lots of warnings in my books. As the people who try to do that, need close supervision from an experienced person, at least in the very beginning. There is some pretty new stuff in my book, and even the experienced person might have troubles with it at first."

I had no idea about what I should discuss with a wizard, or with a modern wizard for that matter.

"Can you predict something for me?" I asked him curiously.

"Predict?" He questioned. "Oh Laura, I sometimes wish to be so talented regarding the predictions as Vanga".

"As who?" I asked.

"Vanga, I said or even like Carmen Harra," he replied.

I thought about for a little bit, but shortly I realized that I know neither of them. I had no idea who Vanga is, or Carmen Harra.

Instead he looked like he was daydreaming for just a moment.

"Carmen, I know all of her music from the time of my college days. She is from Romania too. I was so much in love with her music. Now she is a famous psychic in the USA. She has predicted a lot of stuff, which as of late has become a reality. Regarding Vanga, she was a country neighbour of mine, from Bulgaria. She died in 1996 after 85 years. At the age of 12 she lost her sight when she was swept away by a tornado. The sand from the tornado hurt her eyes so badly, and this caused her the blindness. However, for someone like you who would like to become a witch it would be good practice to check some information on the Internet about Vanga and Carmen."

And he smiled, an enigmatic smile directly at me.

"I can see that, you have a big question for me," he stated matter-of-factly.

So I answered him back in the same tone.

"Yes, how it is it possible that I have dreamt of your niece?"

He smiled and he was looking to Christina.

"My dear, I told you not to play with this kind of stuff." He scolded her in a very serious fashion.

"But . . . Laura is my favourite singer. That is the true Uncle Paul."

"What?" I become sad and excited within the same breath. "What exactly did you do? We have to have a serious discussion about this."

"Actually I did nothing," Christina exclaims as she became a little bit embarrassed.

"So . . . lets try again," Paul said. "There is nothing abnormal here. I don't need any kind of magic powers to see this. You are a great singer. She must have been listening to your songs, and maybe she was somehow thinking of you and . . . you dreamt her. I would like to tell you about a kind of telepathy that has occurred in this situation."

"I dreamt her before the launch of my famous album in the market, before it's explosion worldwide. All this occurred when I was just an unknown singer. Yet I dreamt her, and she gave me the inspiration, the inspiration I needed to create this famous album full of life changing songs."

"Dear," he took my hand, "there is something a little bit strange about the timing of your story. Think about it for just a second. How could a little girl be so talented to create such complex music that you have in your album? And . . . . Even if that is true, as you are so very convinced, all was a success nevertheless. She is supposed to be your best friend."

"She is my best friend." I agreed with him completely.

He was smiling, his most amazing smile to me.

"If somebody in some way or another could give me the inspiration to write a new book, or to compose a great song, to do something interesting, or something after that I would gain lots of money and become a celebrity, I would always admire that person for what they helped me to accomplish. It doesn't matter the way that person inspired you."

"I totally have to agree with you Paul." I said what I thought quickly to him.

The waiter interrupted us briefly by serving us the famous Seafood in the Nest . With professional moves the waiter arranged the food on the table. It looks so yummy. I remember that an old Chinese saying 'you eat the food first with your eyes'. We started eating quickly. I realized that I was so hungry. I was smiling together with Paul, watching little Christina eating in such a terrible rush to finish all of her lunch.

"Christina, please be polite. Don't eat so quickly," Paul asked nicely of his niece.

The little girl made an affirmative sign with her delicate head, and she slowed down her eating.

He served me with some tea and little girl drank her pop.

As Christina was too busy eating her food, Paul found a couple moments for a psychological discussion with me.

"How do you feel today?" Paul asked me in a very inquisitive tone.

"I have a strange feeling," I replied. " I have a very confused feeling inside me I cannot seem to shake."

Paul answered, "Maybe it is because it has almost been one year since you had your latest album explode into the market. Maybe it is time for a new one."

"Yes. I know. There is a lot of work to be done though before I can make that happen." The mere thought of it was very overwhelming to me.

"Don't be mad at yourself. In life there are many challenges, yet there are also many constraints. Sometimes it is very easy to lose your focus because of those constraints. We can be infected and become helpless very quickly. It is our nature. Some people are helpless, but not my friends. I can help you for sure. Life is filled with diversity, and I always teach my friends to take advantage of this diversity. In the diversity of life you can find opportunities."

"You are perfectly right Paul. Yet these constraints are affecting us. They are all around us."

"Take life's constraints and understand the challenges. Where there are challenges there are opportunities. Don't let the constraints transform into problems. Remember, a way to deal with problems is to solve them. Your life has to reflect your efforts. The purpose of life is happiness. If you fix your problems this is your way to happiness." He was so very philosophical. I could not help but admire him, agree, but dispute it all at the same time.

"Oh . . . but that is very hard Paul. There are lots of balls in air at the same time."

"Dear, in life there is never time to do everything, yet there is always time to do all the important things."

I was watching this man so intently. He seemed to be a very good psychologist. His words really helped me. He seemed to observe this in me, so he continued.

"Create a priority list. If your goals are too big don't abandon them, just divide them in small ones; after that solve them one by one. Maybe this is your town. You feel comfortable here. You are a conscience of your environment. This seems to be your comfort zone. Yet at the same time you are reluctant, confused, and this could be because of your environment. Identify the stress in your environment. Maybe a trip will be welcome for you. Your perception now is that you will be far away from your comfort zone, and you have been afraid to make the decision to come and visit Romania. That simply put, is a constraint. You have to try to escape from this small universe, fight with the constraints of your universe. Finally, you will eliminate most of them."

I was very captured by his words. It was like a hypnosis to me. Finally when I awoke from my trance of sorts I said,

"Paul, I am not afraid to come to Romania."

"Or . . . maybe this is still a desire for you, and you have became hostile to the object of your desire. Sometimes we are disconnected from what we want." Paul was grasping at straws for answers from me by this point.

"I don't think so. I do exactly what I want." I corrected him in his thesis of my desire.

"What you want is your current desire. Your current desire represents the next stage in your evolution. What you want, right now, is moving you to the next phase of your evolution."

I smiled at him. This I could definitely agree with.

"I will try to look at the things differently."

He smiled back to me.

"Thank you. That means a lot that you are willing to consider my advice and heed it. Maybe we should speak a little bit about your music. It is a style of Rock music close to . . . witches rituals."

"Yes, it is," I replied.

"Well, if you come with us to Romania you will be more inspired for your next album. We have there a lot of witch's stuff to inspire you."

"Yes, really?"

"Yes, though it won't be all work. It will be a nice vacation for you too," affirming my next question before I even had a chance to ask it.

"Hmm . . . it might work. With the reluctance I felt today I already had fleeting thoughts of . . . and me needing a vacation. Why not Romania? What else I can see there?" Now I was getting excited.

"Actually we can go to the real Dracula's castle even if it is now almost a ruin. I have a place there; a place *near Dracula's castle* where I use to go often."

He started to become focused on what he had just spoken of, and it looked like his thoughts were travelling there, *near Dracula's castle.*

"Really? A castle connected with Dracula? Or his castle exactly? This is wonderful. His history passed the limits of the time." I became more excited with each breath.

His reply was very factual and confident.

"Yes, there is lots of vampire industry in Romania, or starting from Romania."

"I might be very interested to go to Romania," I replied.

"Good. Please be my guest. I know you are rich enough to pay the hotel, but . . . I have some properties there. You don't have to pay the hotel room. It will be an honour for me to have you as my guest. Please accept my proposal." His offer was too sincere to pass up.

"Say yes, say yes. Please Laura. I would like to travel with you," Christina pleaded and touched my hand. I felt like a good energy was touching me.

"I just may accept your offer. In fact I need a guide for Romania, so this would work out perfectly."

"It will be my pleasure guiding you there. We will have a lot of fun. Bucharest is a nice city. You will see some buildings inspired by Paris architecture. A very long time ago it was called the little Paris of Europe." Paul's eyes brightened when he spoke of Romania.

"Really? I didn't know that." His facts intrigued me.

"Don't worry. Lots of people don't know this fact. You will see this with your own eyes very soon. Also the Romanian mountains are very nice, really nice. Maybe even more beautiful than The Rockies, you will truly enjoy them."

I followed with, "I remember in the book of Dracula it mentions that Romania or Transylvania is a very beautiful country."

"True. Also, all my Canadians friends who visited Romania like . . ."

"They like 'mititei' so much," Christina said.

"They like what?" I misunderstood the little girls point.

Paul was laughing and he kissed Christina.

"Dear, this is a very traditional Romanian food. It is somehow between sausages and meat balls, yet nothing exactly the same. However, there you have to be open and ready to eat a lot of very particular and very tasty food and to drink a lot of good variety of wines, all from Romanian production."

"Really? How come until now I have never heard about all this?"

"Well, I know the Romanian commercials are very poor. Yet I would like to tell you again I had friends from Romania. All of them were very surprised, and they want to go back to visit Romania again. I am sure you will enjoy it as well,"

"Please say yes, please," insisted Christina again with her tiny little voice.

"Well . . . it might be a 'yes'. Though you may be busy back there. I do not want to disturb you."

Paul smiled widely, "I will always find free time for you. Of course you can walk on the streets by yourself. It is a very safe country. I don't understand people who travel to dangerous destinations. In Romania though there is no danger."

"Okay," I quickly replied.

"Is it a yes?" Christina was very excited. It was a happy moment for me watching her happy face.

"Well, dear Christina, I do no want to disturb your Uncle. He might be very busy with his work."

"The only business which will keep me busy will be the witches club."

"What?" I have to recognize this gentleman is very intrigued by me, he could almost become a stalker.

"Romania has a very large heritage with a lot of customs and traditions. One of them is in the magic domain. There are lots of witches. So many in fact that the parliament thought of taxing their work. The witches of Romania are organized in a witches club."

"A witches club?" I repeated like I was being hypnotized.

"Yes, there is a witches club. I am chairing it," he said very matter-of-factly.

"That is incredible. You should start with this. I am very interested in that kind of stuff. I have my own wizard. He is a native North Indian. He gave me a couple of dream catchers. He made the dream catchers himself actually."

"Let me guess, and you hung them on the windows of your cabin?" Paul questioned in a strong and unpleasant voice. His unpleasant voice disturbed the little girl. A couple of people from nearby tables turned their eyes to Paul.

"Yes . . . . He instructed me to do it." I was very worried by the tone of his voice at this point.

I was looking at his face for a moment as his face looked quite muddy, somehow bitter. He was taking some food and started to eat it slowly and continued gazing me. It was a terrible moment. I felt like something was wrong in the air, in the middle of the restaurant.

Finally that terrible moment was gone, and he started to speak again.

"Dear, I think that friend of yours is an interesting one. I hope one day you will introduce me to him."

"Yes . . . yes . . . why not?" I was still disturbed about the previous moment. Somehow I felt like I did something wrong, and I felt guilty for it.

"Please tell me more about this witches club." I wanted Paul to continue.

"We meet and debate some strange stuff in the magic domain, sharing our experiences, doing incantations together and stuff like this."

"Wow! I would like to go there" I became very excited as sometimes I have seen Christina become.

25

With an unexpected move he touched my head. He closed his eyes for a couple of seconds. When he opened his eyes he was gazing at me.

"I can feel that in a previous life you were a very strong witch." He sounded very sure of himself.

"Really? Is it possible?" Could I really have been a witch before. Is this where my pull to magic comes from?

"I can feel that in this life you have a gift too."

He was shocking me. If he has some powers as he says he does, I might have a gift too. Maybe it was what I felt deep inside me, and I misinterpreted.

"Do you believe in reincarnation?" He continued to gaze at me inquisitively.

"Yes," the answer came from me without hesitation.

"Okay, we can tell you more about all of this stuff in Romania."

"We?" I was feeling bewildered by that last statement of Paul's.

"Yes, me and my colleagues, the witches. Starting with now you have to admit that in the world are very strong witches and sorceresses and most of them are in Romania."

"How about you? You said you are the chairman of this club." Now my curiosity was peaked.

"Yes. However, I am a good organizer. This was what they was looking for."

"So what are you doing here?" I really wanted to get down to the facts before my final decision.

"Well, I am a dual citizen of Canada and Romania. I very much like Canada. But from time to time I go back to Romania. In principal I like to know about the magic experiences of my colleagues. I like sharing my experience too."

He smiled largely at me.

"I have to share with them my last experiences here in Canada."

"Like what?" I was so very curious.

"There is a family here with a gorgeous house. They have observed that there is a ghost in the house."

"What have they seen?" I wanted to know so badly.

"Unexplainable things like strange noises, moving of objects. You know these things are a little bit disturbing."

He came close to my ear.

"I will tell you more when Christina is not with me" after that he said in a normal voice "and I freed the house from that ghost. Now the family can stay there, without ghost."

"You can do this stuff?"

"Yes, and I am very good." He was smiling at me. "Always remember when you are with me you don't face any fear about ghosts".

"Okay, so when do we leave to go to Romania?" My mind was made up.

"In five days we leave. I will book your flight Laura. We have to switch flights in Amsterdam. We will take the opportunity to stay there five days. These days will be welcome to correct the jet lag we are feeling."

"Okay . . ." and after giving Paul a serious look, I smiled to the little girl.

Christina was applauding with her little hands as she jumped in my arms. She kissed me, and she said,

"I am so very happy".

*   *   *

Once home, even though I felt quite tired, I spent the late night searching information about Vanga. I was so impressed by her predictions. As Paul said, she was blinded at 12 years old. She was alone and suddenly a strong storm started. The sand of the storm hurt her eyes so badly, and she remained blind for all her life. She was in pain and she was very scared. It was for her, like an experience of death. But after that death experience she gained a gift. At the age of 16 she began making predictions. Many of the statesmen visited her to seek her predictions. I found Hitler in the list of the statesmen too. My guessing was right, he was not very happy about her predictions. Oh . . . was it guessing or . . . as Paul said, I have a gift?

*   *   *

We had stayed in touch over the last five days. I was so excited to speak on the phone with little Christina, the source of my inspiration. I will encourage her to sing again for me. It doesn't matter what, only to sing, and maybe I will get inspired once again.

After five days we met in the huge terminal of the modern Calgary airport. Christina had a tiny backpack. She was so excited to see me again.

"Laura, Laura," she yelled after me.

I hugged Christina. After I was done Paul hugged me as well. I had the chance to feel his body. I felt his muscles, and his amazing body. I saw a long smile on his face.

"Okay," he said "are we ready?" Paul sounded as happy as both Christina and I were.

"Yes, yes" Christina said with all her excitement.

"As I said, the first flight is from Calgary to Amsterdam. It will take around nine hours. We will have good meals and drinks on the plane. We will stay five days in Amsterdam. It will be welcome for recuperating from the jet lag. When are in Romania we will be very busy, as there is so much to do."

"I am so excited to see Romania, to visit Dracula's castle, to meet Romanian witches." I could barely contain myself.

"Very good," he answered. "Christina, take Laura's hand." Excited the little girl took my hand. I felt a nice pleasure being hand in hand with her. Paul took her other hand, and with a twinkle in his eye he looked at both of us, and said, "Let's start our trip to Romania."

Chapter 3

Ghost of the ghost,
Mother of the crazy dogs and mother of the pagans,
I tell you this spell; when I am done,
Your only alternative is to leave this house

-Romanian open incantation for throws away the ghost

Amsterdam.

It's hard to admit that I have never travelled here before. Paul told me a lot of things, which in North America are illegal, and are legal here. Also he told me that the people here really know how to party. On our way there he told me a lot of interesting things about Amsterdam and Holland. The flight was around nine hours. We had some discussions, and of course we tried to sleep a little bit. Yet unfortunately as I tried, I was unable to sleep on the plane. Paul was not able to sleep very well on the flight either. Yet the little girl was quite the opposite of the both of us. She was able to sleep quite a long time.

Here the hotels are very small. Lots of hotels are like this, especially in historical Amsterdam or the old part of the country. The people in Amsterdam and all over the country really have this challenge to use the space in their homes effectively. He told me in the small towns and in the villages the homes are more spacious. However, for someone like me who comes from a continent country I hardly understand all of this stuff.

I saw in Amsterdam there are lots of channels and I am not in agreement with this philosophy. If the land is not suitable for building why do people have to build here? Or why do they continue living here if the maintenance is so high? Paul told me to be little bit flexible, and to understand the romantic side of these things. I will try, but I can't promise anything.

Yesterday we were fighting with extreme jet lag. Christina though appears to be very good. She already can normally sleep at night, and stay awake all day.

I had this funny feeling that I would be okay soon. Yet I saw as of four am today that I was not able to sleep. I tried to read something until 6 am. I started walking in this town it being a little bit after 6 am. It is so humid here. This is a thing I like. In Calgary it is so dry. I use a lot of moisturizing creams. I almost had it down to a science by using them. Creams for eyes, creams for face, creams for wrinkles, creams for body, and so on. Almost always, my skin is telling me at various intervals what kind of cream I need. Here I don't think will use them, or at least not as much as I use them in Calgary.

I am looking at a couple of people who were riding their bikes. For sure they must be going to work. This town is so quiet. The street is still dark. I feel like I need to talk with someone . . .

"Hello." A familiar voice said. When I turned I saw Paul. We started laughing.

"You can not sleep too?"

"Yes, it is not a very pleasant feeling. I know we suppose to sleep but the jet lag . . . ." He took on a kind of sad facial expression.

"Maybe it would be a good idea to have a coffee, some breakfast and . . . to try to integrate in the European time." Paul's suggestion sounded like the most brilliant idea at this point.

I accepted it.

We were walking around the channels. To make him a little bit happier I said,

"I am starting to love Amsterdam. Still I find it so different but I try to understand these differences."

"That is so nice of you," Paul replied. "We can visit some museums if you like."

"I am not a museum fan, but . . . yes . . . ." I didn't want to turn him down, though I felt it right I be honest.

"Maybe Van Gogh, or Tulips Museum, or . . . here they even have a Sex Museum."

I felt a little bit embarrassed.

"I don't think I would want, or like to visit the last kind of museum."

He smiled with all his face.

We stepped into a small cafe. There were not too many people inside. We chose a table near the window, and in silence we started to drink our coffees. I was trying to please Paul.

"I love Amsterdam. I don't think I will be able to . . ."

Paul abruptly interrupted with, "you are not here to love Amsterdam."

Good! I thought, this guy is able to read my mind.

I am sure when he was looking at me, he understood my surprise, but he continued to speak.

"Our main objective of travel is to go to Romania and to learn, maybe to do some magic. What do you know about magic?"

"Well . . . not to much, really." I replied.

"Okay, let's think of it another way. When do you think the magic was interfering with your life?"

I tried to think quickly.

"Well . . . maybe after I went to my cabin. As you know it is in the middle of the boreal forest. And I was not able to sleep. There were so many dreams, so many black dreams. At that time I had a dog. The dog was always very agitated."

"Until?" Paul asked.

"Until I found that old Indian wizard. He gave me a couple of the dream catchers he made. After I hung them at each cabin's window, suddenly the bad dreams disappeared. My dog becomes silent, and finally I was able to sleep in that cabin."

"Good. You already had a real experience that involved magic. You will meet Raluka in Romania. She is a horrible witch. In fact she cannot do magic, but instead she is a wonderful analyst. I recommend you talk to her about this fact. She will explain to you everything that was happening."

"Why can't you explain it to me?"

"Well . . . . Just a couple of words. In the woods there were a lot of spirits. Just close to your cabin were very many bad spirits. They tried to come inside your cabin. As the animals have special feeling capacities your dog felt them, and he became agitated. The bad spirits were able to influence your sleep. After you hung out the dream catchers the spirits were unable to pass. That Indian wizard is very good at what he does."

I felt my skin get itchy. I was taught that, yet I refused to admit it.

"So many things are happening near us, and we are not giving them the right importance. We are always in a big rush in our lives. Instead maybe we should stay, and analyze things, maybe like Raluka is doing."

Raluka, what a strange name. I observed that Paul was giving me time to think.

"Don't think that the magic is something foolish. It is very old stuff. It is well known that we only use a small portion of our brain. Maybe the people who can use more of their brains are philosophers, scientists, and even wizards." He accentuated the last word.

"How come?" I smiled an inquisitive smile.

"I will explain this to you. For that, maybe I have to go back in time with you two thousand years."

"Jesus Christ. " I said.

"Yes!" He was happy for my understanding.

"Good. We have progress."

"I don't think we have progress. What are you insinuating? Are you insinuating that Jesus Christ was a wizard?"

"Well . . . walking on the water, multiplying food like bread, fish etc. What do you think?"

I wondered until now how I had never asked myself these questions. I remember that I saw a couple of movies. Yet in that moment I was happy He helped these poor people to get food for their meal. I did not think about how Jesus Christ did such a thing. Regarding the walking on the surface of water. I really don't know.

"Did you read the Bible?"

"No," I said slightly embarrassed. "Have you read it?"

"Yes I have. I have also seen lots of movies about it. However, going back through history, in his time there were very strong wizards, and that is written there in the Bible. Three of these wizards were able to predict his birth. And they come to the exact place at the exact time of his birth to give him gifts. Only wizards could predict the birth of the strong one, their King."

"Really," I would like to read it by myself and so not let Paul surprise me like this again.

"However, in the reign of the Catholic church lots of witches had been killed in totally horrifying ways. I am sure in a country with such a tradition of Halloween like in Canada you know lots of stories. I would like to share with you a particular case in Romania."

"What was this case in Romania that was so different?" I asked very curious.

"In Romania the witches were not punished at all because the Orthodox Church practices differently. As a direct result the magic was freely developed. The Orthodox churches did not punish them."

"I did not know that." I was very surprised as our culture was so much different in Canada.

"I am sure you did not. Even if Romania was rich and a nice country, it's people were poor. For example since in the village there was not a doctor there was always had to be a minimum of one witch. She was able to cure the people using her paranormal abilities, or applying her extremely advanced alchemy knowledge. She was able to help. For this reason the Orthodox Church did not punish them as was happening in the other countries in the time of Catholic Inquisition. You can study a lot of this with my analyst Raluka. She has lots of knowledge about this matter. However, the point here is this. Romania has a very rich heritage speaking of magic. First of all it is in the blood of these people, and second because there was not a radical punishment over the years as it was in other countries. As a result the witches of Romania can grow up stronger."

He was sipping from the coffee, and after that he was looking outside. The town started to come back to life. I was little bit absent regarding the town. I was very much captivated and intrigued by his story.

"I had heard Michael Jackson was from time to time looking for the help of some witches. Our former president Ceausescu even had his own witch and quite often he and his wife were checking in with her for advice. Remember Vanga? She is from Bulgaria a country near Romania. She was as talented as Nostradamus. Hitler was seeking her advice as well."

He smiled, a kind of strange smile and he continued.

"In my family there was a tradition regarding practising the magic."

"This is the reason are you a wizard?"

His face became somehow bitter. For a couple moments he did not answer. He was watching deep inside the coffee cup.

"Romania was so close with the Turkish. There the woman had no rights at that time. It was the opposite in Romania; and especially with magic. It was really understood as it is mostly for women."

He was fixated on me, and he was studying my gestures like trying to understand if I agree or not with his story.

"It was like a general perception that these abilities to the magic powers were directed to the female sex, and rarely, very rarely were they given to the male. My grandmother and her sister were very good witches. They were always thinking one of their nieces would be like them. Unfortunately none of them were. I was the exception to the rule."

I started to become more curious. He stopped talking. I understood this story was affecting him. Due to my curiosity I was going to ask him a couple more things. Yet at the same time I observed his sadness. I decided to wait until he continued with his story.

"Long story short, because none of her nieces had any abilities or attraction to magic my grandmother started to hate me. What I knew is not because of her teaching. All I learned, is because I hid, and I observed her. I will tell you more about this at another time."

"Okay," I tried to find a shortcut. "Is she alive?"

"No. She passed away."

"Is . . . . her sister alive?" I asked.

"I don't know," he replied.

"How come you don't know?' Coming at him with yet another question.

"Well . . . . what I do know according to what my grandmother has told me, her little sister was manifesting very good magic skills, maybe even better than her own skills. When she was a child though the gypsies stole her."

"What gypsies?"

"Oh . . . sorry now I, we, call them Roma. This was their request. I noticed that in Canada still they are still known as gypsies.

"Okay, Okay, but this story . . . . . how is it possible?"

"It happened of course before I was born. In that time it was only a story about a child who vanished from the village. They never found her body. In that time a migrating tribe of gypsies called a *Satra* of gypsies was passing near the village."

Paul paused for a moment, somehow captured by his own story.

"After that terrible incident, my family was very afraid, and did not want to lose another child in these circumstances. I was very worried about this too. I was always afraid of gypsies, ghosts, and vampires."

"Oh, it is fascinating and . . . sad.. look . . . I want to ask you about vampires. Do they really exist in Romania? Dracula existed in Romania?" I had so many more questions to ask.

"My answer is yes. When Bram Stoker wrote his book, I believe he did very good research about these kinds of things. I will go back in time for you, in the time of Vlad the Impaler. In that time the Romanians were standing alone in the front of Turkish. The Turkish were totally superior in numbers. For dominance and defence Vlad would perform special torture methods. His favourite one was to throw the prisoners on a very sharp stake. It was a terrible torture. The stake is stabbed through the body from behind, into the stomach, lungs and ultimately through to the brain. Sometimes they did not allow the stake to go to brain in order to achieve a long suffering for the tortured to obtain a gradual and disparate pain until death."

"That is terrible" I was very horrified. I couldn't understood why this guy was so bloody.

"Yes, he is known to us as the most evil man of history. But think about this in another way. What if the Turkish were able to conquer his country? What he did was just to defend himself and his country. He was an acceptable handsome guy, but his brother was extremely handsome. He is known in history as Radu the Handsome. It is told that he was gay, and he had a sexual relationship with the Turkish sultan. The sultan intended after he would conquest Romania to replace Vlad with Radu. I am sure you can read more about it in Wikipedia."

I thought just for a moment that this is spicy side of the history . . .

"However this is not our subject. Vlad was not really punishing only the Turks, he punished his people like this too, the ones who made mistakes. No matter if the mistake was capital or small the punishment was the same. He really enjoyed seeing tortured people.

What I mean by this, he was so bloody. As bloody as many witches predicted that after his death he would become a vampire."

"Is that really true?"

"Laura what I am telling you is all true. I heard people, compared their words, checking documents and . . . . I have other methods too. According to what I know, he had all the signs to manifest this metamorphosis. What we all know is that after his death a vampire appeared, and started terrorizing the nearby villages."

"How did he get eliminated?" I had to ask.

"Maybe it happened as in Stoker's book. However it is a traditional type of ritual for us Romanians to eliminate vampires. Let's accept the legend as it is, and for now let's not research more. Maybe it is also good to stop the vampires' stories for today. I have to run to the hotel. My niece may wake up, and I want to be there. Would you like to join me? Please come along."

*   *   *

Unfortunately the next day I was not able to sleep in the morning again. When I saw that Paul and Christina were sleeping I decided to go out alone to do some shopping. I met with him in the early afternoon. By this time I was a bit tired and upset.

"I don't need to have magical powers to see that something is wrong. I see that on your face. So . . . what's wrong?"

"I tried to buy . . ."

"Some bananas" he interrupted me.

"Yes, some bananas. How did you know?" I was astonished, he was able to finish the sentence for me.

"Oh dear at one of our last discussion you mentioned that you like bananas. Sorry for interrupting you."

For just a moment I was asking myself again if he was able to read my mind. What kind of powers does he have? Exactly what kind of powers does he have over me?

I tried to control myself and go back to my story, my frustrating story.

"As you said I tried to buy a couple of minor things. It was under 10 euros, and I tried to pay with the visa cad."

"Until now it is all okay?" Paul raised an eyebrow.

"Yes, it supposed to be okay, but she asked me for ID. I didn't understand why she had to ask for ID when what I bought was under 10 euros. I found it to be frustrating."

He was watching me, and was making an understanding sign with his head.

"After that I wend to the second shop to buy some cheese, and at their shop the visa card was not accepted at all. I thought this was a civilized county? It was good because I had some euros changed. I found it to be totally unfair. We are from Canada. Our banks has contracts with all the banks in the world."

He was continuing to make the understanding signs with his head.

"I see . . . however, in Romania you may have these kinds of problems too, or maybe even more than here. I will advise you to make it custom to having cash, or ask them before you buy if they accept credit cards. I see you have not had much fun in Amsterdam. Look my niece is with a friend of mine who has a day care. How about we go for lunch to discuss . . . . Ghosts?"

"Yes," I said almost immediately and totally without thinking.

We chose a little restaurant. It was very small, and cozy. It was a Portuguese restaurant. I don't remember if we have a Portuguese restaurant in Calgary. I noticed a couple Greek restaurants, one Hungarian, but I'm not sure about any Portuguese restaurants within our city.

We chose a window table. From the window I could see the street and the canal. Some tourists were cruising around on one of the nice channel boats. I suppose I could be more flexible and go on this kind of cruise. It might be interesting. However right now I am very interested about our subject on ghosts.

He did not start on the subject until we had finished eating.

"What do you know about ghosts?" he asked me.

"Well, I know they exist, and sometimes they are interfering with our lives."

"Very good. What are they exactly?"

"Well . . . I don't think I have a correct definition in place."

"Okay, well maybe I can help. Think about isolating somebody who inevitably must die, and putting him on a very sensitive balance in a totally isolated room. The room is so closed in, you can even count the breaths of the man, and the water on his breath. What I mean by this is that you can exactly determine its mass when he is alive and its mass when he is dead; again all very precisely. You will observe that the body will be a couple of grams less after death; and again, here I don't include the water lost by dehydration."

He paused and he fixed. After that he said pushing out the words.

"This is the mass of our soul."

Definitely he is a good speaker. I think he must be talented speaking in front of people.

"Really? I never heard about this kind of experiment. How many grams can it be?"

"Just a couple of grams. Or think about the opposite. Take all the chemicals in the human body and mix them in a recipient. The exact quantity and proportion of water, calcium, proteins, iron and so on. Mix them all together. From a chemical point of view you will have the exact composition of the human body in that recipient. But there is no soul. A dead body is a body without a soul."

He took a deep breath and he continued.

"Here we start our journey. What is happens with our soul after we die? We are the most complex creatures in the universe. We can not simply die and all is gone. This is just a phase of our experience."

I felt again that itching sensation on the skin all over my body. I am sure it is because I became very scared about this subject.

"All the religions explain one way or another what is supposed to be happening to our soul. My club will take all these explanations. Let's summarize two principal ideas according to the religions. I will remember to tell you that the main dogma of the religions is to just believe and not to research. We can not prove which way might be more trusted. According to the Christian religion our soul will go to hell or heaven, in accordance with the good or bad things that man did in his life. Yet in Buddhism the soul will have a number of reincarnations, somewhere in the number of one hundred. The essence of these reincarnations is evolution. At this point we have the evolution of souls, less evolved souls and much evolved souls. However in the existence the people observe the ghost phenomenon. They are lost souls; the souls which are not able to go to hell or heaven or not able to go into the next reincarnation, because in the Romanian tradition purgatory doesn't exist."

"Why?" I asked.

His eyes were gazing at me once again.

"Dear, you have to control your feelings when we are discussing these kinds of subjects. If you are not comfortable I can stop here."

He is right. Maybe anyone can see the look on my face or upon hearing my voice, can see that I am scared.

"Are there many lost souls?"

"Oh yes, they are. First of all I will not tell you these kinds of stories during the night. They are very curious, and our subject of discussion can attract them. They can come more and more near us, closer to us, just by listening to us talk about them."

I tried to control myself. He is right. Outside is a beautiful day and I have to try to find energy in the sun's light, in this beautiful day.

"To become a witch you have to find a positive energy inside you. You have to learn to intensify this energy at the highest levels. Otherwise you can easily be destroyed."

His words were otherworldly. It is like they were not a part of the story. It is more like they were a conclusion, an important piece of advice for me.

"The subject is very big. We can discuss a lot about this. I will add this in your training when you are in Romania."

"I know some of these ghosts may be . . . bad." I had to add that in there to get a response.

"Yes. You are perfectly right. They will be bad according to the kind of deed they have done. If they have been murdered, then they feel they don't go in to the normal light because they need to find the man who did this. They want to take revenge, and punish him. If a man died by committing suicide his soul was lost before he did it, from the Christian religion point of view. The priest will refuse to bring or add the body to the inside the church. In Romania they are buried in a separate part of the graveyard. There they can go on to be bad."

He paused a moment and he used this moment to study me better, and longer. I am sure he can easily read my anxiety.

"Usually the ghosts remain connected with an object, or with the house where they died, or a place where they wished to be when they died. Usually my problem is when the ghosts are connected with a house."

"Your case?" I asked.

"Yes, the people know that I am good and they call upon me for help. My recent case was about a very rich family in Canada. They have a huge house, and it is pretty expensive. However the price they received from the previous owner was somehow lower than the market price. When they asked why this was, the realtor was laughing and telling them that the present owner thinks there is a ghost in the house. They both lived in the house, and in less than two weeks they decided to sell it. The reason . . . the house has a ghost, and the ghost is active."

I felt again that itching feeling upon my skin. I tried desperately to control my body. I tried to find that positive energy I needed to fight with this stuff or first to control my own body, to calm it down.

"What does an active ghost mean?" I dared to ask.

"That means the ghost is making noises through the night, moves objects from their places, and so on." He smiled strangely at me.

"They contacted me, and they explained to me that they can not sell the house because the market is totally down. They offered me a very substantial amount of money if I am able to help them out, so I did."

I started to quietly eat my dessert. It was pretty good. I found some comfort, and I was able to calm my mind. Maybe in the future I have to apply this kind of concentration. It is very important for me first to be relaxed, to be able to focus or to respond . . . normally.

"How do you get rid of a ghost?"

"Well . . . First I have to make sure there is a ghost in the house. The way Canadians, North Americans are building their houses now is making them to be somehow . . . very noisy. They are using too much wood in the construction of their houses. In Europe concrete is mostly used. However, the houses will have both situations of course, with wood furniture inside. There will be contractions and dilating associated with the wood material, and these will be heard as noises of various types and sounds. Sometimes, the people are confusing that with signs of ghosts. In these kind of situations I show the people that; and I ask them for less money. Then the opposite, which is a ghost and she is active. Of course your question is about the second situation. In my country the witches have very strong spells. They were transferred from voice to voice by generations. They may differ from one witch to another. Just by saying this spell in the house at exactly the middle of the night, when the ghost feels that it's power is strong you can throw her out. However it is a necessity for strong concentration from the witch's side. Sometimes only talented witches can do this. Also basil, holy water, silver, and crucifixes may work well." Paul definitely knew what he was talking about.

"So if I know the right spell I can throw the ghost out. Will you teach it to me? Or maybe you have holy water I can throw at the ghost?" I wanted very badly to get more into this.

"Probably no. In my opinion there is also a fighting between energies. Our brain is elaborating energies. Think about this little mass of meat. It is able to create complicated equations, questions, or asking about it's own existence or . . . what will be beyond it's existence. Personally I find it to be fascinating. Do you think so too?"

I signalled my approval.

"Think about a solenoid with electric power inside. It is creating around it an inductive stream, a kind of magnetic field. Also our brain is able to create energy. It might be telepathy, kinaesthetic power or some kind of abilities that can be considered abnormal . . . by normal people." His words were very intellectual, and powerful, almost beyond comprehension.

"Coffee or tea?" asked the waiter, and I observed that he was listening to us, and he understood our subject. As result he became scared too. His voice had a fear vibration to it.

"Sorry, for disturbing you," he said to us.

"But?" Paul was demanding.

The waiter continued,

"I think my aunt has a ghost in her house . . . . I was hoping you might help her . . ."

*   *   *

I spent my day walking around the channels, and doing some minor shopping. Some of the stuff here in the shops are really very good. I have been able to find some good things, very nice models

41

that in my country would be much more expensive. I am also happy to walk around the streets without being accosted. Here the people don't recognize me. However, I heard my music in a couple of the bars. I have to ask my director about some remixes of my songs that I have never heard before. Already I started to think of a song, a kind of song for the middle of the night. I also heard if there is a ghost, and you make noises there might be a chance she may go away on her own. Though Paul mentioned nothing about this.

Even though our discussions were about ghosts, and this kind of . . . spooky stuff, I slept very well through the night. That means I hope the jet lag is now almost gone. I am happy for that.

It is almost 10 am now. According to his last phone call, I have to meet Paul here for a coffee. It is a nice coffee shop. It is close to Flowers Street. For me all of Amsterdam is around Flower Street, I have no intention to explore Amsterdam further. I limited my exploration only to couple areas closed to my hotel, and near Flowers Street. I saw that Paul also loves this street. It is really remarkable. I know here in Holland the flowers are a big tradition and especially the tulips. This coffee restaurant is very . . . well how should I say . . . European, and very, Dutch. Small tables, very nice room arrangement, and nice coffee cups. The blue Dutch colour on the cups, I could see a similarity with China's blue porcelain.

After Paul arrived, I told him about my good sleep and my hopes that the jet lag had finally gone.

"Yes it passes within a couple days," he agreed to me.

We start drinking our coffee. It tasted so good.

"I saw lots of interesting tulips bulbs here." I was very sincere with this comment.

"Yes, it is the tulip country. I really like them too. In origin the tulips appears to come from Turkey, yet the Dutch created a tradition by growing these flowers, and making a strong export with them. Also in the difficult war times the tulips bulbs were their main or only food."

"Really? I did not know that they were edible."

"I don't think they probably taste very good, I have never tried them myself." Paul had a funny look of disgust on his face.

He was appearing to enjoy his coffee though. It was quite good..

I was very curious about what was happening. He knows that I am curious, but I have noticed that he likes to play with my curiosity.

"How was last night? You went to the waiter's Aunt's house? Did she have a ghost in her house?" I was full of questions for him.

"Yes," Paul answered very bluntly.

"Yes . . . Which one?"

Definitely today he is enjoying that he can play with my curiosity.

"Both. It was a medium active ghost. Compared to the one from the Canadian house it was a quiet one. The waiter's Aunt is an old lady, and she was very disturbed by these inexplicable noises. Now she will have silence. I will have to introduce into your training lessons about these phenomena. It is quite interesting." He made some notes in his iPhone.

"Well, trying to speak about this as a business is a good one. The people are offering good money as they are really scared, and I can help them to recover their silence in their own house. Not only that, but I am helping the ghost too, the lost soul." Paul's voice exuded with confidence.

"Sorry for bothering you . . . but I need some more explanation."

"I have a different kind of way of dealing with this . . . stuff. The people who are coming with the spells, silver, holy water, they might throw out the ghost and maybe forever. Yet I feel like it is my duty to understand who exactly this ghost is, and to help her. I saw that even in Harry Potter it is known that magic is transmitted genetically inside families. In Romania, it is proven that it is mostly transmitted to the female gender. I believe that if there will be a couple of guys with these powers they might be very strong."

"Like you . . ." I felt the necessity to complete him."

"Thanks. He answered modestly." I don't know how, but I have the capacity to get in contact with these energy manifestations, and to communicate with them. I explain to them that their place is not there. Staying there, they will only disturb the person who is living in the house. Also that they will not find their way to the light. They have to go their own way."

"It appears . . . logical. If . . . I can search for logic here."

"Dear I do believe logic exists everywhere. Even in the paranormal, logic exists and it is very important. I do believe you have important skills, you have that special gift. I can see this. I can feel this. You have to learn to use your powers and abilities. You will understand there are two main logical points. The first is to know what you dealing with, and second will be with what intensity? Knowing these two points, you will know how to react."

I reflected deeply on this. I found this all very right.

"Going back to the ghost, you are thinking to convince them to go on their way. However they need to go away from the houses. Do they listen to you?"

"Not all of them," Paul matter-of-factly replied.

"How do you deal with the ghosts who refuse you? How do you make them leave the house?" I had to ask.

"By forcing them." Paul's answer was very simple.

He started laughing. His laugh was this time strange, and unknown to me until now. There were very few people present in the small cafe, and yet the ones that were there raised their heads, very disturbed by the strident laugh.

* * *

Finally, we are in the plane on the way to our final destination – Romania.

I am so excited about this. I was so happy today. I was laughing with Christina. She is very happy too. The check-in point though the airport were very long compared to what I was used to. I was talking with the little girl. She was so happy telling me about her play friends, her toys . . . she was so full of energy today. Paul was always admiring his niece. I can see in his eyes how much he loves her.

"Don't worry. When we are on the plane she will immediately fall asleep. She seems to really enjoy sleeping on the plane."

That was very true.

"It will be a short flight compared with the one from Canada. It will only take around three hours. In three hours we will be in Romania."

"Halibarda," said the little girl.

I looked at Paul's face for explanation because I totally misunderstood the word. He was smiling with satisfaction.

"Dear niece, Halibarda doesn't know exactly when we will return, so . . . this time we will take a taxi from the airport and we may see her over the next few days.

The little girl nodded with approval from her tiny head and she felt almost immediately into a deep sleep. She was like a little angel.

Chapter 4

The vampires are described in the old books as quite evil looking guys. In the new books and movies the vampires are presented as very handsome. However, they both have something in common. They like to suck your blood.

-Raluka-magical annalist

"Good Morning. My name is Halibarda, and I am very happy to meet you Laura."

The woman was standing in the front of my door. Her face was covered in a huge smile. She was ringing the bell at the right moment. Despite her strong Romanian accent, her English was very good and perfectly understandable.

Last night Paul put me up me in a condo, which was one of his properties. He had another one in the same building. Last night after I took a shower, I immediately fell asleep. In the morning I heard a couple of birds at the window, and I woke up. I managed to prepare myself a coffee, and I was watching out the window. I found the view quite interesting. This condo is situated at the upper level of the building. I think the building has ten levels or so. At the back of the building are only smaller buildings, so I have a large view from here. The other buildings have only four levels, and the trees are a bit taller than them. I am really happy with this view. The building is quite large. It is like a "U" shape, and I am in the middle part of the letter. I can see from here the inside of another person's condo. I think these people don't use their dryer very much. I can see lots of clothes arranged on their balcony, drying in the natural air. This is unusual for me as a Canadian.

I spent time enjoying my coffee, and watching the view from my living room window. I found it to be different from my Canadian cityscape, and I decided that I was happy because I came to Romania. I don't know exactly how long I contemplated this nice view, but according to my custom I need to eat my morning banana. It is my morning custom after I am done with my coffee. It has been my breakfast for more than twenty years. I thought that now I have a problem, as Paul has no bananas. To go through today, through this wonderful morning without my banana might mean my entire day will be a disaster. I am quite superstitious. Maybe this is a sign I am good witch. I am able to interpret signs, starting with small signs of the day, and how it will be. This trust gave me some optimism.

I looked at the women. She was a medium sized, yet tall woman. Her skin was a little dark. Maybe she is a gypsy, I thought. I think she was just a little bit older than fifty. Her body was proportionately acceptable. Maybe it was because of her age. Her belly was little bit big, but other than that she was acceptable looking.

"I know you don't know me . . . yet. I am a good friend of . . ."

"Paul's." I completed her sentence.

"Yes," she replied.

She was gazing at me. Her face was full with that wonderful smile.

"I have some bananas for you." She reached out her hand with the bananas.

I took one immediately, and I started eating it. I felt like myself again. How could I pass through a morning without my banana? I was already starting to love Halibarda.

"I tried to clean this condo for you. I hope you find it acceptable," she said.

"Thanks," I smiled at her. "It is indeed clean, I have seen no dust."

Her smile became bigger and I felt very welcome.

"Dear, I'm not speaking about dusting, or stuff like that. I cleaned it from spirits and other magical entities. My wish is for you to have a wonderful sleep, and to be relaxed in the morning. I tried to eliminate any disruption here. I am telling you about a magical kind of cleaning . . . of this zone. You know . . . here we don't use the dream catchers. Paul told me that your Indian wizard is a strong one. He made those powerful dream catchers you have in the window of your cabin. I hope you will introduce me at some point to him. I understood from Paul the he is a great wizard."

"I think he is," I am not very convinced, though I don't like to contradict this woman.

"Take your time," she said. You have lots of bananas now." She started singing as she walked into my bedroom. I watched her making my bed, and arranging things inside the bedroom.

"I am little bit confused. Are you the house keeper?"

Her face was lighted again by that wonderful smile.

"No," she replied. "I am a witch, and I am Paul's greatest friend."

I could not breathe for a couple of seconds. The words came very normally from her mouth, yet their impact on me was huge. To be a witch seems to be very normal here in Romania.

"Yes, indeed." She said in a very matter of fact fashion.

"What?" I asked.

"Yes indeed," she said again. "Witches are very normal here. Some of us are so successful that the government was thinking of taking taxes from our activities. They tried to do it but the law failed."

"How are you able to read my mind?" I was very confused.

"Dear . . . Paul is much more gifted than I. I do have some abilities here. Though I am not like him. Well . . . forget about these for now and eat your banana. Would you like more coffee?"

"Oh . . . no thanks I think I have had enough." She was very sweet, and yet very mysterious to me.

"Please let me come tomorrow to prepare the coffee in the Romanian style. You will be very impressed. It might be a huge change for someone like you who likes filtered coffee. We don't use filters. It is almost like a Turkish coffee, or like Arabian sand made coffee, yet somehow . . . different. I hope you will like it."

"For sure. You have made me very curious."

"Okay, I think we are done here. How about a walk in the park? We are very lucky to live in the neighborhood of a great park."

"I would like very much to take a walk in the park," I said.

"The park is very close to our location," she said on our way to the elevator. "It takes only 2 minutes by foot."

It was around nine am. In the spring morning I discovered a corner of Bucharest that was quite beautiful. The people were walking around. The street was nicely cleaned. From place-to-place, they were very nice, relaxing, and very well maintained. Between buildings were lots of green spaces well protected by pretty metal fences. I think the designer of this corner of Bucharest did a good job. Halibarda was right. The walk to the park was very short. It was in fact at the very first intersection. I realized it was really nice, as Halibarda said. We started walking in the park. Her face was lighted by her big smile. She seemed to really enjoy my presence. I enjoyed her presence as well. She seemed to be a very nice lady. Oh . . . sorry. I should say a very nice witch.

Little by little I started to be impressed by this park. I thought from the corner of the park I could see its end. Yet . . . this park is huge. I have this awesome sensation since in the middle of the park there is a huge lake. The way from here to the lake is in fact through a small valley. I was very impressed by the dimensions of this lake. In fact it was centered in the middle of the park.

"Is this park the biggest park in Bucharest?" I asked.

"Oh, no. It is not the biggest, nor is it the nicest. Tomorrow or the next day, I will bring you to the nicest park of Bucharest. The name of that one is Cismigiu."

"That seems to be quite a difficult name for me. Which is the name of this one?"

"This one is an easy name for you. It is Titan. It is very easy to remember, I guess. If you are alone in the town and you have to take a cab you can easily remember to tell to the driver to go to the Titan Park. From here you will be able to guide him to the access door of our building. Though don't forget to ask the driver when he starts the car to start also the pay machine, and pay him exactly the amount of money that appears on the machine. I would suggest for you to have the exact amount of money. Otherwise they may take advantage of you. However, we will always manage to make sure you are with one of us."

We were walking very close to the lake. To go there we chose some fancy stairs.

"There was a time when water was here," Halibarda said.

"How come?" I asked Halibarda. I was very curious.

"There used to be a waterfall. It was an artificial one. It was so very pretty with lot of flowers around. It was quite nice." She appeared to be day dreaming for a moment of the previous waterfall that was here. It was like for just a brief moment I felt the nice sound of the waterfall too.

"Why did they change the design?" I asked her directly.

"I am not sure. However, I think some changes are welcome from time to time. Maybe the main duty of the artificial waterfall was to take the water from lake and to re-circulate it back. Like this was done with the oxygenation of the lake's water, which is good especially for the fish."

"It was a wonderful idea," I said to her, envisioning the presence of the waterfall.

I wondered a little bit about her perception. Most of the time I don't even think that deep about the oxygenation of the water in parks, and such things.

"Yes, and now it is better. A huge fountain helps with the oxygenation of water. You will see it soon." She smiled to me like she was proud to show me the park, the lake, and the fountain.

We were walking around the lake. It was very well maintained with lots of benches around.

"There on the south side is a small and wild island. It is so wild, and I thought there is some . . . wild stuff too. Last summer I saw a guy and girl naked there," Halibarda said, as she winked at me. She smiled at me nicely from time to time. She was studying me with her curious eyes.

We started to walk on the opposite side of the lake. I was impressed by how many roses could be on this site. They were nicely disposed around a huge fountain. It seemed to be quite a large vessel with lots of other vessels circularly disposed around the big one. The water is flowing down from the big vessel to the smallest vessels. Usually I don't like symmetry. But here, it is a nice design. The artist had done a very good job. Maybe this is the fountain for oxygenating the lake water.

"It is not the big jet fountain I told you before," Halibarda stated at me. "I used to come here before this fountain was made. It was only a place for roses. Quite interesting, but it was like something was missing here. Now with this fountain, it looks like we have the missing item."

I checked the disposal of the roses around the fountain. They were indeed nicely arranged. Definitely the artist who projected it had particular talent to use the symmetry to create wonderful effects. Now that it is early spring, I am sure that this place would be gorgeous in the summer.

The sound of falling water is so relaxing. I felt like I could stay here for a whole day just to listen to it.

"I, myself enjoyed listening to the sound of the water in the waterfall more."

Again I had the sensation somehow this women was able to read my mind.

"When you look around you can see roses, trees, herbs and so on. I know almost all their chemistry. I know how to use the roots to do interesting and efficient nepenthe. In fact maybe the correct word here is alchemy."

"How do you know all of these things?" I asked inquisitively.

"My mother taught me. As per my origin I am a gypsy. I do believe we gypsies are very talented. My mother definitely was. She taught me all that she knew."

"Halibarda, it's fabulous that you are so proud of your heritage. Maybe you could teach me some stuff about nepenthe one day."

"Yes. It would be my pleasure. We are always looking for talented students." She seemed very confident in her statement of teaching me of such wonderful magical talents.

I tried to have my own silence by listening to the sound of the water falling from the large vessel to the smaller vessels, and after that in the big basin of the fountain. We stayed together at the base of the fountain basin. The base was quite large. Halibarda was focusing her eyes . . . to something. Maybe she was trying to read my mind again.

"It is important to learn to do silent meditations. Try to calm yourself. I am telling you about a kind of yoga meditation. I know you have practiced yoga. I have practiced it too. Only a couple of meetings because . . . in my position I observed the level I am doing all that stuff is . . . far superior." She made a long pause, and she was looking at me like she was drawing a very large conclusion.

"Don't forget, your concentration determines your reality. In yoga and Buddhism its called meditation. Here in Romania we are mostly Christians, and mostly orthodox. We have a part of Romania called . . ."

"Transylvania." I completed her sentence.

"Dear Laura . . ." she was smiling, and after politely laughing she continued.

"No. Transylvania will be another subject. I am speaking to you now about Moldavia. There are a lot of churches. Paul told me that there are so many and so close together they almost form a great wall like in China."

She paused again, and was gazing at me. I understood now that when she has done this before she is allowing me to conclude something interesting. I started to understand her and started to like her as well.

"Maybe I should visit them."

"Yes. I was there with Paul a couple of years ago visiting all of them."

"You and Paul? But you are . . . wizards. Why would you visit?"

"That's right. I told him that too. He said we are two Romanians who are going to visit Moldavian churches for praying. I remember we started our trip with one monastery called Dragomirna. In the middle of the immense land the church rose tall and imposed like a prayer. The priest told us ,'Thanks for coming. God will reward your patience.

"Oh so nice . . ." she seemed truly impressed.

"Yes, I took from that trip lots of soulful words. Deep in Moldavia we also have a monastery completely colored in blue inside and out. Until now we did not know the formula or the essence of that paint that was used for painting. It is like a magic. For years and years the blue color has still been there, even the external walls despite the wind, rain and snow. It was built more than five hundred years ago. There was something . . . it was indeed magic. Like a big tear dropped on the earth, and it created this monastery."

She paused again for a couple of seconds.

"We were trying to sleep in their very small accommodation rooms. I tried to pray with the monk men and women. By my education I am a religious woman. I like the morning praying. But staying there with the monks and praying with them, well, it is like meditation. In that time it is possible to pass in into a superior level of concentration. Having a wonderful sensation like touching God."

She paused again listening to the sound of water.

"What I mean by all of this is it doesn't matter if you call it meditation, concentration, praying and so on. If you are doing it well, it will help you pass to a superior level of concentration. I have realized it is very important especially in . . . magic. If you are not able to do it, you cannot do magic."

"And opposite," I added.

"Yes. When you are at this level you can focus to the superior stuff and in our situation to do . . . magic. Try to practice different kinds of concentrations in your room. I recommend you start with a kind of relaxation concentration. Try to be able to pass as quickly as possible into that stage. It is essential." She was gazing at me deeply with her dark eyes.

"I am sure you can do it. You are a gifted person. I can feel it."

We continued to walk in this nice park. The spring made the park much nicer. I am sure I will love the summer when the roses are in full bloom. This side of the park will be gorgeous. I intend to come to see it.

"In the summer when the roses are blooming this side of the park is gorgeous," Halibarda said.

"Yes, that is exactly what I thought."

She gestured approval with her head.

We were walking down to the lake. We went onto a very big concrete plateau, very well arranged. It gave us a large preview of the lake. From here we can see the gorgeous jet fountain too. I think the jet is taller than twenty meters. It was a wonderful spring day.

"In Calgary during this time it is still winter," I mentioned to her.

"Yes I know. Here the spring starts in March. We have a nice celebration of spring arrivals on March first. Of course with the climate change now we have surprises here too, but still the spring comes here earlier than it does in Calgary, than most of Canada actually. Here it is a wonderful spring and especially in this park. Maybe we will have this opportunity to follow the spring together."

"Yes," I agreed with her. This idea made me much more optimistic.

We were spending a lot of time staying on this nice patio, and enjoying the spring sun.

After a time, we walked down to the lake by some large stairs.

"I think you have already observed that in the roses zone, and most of the other parts of the park are paving stones. Here is mostly asphalt."

"Why the difference?" I asked.

"Because, the guys with roller blades, skateboards, bicycles can ride easily here."

"Oh . . . yes," I was little embarrassed that I didn't realize that sooner.

"Of course with the bicycles they can come in the roses zone but it is mostly a walking zone. I like the paving stones. I think they did a good job here with the paving stones."

"Yes," I agreed with her.

"I was in Paris, Champs Elise, Le Jardain de Luxemburg . . . I don't like the paving there . . . at the time when I visited there was a strong wind and it was so very dusty. I felt much better when I walked in this park. Maybe because it is close with my current philosophy."

She seemed to be very silent in her thoughts.

"You seem to travel a lot, Halibarda."

"Yes. I visited Paul in Canada too. We went to Banff, Drumheller, Radium and so on. We did house boating on the Shuswap Lake. Maybe we can meet in Calgary once." She smiled to me.

"It would be my pleasure Halibarda." I liked conversing with her very much.

"Thanks dear. Paul also told me about that Indian wizard, I would like to meet him."

"Do you like to meet people?" I asked her.

"Yes, I like meeting people. I always try to meet people. I like to listen their stories. I try to understand their universe, explore their philosophy. The possibilities are endless."

I really liked this woman, her thoughts, and her philosophy. I knew instinctively she was going to become a good friend of mine.

"Laura, we have been walking for a while. It is almost eleven, and we did not have breakfast before. I know that your breakfast is only coffee and bananas." She smiled again. "Mine is only coffee. Maybe we can walk around to the park's restaurant to get something to eat."

"I think that is a splendid idea," I replied without hesitation. Halibarda smiled at me.

"Okay then . . . lets go." We continued to walk around the lake.

"Paul can't join us today," she said. "He is little bit busy with the club business. He asked me to send his apologies."

"That's okay." I replied shrugging my shoulders nonchalantly.

She stopped in her tracks briefly for a moment, and gazed at me. Accentuating the words she said,

"I am one of the founding members of the club. Maybe we can chat more about this club over lunch if you would like?"

"That is a wonderful idea," I replied very quickly.

Finally we reached the restaurant. It was a very nice building inside the park. The walls were totally made of glass, as we are able to see the park from our table. The inside was really very elegant. I can see the traditional Romanian arrangements are in very good accordance with the modern window walls. All were very well arranged, and very well maintained. The waiter was a very young and handsome guy. I enjoyed watching him.

"Here there are lots of handsome guys," Halibarda said. "As Romanians seem to be very close with the Italians; also our language is very, very close with Italian. Well, as closely as I can easily understand Italian."

We ordered steak and red wine, and we continued our discussion about the witches club.

"Because in Romania are a lot of witches, Paul and I decided to found this club. The first members were our close friends who were witches or wizards as well. The main reason was that sometimes in our magic there have been . . . strange experiences, and we have found that it is very useful to share them between us. We found it useful to learn from our various experiences and to conclude how we can safely go on."

"That is very interesting, and it is definitely a wonderful idea."

"I think now we are around one hundred members, and I think more witches will join our club. However, very famous witches of Romania are not members at all. I guess they are busy with their work, and of course I understand this. It is not mandatory to be a member of this club to be recognized as a wizard. Though it is important to be a wizard or very interested in these kinds of activities in order to be a member of our club"

"Would you like to become a member of our club Laura?"

"Yes, I would really like this. You know Halibarda, I was always attracted to the magical arts, and the dark places, being alone in a woods and so on." I felt it necessary to give her the whole truth at this point of what, and how I felt, and what I truly was seeking.

"Good, that is definitely very good Laura. I will give you a document paper to sign."

"Do I have to pay a fee?"

"No. There are no fees. Our witches are rich enough. If you would like to do an activity the financial participation is only on a volunteer basis. For example if I would like to organize a conference, I can do it at one of my residences and all at my own expenses if someone wants to contribute with money of course he is welcome. Money is not a big problem for us, but regarding the magical research is another story."

"How do you know which ones are real wizards? Is there a criterion to segregate wizards from fakers?"

"Firstly, not all the guys who are pretending to be witches are witches. There are many fakers. Or at least guys who believed they are strong wizards but their power and their abilities are not so . . . strong."

"I guess it is difficult to guess that."

"Well . . . let's say Paul and I, have special abilities in terms of this subject. We can feel when a wizard is strong. Secondly, if one particular guy already has made a business from magic, and the people are visiting him then we can understand that he has special talents, and he can be accepted in our club."

"Are there strong wizards in your club?"

"Oh yes there definitely are. We have made an exception for Raluka."

"For Raluka? Why?"

"Well, she has lots of theoretical knowledge . . . but she is not a witch. You will soon have some training with her. You will study the history of magic in Romania, theoretical knowledge about spirits, ghosts, vampires, and spells. After that I would like to start you with some practical magic."

She gazed at me and smiled.

"I am very excited about this. Yet I am afraid with Raluka I will accumulate lots of knowledge and still no magical power."

Halibarda was touching my hand at the table. She was closing her eyes and she tried to meditate for just a few seconds. Finally she opened her eyes and she said,

"Dear, you will be a strong witch."

*　　*　　*

The lunch was gorgeous, and to die for. The Romanians definitely have very good red wine. After lunch Halibarda said she wanted to show me downtown Bucharest. The Titan Park has underneath it the underground subway train station. They call it the Metro here. I have to become familiar with these key words. Halibarda had with her two monthly pass cards, one for each of us. She explained to me that the underground transportation, The Metro runs very good, and you can go almost to any side of the city very quickly.

The inside of the Metro train was very modern. I saw very many attractive guys. Halibarda was looking at them too.

"The Metro transportation is very good as I said. Unfortunately, as it is underground, we cannot see the town. For this I recommend you to take a cab. I would not recommend you rent a car. The town is very crowded. Driving here requires very special skills." She confidently stated.

"I am a very good driver though," I objected

"Dear, not here. You will see soon what I mean."

She paused looking at two guys.

"I told you the Romanian guys are very handsome here."

We stopped at the station called 'Unirea'. This was in the core of the town. Once we reached the surface I observed that the town was definitely very crowded. I looked in the roads and I started to agree with Halibarda. It was definitely better not to drive here. We were walking in the front of the complex called Unirea. I saw many wonderful fountains. They were so wonderful, as they made me think about Paris. After that I saw a very big building.

"It is the 'People House' or in Romanian 'Casa Poporului'." Halibarda explained that it was quite a large building even for Europe.

We were walking around the fountains close with 'Casa Poporului'. I was fascinated by it's dimensions, and it's architecture. After that we were walking back to Unirea and inside the mall. There are so many things I would like to buy. They are of very good quality. I saw a lot of artisan things there with the face of Vlad the Impaler. I decided to ask Halibarda about this Impaler at the first opportunity.

I think we were walking like this for more than three hours.

"After walking so long dear, I think we need to have a drink," Halibarda said. I accepted immediately.

"It is about fifteen minutes to a really nice bar I know," Halibarda said as we kept walking.

We were walking from the Unirea to the direction of a nice tower.

"What exactly is this tower?"

"Dear, this is the Intercontinental Hotel. It is quite famous. The bar I would like to go is very close to it.

Near the Intercontinental Hotel there are lots of nice buildings. One of them is the Theater Place."

In the Theatre building we went for the dink.

The bar is called 'The Actor's Coffee Shop'.

We asked our waitress to bring us a round of beers. Halibarda recommended I try some Romanian beer. She asked for a beer called Bergenbeer. I remember Bergen is in the German language the word for mountain.

"Cheers Halibarda," I raised my glass towards her.

She pointed a finger at me.

"Dear Laura. It is the time for you to learn a couple of Romanian words. Cheers in the Romanian language is 'Noroc'."

"Okay . . . 'Noroc' Halibarda."

"Noroc, Laura."

The Bergenbeer tasted very good. Halibarda was right. It was good beer.

"It is my favorite beer," Halibarda said.

I looked around the inside of the bar. It was arranged in a old western style. The bar was quite large inside.

"They have another level underneath," Halibarda explained to me.

"It is indeed a nice bar," I replied.

"Yes, it surely is," Halibarda approved watching around the bar. "I suppose it could be the equivalent of a Calgary bar called Out-burn."

"Yes," I approved, though a little bit embarrassed because Out-burn is not quite large as this one.

"Halibarda, what do you know about the Vlad the Impaler?"

"Which of his lives are you asking about?"

I was little bit shocked by Halibarda's question.

"Tell me anything you want. Tell me all that you know."

She was gazing me.

"Why are you so interested in this subject?"

"I think it is . . . interesting. I feel that a lot of people in my country are very interested in this subject, as am I."

Halibarda's face became very serious.

"Very well. From history point of view he was a very famous king. He was fighting with Turkish and he was very bloody. So bloody, our club believes that after his death he became a vampire."

"Paul told me about this hypothesis."

"Yes. However he is gone now."

"What do you mean? If he was truly a vampire they don't die."

"I meant that after he became a vampire, a nice girl, who he fell in love with, killed him. She killed him using an old Romanian tradition. She used a large stick and implanted it in his heart."

She became silent for a moment taking a long sip from her beer.

"I have asked myself what level his spirit is on. This is a question for Raluka." Halibarda became silent again.

I tried focusing on her words and I tried to fixate directly on her. Then . . . I saw behind her, at another table, a handsome guy. He was looking at me too. After couple moments of silence I observed that Halibarda caught the direction where I looked. She was looking behind her back at the handsome guy. She was looking back at me.

"Laura, I think I have to go. You can finish your beer, and after you may take a taxi back home. Remember go to Titan Park, once in that zone you will be able to guide the driver to our building. I'll give you some Romanian change and . . . have fun."

She was smiling at me and after hugging me she left the bar.

Immediately after she left the bar the handsome guy came directly to my table.

"May I introduce myself? My name is Vlad."

I shook the hand of this handsome gentleman.

"Vlad, like the Impaler?"

"You are?"

"My name is Laura." I replied.

"That is a very nice name. Laura, may I offer you a beer?"

"No thank you."

He was confused for a moment.
"Vlad may I offer you a beer?"
He smiled, a captivating smile right at me.
"Yes please," he gracefully accepted.

*   *   *

The strong smell of coffee woke me up and . . . God . . . Vlad was not here.

I had a gorgeous, fabulous night in my condo with this handsome guy, and in the morning he left me. Tears flooded my eyes. In the kitchen Halibarda was preparing the coffee. She was very easily singing a song in Romanian. She seemed to be so happy. When she saw how sad I looked she gave me a huge smile.

"Good morning dear Laura. How did you sleep?"

Though the smile faded from her face as soon as she observed the tears streaming from my eyes.

"Laura . . . what's wrong?"

"Halibarda, I said, I am so sad today. I am sadder than I have ever been in my entire life. Yet I think, I have just lived the most beautiful love story of my life."

"Oh dear," she sighed, and she strongly cuddled me.

Chapter 5

The way Halibarda prepared coffee was quite interesting. It was somehow the total opposite of filtered coffee. She boiled the water, and when the water finished boiling she stopped the fire and added the coffee grounds. After that she let the coffee sit in the vessel for ten minutes to allow the sludge to be decanted. After ten minutes she put the coffee in the cans so as not to disturb the grinds in the bottom of the vessel. After that she waited another 10 minutes before serving the coffee. We were supposed to drink the coffee without tilting the cup as it still had some grinds in the bottom. The coffee was quite concentrated it tasted like an espresso but with more water, like a café americano. I was afraid of this way of preparing the coffee, I was worried that maybe the grinds would remain stuck in middle of my stomach. She was laughing, telling me that she has been drinking coffee prepared like this for years and she is just fine. She explained to me that this coffee was better tasting, and almost all the grinds were gone because of the successive decantation.

Also, she told me that the remaining grind at the bottom of our cup allows us to see into the future.

At home were only Halibarda and I. Yet she prepared three cups of coffee.

I looked at the third coffee cup on the table.

"Paul is going to come over to have coffee with us this morning," she added.

We were taking some sips from the coffee prepared by Halibarda. I have to admit that this way of preparing coffee was definitely becoming my favorite, and because the taste of this coffee was so good and so different. It appeared to be more natural. Definitely I have to try making this coffee for myself one day.

The couple moments of silence we had helped me to pass the tragedy of this morning, the tragedy of my life. Vlad was gone.

The discrete doorbell was ringing. Both of us knew that it was Paul. Halibarda made an affirmative sign with her hand, and I walked to open the door.

He was standing in the front of the door smiling.

"Dear Laura," he was hugging me and kissing me. Paul then continued with a very low voice "he will come back to you . . . today."

His words made me my day.

Suddenly I started to become happy. I loved Paul. He came with great news. Vlad would come back and that would happen today. I know Paul was a wizard. I am sure he is right. This really was the news of the day. I had something very useful to do today. It was waiting for Vlad's return.

"May I come in?" Paul asked.

"Yes, of course," I said. The manners I had been taught left me for a moment. I totally forgot to invite him inside. His words were so spectacular for me though. They gave me a new perspective for my life. Vlad will come back to me.

Paul walked in the living room and he showed me a bottle,

"Actually I have a gift for you today dear Laura. The name of this Romanian plum vodka is Vlad, like the Impaler. The name of it is 'Tzuica'. As you know vodka is 40% alcohol. This one is 45% alcohol. However, if you go into Transylvania we will find homemade drinks called 'Palinca', and it is distilled a minimum of three times.

As a result the content of alcohol in this Palinca is more than 45%. I do very much like this 'Vlad Tzuica'."

"I will advise you to not drink as much as he drinks," Halibarda intervened in our discussion.

He was looking long at Halibarda, and after that he looked back to me.

"That's right, my focus increases when I drink more alcohol, and in order to increase my focus I am digesting huge quantities of alcohol."

"Huge quantities!" Halibarda repeated his sentence.

"You might be able to drink the same amount like me Laura. Who knows?"

"No, no . . ." Halibarda was persistent in her thought. "Never try it Laura."

Ignoring Halibarda, Paul continued on with his ideas.

"Digesting huge quantities of alcohol is like doing magic. You have to direct the alcohol molecules in exactly these zones of your brain you need. You have to use the power of these molecules to increase your magic abilities, and to do what you intend to do."

He was gazing at Halibarda. The woman became silent. Her face was showing instead that she totally disagreed with Paul.

"We have to understand the possibilities of our power. We need to take the substances we need to increase our powers, and I do believe that the alcohol is one of them."

He paused a little bit, moving his eyes from me to Halibarda.

"Now, after interrupting me so much Halibarda, may I have my coffee?"

Halibarda said nothing. She only made a big affirmative sign, and disappeared into the kitchen.

After a couple of moments she came in with the coffee pot and she filled Paul's cup. Also she completed the coffee in our cups as well. Here they used very nice European cups for coffee. They were really very nice. I think I've only kinds of cups only in the movies with kings and noble families. They were nicely painted, not only on the outside of the cup, and on the inside as well. Actually I found that to be very nice; you are drinking coffee, and little by little you discover the design on the inside cup.

We had a couple moments of silence, a couple moments of peace. I don't know why but I had a strange feeling. It was like this peace that was in fact about to precede a storm.

"It was in accordance with my thinking," Paul said.

"You have to go back somehow to your yoga teachings. I can teach you more kinds of meditation to become calm. You have to know how to gain energy from these kinds of moments. Sometimes this peace is in fact the silence before a storm. I remember it from my childhood. After each terrible storm I realized in fact the silence of the moments before the storm. After that, I was able to foresee the future through the tragedies; both with natural and human futures."

"He is pretty good," Halibarda said very quickly after him.

"How do you do it?" I dared to ask him.

"Well . . . nobody can explain it correctly. There are some theories in place, though nothing sure until now. It is like I am able to come in contact with some resonance energies, and I can extrapolate the future. It is like if a big tragedy happens, and a lot a people suffer, there is a king of . . . an energy, a resonance energy . . . a kind of . . . impending regret. After that then the inevitable tragedy is happening. The people suffer so much that it creates an energy that surpasses the barrier of time. I can catch their suffering before it happens."

"Is it possible to prevent it?" I was very curious, and I thought there might be some possibilities to prevent it.

"I don't know . . . The warnings exist, therefore I can catch it. I have to understand after that when, where, how . . . It is not always easy to answer to these capital questions. If my predictions are close with that specific thing I might be able to take some actions . . . we might discuss more about these practices."

We were almost done with the coffee.

"It has somehow gotten very late. Halibarda intended to cook for us today. It might take her around two hours. We could go for a walk in the park. What do you think?"

"Yes, of course." I accepted.

"Do you need anything that we could buy on our way back Halibarda?"

"No, I think I have everything I need. Or . . . if I remember something I will call you."

"Okay . . . let's go Laura."

The park was so beautiful this fine morning. In fact it was almost eleven in the morning. It was such a beautiful spring day.

"Soon it will rain. It will be a little storm." Paul said very nonchalantly.

"Really? Did you watch the forecast?" I asked.

"No, I feel it. I told you I can feel the storm."

We were walking around the lake. I found it to be very familiar, and knew the park from the day before. Halibarda introduced me to these places. I felt like these people knew and understood the nature well.

"You can always ask me about what other people tried to explain to you before about magic, witches, the witches club, and any other things you may be curious about."

"Thanks. Actually I have some questions about Halibarda. Is she really a gypsy?"

"Yes, as I said I will call them Roma. If you don't call them Roma you might upset them."

"How come?"

"Maybe because before they did some kind of . . . regrettable stuff, and they would like to change it. Yes, she is a Roma. I don't know any more about her family. Though I think she was born as a witch. That means her mother was a witch, her grandmother was a witch, the mother of her grandmother was witch too, and so on. It was somehow demonstrated that this was a genetic heritage. In the Gypsies and Romanian families this magic tradition this was part of their heritage. Usually this was transferable only for the women, not sure for males. There may be a few exceptions however."

"How about you?" I asked.

He smiled largely at me.

"As I said there might be a few exceptions. It might be a guy from a family with not a strong magic tradition, and he could be a very strong wizard. However, I don't know one. I always say it in the club though. If I don't say it, then the witches members of my club might be ignorant, and I don't want this."

We started to go to the rose side of the park. Suddenly Paul's cell phone started to ring. He had a short conversation in Romanian. A couple of times he increased his voice, sometimes he was laughing. Finally he ended his conversation and closed the phone.

"It was Halibarda. She needs us to buy something for her. We have to go back. I know in Canada we don't have many farmers markets but here we have many. Almost each community of Bucharest has one of these kinds of markets. We have a very nice one in our neighborhood."

"Is it called the Titan farmers market?" I asked taking what I thought was a good guess.

"No . . . here we have a lot of history, stories, and names of people. We have a lot of choices. Each street has it's own name. There is a wide variety. It was also hard for me, when I moved in Bucharest. Sometimes I was embarrassed by my lack knowledge of history. The name of the farmers market is Minis. It might not be an easy word for you compared to Titan. Don't worry though, you don't have to remember it."

The farmers market was close to the Titan Park. I was very impressed by that. There were lots of Romanian farmers with apples, lettuce, veggies and other spring stuff. It was very big. So I asked Paul.

"Is this the biggest market of Bucharest?"

He smiled almost laughing

"Oh, Laura, in fact it is one of the smallest ones."

Some Romanian farmers were addressing me in Romanian. I was able to conclude that they were asking me to buy some of their products.

"Their products are pretty good. It is exactly what we call organic products in Canada. On their farms this is the way they grow all of their fruit and vegetables. I found them very tasty. I have really been having a nice time from this point of view since I have been here."

He was exchanging a couple of words with some farmers and he bought some lettuce, some kind of strange herbs, I don't know the name exactly, some kind of pickled tomatoes, and some bananas too. I was not able to resist having one. He also stopped in a front of a farmer with some apples. They were so yellow they appeared to be almost gold. He bought one kilo and he offered me one. I accepted it, as I was done with my banana. It tasted so very good. It is unbelievably sweet and its smell was just so wonderful.

He smiled at me.

"As I said, it is all totally organic."

When we stepped back in the house I was impressed by the nice smell that was coming from the kitchen. I could not resist congratulating Halibarda on it. She started to explain me about the soup she was preparing that was a very famous soup in Romania. In fact it was a kind of a meatball soup, but very sour. She explained to me because it is sour they don't call it soup. The correct Romanian word for it is 'Ciorba'. I found it to be a funny word.

Suddenly the door's bell started ringing.

"I think is Raluka. We invited her for lunch. Let me to introduce her to you."

Raluka was stepping inside. She was a medium height lady, and slim. Her hair was long almost to her shoulders. She looked very well, and she was very professionally dressed. She looks like being 50 years old. Her face had a grave air to it.

Halibarda was making the presentations. "Laura please meet Raluka. Raluka please meet Laura."

"I am so pleased to meet you Laura," Raluka said smiling very professionally. Consciously correcting her Romanian accent she added "I brought the dessert. It is a very popular cake here with sour or tart cherries. In some dictionaries the sour cherry appears like morello."

She showed me the cake on a very nice plate, and I have to admit that the cake looked really good. I could hardly resist eating a piece of it almost immediately. That could be the reason that Halibarda covered the cake immediately and took it away.

"The Ciorba is ready." Halibarda announced in a grave voice.

"Somehow to make peace," Raluka added.

"Oh that is wonderful, sour meatball soup. Thanks Halibarda. I die to taste it."

We stepped into the very nice living room. The candles were on the table. Halibarda put the Ciorba on the table in a nice large ceramic soup pot. The Ciorba smelled so very enticing. This was a little bit strange for me and I don't think I have smelled this in my county.

All was so nice and cozy. I could not resist recording a few moments with my camcorder. I thought that it was too bad because the camcorder could not capture the smell as well.

"Sometimes the best record for our memories is the recording we are doing with our brain. We call it mnemonic record," Paul added.

I have to admit that he is right. Usually I get mad when I look for a particular video, and I always seem to have troubles finding it. Lots of times I just play it from my own memory.

We sat down around the table. With grave gestures, and using a huge spoon Halibarda filled my soup bowl with Ciorba. She served after that Paul, Raluka and herself.

Paul filled up our shot glasses with Tzuica. Now I know the name for their vodka. Raluka was looking little bit confused.

"Noroc," Paul said.

Now I know 'Noroc' means cheers. We toasted but I could hear a fear in Raluka's voice. Nice crystal sounds were filling the room. At that same moment a very bright light flashed outside. After that I heard a violent boom. The storm started.

Paul smiled at me,

"This is the storm I foresaw."

Outside the storm was quite violent. But inside was very nice, the candles were lit at the table, the smell of Ciorba was so nice. It is like we were protected here against the storm by a powerful magic.

We drink the Tzuica in silence. Raluka was not able to do the same. Her eyes were looking very confused, like she was asking for an apology.

We were looking at the outside disaster. The storm was pretty strong. Paul was checking for the content of what was left in the glasses. Paul's and Halibarda glasses were empty. I decided to do the same as Raluka, and that was only to sip from the content of the shot glass with the strong drink.

They also passed me a small bowl with hot chili peppers. I remember this from the Chinese market. It is unbelievable that they have it all here. All of them were taking a piece of hot pepper. They started with a small little bit from it. Paul was watching all the time that the glasses don't remain empty. However he and Halibarda were drinking . . . a lot. If I was to drink that much I would be drunk already.

I started to eat the soup. I have to admit that it was sour and unbelievable tasty.

"Raluka," Paul started, "Laura has wonderful abilities to become a strong witch. Her best friend is a north Indian wizard. She has a couple of dream catchers made by that wizard's hand and . . . I have to admit that she is almost totally protected by them."

I do not know why but I heard a strange tone in his voice.

"Oooh . . ." Raluka wondered, "that kind of north Indian magic is to filter the dreams. Laura did you understood the way it works?" She was fixing her hazel eyes on me. Professionally, she started to explain me.

"Our dreams come from outside. There are lots of factors which determine our dreams. Usually they come from the outside. Sometimes they are sent to you by people with bad intentions, wizards, witches or just some bad spirits that try to catch you. If the dream catchers are the right ones they will protect you against this bad stuff. They will filter the bad content of the dreams. I intend myself to come to North America to find an Indian wizard to buy a couple of dream catchers from him for myself."

"You have bad dreams?" Halibarda asked

"Sometimes . . . But you know me Halibarda. I like having dream catchers."

"Yes," Halibarda said while she filled up her second bowl of soup. She did that with my bowl even though it was not totally empty. I thought this was a polite Romanian custom.

"I want to receive bad dreams. I am a witch. I like to feel who is trying to attack me, and who I should be connected with. I need to see the reality, to feel it. Once I know who I am dealing with, I will know what to do."

"Not all of us are strong like you Halibarda," Raluka said. "Lots of us need dream catchers."

"I would be happy Raluka to invite you to my home in Canada and introduce you to my wizard friend," I said to her very sincerely.

"Thanks Laura. That would be great."

"Raluka, Laura is at the beginning. She is just starting to learn about magic. Maybe you can help her in gaining some theoretical knowledge." Paul was filling a Tzuica for himself.

"It would be my pleasure," Raluka said smiling.

"Good, good," said Paul satisfied.

Halibarda stared to collect the soup bowls.

"Laura, you have to be aware that Raluka has very good magical knowledge. She is a wonderful magic analyst, but her magical powers are somewhat limited."

"I admit it. You will be able to take a lot of knowledge from me. Unfortunately I am not a witch."

"If you are not a witch, how come you are so close to all of this stuff?"

"Laura, even when I was a child I was attracted to everything about magic. It is amazing for me. Maybe the things I can do are very few, but I always will enjoy collecting knowledge."

I smiled at Raluka.

"Me as well, Raluka. I don't know how strong I am with this stuff. I know for sure that I need knowledge. Thanks for accepting the responsibility to teach me."

Raluka smiled at me again.

Halibarda was arriving with a big bowl that was filled with cabbage. She explained to me that it could be called 'lazy man's cabbage rolls' or 'cabbage a la Cluj'.

"Cluj is the name of a big town in Transylvania. The meat is mixed with rice, tomato paste, and salt. In the bowl the cabbage is arranged layer by layer, one layer of mixed meat, one layer of cabbage, and so on. All of it is cooked in the oven with a small fire for almost three hours."

"She said lazy mans cabbage rolls because she is . . . lazy." Paul added. I did not know how to react. Halibarda was being so nice doing this great cooking for us and he was so . . . rude with his remark towards her.

Taking a diplomatic face Halibarda said,

"It will be my pleasure next time to cook cabbage rolls for Laura. Today the time did not allow me do this." She passed me the cabbage bowl, and she also gave me some hot corn meal called Polenta. To top it off Halibarda added sour cream to my plate. She also passed me a new hot green pepper. I saw that they did the same. Paul filled out the glasses with Tzuica. We toasted again. After that, all of us started to eat with great pleasure. I have to admit that Halibarda's meat cabbage was awesome. I was definitely going to be asking her for more.

This particular combination of hot green pepper, meat, cabbage, Polenta, and sour cream works just perfectly together.

"I think that the meat cabbage would work very well with wine," I observed.

All eyes were gazing at me like I made a terrible mistake. Raluka was the one, who clarified this.

"No dear, that is totally wrong. The meat cabbage works only with Tzuica. We have been eating like this for more than two thousand years."

We continued to savour the delicious plate, and from time to time having sips of Tzuica. I lost count of how many times Paul filled his glass. At this point I could see that the Tzuica bottle was almost empty. Also he had eaten three green hot peppers. He filled his plate two times.

"I have to admit that Halibarda makes a great meat cabbage." I said out loud in order to compliment her cooking.

Our eating was somehow rushed, and that was more than likely because it was all was so good. In a pause after we were done eating Raluka started to talk.

"I brought over some paper work. Laura, we thought maybe you might want to become a member of our club."

"Yes, why not?" I approved. "Paul told me that there are no fees."

"This is very true. You just have to sign the admission paper and you can enjoy our meetings, chatting, experience the changes and so on." She had a nice professional smile again.

I read the paper. It was in English and I declared that I wanted to enjoy the club. There were also some explanations about the activities of the club as the people are practicing magic, sharing their information, chatting, exactly as Raluka said. I signed the paper and I gave it back to Raluka.

Paul put on some music. I heard a kind of language that seemed somehow strange. In fact I started to recognize the Romanian accent and I deduced that the music that was being played was not in the Romanian language.

Raluka helped me, "This is in gypsy, or Roma language." I was watching the screen of the big plasma TV and I saw young and nice gypsy girls dancing and singing in a very timed music.

"Maybe this is something you can add to your music Laura, some color and influences from the Romanian gypsy music. I am sure it will work for you."

"I think you are right Paul. I really like this music. It is so . . . happy."

The happy music was refreshing the air in the room and I could not believe it. Halibarda was starting to carry inside lots of other plates. God . . . these people eat lots.

Halibarda was arranging in the middle of the table a big plate with meat, of which she called 'Pastrama'. Also there was still Polenta, a very nice smelling bread, and on a big plate held the pickled green tomatoes which Paul bought from the farmers market. They were very nicely sliced by Halibarda.

I started to eat first, and I was totally impressed by how tasty this Romanian Pastrama was in combination with the Polenta. I felt like I was able to eat a big part of the meat on the plate. Definitely after this vacation I will have gained some weight.

Paul opened up a bottle of red wine, and he filled our glasses.

"Let's drink to the newest member of our club, Laura."

"To Laura . . ." they saluted me first with their eyes and then they toasted me. We each had one long sip from the wonderful red wine.

"It is called Cotnari," Raluka was happy to share this information with me.

Halibarda came over to me and hugged me.

"Dear Laura, welcome to our club. I am very happy for you. I am sure very soon you will become a remarkable witch."

"Also," Paul added, "we will have a meeting very soon, and as a member you will be of course welcome to come and join us. We are going to start doing our group incantations. Maybe you would like to come do this with us."

"Yes. I am so curious about all of this. I would like very much to attend these group incantations. I guess they are done over the night."

"Yes," Raluka tried to help me, "usually the strong magic, the spellings, the incarnations are done in the night."

"Okay, it sounds so interesting . . . magic incantations in the night. Do you have a place where you are doing these incantations?"

"Yes . . ." Halibarda answered.

"*Near Dracula's castle,*" Paul words were like a flying sword in the room.

My throat felt suddenly dry. I emptied the whole wine glass. Paul was filling my glass again with wine. I was staring at the wine. It was as red as . . . . blood.

I felt a kind of strange and horrific energy was in the room. A terrifying energy which was growing in intensity, despite the happy gypsy music, and the happy gypsy girls who were dancing on the TV screen.

With a small effort Raluka was trying to break this difficult moment.

"Please, don't forget we have dessert too. I will feel very offended if at least one of you doesn't taste my cherry cake."

"Raluka, I very much like your cake."

Halibarda was so enthusiastic about the prospect of having Raluka's cake on the table very soon.

Soon after we were done with Pastrama, Halibarda was clearing the table, and Raluka was arranging the nice plate with very nice smelling cherry cake slices.

Even if I was so very full, I felt like I needed to eat a big piece of this cake.

"Let's finish the wine first. We will have mineral water for refreshments, but only after Raluka's cake. I would recommend Borsec."

We emptied the wine glasses.

At that moment the doorbell rang.

"Are you expecting somebody?" Halibarda asked me.

"Yes," Paul answered Halibarda question, "she is expecting somebody. You better open the door Laura."

I felt a little bit drunk. In the morning he foresaw that Vlad would come back to me. It could not be true. I could not expect to be so happy. My morning started out like a disaster when I woke up, and he was not there.

Unsure I walked to the door. I opened it and . . . Vlad was standing there. There he was with his beautiful face, his gorgeous body, and of course I hugged him. I forgot all my friends could see us from the living room. He was carrying a small bag.

"May I come inside?" he asked.

"Yes, yes. I am so happy that you came back. I have some guests, but please come in."

He left the bag near the door and he stepped inside.

"Buna ziua" he said fixing his eyes first to Paul and after that the two women.

"May I introduce you . . . I tried to start the introductions," but Paul interrupted me.

"We know Vlad. You don't need to introduce him to us. We met him at the same bar you met him."

There was a silent moment. Almost everyone looked confused, all except for Paul.

"If you don't know, Vlad is a big sweet eater. You may offer him a piece of cake."

I observed a big smile flourishing on Vlad's handsome face. He took a chair, and he accepted a big piece from Raluka's cake, and also a big glass of that sparkling water called Borsec.

We did the same. I saw that Raluka was really enjoying seeing us eating her cake. In fact it was so very good. Sweet but not too sweet, and at the same time the sour cherries gave the cake a kind of refreshing taste.

"Okay," Paul said, "how about . . . let's say in three days Raluka can start the magic theory lessons with you. What do you think Laura?"

"Yes. I think that works well for me," I replied.

"For me too," Raluka added.

"Good," said Paul joyfully, "all sounds good. Anything more to add?"

"Yes," Vlad said.

All the eyes in the room were gazing upon Vlad. I was very surprised too.

"Paul, I know this is your condo, so if I may, I would like to ask if I can live here for a while?"

"Would you like that Laura?" Paul asked me.

"I would like it very much," I added unable to hide my happiness as a huge smile came across my face.

Chapter 6

I have the power to cure you,
Even if you are affected by,
Vampire man or vampire women,
Werewolf male or werewolf female
Ghost man or ghost woman
                    -Romanian spelling

The room was totally empty, and very dark. The windows were covered with black and heavy curtains. I was standing directly in the middle of the floor face to face with Raluka. Now it had been thirteen days since our nice dinner. For three days I had just stayed inside the condo with Vlad. From time to time we walked in the park. He didn't talk much. Though he doesn't need to. He was a wonderful lover. I had never met anyone like him . . . he was so good, and so lovely. After that I had already had ten days since I started studying magic with Raluka. In fact I was learning a lot of theories of magic. Raluka made it very clear she had wished to be a witch, though her powers and abilities were very low. Instead she had become a very good theoretician. After ten days of theories we decided to practice something.

The room was totally empty, with only Raluka inside. Between her and I was a tall candle stick with a white candle.

We waited just a couple more minutes until our eyes became more comfortable with the dark of the room.

I was silent and very respectful, exactly as Raluka wanted me to be. She started her lesson.

"There are many theories regarding the magical parts of our body. However, in our club we make things simple. We accept that there are mainly two parts, the physical body and the soul. The physical or biological body is quite well known, and relative easily to study as compared with the soul. I read about experiments that have been done. For example, isolating a dying subject in a very insulated room even the evaporated water in this process is counted. We can have the exact mass of the body before and after the subject passed away. The difference is a couple grams. These couple grams are in fact our soul or the mass of our spirit after our body has passed on. We can say after we pass away the soul becomes a spirit. The study is very difficult, and that is because it is not a physical matter. It might be a form of energy but hardly enough to be analyzed. And because of this, we have a lot of speculations."

Raluka made a pause and she took a couple seconds to study my face in the darkness of the room.

"Let's say after we die our biological body is gone, and the spirit is the one which is remaining. Where is it going? Here we accept two theories. The spirit can be reincarnated or go into a place. The second possibility has a couple of alternatives, like going in a good place such as heaven, or going to a bad place like hell, or to get lost somehow in between. Reincarnation supports the theory of evolution. If in a preceding life you were an inferior person, in the present life you may be quite superior. Somehow reincarnation can be proved. I know of situation where children were born with preceding memories, the memories from their previous life. A good example is Paul. He can very clearly remember memories from another life. You can ask him. Also we know of cases of children born with signs on their bodies. When our witches saw them, they were able to determine who this child was in his or her previous life. Drina and Chlorinda are quite good at this. On the other hand, if in your life you did good stuff or bad stuff you might go to heaven or hell. This was a long introduction. Sorry about that. Our discussion here is about the very last category."

"The lost spirits," I said.

"Yes," Raluka approved in a very natural voice.

Still I cannot believe that I was here, that I was actually doing this. It was like yesterday all I thought about was all the things that might be, that might exist. Here I was, studying them, with a Romanian teacher.

"On their way to reincarnation, or to heaven or hell, the spirits remain for a time around us, in this world." Raluka paused a couple of seconds, and after that she raised her voice. "In this time they are vulnerable, and they accept commands from a qualified and talented sorceress. In fact this is the essence of the magic, to have the ability to manipulate the spirits."

I got excited about Raluka words, which were somehow scary. I felt a cold feeling. It was like all my body was freezing under these scary emotions.

"Be very clear, I am not talking about ghosts for now. There will be another discussion. I am talking about spirits who may accept commands. By chance, in your life did you ever learn some theories about these spirits?"

"Yes," I said in a strange voice, even for myself

Raluka was gazing at me, and finally blinking at me with her eyes.

"Could you please relate to me your experience? Please remember I am the club analyst. People who experience strange things relate it to me. I do the classification of it, and I will try to categorize it. Finally we found someone in our club with suitable powers who would be able to help the matter."

Quietly she was waited for my story. I was desperately searching inside my body for some resources, for some energy to be able to speak and to relate to Raluka my story. She was watching me in the dark room. Her study was quite well. Maybe she was catching my feelings. She was bending a little bit toward me.

"Dear, in these situations when you feel yourself weak you have to find energies inside of your body. What we are doing now, it is just an inoffensive discussion. Though in magic these kind of hesitations can be . . . deadly. I am sure you can control yourself. Never allow this stuff to take place again."

She was such a remarkable person, always polite, always an entertaining person. Her words were helping me to focus, and to coordinate the lost energy of my body. Once recovered, I started my story.

"Once I went house boating on Shuswap Lake. It is a huge lake in Canada, in British Columbia. I was there with couple friends on a very luxurious boat. It was late in the evening. I became very friendly with a girl there. In that evening we stayed a long time in the hot tub watching the beauty of the lake. We were chatting about life. The evening was wonderful. It went by so quickly, and night came very soon. After that we had dinner with the friends, and a gorgeous dinner. Finally we lit a fire outside. Soon all of our friends were gone. I spent a long time with her that night, and we started to chat about ghosts, vampires and spirits. She told me that she always had troubles in her house with ghosts. She spoke of spirits, and told me that she would be able to show me a couple of spirits right away. She started walking around the beach and taking some pictures in the terrible dark night using her camera with the flash on. When she came back she asked me to watch the pictures. However she was a little bit disappointed. She was looking for some lighted points on the pictures but . . . there were only one or two. She told me that in that night the spirits were . . . quite lazy."

"That is not true," Raluka interrupted me.

I was gazing at her, somehow amazed about her observation. It was like she was there with us at Shuswap Lake watching us, seeing the mistakes we were making. Maybe she was amused by the low level of our discussion regarding this stuff, and compared it to her vast knowledge.

"How do you know?" I asked her.

"If she was taking a picture close to the fire, you would have a good chance to see spirits. According to what you said 'she was walking on the beach taking pictures in the dark', not close enough to the fire."

"Yes," I replied.

"Did she take a picture close to the fire?"

"Yes."

"Did you observe a difference?" She asked me wanting to gather all the information.

"Yes I did observe a difference," I stated.

"Okay Laura, do you have something more to relate here?"

"Well, of course there was the influence of the fire. Yet there we saw lots of unexplainable light points and there were so many. She told me that was what she was looking for. She told me in fact those lighted points are spirits, and that they were watching us."

"She was right."

Raluka paused, and with an expert gesture she lit the white candle. We remained in silence watching the candle. Its flame lit a little bit of the dark room.

"Think about the spirits that were dispersed in the room, and now moment by moment they are coming close to the light of the candle, or to the light of the fire in your story. As your friend knew it, we can have on the pictures some signs which show us the evidence of the spirits or ghosts. A good sorcerer will find them, and will be able to manipulate them."

"Why do they come close to the candles flame or fire?" I asked her.

"They do this because they are very curious," she paused like she was giving me some time to think.

"If they are around, and with magic and distance, about distance, huge distance may mean nothing. The lighted candle in a dark room means a strange event. They of course will be curious. They will come closer. In their dark world this is an event and they will want to attend it in one way or another. The first way would be to come as close as possible."

I was gazing at the candle's flame.

"I totally understand you Raluka."

"Thanks dear. However we are at very beginning. We have to discuss now about the levels of the spirits. Lots of them are elementary spirits."

"Elementary spirits?" I asked curiously.

"Yes . . . Let's take a newborn that is only one day, or just a couple of days old. Let's just say either because he is not healthy enough or because of an accident he will die. His soul will become an elementary spirit. This is opposite of a monk who was living for example close to one hundred years when he passed away. His spirit will be a superior spirit, a superior spirit in a good way. Now on the opposite side think about a medium age man who was a criminal. He was killing a lot of people until he died. His spirit will be superior a spirit too, but a very bad one."

She paused again watching me.

"A sorcerer will be able to use these spirits according to his needs. In your situation, in order to be able to use them the first step is to see them, to feel them and . . ."

"Raluka . . . I am sorry. Can we stop for now?" I felt overwhelmed.

Raluka was watching me reacting very surprised.

"Yes, of course," she said.

She took my hand, and she led me out. I was very sure she observed my hand was very humid because of my sweating.

I spent all the rest of the next day, evening and night with Vlad, my Vlad. The hotness of his body was bringing me back to this world.

*   *   *

The next morning around nine am the door bell rang. Vlad was sleeping so deeply. I guessed that it was Halibarda, and I went to open the door. Yet . . . there was Paul. Gravely he was smiling.

"Hello Laura. May I come in?"

"Yes please," I said embarrassed, and tightened the housecoat to my body.

We went to the living room.

" I feel like I need a coffee," Paul said.

"Yes, sure. I will prepare you one immediately."

"What?" His voice was tense. "You? Why do you keep that guy with you? Vlad! Vlad!" Paul started screaming Vlad's name.

Scared, Vlad arrived naked. His face was sleepy and confused.

"Yes Paul. What can I do for you?"

"We need coffee here!"

"Y . . . yes," Vlad said a little bit terrorized by Paul's screams.

"And quickly please! Don't keep me waiting you lazy bastard!"

Without saying a word, Vlad hurried into the kitchen. Shortly, I heard the water running, the gas oven starting. I wondered what was going on. He never prepared coffee for me.

"Dear, you are on vacation here. He is supposed to be more helpful with you. Try to get him to help you in other ways, or he will become lazy."

I was confused. I did not know how I should answer.

"I would like to speak about yesterday with you. Raluka told me about your reaction. It is okay if you can't handle this stuff."

"You said I can become a strong witch though," I firmly retorted.

"If you want. I said you have the gift, but also you need to make an effort. If not . . . it's okay. You may come once with us to see a kind of co-active incantation at night, and then you might want to go back to Canada."

"Well . . . I am still very interested still about Raluka's lessons, I would like to go on."

Vlad came with the coffees into the living room. They were very close to what Halibarda usually did.

Paul looked deeply as if he was trying to find something wrong, a reason to start screaming again at Vlad. After that he finished looking at Vlad. He started to drink his coffee, tasting it. "Good job. You see? If you want you can help. You just need to put forth some effort. Now go back to the bedroom." Paul commanded to him very firmly.

"But I want a coffee . . ." Vlad said directly to Paul.

"Take it with you into the bedroom! I am advising you! I don't have the nerves to deal with you today! So, do as I say!" Paul was screaming again at Vlad. For a moment I thought in fact he was mad at me, and he was taking out his anger on poor Vlad.

I was very embarrassed about the scene. Quietly, Vlad took his coffee and disappeared into the living room.

After that Paul looked very seriously at me.

"Laura, I would be very happy if you would like to go on with the magic lessons. Though if you would like to give up it that would be okay too. You might be a better witch in your next life. In this one you are an wonderful singer."

"Well, I was a little bit scared, I have to admit that, though I know I can go on. I really want it."

"Okay . . . Good news. I really like Raluka." Paul seemed to calm down a little at this point.

"I like her too." I replied in a much softer tone.

"If I had not been born with this gift to perform magic stuff, then I would have been just like Raluka. I would simply have been a man very interested in paranormal study. A lot of stuff we perform is considered to be unnatural. Raluka is the one who helps us to understand what exactly was performed, in what category it is situated, and with what intensity. I think it is difficult to have some instruments needed to observe this. An example of this is you may catch some elementary spirits on a camera when you do a picture in the dark. But we have very qualified people like Ivanka, who are able to see all of them. All this information is explained to Raluka, and she keeps a database. However, she has a wonderful memory, and she is able to interpret, and do comparisons, and at the very least to generate conclusions. I have to tell you that, for a person without magical powers she is really talented in understanding the paranormal phenomena, and seeing the associated connections."

"I think that she is a great person," I replied.

"Yes, you have to understand a couple of the fundamentals in order to perform magic."

"Like seeing and using elementary spirits," I added.

He made a couple of yes signs with his hand.

"I can see that you may be a strong witch. I can feel that energy inside you. You have to learn to control it though. You have to start out with the theories, as long as we know these theories, and to start to perform some stuff. I have to tell you that some stuff involves more than just a dark room and a candle."

He paused, as he was waiting for feedback from my side, and yet I decided to be silent.

*   *   *

"I am so sorry dear Laura. It was all my mistake. You are such a wonderful student and when I am starting a magic lesson I am unable to stop myself. I can speak about magic for weeks, without food and maybe even water."

"Raluka, you are a wonderful person. But sometimes your personality, your delicate gestures are contradicting with what you are teaching."

We were having our coffee in Raluka's nice living room. She lives just a couple of blocks from the Metro station by Paul. It was very easy to reach her address from Paul's place. She had a condo in Bucharest that was made up of two bedrooms, this wonderful living room and that dark room which Raluka used to perform magic.

Her living room was really interesting to me. It was like almost all the stuff inside her house was made of glass, or other transparent materials. The big table in the living room for example, the chairs, the shelves filled with glasses, and strange forms of bottles.

Raluka was looking around her living room contemplating the transparent objects. Finally she started to talk.

"My living room is supposed to be like a magic lesson. For someone with good magic abilities it is easy to see the objects as they are. For someone like me with less ability in magic, I only see only an empty room. I find as a magic analyst it can be a challenge. I can listen to what others are relating to me, what they can see, and I can have a picture. When I make a . . . picture I ask a couple of the witches about what they saw or felt regarding the same subject. No story is identical. Here their emotions, their imagination will affect my picture, my understanding. But finally I can see possible explanations regarding this fact." She seemed so self assured.

"If these things are so hard, why do you need to have a full picture?" I asked Raluka.

Raluka was looking at me very surprised as my question had a very obvious answer, and I did not see it yet.

"Because Paul asks," she simply replied.

She was taking a sip of coffee from her transparent coffee cup.

"Maybe today I should start with something not so dark. Did you read the Bible?"

"I read a little bit, and from some pages. You?"

"I have read the Bible entirely, and actually a couple times through. I have also read the gospels of Judas and Mary Magdalene. Already you know about the spirits. I would like to go to the end of the Bible story. Jesus died. In that moment his soul became a spirit. However, in a very short period of time his conscience disappeared from his body. I do believe his spirit was going back to his body and took it again. He died violently. That is so he could be converted into something else. When someone dies so violently his spirit becomes very excited, somehow in a superior level of energy. I told you until now about elementary spirits, at the opposite and positive end of the scale I will situate Jesus as a superior spirit. We have a scale going from the elementary to something very complex. Using his good energies and powers he was able to take his own body again. From that time he showed himself from time to time to his disciples as a vision and he guided them."

Raluka again took a sip from her coffee and she continued.

"For example, you are from America. In South America lots of people pray to the Guadalupe Virgin. There may also be a couple versions of this apparition. Which one do you know?"

I decided to hide my embarrassment.

"You are the teacher Raluka, you tell me the right version."

"I know a version. I am not sure if it is the right one. One day a Shepherd was with his lambs on a hill and he had a vision of the

Guadalupe Virgin. She saw his sadness and she tried to talk to him. He talked about his father who was gravely ill. She did her first miracle by curing his father. After that she asked him to request the church representatives to build a church there, exactly on that place. The representatives of the church refused him telling there are lots of requests to build churches in various places, and of course not enough funds. The Shepherd went back to the Virgin Maria as she was known at the time telling her the story. She asked him to go again to tell them this time how she cured his father. The church representatives told him to ask his vision for proof that she is the right Maria. Embarrassed the shepherd told her what they wanted, and she said that was very easy. She commanded the shepherd to collect the wild flowers, which were growing around that hill. Unconvinced he collected in his large coat the flowers and herbs from all around. He went in the front of the priests telling them that he now has the proof. 'Show it to us,' they said. He did as the Virgin Maria taught him, there he just threw down the herbs and flowers in front of the priests. He looked down, and of course he saw the same flowers and herbs he collected little bit earlier but . . . The priests instantaneously began to kneel, and fanatically they started to pray to the Virgin Maria."

Raluka stopped talking, and she looked at a strange transparent bottle at the top of one of the shelves. The bottle had the shape of a woman. She had no intention to continue the story. So, I missed the point.

"Raluka, so what really happened?"

"Oh . . . From his angle the Shepherd was seeing the herbs, flowers and the priests praying. But when the shepherd threw down the herbs and flowers, the priests saw on impressed upon his large coat . . . the face of Virgin Maria."

"Oh . . . dear." I was really impressed by this story. Maybe I should have known this story before.

"It is a really nice story. It is there a similar story?"

"Speaking about this phenomenon yes. There is one known as Jesus Christ's face which was impressed on the veil which covered his face. There are lots of stories and facts in religion. However, as I said we have a scale from something elementary to something very good, positive and complex. Also we have this phenomenon of returning back to the physical body."

"Do you mean there is a negative example of something complex but . . . negative?"

Raluka was turning to me somehow frustrated this time about my lack of knowledge.

"Yes of course . . . vampires," she stated abruptly.

I became scared again.

*   *   *

The closest park to Raluka's house is called Carol Park. I have to admit that it looks nicer than Titan Park. When I was walking with Raluka in this park my imagination was flying like the wind. It looked like a science-fiction garden. Raluka explained to me that Carol Park was built in the communistic era, and it is supposed to be in fact an edifice communism. At the top of the hill is the big edifice. On the way to the big edifice, I was able to admire the nice view of the well-organized garden. The waste pools were so wonderfully disposed, and I was totally impressed. I wondered why this park was not as well known as other parks of Europe, so I asked Raluka.

"The Romanians are not so good at promoting their products as well as other countries," Raluka answered my question with confidence.

Finally we arrived at the top of the hill near the communist edifice. From here I had a nice view of the entire park. It was so beautiful and unbelievably large. I have to admit after walking so many stairs I got tired.

"Maybe this was the target of the architect. The people who reached the top and are tired take the time to think about the immense significance of the communist era." Raluka added.

"Were you happy during the communist time Raluka?" I asked.

"No . . ." She paused.

"Think about all the restrictions, having no continuous hot water, the electricity was often cut off, the TV only had two hours of programming from eight pm to ten pm, and almost all of the time it played patriotic songs." She paused again, and she smiled a sad smile to me.

"After a couple of weeks of watching this TV program you realize how small this universe really is."

She looked down at the nice park. The weather seemed to be wonderful in this country. So far all the days were just gorgeous spring days. After a short pause Raluka added.

"Once I told Paul that if I had to torture the communist leaders, who made our lives so impossible for such a long time, I would collect them in a room with a big screen TV and all the time I would project all of those communist emissions for the rest of their lives."

Down in the park two twins boys were happily playing with a big ball. She was becoming little bit optimistic watching them. The twins were around four years old, and their faces were so beautiful. A lady was closely watching them while they played. Near us a young couple was taking pictures around the park. The girl came to me asking me something in Romanian. I did not understand the words but I guessed because she was showing me the camera, she was asking me to take a picture of her and her boyfriend. I regretted that I did not know very many words in Romanian, so it appeared like I didn't belong here. So I improvised a 'yes' sign with my head. Raluka exchanged a couple words with them, and they started laughing. I was able in this happy moment to take a couple nice pictures of them. They were a wonderful couple. I thought for a moment of my Vlad. I could see these people are very well balanced. The guys and girls are very cute. They look like Italians.

"Raluka I take it that Romanian is a Latin language?"

"Yes Laura, you are perfectly right. It is extremely close with Italian. Actually with a little more attention we can catch the main ideas from a conversation in Italian language. For example 'good evening' you will say in Italian language 'bona sera', and in the Romania language it is 'buna seara'."

"Is it close with Spanish too?"

"Yes, you are perfectly right Laura, and somewhat with French too. There was a nice connection between France and Romania over the years. I mean before the communist era and after."

We decided to stay on a bench. From there we had a wonderful view of the park.

"It is a wonderful and shiny day."

She paused looking at me.

"I said shiny. I will use it to teach you a lesson about vampires."

She paused little bit, as she was waiting for my acceptance.

"Okay, I am ready." I said.

"The light, the sun shine, was always considered to be the capital defense against vampires. When the sun rises their power is over. You might go with Paul for some night incantation near Dracula's castle. If there appears a vampire, and you can not defend him right away, the only solution would be to fight with him until morning, until the sun rises over the horizon. Then there is the light, I heard about guns with light bullets that are able to defend the vampires."

"My I ask why somebody would become a vampire?"

"There might be a couple of reasons. For example a boy loves girl. But he dies before he gets a chance to marry her or even before having . . . sex. His soul feels like it needs to return to search for that girl. Yet this time this will involve a bodily pleasure. He needs his body too, otherwise he can be only a ghost."

"Really?"

Raluka was philosophically approving with her head. 'Yes.'

"However the solution for defending this kind of vampire is relatively simple and very applied. On his grave the girl will bury a bottle of wine and after six weeks she will come back, dig it up and drink the wine with the relatives. This method however has some inconvenience. The girl has to go herself in the grave. To eliminate this inconvenience, usually they hire a witch who will do a kind of different magic."

"Like what?"

"The witch will take a bottle of a very strong drink. It can be whiskey, or vodka or our traditional Tzuica. She will start saying some particular incantations and she will get the girl to drink from that bottle. In the middle of the night the witch will go to the grave and she will continue the incantation. Also, the witch will fix to the bottle a special plug. She will bury the bottle with the strong drink with the top down. The special plug will allow the strong drink to drop from the bottle by droplets, as it will take a long period of time to empty. It is said that the vampire will drink it and never return home."

She paused again watching the sunny sun. Somehow I was happy because she chose to teach her lesson here.

"This was an example of someone becoming a vampire. There can be other reason much more frequent. We know the newborns who have the capacity to become vampires. I believe Chlorinda will explain to you more about that. I would like to make a classification.

87

Here I see two categories, live and dead vampires. A living vampire is the person who is a criminal or psychopathic people who like to drink the blood of their victims or . . . they might be people with certain magical powers. He or she can have magical powers and use them to catch the victims to drink their blood."

She paused again, gazing at me.

"We have in history these kind of examples, maybe the classical one is the Countess Dracula or Ecatherina Bathory. The dead ones are the main category. As I mentioned they are spirits who are returned to their body and they can walk over the night searching for their victims. During the day they will stay buried in their grave or, in the places very dark and without exposure. Again it is a very sure method to kill them, by exposing them to sunlight or with our technology to expose them to a very strong source of light. Another method might be to spit on him with holy water, some certain incantations, a sharp knife or stake through his heart. Silver bullets, light bullets, silver needles and so on can work too. "

She paused again a little bit confused this time.

"Unfortunately we meet up with situations where vampires had two hearts."

"Two hearts?" I have never heard of such a thing.

"Yes, Halibarda had lot of troubles with this at one point. Paul had helped her and they dug it up, and opened up his body. They were concentrating mostly on the one heart. Maybe that was the reason why Halibarda was unsuccessful in defending the vampire initially. She was implanting her knife only in one heart, as she did not know before hand that this vampire had two hearts. Here looks to be a very general problem."

"What kind of problem?" I asked getting very scared.

"The members of our club, or another sorceress who have to fight with the vampires, know now the only sure method to kill them is with the strong light. Other methods can be successful or not according with particular cases. Of course all this is happening in the night. The vampire is a night creature and he will be strong in the night."

After a short pause Raluka continued with her distinctive and professional air.

"Maybe it is better to stop here today. Tomorrow I would like to present you another entity of something that may be worse than vampires."

*   *   *

I decided tonight just to sleep, to not even think about vampires or any other kind of entities. I just wanted to have a quiet night with Vlad.

Maybe Paul was somehow right, Vlad started to be lazy. I think he was staying all day just inside the house, and almost always was in bed. He seemed to enjoy it. I was always happy to be with him, the question is 'could I stay all my life with him?' Touching his body give me a very comforting sensation. Sensual of course, right now I need somebody to be with me. I am not so sure about how I would be if I were alone in a room . . . how scared I would be. With a ghost, or a vampire . . . I just said I would not think about that stuff. I tried to stay tight by Vlad's body, and I was watching the TV with him. I think it was a Romanian news channel. Sometimes I like their language, and this was because it sounds like Italian. I saw the news was about a country village. The people were scared and they were speaking so quickly with the reporter. It looked like all of them had to relate something about that story.

"Oh . . . Unbelievable . . ." Vlad was almost screaming.

With quick movements he was commanding to the record system to start recording the news.

"What's going on?" I asked somehow amused about his excitement.

"That is happening in a village close to Paul's village."

"But what is happening?" I asked.

"An old man died there a couple of days ago there. And the habitants of the village believe that he has become a vampire."

"Unbelievable . . . How could this be so real here?" I asked.

Suddenly I stopped talking. Vlad was looking at me with a harsh eye as if to tell me 'don't be stupid'.

At that moment there was only one person on the TV. This one showed to the reporter his hands.

"He is the one who extracted the heart of the vampire and he burned it at a cross of the roads." Vlad repeated to me.

I think Raluka had mentioned this method to me. I have to check my camcorder records. I decided though at this moment to just look at this unbelievable news on TV, and then I would ask Vlad a little bit later to summarize it. Then he started to explain me about what they were saying on the TV.

"It all started with the night when he died. The families who lived close to the graveyard were unable to sleep. Almost all of them had some animals around their homes. It started with that night the animals were unable to sleep. They were always screaming, like a big animal was around. A family had two dogs, and the dogs were running in that direction, but in a short time the dogs had been killed. As a result the nearby community decided to dig up the body of the man who died, and to do the requested stuff."

"Really?"

"What do you mean by this? We were just watching the news. This seemed to be a common experience. It was not just one single person who had hallucinations."

"So . . . the old man was extracting the heart of that . . . vampire?"

"Yes . . . Now there looks to be a conflict with the relatives of the dead man who was the vampire. They don't believe this story and they intend to sue the nearby community who dug up the body, and especially the man who extracted the heart."

"Vlad please shut off the TV. I am very tired. I would like to relax some now."

*   *   *

I spent almost all the next day with Raluka. She encouraged me to search in Wikipedia for some explanations, definitions about vampires, strigoi, mori and other kinds of entities. I was quite surprised to see who was rich in the Romanian folk culture of this matter.

In the afternoon she said that we had to go downtown to meet Paul.

We were going to go into the historical center of Bucharest. They were rebuilding this historical center. It was not totally finished but I was sure it would still look very nice when it is all done. There were a couple of streets with old buildings, and with the particular architecture of the old Bucharest. A couple of them were redone, and the others were still being redone. Almost all of them were converted into restaurants and bars. There were very nice people, very modernly dressed and very happy. They really liked to speak a lot, laughing and spending their time with friends. We met Paul, Vlad and Halibarda there. It was a wonderful and warm spring evening. They were already drinking beers. Immediately we were seated, the waiter brought us beers, Bergenbeer. I wondered how he knew, as he did not ask.

"We have asked for what we call the littles, or mititei," Halibarda informed me.

"They are a kind of particular sausage very specific for Romania. And they go perfectly with beer. So . . . Noroc."

I remembered now very well this word meant 'cheers' in Romanian. We toasted with our beer bottles. Raluka was embarrassed, as I knew she didn't like to drink directly from the bottle. Though it looked like Paul always intimidated her, and she didn't dare to ask for a glass.

"I guess you saw the news yesterday?" Paul looked over at me and asked.

"Yes, they seem to be having a problem in a village with a vampire." I said. "I was quite impressed about . . . the reaction of the people."

"It is maybe because back in time, we Romanians we had really big problems with vampires, and according to the experiences we have gained over the years it is better in this kind of matter to take immediate actions."

"Also waiting may be deadly in this matter," Raluka added.

Paul had agreed with Raluka on this.

"However, there they will have problems with the family of the supposed vampire. You see Laura, here is not like in Canada. Here the people are buried in the cemetery. I mean, most of them are not cremated like in some other countries. Sometimes I think burning of the body is a much more civilized mode. At least with cremation we would be able to avoid the possibility of the returning of the spirit to the physical body. Mostly vampirism."

Halibarda was just listening and watching the nearby tables filled with young people. She was absent for a couple of moments. Paul observed this. He was looking at us and finally asked Halibarda a question.

"Something to tell dear?" He asked Halibarda inquisitively.

Like she just woke up from a dream, Halibarda was looking around our faces at first like she misunderstood Paul's words.

"Oh . . . sometimes I think we have to go deeper with the actions
of our club."

"Like what?"

"In these kinds of moments these people need qualified assistance.
Our club is able to provide that kind of qualified assistance."

"I agree with you," Paul said.

"Me too. Sometimes in these kinds of situations the people are
going to the priests, some of them are inexperienced, and to fight
with these entities you need adequate knowledge and magic powers,"
Raluka added.

"You guys have to make decisions very quickly to act like this,"
Vlad said.

Paul was glared at Vlad, and Vlad became silent immediately,
even if he was originally going to say more.

There was also a long silent moment, as the waiter came with
a huge plate with those Romanian sausages called 'mititei'. On the
big plate was also a sliced French-type bread and mustard. The guys
started eating with an unbelievable appetite. I start doing the same. I
was very surprised about the awesome taste of these littles. I think
I ate three of them with a terrible speed. As good as they are, I think
I would have been able to eat the whole plate. All of them were
watching me, and they all had the happiest faces. Paul decided to
speak in the middle of it all.

"We can see that you really enjoy eating our mititei."

"Well . . . they are just gorgeous."

"It is a kind of mixed meat and it is roasted over coals."

"I can see these mititei has no cover. How do they stay on the
BBQ without falling apart? Do they have some eggs in the meat
composition?"

All of them started laughing. They were laughing so loud that
the people from the nearby table turned their eyes toward us.

Raluka stopped first.

"Oh . . . sorry dear. But for us it was like a very good joke.
There are no eggs in the composition. It is a kind of bonding juice,
bicarbonate, with some garlic and a lot of spices. The composition
has to stay like this for a couple of hours, and it will become quite
compact to prepare on the BBQ. However, it is easy to tell but hard

to be done. None of us prepare them at our home. We buy them already prepared."

"Unfortunately we can not buy them in Canada," Paul added. " I miss my mititei there. However, going back to the recent case with the vampire, maybe the situation was quite desperate, but I find the action being quite . . . uncivilized."

"And to meditated on," Halibarda added.

"Yes," Raluka agreed.

"According to the news, the situation was desperate, the vampire was attacking the animals of the nearby houses," Vlad observed.

I was afraid Paul was going to stop him again and I tried to save the moment.

"If you were there what would you do to stop the vampire in a civilized method?"

"Maybe the method with a bottle of strong drink buried . . ."

"No . . . Paul has a special method. I started to use it too." Halibarda said.

"Like what?" I asked.

"Implanting five sharp stakes on the vampire's grave mound. When the vampire body tries to get out it will be impossible because he will get hurt on the sharp stakes."

"Yes. This is a method that doesn't involve so much barbarism. If our club would be involved in these kind of stories, this would definitely be a recommended method. I agree with all of you. We have to move up to a new stage with the club," Raluka suggested.

"We will discuss this at the meeting tomorrow," Paul was fixing me his eyes on me.

"Tomorrow's meeting?" I asked.

"Oh yes. Tomorrow we will have a club meeting. Finally you will meet the members of the witches club."

"There will be lots of gypsies," Vlad added.

"Yes," finally Paul was agreeing with Vlad in a matter. "There will be some particular people there as well."

"Particular? Like who?" I asked.

"The twin sisters?" Raluka tried to guess.

Paul and Halibarda exchanged a strange smile. They looked enchanted, in a kind of contemplated look toward each other.

"Somebody . . . with some unbelievable green eyes. Hypnotic green eyes." said Halibarda.

"Green like a poison." Paul added

"She is a poison," Halibarda agreed.

"She is a green poison. She is Chlorinda," Paul finished.

Chapter 7

In magic when we do something; we deal with the unknown and terrible forces. Some of them can be very unfriendly, a real representation of the evil or evil itself. Don't take this like a challenge. Take it like a warning.

-Halibarda – Club speech

"Call me Chlorinda."

She was gazing me with her unnatural green eyes. I looked at her. Her eyes were so green, unbelievable green. I have never in my life met somebody with such natural green eyes. "Avoid looking directly in her eyes for a prolonged period of time. She has terrible hypnotic powers. Don't allow her to penetrate your mind. Always resist her." Raluka had advised me before meeting her.

Near me Halibarda was intervening,

"Chlorinda, you better take a seat. Now it is not the time for hypnoses and stuff like this. You know I am easily irritated when you do this in my presence."

Somewhat upset, Chlorinda was moving her eyes to Halibarda. I felt like I could start to breathe normally, immediately she moved her eyes from me. When she was gazing at me, I had a sensation, as all around me was only green . . . . poison and no oxygen; no air to breath. I think the other guys are correct, her eyes have a hypnotic quality to them. She was gazing at Halibarda as though she was trying the same trick with her. Instead Halibarda had started to laugh.

"Don't be stupid Chlorinda, now it is not the time to play." Halibarda was stepping close to Chlorinda and she said, "Especially don't play like this with me or Laura."

As though she was ignoring her, Chlorinda was moving her eyes back to me. My eyes met her green ones again. Again that flooding green poisoned sensation was around me . . . but like a wind from behind me, even if around me I had that green poison sensation, I found enough air to breathe, and enough energy to deal with Chlorinda.

I was analyzing her. She was a tall and solid woman. I thought for a moment about her origins, I determined she was a Russian lady; definitely her breasts were quite large. She was quite elegantly dressed, with blond hair, and a weathered look to her, as though she has been affected by her age. If I had to guess, I would think she is the same age as Halibarda.

Finally Chlorinda was smiling at me and she took from her purse a massive bracelet.

"Laura, please accept this gift from me. It is blue gold, and the green rocks are sapphires. Wear it. This bracelet will protect you against dark magic."

"Oh . . . I am not sure I can accept it Chlorinda."

"Yes, you can." Paul said from my behind. "It is a custom, a tradition for the people here to offer gifts, like this they show you how much they appreciate you. You are the new member of our club and a potentially strong witch. You should accept any gift they will give you. Some of them are really valuable, like this bracelet. I cannot guarantee its supposed magical powers but there is a guaranty about how valuable it is." Paul was looking at the heavy bracelet. I was interested in the manufacturing of the bracelet too.

"I bought it from Egypt." Chlorinda was obviously proud to mention that.

"It is really nice. Thank you so much Chlorinda." I added. She was smiling. I felt like even her smile was cold.

"You are welcome Laura. Now with your permission, I would like to take a seat as it was indicated to me." Chlorinda was feuding with Halibarda with her eyes. Halibarda was smiling at her.

"I missed you too Chlorinda."

I was checking out the bracelet from Chlorinda. It was quite heavy. Or heavier than any bracelet I have ever owned. I thought mainly with respect to the quantity of gold and precious stone used to make this bracelet, it was definitely very expensive.

Finally Chlorinda walked inside the room, and I was able to analyze the people that were already inside the room. There were around 50 people; mostly women and a few men. All of these people I guessed were sorcerers. Paul, Vlad, Halibarda and Raluka were with me. Raluka continued to work on her iPad. From time to time she was taking pictures or movies of the people who were present in the room. However in a corner I saw also a camcorder which recorded the entire event. The room was quite spacious; Vlad told me that it is usually a room used for fitness. For this even they moved the fitness equipment to another room. I remarked to the others that this meeting was taking place near the zone of Bucharest called Obor.

Paul was staying close with Raluka giving her lots of instructions in Romanian. Finally he turned to me and he said "Laura can you go around to socialize with the people. Halibarda, Vlad please help Laura with this."

I was somewhat intimidated. There were a lot of gypsies' ladies. They were dressed in their traditional dresses; very long, large dresses with lots of colors. The color on their dresses was randomly arranged. I noticed that lots of them had around their necks a particular necklace that had lots of big golden coins on it. However, it is important to remember that I just thought it looked like gold from a distance. I pride myself on being able to recognize gold because I like gold so much . . .

I looked at them, and they were curiously looking at me. Even if their look was curious I was able to see some respect in their eyes. Trying to fight with myself, I started to walk around the room, Halibarda and Vlad were walking a step behind me. Very close to me was a group of gypsy ladies and they started to speak almost all together in their language. I figured out that it was not even Romanian. Halibarda also started to talk loudly with them in the same language.

"They are speaking right now in gypsy language. Some of them are pretending they know you." Vlad translated for me.

"They know me?" I inquired.

"Yes. This is what they are pretending, but Halibarda is explaining to them that is impossible because you live in Canada and you never been in Romania."

"Okay, but maybe some of them were once in Canada and they saw me at a concert or something."

"Laura . . . none of them were in Canada." Vlad was smiling.

"How do you know that? How you can be so sure?"

"Raluka is monitoring them very close. None of these people were ever in Canada."

"So why would they pretend they know me?"

Vlad was unable to answer my question they were coming around me continuing to talk all together and almost each one of them gave me a heavy ring. Each ring was considerably heavy. I found the rings to be hideous to look at, but I realized the quantity of gold used to make them is a lot. I took the rings and told all of them "thank you. Thank you very much. I appreciate it very much". They were all smiling at me.

We were moving close to the next group of gypsy ladies. They did almost the same thing as the previous ladies and offered me golden rings and smiles. Halibarda was speaking quickly with them with a lot of energy. They were trying to hug me, but somehow Halibarda was managing to avoid this. From time to time she was making signs to Paul. I thought that she might instruct to them that if they continue in this manner Paul will become upset.

Next was a lonely lady, sitting by herself, although she was a gypsy too. She was dressed in their traditional dress, and was very tiny. It appeared to me that she had a very strong personality. She was smiling to me, and she offering me a heavy golden necklace.

"My name is Drina. I am so happy to meet you Laura. Please accept this necklace like a gift from me."

"Thanks . . . thanks Drina," already my pockets were full of gold rings. I decided to use my purse to carry all of my new found jewels. Even if I was so unsure about what to think about the people around me, I remembered Raluka, and mentioned her name. She is the one with remarkable kinesthetic powers.

The next group was a group of gypsy witches. They also gave me gold rings. There was one other lonely lady who was obese, and had really white skin. She gave me only a glass with honey.

Halibarda translated for me, "She is suggesting that each morning you should eat a spoon of this honey because she did some magical stuff to it. This will help you to accelerate your magic abilities."

"And her name?" Nobody was answering me because the next group of gypsy ladies was very noisy, and could be heard over the others. In this group I saw two identical young ladies. They were unbelievable nice. A gypsy lady was trying to ignore Halibarda and she tried to speak to me in their language. Of course I did not understand either one of them because she spoke a language I did not understand and the room was so noisy.

The two sisters were also stepping close to me "Be welcome Laura. My name is Gina, she is my sister Geta." They gave me a necklace. I was somewhat embarrassed. The quantity of the gold, and the cost of it was too much . . . I appreciated that they were trying to speak with me in English.

"I am sorry Gina but there is so much gold here, I will have to refuse it."

Near me, almost in the same time, Vlad and Halibarda were touching me with their elbow, in a way to indicate to me to not be stupid and just take the gold necklace anyway.

"It is not only from my side and my sister's side, it is from the side of my entire family unit and my entire village."

"But girls . . . I have done nothing for you. I don't think I will be able ever to do something for you to compensate for that you have given me."

"Don't worry, we feel that just being your friend is enough compensation," said Geta.

"You have to come to visit us in our village. We will have a good time together. Why don't you come by next week."

"Well . . ."

"Yes, she will come next week," Vlad said. "I will make sure we will visit you." And he was pushing me to the next group of gypsy ladies. They also gave me rings.

The last people in the room were two guys, who looked like they could be twins. They were very tall and slim, however one had white skin and the other had dark skin. They gave me two nice bracelets and explained to me that they were made of white gold.

All the people in the room were now around me. There was a strong and loud conversation in Romanian, gypsy and English. Vlad was making sure I fit all the gold I'd received into my purse. Halibarda seemed to enjoy very much dialoging with everyone in all three languages. I put the necklace I received from the two sisters around my neck. I could tell that they appreciated it. Vlad told me to fit at my fingers with some rings I received. I was quite embarrassed because this was not my style at all. However, I agreed with Vlad that they would be very happy seeing me wearing their gifts. I fit two big rings on each finger. Even wearing all of this jewelry, my purse was still heavy with the other gold rings inside.

I was trying to make eye contact one by one with all the people present in the room. It was as a way for me to visually thank all of them. I felt that most of the people were ignoring me, and discussing things very loudly between each other.

"How do you like Bucharest? Somebody asked me?" He was the white and tall guy.

"It is nice."

Touching in a totally familiar gesture Vlad's shoulder the tall guy said, "I am sure Vlad is a good guide to show you the town."

"May I have your attention please?" Raluka asked in a loud voice. Some of the people became quiet, but the majority was continuing to talk. Halibarda was trying to calm them down but was unsuccessful. Paul was near Raluka, he was walking to the direction of the mostly nosily people and almost instantly they all become quiet.

All the eyes in the room were directed to Paul. He was smiling in a strange way. I never saw it on his face before, a kind of diabolic smile. I observed even Chlorinda was intimidated.

"Good," he said. "Maybe we can discuss things now in a civilized way."

He was speaking in Romanian. Close by me in a low voice Raluka was starting to translate. I had been told before by Raluka that all the gypsies in Romania speak in the Romanian language too. But not all of them speak the gypsy language. So no one in the room, except me, had a problem understanding what Paul had to say. In the room the people were gathering close around him in a semicircle. Lots of the gypsy ladies were standing directly on the floor. In the back a couple of people, like Chlorinda, were standing on chairs.

"The first point in the agenda today is to introduce Laura to all of you. I can see you have all introduced yourselves to her, so this won't be an issue. I would like to thank you for the . . . rich, golden welcome you made to her. A little bit about Laura, she lives in Canada in the same town I live, although I did not meet her face to face until last month. However even if there was such a short time, I can see that she has the gift, she is going to have very good magical abilities and I can predict she will be a strong and very talented witch."

He was interrupted by the applause of the people in the room. "Already Laura signed the papers and now she is a member of our club. She started the theoretical training with Raluka. However, the next step will be to start practicing . . . magic." He paused and he faced me again.

"I will need help from some of you. As you know the magic is something different from witch to witch. We have to show her all of the things that we have learned and the skills that we know. We have to study her in which zone her abilities are strongest. After that of course, we will help her to increase her abilities. I have to tell you dear Laura, there is a lot of work from your side too."

"On another hand, in a previous life . . ." Chlorinda started.

"I speak about this life . . . you stupid woman." With a cold and heavy voice Paul interrupted Chlorinda. "And stop talking in front of us if I don't give you permission first."

"But . . . ." she tried to protest.

"Shut up, witch!" Halibarda cried to her. The room was filled up with the disgusted faces directed to Chlorinda.

"Why are you constantly the problem Chlorinda? When will you be able to watch your manners?" The room was flooded a cold silence.

Without being intimidated Chlorinda said, "If I am so bad why do you not just reject me from the club?"

"I can do this at any moment. Is it what you wish?" He was looking evilly in Chlorinda's direction. For sure I would make sure to never be under his gaze when he was mad like this. "I won't hesitate to do it. But still I believe you can put some efforts towards improvement on your behalf." He was constantly gazing Chlorinda. She finally became silent.

"As I said before, I would like some of you to help me with Laura's training. We will discuss it at the right time. Next item up for discussion . . . ." And simply he took my hand and he directed me to sit in a chair. He did the same, and sat down beside me. All of the eyes in the room were watching us. Raluka took a chair near me ready for another translation.

"With your permission Paul," Gina said. Paul approved her with a nod.

"Thank you," Geta said.

These twins are so identical and so beautiful. If they were not wearing different colors in their gypsy dress, I might not have been able to tell them apart.

"Because we are a good club, a good and friendly team, we would suggest to do some stuff in common."

"Like what?" Chlorinda asked.

"Like group incantations." Gina simply answered. "What we are trying to propose is a way to unify our magical power in order to create . . ."

"I agree," Paul said. "Opinions?"

Chlorinda stood up, along with a few of the gypsy women. Without waiting to be invited to speak Chlorinda tried to talk, "I believe . . ."

"Silence!" Paul cried. Chlorinda voice died almost instantly. "I am not interested in what you believe witch. Other people want to talk here. I want to know couple of opinions." And he pointed out a gypsy women.

Smiling, proud because Paul chose her to talk of she started, "I agree . . . ."

"Stop." Paul screamed again, and he pointed to another gypsy lady. Almost in the same way she smiled and started, "I agree . . ."

Halibarda started laughing. Instead of being disturbed by her laughing Paul started laughing too. Lots of people in the room did the same. Their laughing was so colorful. Maybe some of them were just laughing because of how everyone else was laughing. It was a happy moment after so much tension. Happily I enjoyed them.

"We will vote. Who is for yes?" All of them were for yes.

"Who is for no?" No one voted.

"Okay." Paul said. "We will do collective incantations. It is decided. Now we have to decide the place and the time. What is your proposal for the place?"

"*Near Dracula's castle.*" The two sisters said in almost the same voice.

All the faces were directed to them. Paul waited a couple moments. The room was flooded again with a cold silence. The two girls were standing in front of all people, and took all the questioning eyes.

"Why there?" Halibarda asked.

"Because this is the most exciting place in all our country." Gina said.

Geta started laughing.

"Guys this is a challenge. I hope you are not afraid of this challenge, I have to admit it is enormous."

"No one is challenging me." Chlorinda said proud about herself. "I will attend these collective incantations."

"Good girl!" Paul said. "Finally we agree on a point Chlorinda." And he was smiling nicely at Chlorinda. After that he made eye contact with all of the people in the room.

"If we choose to do this in that particular place I have to warn you about the danger." Paul said in a low voice.

"Guys, there is no danger." Chlorinda said. "I will be there with you. And I will protect you."

"Chlorinda is right." Drina, the short lady, said. "I will be there too. It doesn't matter what entity will showed up there. I will smash her with my kinesthetic powers. And remember, together we are strong."

"Yes, yes!!" Raluka translated for me. In fact it was "Da. Da." Vlad taught me this word, and I liked it so I decided to use it in my conversations.

"Yes." A gypsy lady was standing up speaking loudly and with enthusiasm.

"We are Romanian witches. And we are strong."

"Da. Da.", I heard a core of voices strongly agreed with the woman. In the room we heard a satanic laughing. Paul was laughing so loud and unnaturally.

"You're strong . . . Bull Shit!" he said it in English.

Raluka translated it back in Romanian language. Her voice was sharp. The enthusiasm of the people suddenly disappeared. They gazed Paul with very disapproving faces.

*   *   *

I was happy to observe that they had a second part of the meeting. Some catering guys were showing up with huge plates with food that were very ornate. Also there were a lot of drinks. All the people including me stared to eat and drink and eventually some of them started to sing. They had a couple of musical instruments and I was wondering how nicely rhythmic their music would be?

"This is mostly gypsy music." Raluka explained me. "It might be indeed a source of inspiration for your new album of songs." I saw that they were also enjoying the dancing. The music and the dancing looked so colorful. I saw the two sisters enjoying singing and dancing. They took me with them. First, I found the beat difficult to dance to, and they had a particular style. But after thirty minutes of practicing I was quite good at doing some dance movements. I had also a very nice surprise from Vlad. I observed that he was an awesome dancer. He was teaching me some movements, which initially appeared to be quite difficult. Paul was still enjoying chatting and drinking with various women in the room.

Gina said within hearing distance "try to make him to drink more. " And her sister replied to her "We want to get him drunk."

"Why?" I was wondering.

"Because . . . the party will be much nicer." However, after this short discussion they went to Paul and started filled his glass with Vlad vodka, or now I know it as 'tzuica'. Paul, was really enjoying his time and drinking with them. Finally he started dancing with Vlad and other girls in their gypsy style. Chlorinda started to dance with them, and the surrounding people started to applaud. This somewhat upset Halibarda and she stopped dancing and she came near me to watch them.

Intending maybe to make me a surprise, Vlad stopped their singing and he put on couple of my songs. I was quite amused seeing the women trying to dance to my music. Their improvisations were quite nice. I thought that lots of their gestures and movements would have to be introduced to the repertoire of my dancers.

Forgetting that I cannot speak Romanian, lots of women were trying to talk to me. I was just smiling at them saying, "I am sorry I don't understand."

Raluka was quiet. She did not sing, or dance. She was staying close with me when I was not dancing. A woman dressed in gypsy costume was coming to me a lot talking in Romanian, even if I told her, "I don't understand".

As Raluka was near me her first intention was to translate, but after she was listening to the women a couple of moments she said to me,

"Oh . . . I have to change it."

She immediately went on the dance floor where Paul was happily dancing. She stopped him roughly, I have never seen Raluka upset like this. She was arguing in a quite strong voice with Paul. Maybe if this was happening in the first part of the meeting it was a terrible issue. But now all the people were dancing or singing, or drinking around them as though it was normal for people to argue sometimes. I thought again these people are speaking more quickly then the Italians and they like a lot to argue. Raluka continued to be upset and she tried to pull Paul into a silent corner of the room. But he refused. By their gestures I could tell he was encouraging Raluka that it was better to come to me and to entertain me. Friendly, unhappy she came back to me.

"What is so wrong Raluka?"

"Well the situation was going to be quite bad, but I changed it" Raluka said smiling to me, as though she was trying to show me a small victory. The gypsy woman who was tying to speak to me, started to argue something with Raluka. But Raluka was quite imperative with her.

"Nu. Nu . . ." I caught some words from their conversations. Vlad was teaching me that 'No' is 'Nu' in Romanian, in the latest days. Finally the gypsy woman became silent, and Raluka started talking with me.

"Laura, please meet Ivanka"

"Ivanka . . ." and Raluka continued saying some words in Romanian to the woman. I figured out that she said " Ivanka please meet Laura."

"Nice to meet you Ivanka," I said. The woman started talking a lot not being very pleasant to Raluka. But with an imperative gesture Raluka stopped her.

"Ivanka will be your next teacher. Paul decided it, and our big argument was that he decided you are to go to Ivanka's village for that."

"But this is Okay. I would like to see a Romanian village."

"Oh dear . . . we will have lot of time to travel around Romania, but . . . let's start with pleasant things. Romania is a nice country. I think on our way to *Dracula's castle* you can see lots of Romanian villages. But, I would recommend you to avoid going to Ivanka's village."

Ivanka was again starting to argue. Taking a superior air Raluka just ignored her.

As my music continued to play, Raluka took my hand, and we were walking in the middle of all the people. She tried to dance near me. I noticed that she was not a good dancer but she did this just to escape from the arguing woman.

The party was wonderful. I haven't had so much fun in long time. In my head a lot of the melodies played, long after the party was over.

As I drank, I started to see Vlad dancing in the front of my eyes. His body is so handsome, and especially when he is dancing. I thought that I would be happy to bring him with me to Canada.

From time to time I also thought I was a little bit scared of my new magic teacher.

Chapter 8

My friendship with him is like the friendship with a venomous snake. I will end by being bit.
-Chlorinda – Teaching to Laura

I was quite drunk last night, and I don't remember much. I decided to take my morning shower and have some coffee. I noticed some voices in the living room but I decided to have a quick shower before seeing who was there. When I stepped into the living room, I saw everyone in the house, Paul, Vlad, Raluka, Halibarda and Ivanka! Also nice cup of coffee was waiting for me.

"I made the coffee the way you like it" Halibarda said smiling nicely at me.

They were all watching me with protection; all except my new teacher. This woman had something wild, rude in her eyes. I felt like she is dominant over me but I could not understand how. I saw that she did not drink coffee, the smell coming from her glass made me think she was drinking 'Vlad tzuica'. 'Gosh so early in the morning . . . in fact in the day . . . '

Paul was talking to me.

"Laura, I know that Raluka introduced to you Ivanka, she will be your new magic teacher. There were some arguments but I've already decided. You have a lot of theoretical knowledge to learn now and you need to form a strong relationship with a witch. I would like to introduce you an archaic witch."

"Yes," Raluka said upset, "but maybe you've chosen someone too raw."

I felt there might be a new argument, but Paul was not upset by Raluka's interruption.

"That's right, I would like you to see someone authentic speaking about magic, because those of us outside the tradition have transformed it. The way Ivanka knows and thinks is, somehow, like those witches from thousands of years ago. We've changed a lot of things, but because of the tradition she didn't."

Raluka was still upset. She walked to the window to look out as if the exercise would calm her.

"Unfortunately, Ivanka cannot speak English. Raluka will be translating for you."

I thought Halibarda would be a better choice as I could see Raluka didn't like Ivanka at all.

"When you don't understand something please ask Raluka, she will ask Ivanka to keep explaining until you understand. I would like her to introduce you to some basic magical concepts, it is very important for you to memorize them all. You can use your camcorder to record and replay the lessons." He was paused smiling at me. "Now I will discuss with the group. Vlad please translate to Laura what we are saying."

Vlad came closer to me, making me feel more comfortable.

"Ivanka, do you know where you are?" Paul asked Ivanka as Vlad translated for me.

"Yes. I am in Bucharest."

"Do you know why you are here?"

"Yes, to teach Laura."

"I agree. However, the people around you don't like you. I would like you to pay attention to the people who don't like you and ask yourself 'Why?' Do you know? No? I will tell you. You are not up to date with your bathing. Try to have minimum two baths per day."

"What?" Ivanka said. "I will get a cold if I have two baths a day."

Paul was laughing loudly.

"You might get a cold, but having two baths per day is a command from me. I will have Raluka watching you. You have to understand that here people are much more civilized than in your village. I know that in your village you have no water, and maybe this is the reason for your habits. Here, we have lots of water and I ask that you use it. Starting now do as I say, have two baths per day, and don't argue again. Understood?" There was a silent moment. The woman refused to answer.

"Paul asked you a question Ivanka," Halibarda said. "I suggest you to answer with 'yes'."

"Da (yes)", the woman said in a gruff voice.

"Good," Paul said thankful. "I would like you to obey this command to the letter."

"Yes. I will." Ivanka looked scared.

"I want you to understand that we have to focus to bigger things. Don't upset the group further with your poor manners."

Ivanka became suddenly angry, "I already said I will!"

"More than that, Raluka will teach you to use the cosmetics we all use daily. While you are staying here please use them." I could see that Ivanka became angrier almost ready to explode but still watching her Paul added in a normal voice. "You may have noticed I said 'please'."

Ivanka remained completely silent.

*   *   *

The next morning Vlad gave me a ride to Raluka's house. There I began my new magic lessons with the new teacher chosen by Paul and with Raluka as translator. Ivanka was changed today. She was dressed in gypsy's clothing but extremely clean and smelling nicely. Her style was quite rude, but she was trying to be a nice person today; or as much as she could. I looked from Raluka to Ivanka. These two women were total opposites in personality and habits! I had some discussions with Vlad; he told me that Ivanka lives in raw conditions; like the Indians who lived years ago in teepees. Vlad told me that the two types of tents are quite similar. I was wondering how it was possible that in our day people could live in tents. He explained me that there are a couple of gypsy families but very few houses. Ivanka already has a house but she prefers to live in her tent and because she does her magic there too.

The three of us women were now sitting on the floor of Raluka's condo in her magic room. Ivanka asked me something in Romanian and Raluka translated for me,

"Ivanka asks if you believe in fate."

"Yes. I do."

"When does our fate begin?"

"When we are born," I answered.

"Very good, I will tell you about our tradition in this matter. When a child is born we believe there comes three entities called 'Ursitoare'. They appear in one of the first three nights after a child's birth to determine the course of its life. We don't know exactly if they come once in the three nights or in each moment. But over the years it was important to find a method to listen and understand what they would foresee for the newborn. It was considered to be of capital importance as it cannot be changed," she paused, "even by a strong witch."

Raluka started to argue with her in Romanian. The argument lasted a few minutes, finally Raluka looked at me, "I had an argument with her as not all members of our club believe this. Just remember, you will have other teachers who will each teach you something different. However, Paul wishes you to understand this old point of view on these entities." After that she looked to Ivanka letting her know to continue.

"Over time we had stories about women acting as if they were sleeping but in fact they were focusing to see or listen to the three entities. It is said that if a mother would know her child's fate she would be able to take some action."

"How many women have succeeded?" I asked curiously.

"None!" The two women looked at me strangely.

"Oh . . . really?"

Ivanka was focused on me with a rude expression and she continued, "Yes! Some of them, who hoped to see something were temporarily blinded, lost their hearing, or were not able to speak. Now, we believe they are the three powerful entities of the universe, and they cannot be tricked. For this reason in the first three nights of the newborn's life all the women put gifts for the Ursiorate near the child's bed."

"Like what?" I asked

"A cup with honey, a big vessel filled with very fresh water in case the entities are thirsty and they need a drink, some good food and so on. These days if the child spends his first days in the hospital's maternity ward it is not possible, but the three entities still come and they will determine the future for that child. Because our fates are sealed at birth we are very interested to learn the future. To my tent come women with children, or alone, or mature people asking me to read their future," she paused longer. "And I am quite good at this."

"How do you do it?" I asked her fascinated.

She was no longer looking to me and she smiled proudly. "I don't know the exact word, It is chiro . . ."

Raluka was smiling and she said to Ivanka and me. "Chiromancy. She is looking for the word Chiromancy. It is the art of foreseeing the future of a person by studying the lines in the left hand."

"Yes! Maybe the mother of the child was not able to hear what the Ursitoares had commanded. However we are wonderful creatures in this universe. Also the child, the newborn has wonderful abilities. Even if the child has, at that moment, only been alive a few hours he understands what the Ursitoares are saying. I believe it is like a curse. The Usritoares judge him according to what he did in his previous lives, they are also aware of his current parents."

Raluka raised a hand to stop Ivanka because she felt that she needed to give me further explanation. "She is trying to tell you that the main criteria which the Ursitoares take into consideration are the evolution that child had in his previous lives and second, the genes which come from the parents. They will also look in the room of the child and if they will find gifts they will be kinder in their choices for his fate."

Immediately when Raluka was done Ivanka started to speak.

"Yes. The Ursitoares will determine his fate. Even if the Ursitoares are stronger entities than us, they are not perfect. In that moment for they might be upset and they will determine a bad life for the newborn even if his parents are good and he had a positive evolution; or they might be very happy and even if his parents are bad or in his previous lives he made bad decisions his fate will be good. And it cannot be changed! But as I said, we're wonderful creatures, with very early understanding the child will make lines in his left hand according to what he hears from the three entities. I can see, understand and translate these lines. Therefore I can read his future extremely accurately to what the Ursitoares commanded."

I looked at Ivanka with respect.

"An easier way to explain," Raluka trying to complete Ivanka's explanations, "is in school, you heard some important information but you are afraid you will forget it. You have a pen, but no paper. As this information is vital you write it on your palm. Ivanka believes at that stage of life the newborn is able to modify his palm skin and these modifications can catch the pattern the Ursitoares foresaw for his life."

I tought about this possibility. It is known, even in my country, that there is a terrible coincidence between palms lines and our future. I believe in coincidences, but not at this scale.

"In my country we also have people with the same abilities," I said.

"Sorry to say Laura but, there are a lot of amateurs," Raluka said. "I also believe these signs are an indication regarding how our life will unfold. All of the palm readers might be able to understand and interpret these lines more or less but, I have to tell you Ivanka is very good. People have gone to her a second time after ten years or more and she told them absolutely the same words. They were not happy with the first reading and they came after years hoping she was wrong the first time and that she will predict something different. But the prediction or the reading was exactly the same."

"Yes. Until now all my predictions were true. I would like to tell all the people who come to my tent only good things but if the lines tell me different, I cannot lie."

"Okay," I said. "Could you please have a look in my hand?"

There was a terrible moment of silence. Ivanka was looking to Raluka as if asking for her permission. Instead Raluka was gazing the empty wall in front of her as if she was not present in the room. I offered Ivanka my left hand.

Unsure, she took my hand. First she looked at me for a long time, and then her black eyes came down easily to check the lines of my hand. Instead of telling me something she made a terrible sucking sound as if affected by a strong demon and screamed as loudly as was possible.

*   *   *

The room was dark.

Only a single chair in the middle of the room, Ivanka was sitting on the chair, Paul and Halibarda were standing in her front. Ivanka was exhausted and afraid of the two sorceresses present in the room.

Paul was discussing with Halibarda.

"So . . . . we begin. We start our race. Put on your belt Dorothy."

"My name is Halibarda."

"I promise you we will have fun." And Paul started demonically laughing.

Halibarda was smiling down on Ivanka like an eagle looking at his victim. The echo of the empty room amplified Paul's demonic laugh. It was a long time before Paul stopped laughing.

"Ivanka, I need to know all about what you saw." Paul said in a commanding voice.

"But . . . but, I already told you. Halibarda also asked me a lot of questions and I told the story again and again."

Halibarda said in a grave voice, "Yes. She told me things. When she tried to do her chiromancy she was in touch with an entity, an entity unknown to us until now. We know almost nothing about that entity because this stupid woman instead of dealing with the entity like a professional witch, she started to scream like a crazy child."

Ignoring Halibarda, Paul said, "Ivanka, I need to know more about the entity you met."

The wound was deep, and fresh. She was beaten, confused too. She was tired, scared. She looked like a man overdosing on a strong drug. When Halibarda was interrogating her earlier, the room was so bright and Halibarda was studying the expression of her face. Now the room is so dark Paul could see almost nothing.

"Okay. I will tell you again about the feelings I had in that moment." Ivanka tried but it was a huge effort to speak.

"It is not enough" Paul said. "I need more"

The woman looked at Halibarda, unsure.

"But there was only a moment, like a blink of the eye." With the last of her power Ivanka tried to protest.

"We need to use our methods to extend this blink of the eye as long as we can to grab the important information." Halibarda raised her voice, and breaking the previous silence the empty room started again to vibrate.

"In order to know more about what you saw, I will use hypnoses with you Ivanka." Paul said.

"What? But . . ." Ivanka was totally terrified. "I cannot experience again these feelings. My heart . . ."

113

"Silence!" Paul was screaming in the room. "I don't have the nerves or patience for your stupidity. Do I will command!"

Halibarda was pacing in a corner of the room and she sat down on the floor. On her chair Ivanka started shakeing. Paul came close to Ivanka. He bent his body so his eyes were at the same level as Ivanka's eyes.

"Now look in my eyes. Look deep. Relax. Relax." His voice became soft. "You see a river. It is large river. See its water. It is flowing down. It is a silent flow. No wind, no turbulence. On the river is a big cylindrical log. The log is floating in the middle of the river. You can see it. See the details of the log. It is calmly floating in the river; the water is calm. The log is in balance and harmony with the river's water. I will start counting from ten to zero. When I will reach zero you will be the log, and all that you hear will be only my commands . . ."

Chapter 9

41 corn beans, 41 brothers
Be good friends, be good comrades
As you well know to feed the entire world.
I command you to be good friends, good comrades.
I command you to help me to read the future.

-Romanian spelling for reading of the
future using 41 corn beans

"It was our intention to have this part completed with Ivanka," Raluka said in a low voice, "unfortunately she refused to come back . . ."

"Why?" I was so confused, I did not know if I made a mistake, I felt guilty.

"If you remember, I was not very happy having her as your teacher. She is a strange woman. Please don't let the sadness interfere with your lessons. We're dealing with a lot of strange things; we have to keep a clear mind. It is essential."

I still wondered, "Is she okay?"

"Yes. She is back . . ." Raluka snorted "in her stupid tent. I don't agree with living that way in this century."

She kept pausing as if she was upset about discussing the subject. After few moments she continued.

"In fact, I am happy I will teach you this part. It is not necessary to have the presence of a confirmed witch. I have to tell you some of our witches are not well . . . mannered, and I am afraid you will not have a . . . ." She stopped to consider her words, "very easy time with them. Sometimes they exaggerate, and only Paul is able to command them. I am happy he is the president of our club, and I think in regards to the work he does, he is the only one capable to do it." She smiled at me, friendly, "Now the lesson."

She took my hand and brought me into the dark room of magic. I was quite surprised. There were two comfortable chairs, a table with refreshments, Raluka's iPad and a projector. "I intend to spend the entire day here, there is much to tell. We will pause only to use the washroom. We might extend the teaching to the other days if need be."

I was confused. I did not understand why there was so much work to do, but I really liked Raluka. She was a wonderful teacher.

"In fact Ivanka's main task was to tell you about the witch's history in Romania, to show you her magical tools and to discuss their usage." She paused a moment delicately touching her iPad. "Over the years so much knowledge has been accumulated that is difficult to explain the tradition and history. It is so difficult that there are no books."

I was confused, "Why is that? The people are fascinated by old books? I have never encountered this situation." I wondered, "Fantasy literature is full of this kind of story. There are always books; sometimes these books are very valuable. How is the information kept if there are no books?"

"I will assure you that the information was passed from generation to generation without losing any knowledge. A witch would teach her daughter or her niece all what she knows and so on."

"What if someone in the family was not interested in learning?"

Raluka looked at me as if my question made no sense.

"We have never had that situation." She paused taking time to think. "Think logically; in the old times in very poor villages a woman with these abilities was very good at preparing different types of medicines using herbs or alchemy. As a result that woman was much respected in the villages. It was like having a good job. In her family there was always somebody very interested in taking over this job. We are talking about times when people didn't have enough food, or money; it was not a suitable way to live at all. Having this job was like gold. As a result there was always somebody, usually a woman, to continue in this golden occupation."

Even if Raluka's arguments were good and logical I was not totally convinced.

"What about the inquisition? I know being a witch was a terrible accusation. Lots of women had been accused and killed during those times."

Raluka was confused yet again. I was able to read from her face that she totally disagreed with me.

"Not in Romania; or in the countries which consisted then of what we know now as Romania today. The witches were respected. There was no contradiction between the witches and religion. Most of them respected and believed the teachings of Jesus Christ; even today they are often Christian. If there are no contradictions why punish someone?"

She paused again gazing me. She was waiting to see if I had another question. But I was quite pleased by her explanation. Here in Romania and old Romania things are different in comparison with the other side of the world. I decided to ask nothing for the moment and to let Raluka to continue the lesson in her logical way.

"For witches like Ivanka it was like all the knowledge already existed in her mind, as her mother taught her everything. But for someone like me or like you, we might need books. I have collected this kind of information for years. When I first started I learned from an old lady in my village, she is now dead. I recorded all the information and knowledge she had in an old computer, now I've transferred it all in an iPad. Over the years I've added new information from other witches as I met and learned from them. I was surprised to find the details were consistent and that all the main information is the same. There are of course some regional influences but otherwise they are the same."

"What do you mean by *the same*?"

"Some tools, some understanding about the chemicals inside the plants, name and spellings of words, the main criteria about alchemy and so on. I would like you to remember that in the old times having this knowledge was a not challenge. These days things are quite different. Now we have good medicines, the alchemy is almost totally ignored. Being a witch requires a lot of work, even if you are a gifted. Why should the people come to you if they have a headache or feel sick? They will go to the doctor. But! If the headache, or the illness persists and the doctor is not able to cure the person it is very possible that they will seek out a witch for help. I feel it's important to collect the information from the witches and to keep them in a computer. Who knows when these traditions might be lost and then only my records would remain!"

This time I was the one who did not agree.

"But Raluka, the people will always be interested in methods to predict their future and it is still unclear if there is another world for our soul to go to when we die."

"That's right, I would agree with you. For argument's sake let's say some interest will always exist. But when there is someone like you born with the gift, the information I have collected might be very useful. It will say things which are not in books, only oral traditions but now are recorded so people outside the witch's family can learn."

"Okay, I agree."

"Perfect. Now let's begin by talking about the very common things. Let's see some pictures. I have been very fascinated by collecting pictures of the old witches. Unfortunately I cannot go too far back in time and the quality of the images is not great, but let's watch anyway."

Using the projector she started to show me the pictures she had of the women who were witches a long time ago. Most of them were gypsies. They had very common dresses, unfortunately the pictures were only black and white, and I was not able to see much detail. Usually all of the women were old. I saw a few that were young and beautiful. When Raluka came to the images of the young women she commented, "They were always creating trouble in their time with the high situated gentlemen of their regions. As they appear very smart and as you can see in the pictures very beautiful."

She was showing me more pictures, but suddenly she stopped and she stood in the front of the projector looking at me. She looked like she was searching for the right words for what she wanted to say.

"Dearest Laura, Paul instructed me to ask you this, please look closely at the images you will see. If you notice some peculiar feelings or emotions associated with an image please let us know. We have methods to understand what kind of connections there are and in what life."

"I am not sure what you or Paul means by connections."

"Okay. Let's say this is not your first life. Who knows? Paul is convinced as you have a significant potential, you might have been one of these witches in these pictures."

I felt my mouth go dry, and I took a big sip from the ice cold coke I had in my glass.

With a more professional voice Raluka added, "Please don't be scared. We can manage a lot of complicated magical stuff. It would also be interesting for you to know your ancestral origin."

"But, Paul already knows that I was a strong witch in a previous life." I said almost indignant because this might be doubted. Actually I had to admit I like this hypothesis that I was a strong witch in a previous life. "And at the last meeting the other sorceress confirmed that I have something special. I also believe that I was a strong witch in a previous life."

Raluka was patiently listening to me. "Yes, but which one?"

"You . . . you mean that there is a possibility to find me in . . . one of your pictures?" Raluka did not answer but emphatically nodded.

*   *   *

We spent all day watching the pictures Raluka had of the old witches and the next day we started to do the same. I felt no particular attraction to a picture, or a face or to someone in the picture. After many hours Raluka decided to give me a copy of the folder and if I wanted I could continue this exercise by myself.

"However" she said. "If Paul is so sure and other people saw a particular kind of energy in you, you might be an incarnation of a witch in Egypt, or in China or . . . However, I cannot pretend I have all the pictures of the all witches that existed. Now, let's move on. We have seen a lot of photos of witches; let's have a look at their tools."

"Are they very common tools?"

"Yes." Raluka started to laugh. "Please don't be surprised if they are different than those used in Harry Potter."

"You don't like Harry Potter?" I asked her.

"Yes, I do, I do." She said turning her face.

"I can see that you have a different opinion."

"Well it is a good children's movie. But let's go back to our studies. Not only compared to Harry Potter, but even with another witches from old European times, the Romanian witches are different."

"In what way?"

"Well, for example flying on a broomstick totally doesn't exist in our culture. I find it ridiculous. I know it is in legends from other countries but, in Romanian culture it is nonexistent. Let's focus on what we have here and to understanding the mandatory material we have here."

"Ivanka has already taught you about the art of seeing the future. Through history even now people are always interested in seeing into their future. The witches have the tools to read the future. Of course for chiromancy you need no tools, but they are necessary for other practices. A very old and common tool is the water vessel. This vessel has transformed over the years. It looks like a soup bowl but quite large. Let's look at some pictures," and she started to display the pictures. "Beginning with the most ancient vessels, the first vessels were made of mud. After that, the ceramic vessels began to be used because the vessel is meant to be fully filled with water. The witch will study reflections of the light in the water. She will interpret these reflections into a reading of the future."

"So . . . the light is showing her the future? Is that correct?"

"Not exactly, I spoke to you about spirits, elementary or complex; also Ivanka told you about Ursitoares. It is thought entities are playing with the light or they are trying to communicate with the witch. The witch is able to catch this energy manifestation and to interpret them into how we will experience future events. The witches of Romania are still to this day using a water vessel to read the future. A modern tool that you may be familiar with is the crystal globe. The principle is absolutely identical."

She started to project the images of crystal globes and some images had witches in a trance looking into their crystal ball.

"Another common tool to read the future is the cards. They use either tarot cards or normal playing cards." She smiled, "here I have a lot of pictures." And she started to show photos of the cards and witches old and young arranging the cards in various ways. Also in these pictures there were ordinary people around the witch.

"Here is a theory, I don't fully agree to it but best mention it; the theory that in order to read the future properly the witch has to create the cards herself."

"But how we can explain reading the future in the cards? There is no a mechanism involving the light."

"True. But don't forget, using the water vessel or crystal globe, the brain and the body of the witch might be in touch with entities who help her to read the future. This principal is the same for reading cards" She paused and then continued to show me further pictures. Some of the women looked quite nice. "The twins are famous for this kind of future reading. I do believe you will have a lesson with them soon. Think about how complicated it is you need to know the significance of each card; there are so many combinations and possible interpretations of the combinations."

She smiled professionally at me.

"Whenever we are thinking about our decisions we are creating alternative possibilities. The witch has to identify the improbable possibilities and ignore them. She has to focus on the most likely possibilities. It is akin to completing mathematical equations."

Raluka continued to show me images. "I have a lot of photos; I will give you the folder to be watched another time. Historically speaking the tarot cards were first and the playing cards come from tarot cards." We spent some more time watching the pictures of tarot cards and the pictures of witches who was reading the future in tarot cards over the years.

After that Raluka continued, "A very old method used in Romania and particular to this region was reading the future with 41 corn beans. It is believed that before the corn beans go in the earth, grow and fructify, the corn beans can be used by a witch to see the future. Using this method the way the corn beans are stuck together in various combinations will help the witch to see and understand the future. Paul's grandmother used this method a lot. I think he is also quite good at it. I heard that he has a friend; she is able to read the future with an unbelievable accuracy. But be sure not ask him about, we know he doesn't like to speak about it!" Here she paused to make sure I understood the subject was off limits.

"Another method used to read the future is a sea shell like this one over here. The witch will listen to the echo in the shell and she can hear the future."

I had a look at Raluka's sea shell and I could not resist holding it to my ear to listen the echo. I agreed with Raluka it is like solving equations, there are so many possibilities of interpretation.

"The there is also the receptacle for magical drinks."

And she showed me various pictures, first what I saw was almost like a goblet made from mud. After that it evolved as the water vessel had over time.

"Now even plastic glasses are used! I think my favorite one is the metal glass or the goblet. Silver is often used, but most people like Chlorinda use gold."

"Why exactly do they need a goblet?"

"Often witches have to drink various magical nepenthes. It is believed that it must be done with the right receptacle. Otherwise the material of the goblet might interact with the nepenthe. The witch's particular goblet is meant to have magical powers."

As Raluka was continuing to show me various pictures I saw there are beautiful goblets made from silver, gold and other metals. I thought I would choose to have a silver one.

"Next tool is?" Raluka asked me.

"The wand?"

"Yes, it is not used often by our witches but I have to mention it. In their work sometimes they come in resonance with various energies and when combining these energies or sending them in various directions a wand is a very welcome tool. If there are male sorceresses they will have a rod. The rod is sometimes used by the very old witches too. They are most often made from wood, but there is a big variety in types of wood. I will mention only one of them. Usually a wand is made from filbert. It is known that the filbert has wonderful magnetic proprieties. An old method involved the usage of a filbert pendulum over a village surface to find where the water reservoirs are located before drilling a well. The rod has to be a strong type of wood. A pin rod is definitely not recommended."

"Paul has one?" I asked.

Raluka, surprised, looked at me like I was crazy and ignored my question, continuing "A very used tool is the knife, or the sword." She started to show me terrifying tools. There were no Japanese curved swords, but a rich variety of other knifes and swords.

"Why would they use a knife like a magical tool?"

"Because they don't use a wand as much, the knife can be used like a wand. Also a lot of the entities who surround us have a fear of knives or swords. If you are so interested about Paul, you may like to know he is highly practiced in the martial arts. He is very skilled in using the sword or a knife but I never have seen if he has these tools in his magical requisite collection." She made a pause as if to tell me we are now done with a big part of the theory.

"If you want to become a witch, you will need to have your own tools. It is important that you first become familiar with them. They have to be very practical for you and you have to be very confident with them. I would suggest you start with the blade."

"Why?"

"Because, the list of entities that is afraid of a knife starts with vampires, and here . . ." she paused, "we are in Romania."

Her words impressed me. It made me think about a battle!

"Also together with knife or sword we are going to use the stake or peg against a vampire; and there can be a huge variety. There are various types of pegs. They can be made from many different woods and very sharp or silver pegs are also commonly used.

Please take your time and think about having your own magical tools. You might also have questions about all this and . . ." She paused, "we don't have much time."

"We don't have much time?" I wondered, "how come? And why?"

"Because we leave in three days in for our trip *near Dracula's castle!*

Chapter 10

You are my trusted witch,
I know you can use the magic to bring him back to me.
But, may I suggest to you,
Do your magic on a Tuesday.
I know your magic needs one day to travel,
It will touch him on Thursday.
Friday he will feel bad, and he will start complaining to me.
Saturday I will cure him,
And Sunday I will make love with him.
And, thanks to you . . . I will start to live again
-Romanian folk song

After we had our morning coffee, Paul, Halibarda, Raluka, Vlad and I started our travel to the Romanian mountains *near Dracula's castle.* Vlad was our driver and this time we used a van which belonged to Halibarda.

The trip between Bucharest and the next town nearby can typically be completed in almost one hour, depending on the amount of traffic. It is a very scenic route. We passed the Romanian domestic airport, the international airport and after that I observed attractive and well kept houses on each side for the rest of the way. I do not know why but they evoked romantic feelings in me. Paul explained to me that the name of the town is Ploiesti some oil refineries are located there. The oil university is also there. It was initially in Bucharest but was moved to Ploiesti by the communist regime. They believed it would be welcome but as all the main teachers were living in Bucharest it didn't turn out as well as they had hoped.

However, before going into this town we took a back road to go to a church near this town. Unfortunately as the name of the church was quite difficult for me, I don't remember it. I recalled that Halibarda mentioned this church as she and Paul go there from time to time. And as she had told me, the church is very beautiful. It is surrounded by townhouses with rooms for the mantis who live there. Around the church are lovely gardens and a small patio painted with religious scenes.

Halibarda explained me that on Saint John's Day, the priests make holy water and share the water with the people on the patio. "We use the holy water against vampires," she said in a low voice near my ear.

The architecture of the church was remarkable. "Please keep in your mind this is not the most beautiful church in Romania," Halibarda clarified.

Inside of the church all the walls and the ceiling were painted with religious scenes. I have been told these are unique and they are painted by a very famous Romanian painter. I could see that he was very talented.

Last but not least were the icons. "It is told that the one over there, the Virgin's icon, is able to perform wonders," Paul said softly. "Many people come here to tell their wishes to the icon. There are a fantastically high number of people whose wishes are becoming reality."

"What kinds of things are they wishing for?" I asked curiously.

"Health for themselves and their families, prosperity, longevity and . . . help in their fight against bad spirits."

"What?"

"Remember in the car I told you a story about this. Now you have to focus and feel the positive energies which are in this place."

After we passed around the church and viewed all of the icons we all bought candles. Outside of the church there were special places to light the candles.

"As you light a candle, please focus and say a prayer for the person you are lighting it for. There are separate places for people who are still alive and over there for the dead," Raluka explained to me as she gestured to the areas.

"I hope you remember in the Christian Orthodox church we believe after death a person's soul goes to another world in heaven

125

or . . . you know," she stopped speaking. I watched as they lit candles in each area.

"They have a museum near the church here," Paul said.

"Yes. But I saw that it is closed." Raluka was looking toward the closed museum's door.

"I will ask that they open it." Halibarda said and she stopped a mantis, asking something in Romanian. With a welcoming smile the woman was making affirmative signs with her head. Shortly another one came with keys and opened the museum door for us.

Near me Raluka was starting to tell me about history, years, names of people, priests and about the religious objects I saw there. After a few minutes Paul stopped her. He suggested that she give me information only if I ask . . . his observation was quite welcome as I was becoming quite lost in her details.

Finally we went out. There is a very nice market with icons and religious items. I was impressed with their high quality and I decided to buy an expensive icon of the virgin as a memento.

"I have some icons from here too," Paul told me. "Initially many of the things at this market were hand crafted in the ateliers of the church by the mantises here. But last time I bought a very similar icon and I saw that it was made in Greece. At least it was not made in China," he said with some sarcasm.

It was noonish and I felt hungry. Vlad drove us to a nearby village restaurant. As it was a beautiful day we took a table outside. We toasted with Bergenbeer and after a short wait we had the delicious 'mititei'. I ate the mititei hungrily and decided they were now my favorite food. I thought I could never tire of eating them.

"Thanks for bringing me to the church, guys. It is a wonderful place."

"You are most welcome, Laura," Paul said, "did you feel something special when we were . . . inside of the church?"

"Well . . . maybe as you said a kind of positive energy around me . . ."

"But nothing special?" Halibarda asked.

"No . . . sorry guys, maybe you expected more."

After a moment of silence I said, "I saw that you somehow ignored the priest of the church. I saw that he was there and the other people were socializing with him, but not you."

"Maybe because he was busy socializing with the others," Halibarda suggested and Paul chimed in.

"I see a priest the same way as Raluka is for us. She knows a lot about magic but she has no magical abilities. She cannot perform magic. Sometimes we have assistance from the priest's side, especially with the exorcism cases. Maybe Raluka told you abut . . ."

"Not yet. I have not had enough time to cover this section," Raluka said somewhat embarrassed.

"Of course the priests have no magical abilities even if they think they do," Paul said, "or perhaps just a few of them have some magical abilities, speaking about exorcism and possession cases. But maybe the place of these priests is in our club too. Unfortunately none of them have contacted us. I think this is an unfortunate situation. But . . . I found that place to be really interesting from the point of view of positive energies existing there. And that icon looks to be indeed a wonderful one. Vlad?"

"Yes," said Vlad.

I was quite surprised. Usually Vlad was not asked about these types of subjects. I became interested about what he would say.

With an enigmatic voice he started to tell me the story.

"Once I was walking in the park and I met a woman who was crying. She told me that she has a daughter who is possessed. She tried many methods to exorcise the evil spirit but nothing was working so far." He was looking one by one to Paul, Halibarda and Raluka. "At that time your club did not exist, and I did not know any of you. I had no idea what I could tell the woman, but at the same time I wished to help her. By chance, I remembered being told that the icon can perform wonders. I suggested she go there with her daughter to pray. She told me that until that time they had visited many priests and nothing was working. I insisted they try this church and pray to the Virgin's icon. She was disapproving of me as she observed that her daughter would have to go inside the church which would make her more agitated. I thought while standing there with the woman at the bench in the park that it was a cold winter day. I felt like the cold of the winter had also overtaken the woman's heart. I felt again that I had to do something to help her.

"I offered to drive them to the church. Our agreement was that she would go by herself into the church and prays to the Virgin's icon and when she came outside she would light 33 candles, all for her daughter. Each time she lit a candle she was to pray 'Please Virgin Maria help my daughter.' I stayed in the car with her daughter while the woman was in the church. I was in the back seat of the car trying to speak with the girl. Her eyes were wild, but I think she liked me. She was trying to speak with me and she broke into a sweat. But her words were barely understandable. Her words were like she was speaking an alien language. I thought it was because of the possession. I tried to continue to talk with her. I told her that her mother will help her by praying to Virgin Maria. There are people who love her, and Virgin Maria loves her too. She was fighting with something inside her. It was horrible for me to watch her. Finally with a convulsion she fell into a kind of sleep. I wiped her sweaty face, trying to dry her off. It appeared to be under control.

As I was focused on the young girl, I did not notice people were coming and gathering close to my car. Finally when her mother arrived . . . she started to scream. I become scared, and I stepped outside of the car. What I saw there was . . . terrifying."

"What did you see?" I asked him, completely captivated by his story but little bit scared too.

"I had kept the engine of the car running to have heat inside of the car for the girl; outside it was starting to snow, but some of the snow started to melt. The icy water was creating on the windshield of my car a portrait of the face of an ugly man with horns."

I took a strong sip from my cold beer. Usually in these kinds of moments when I am horrified I feel like my mouth is very dry.

"As I had my cell phone with me I took a picture," and he searched through his cell phone until he found the photo.

"No thanks," I protested. "I am not curious to see it."

"Why not? It is just a picture," Paul said. "I would like you to be much stronger and find power within you in these difficult situations."

Vlad showed me the picture. It was indeed terrifying. I could clearly see that it was a face of somebody like a man, a hideous one with horns.

"Some explanations, Raluka?" Paul asked, politely smiling at Raluka.

"Yes," she was smiling back at Paul with her professional air.

"Here it is quite clear. The positive energy of Virgin Maria's icon exorcised the evil spirit possessing the girl. On its way out, the image of the evil spirit was captured by the snow which melted on Vlad's car's windshield."

"But Ralu," Paul tried to corrected her "there we have images. You should be able to interpret them. There was not a spirit." And he smiled at Raluka with some superiority. "There is another kind of entity."

"I don't need any picture," she said, "it is common in these possession cases, it is not a spirit. You are perfectly right Paul. It is a hell."

*   *   *

The way to the Romanian mountains was silent. I continued to think about Vlad's story. "How is that girl now?" I asked.

"She is perfectly well," Vlad said focusing on his driving.

"Why is she not supposed to be well?" Paul asked. "The hell which possessed her was exorcised, she is free. There is no reason for her to be ill. From a medical point of view she was in good health. The only reason for her sickness was the possession. Sometimes people are unwilling to accept these types of . . . paranormal situations," Paul added. "We also experience the phenomenon of weeping icons. Sometimes they are clever counterfeits but occasionally . . . perhaps you have heard the legend that during Dracula's birth the icon in the room was weeping bloody tears."

"I was not aware of this information. However, it is extremely . . . interesting." I was quite embarrassed about my lack of knowledge.

"Maybe we can have some music, Vlad? In fact we are going to the mountains, it's not a somber event," Halibarda suggested.

"Oh yes," Vlad said pleased by this suggestion. "May we Paul?"

"Yes, but try to find something . . . interesting." Paul added.

"Like my music," I said.

It was extremely enjoyable to listen to something very familiar like my music while viewing the beauty of these mountains. They are so beautiful, I thought. Maybe because the winters are not so hard and long as they are in Canada, the pine trees are taller and impressive.

No one was speaking; we were all just admiring the scenery. The villages we saw along the way were unbelievably nice. There was a lot of traffic and I deduced these mountains are visited often. They are the Carpathian Mountains and they are gorgeous. I wondered how until now I had heard nothing about how beautiful they are, through the media or another source.

"These mountains are breathtaking. I hope you agree, Laura," Paul said.

"Yes. I totally agree."

Going to the Carpathian Mountains and listening to my music; Carpathian Mountains and my music, what a wonderful combination.

"I told you little bit about my friend from Malta. As we are good friends I invited him to ski in Canada. I told him about Calgary Olympic park, about Banff, about cross country skiing," Paul explained. "But he told me somewhat sadly, 'I told you my friend, when I go skiing I do it only in a place away from the entire world. It is in Romania at Poiana Barasov. When I go there, I take a taxi from Bucharest to the mountain. On our way where I see the first place where it is possible to eat mititei I always ask the cab driver to stop the car and I invite him to share some mititei with me.' I always enjoy listening to him tell this story."

I smiled at this. "You know Paul, I totally understand your friend now. I may do the same."

We were passing through the spectacular Romanian mountains. In a few hours we reached the villa which Paul rented for us. The villa had a quite large living room and many bedrooms, most of them with its own bathroom. Lots of people had already arrived there. It was like they were waiting for us.

Paul was entering the living room. Several of the women present there tried to salute him but instead he just raised his hand and said "Don't talk." He was looking around and with a disapproving gesture he said, "There is a bad odor here. Please open the windows." The women hurried to follow his command.

"That's better," he said thankfully. "I will go to my room and have a quick shower. I will be back in 40 minutes, and we will start our meeting. I suggest all of you call the people who are missing now. Once I start the meeting I will not accept people who show up after."

Saying this he turned around and started going upstairs to his bedroom. We did the same, hurrying as much as we could. We got a very nice room. It had two bedrooms and a bathroom. Vlad and I chose one and Halibarda and Raluka took the bedroom next door. I had a quick shower. I dried quickly, gazing outside at the small but pretty balcony attached to our bedroom. The view was amazing. The beauty of these mountains is very difficult to describe in words. I was quite shocked to see how tall they are. I wondered to myself if they are bigger than the Swiss Alps. I made a mental note to ask Raluka about it as I was sure she would know the answer. But for now, for me these mountains were the biggest, and the most awe inspiring mountains in the entire world. I was happy to be there.

I continued to admire them closely, but also checking my watch from time to time as I did not want to be late to Paul's meeting. As my gaze drifted over the tallest mountains I saw a cross at the top of one. God, I thought to myself, that cross must be huge if I am able to see it from here. That is . . . incredible. I wonder how I never have been told about that before. I spent a few more minutes contemplating the mystery of the cross on the top of the mountain.

"When a festival is occurring the cross is lit." Someone spoke from behind me and I recognized Raluka's voice. "You had better get dressed; Paul is strict about the start time of the meeting."

"But he said in 40 minutes. We still have time."

"Believe me, he will start the meeting early, and he will yell at the people who are late. He quite often does this. We had better be early."

"Oh . . . I see . . . I will be ready in just a moment."

As we returned, almost the entire group was already in the living room. Paul was there too. He was looking around. Many people were watching me and they were smiling at me and making 'hello' signs with their hands.

"My car is so bad," somebody said near me with a voice full with frustration. I saw that it was Chlorinda.

"So sorry to hear about that, Chlorinda."

"Yes . . . and also some stupid cops stopped me. I was almost late arriving here. It was my intention to use hypnosis against them but finally I decided it would be quicker to just get the ticket. But . . . if I tell this to Paul he will never understand or trust me," she said with a kind of regret in her voice. I was unsure if the regret in her voice was due to her situation with the cops or Paul's lack of understanding.

Everyone was chatting with each other, but soon their voices become silent.

"Okay, let's start," Paul said, raising his voice. "Raluka, could you please translate for Laura?"

"It is my pleasure," Raluka said smiling in a polite gesture to Paul and me.

"Good," he said, satisfied. "As we decided at our last meeting we are here to go in a special place to perform spellings. I would like to explain to you about three things: the time, the place and the scope. Please hold your questions until I am done. In my experience with this club there will be questions. Usually when someone is beginning his speech you may think you have questions, but by the end of the speech you might be surprised to learn all the things you were curious about have been answered." He paused, fixing Chlorinda in his stare. After that, he smiled to the people in the room and continued.

"The first factor is time. All of you practicing white or good magic," he was looking again at Chlorinda, "begin your magic when the new moon occurs. You cast your spells each night with increasing intensity until the full moon. In that particular night you release all the magic that you started one month ago. Tonight is the full moon. It is the time when the power of practicing of white magic is at its peak. It may be the right time for us. I hope you did your nightly spelling; tonight we will do our common spelling."

He paused, looking around in the room.

"Second on my list is the place. Some us determined that this is a place with . . . ," he was searching for the right word, "high activity, but I found it to be quite normal. As we are *near Dracula's castle*, numerous people have been killed in this place or close by. Their spirits are still here. We expect there to be . . . activity here."

Paul paused again, checking the room.

"And for the final factor, we are looking for synchronization. Try to find the energy which comes from the sorcerer next to you; try to unify all these energies into a common one, into a stronger one."

"Da, da . . . Bravo . . ."

The people in the room started to show excitement.

Paul was smiling widely as he enjoyed what he saw. The excitement in the room grew. He was looking around, proud of himself, and there were a few good minutes as he was took in the glory of the victory. Finally, as the room calmed down he said "Finally, I will answer questions if you have them, if not you can proceed to Raluka to sign a form that you are in good health and are freely participating in this activity. So, questions?" He was looking around the room.

Near me, Chlorinda raised her arm. I saw tosses of the head and faces becoming ugly as people looked in Chlorinda's direction.

Paul was scowling as well, looking at Chlorinda.

"Chlorinda, put your hand down."

Chlorinda's face became red, and she was ready to protest, but she ignored Paul's words and continued to keep her hand raised as she was the first to ask a question. Paul moved his eyes toward Drina. Drina was turning her eyes toward Chlorinda. With a terrible effort, Chlorinda was putting her hand down; it was like she was fighting a great force. Undoubtedly, Drina was using her kinesthetic powers against Chlorinda. Some gypsy women began to speak in Romanian, making signs to Chlorinda. They were obviously not agreeing with her way.

"She is always arguing," said Halibarda at my ear.

Tired after trying to resist Drina's kinesthetic powers, Chlorinda was lying in a chair. The gypsy women were going in front of Raluka and they began to sign the form. All of them did the same. Finally Chlorinda signed it too.

Coming close to Chlorinda, Paul started to speak to her.

"Chlorinda, I might need you to drive me there with your car. On our way you can ask me whatever you wish."

"Okay," she agreed, slowly, as if waking up from a dream.

I felt like I should do as the other people, and moved to sign Raluka's form. But Paul came over to me and said "Laura, what are you doing? This is a dangerous thing. All these people have magical powers. It is too dangerous for you to participate now. Maybe . . . another time. Maybe after you have received some more training."

"But . . ." I tried to protest.

"Here I agree with Paul," Chlorinda added.

"Thanks, Chlorinda," Paul said, pleased because Chlorinda was on his side now. "Do you see we can sometimes be on the same page? Halibarda, Vlad and Raluka will stay with Laura. All three of you please watch Laura carefully. If she needs assistance please don't hesitate to help her immediately. However, I will consider Halibarda to be the leader of your group. Over the night when we perform our magical spellings it is possible Laura will feel . . . strange. If that is happening, I am sure you will be able to help her."

"All will be Okay. Laura, you are with me," Halibarda said.

The people around us began to prepare for their departures. I was able to see in few of their bags the types of magical items that Raluka had told me about. I saw candles, goblets, and knives. Some gypsy ladies were carrying quite big knives that might be considered swords. I also saw large stakes and wands.

Happily, the sorceresses were going in their car pools. The cars were leaving one by one following the car which held Chlorinda and Paul.

*   *   *

It was a wonderful evening outside. The air was clean and fresh as I appreciatively took deep breaths. A quiet peace had descended on the villa as all the people left.

"Okay guys," Halibarda said, "it is our turn to celebrate. I am inviting all of you to a nearby restaurant for a party."

"I am not sure that is a good idea," Raluka said. "We are supposed to stay here and try to focus to see if we can catch some signs or energies during the group concentration."

"Exactly as I said Raluka," Halibarda smiled at her.

Raluka was watching Halibarda as she was asking "Am I crazy?"

With a big smile Halibarda added, "I said we can go and focus on all this from a restaurant. Why must we remain here?"

"Because it is quiet here, and that will assist us in achieving better focus," Raluka tried unsuccessfully to make her arguments to Halibarda.

"I am the leader of this group, let's vote. Who is for going to a restaurant in town?"

I thought in fact Halibarda's idea was a good one. I raised my hand. Immediately Vlad did the same.

"Good guys!" Halibarda said enthusiastically. "Let's go."

* * *

Halibarda was right; the restaurant to which she invited us was indeed very nice. It was quite large, with a dance floor, and we could see two handsome guys singing. As soon as they saw us they made friendly gestures towards us. Vlad and Halibarda answered them back with the same friendly signs. I noticed here it is not a custom for people to wait to be seated. Halibarda chose a table in the middle of the restaurant. Immediately a handsome waiter showed up.

"Buna seara," he said, grinning at us.

"Viorel!" Halibarda almost screamed his name. "How are you, my friend?"

"I am good. How are you, Halibarda? Where have you been? I miss you."

Saying this, he hugged Halibarda in a very sexy way. I was quite embarrassed as it was not very polite in a restaurant, and especially a nice one like this. Next in line was Vlad. They were also hugging in a very friendly manner.

"How are you Raluka?" Viorel asked Raluka as he placed a big kiss on her hand.

"It is considered polite here in Romania to kiss the hand of a respected lady," Raluka explained me in a low voice.

"I am good. How are you Viorel? You all right?"

"Yes, thanks for asking Raluka."

"Viorel, I would like to introduce you to Laura."

"Oh . . . Laura . . ." Viorel became totally intimidated.

"Viorel! Boy, are you Okay?" Halibarda asked in a maternal voice.

His skin color had turned yellow.

"No, I said he has troubles." Immediately Raluka took a glass with iced water and forced him to drink. Vlad helped him to sit on a chair. The people around us were watching with interest. After a few seconds Viorel became a little better. He drank all the water from the glass, and he commented to me, "Laura, it is an honor to having you here. I would like to make a public announcement about your presence here."

"You better not." Halibarda said. "Or not yet. Where is my . . ."

"I have your Vlad tzuica immediately Halibarda," Viorel said as he almost ran out.

"He is a good kid," Halibarda said watching me. "I love him."

Shortly Viorel was back with an icy Vlad tzuica bottle.

"Good." Halibarda became very happy.

Viorel filled our short glasses with tzuica.

We were going to toast but Halibarda had already finished her glass. Quickly Viorel filled her glass back up. We toasted. This time Vlad, Halibarda and I finished the shots. Raluka just sipped the drink.

Halibarda filled her glass herself and drank the shot. After that she smiled nicely at Vlad.

"Vlad, can you make sure my glass is never empty?"

Vlad winked at her.

As there was some lively music playing, Halibarda stepped to the dance floor where people were already dancing, and she started to dance. Vlad and I began to laugh and we did the same.

Now I know a few Romanian dances and I think this time I did a good job. We were dancing there for more than half hour and I became tired.

Immediately when we took our seats, Viorel served us cabbage rolls, sour cream and polenta. "As all of you were busy I decided the menu for all of us by myself. Now you must eat what I chose," Raluka said, making eye contact with all of us. I saw that she had emptied her glass too and was in a joyous mood.

The cabbage rolls tasted wonderful. We ate quickly although we did not forget to drink too. Our Vlad tzuica bottle quickly became empty.

During this time, the nearby table had filled with almost 20 guys.

"I think they are football players," Vlad said.

"Yes, for sure," Halibarda agreed.

They were very noisy. Some of them were looking over at me. Finally two of them came to our table and tried to talk to me.

"If you can speak in English you can talk to her, otherwise you are wasting your time," Halibarda said to them.

"You look like Laura," said one of them. Even if there were just a couple words in the sentence, they were hardly understandable as they spoke.

"She looks like Laura because she is Laura. Idiot!" Halibarda became angry with them. "Somebody told me that football players have no brains."

We spent almost all night dancing and drinking heavily.

"Don't worry when we get back I have mouth spray," Halibarda said, like she was telling me a secret.

"For what?" I wondered.

Halibarda was laughing at me. "We are supposed to be prisoners staying alone in our rooms and waiting for Paul's return; not drinking heavily here. Do you want him to smell alcohol on us in the morning? We will not give him the chance." Halibarda filled my glass. "Let's drink."

We toasted with our glasses, "Noroc," and emptied them.

"Now let's go dance."

And we partied all night long.

*   *   *

The people were returning to the villa. They were quiet, tired and unhappy. In the living room was a breakfast buffet. Some were eating, but without any pleasure.

"Guys, you can have tea if you want. I ordered only caffeine free tea," Paul said. "As we are tired, I would suggest all of you take a nap and let's meet here at 1 pm. It works for all of you?" he was looking around at everyone.

"Da, da . . ." I heard around me.

"It works for you too, Laura?" he asked, looking at me. I was quite surprised as I was not a participant at the group spelling. But as it was a good plan to not sleep all day long I said "Yes, Paul. It works perfectly for me."

"Okay, let's meet here at 1 p.m." Suddenly he turned his back and went to the stairs. He was looking very upset. As his movement was quick, Drina did not have enough time to move out of his way.

"Get out of my way, you stupid woman," he said in a loud voice to Drina and he shoved her hard. The woman was losing her balance and was going to fall down. As Chlorinda was near Drina, with a surprisingly fast move she caught Drina's small body. Drina was already on a step of the stairs; if she had fallen as Paul pushed her she could have been badly hurt. All the people in the room were surprised by his gesture. A terrible silence fell over the room. Drina was looking at Chlorinda as she was saying 'thank you' without words.

"Learn with this: none of you stay in my way. None," he said. Raluka's voice was shaking as she translated these words.

"I am sorry I had not enough time to avoi . . ." Drina tried to save the moment.

"Silence!" Paul screamed at her.

But Drina was stepping toward him. I noticed Raluka was sweating beside me. Somehow I was afraid that Drina would use her kinetic powers against him as she did with Chlorinda yesterday. The small woman was stepping close to him and she said, "I am tired and upset too, it was not at all my intention to stay in your way."

Paul merely glared again at Drina, and then at everyone in the room. Without another word he swept off to his bedroom.

*   *   *

I slept well. I always sleep well with Vlad near me. He set the alarm on his iPhone to go off 20 minutes before 1. We had time for a quick shower. We made it downstairs a few minutes before one. In the living room Halibarda was serving coffee. There was only coffee. Like he had calculated his time with mathematical precision, Paul showed up in the living room at one minute before 1 pm. The chairs and couches of the living room were arranged in a semicircle. Most of the gypsy women were sitting down directly on the floor. Raluka, Vlad and I took places on the central couch. Paul stepped into the created semicircle. The room was oddly silent. We waited like this for a long couple of minutes for Paul to start his speech.

"Let us speak today about yesterday." He stepped out and took a comfortable seat in the only large king chair near my couch.

With theatric gestures, Halibarda was taking Paul's place in front of the group. She was wearing a new dress; it was pretty but maybe too tight on her body. I was very surprised about that and thought to myself *God! This woman is crazy.* What the heck does she have to report here? What does she want to relate? She was dancing, partying all night and getting drunk. I was worried she would tell everyone stupid things and Paul would get angry.

"I have to tell you during the night Laura was normal. We don't have much to report. I was watching her closely and her health and psychology were stable."

"Did you feel any entities around?" we heard Chlorinda ask. Chlorinda was standing up on a platform. Her body was quite imposing and she was like a judge questioning the defendant.

"No," Halibarda answered simply. I did not understand why she would report about me. I wondered why it seemed I was so important as I did not participate at the incantations; in fact I was partying with Halibarda all night long.

As there were no more questions, using the same theatric gestures Halibarda stepped out of the circle.

Her place was taken by a young, tall white guy.

"Something was around us." He was trying to control the emotion in his voice. "It was like something . . . curious was watching us, observing us. If someone," and he was looking to Chlorinda, "wants to ask me if I am sure, my answer is yes." He was waiting for someone to ask him questions. When none came, he stepped back.

In front of us came the twin sisters. These girls were nice indeed. The twin sisters were looking around the room. I saw the gypsy women near me studying them with curiosity. Smiling nicely at all of them Gina stated "Usually when we are performing magic I can feel my sister."

"How?" Chlorinda asked. I was quite surprised that Paul was allowing Chlorinda to ask so many questions today.

"It is like an energy, which is coming from her. I can feel when she is weak and I can help her; I can feel when she is strong and I decrease my concentration accordingly." She paused as Paul raised his hand.

"This is what we have to do when we are doing our group mental concentration; we have to feel each other. We have to help each other in emergency situations. Please continue Gina."

"Yes," she said, smiling at Paul.

"When we began the incantation, as usual we were together in good harmony. But after about an hour . . . it was like a entity was between us, and moment by moment that entity was separating us."

"When you were completely separated, did you feel that you were weak?" Paul asked.

"No," Gina said. "But . . . I felt like I was alone and I might be vulnerable."

"It was like having a power and suddenly you have only half of it," Geta completed.

"And all night long we were separated like this," Gina said.

"When we were back in the room we tried again to concentrate and sense each other. All was working as we are accustomed to," Geta said.

"What do you conclude from this?" inquired Halibarda.

"There was an entity. It is capable of separating us," Geta declared.

"The entity is not aggressive. Even as it was separating us it performed no negative actions," Gina clarified.

"The entity was not negative and aggressive . . . yet," Chlorinda muttered.

"Thanks, girls. Your account is of the events is clear. Who else has a report?" Paul carried on.

A gypsy woman from the group in front of my couch stood up and walked in front of us.

"Her name is Joanna or in Romania, Ioana," Raluka whispered to me.

"On the way back, I was speaking with the other members of my group. We started to perform our magic but there was something that broke what we tried to do."

"This something has a form?" Chlorinda asked.

"No. We felt a presence. And that was all. But, to be very clear, things which we had previously done very easily before were very difficult to accomplish last night," Joanna said.

"Can you classify in any way that is an entity? Is it positive or negative?" Paul queried.

"At this stage it is neutral," Joanna replied.

"Try to think deeply. We need more information here. Your feelings during those moments are necessary for us to understand what was there. Paul, I suggest you allow me to hypnotize Joanna to gather more information," Chlorinda said, trying to dig deeper.

I was very surprised. God, these people were speaking about hypnotizing someone as if it was a normal morning coffee conversation. I continued to watch Paul.

"I agree with you Chlorinda. You can try. But I don't think there will be anything more to catch," Paul said.

Joanna stepped back to her place on the floor.

"So . . ." Paul was trying to say something but a voice interrupted him. I was trying to remember that voice, it sounded familiar and yes . . . I recognized my former teacher Ivanka. A little frightening but in control, the woman stepped in front of us. She stayed there without speaking for a few moments. Her sharp gaze wandered over each face in turn like a warning 'be careful. I am going to tell you something of utmost importance'. The tension rose in the room and several people shifted in their places uncomfortably.

Finally she spoke. "That entity is connected with Dracula."

I was terribly impressed. Even if Raluka had not translated these words for me I felt their gravity in Ivanka's voice like a weight on my shoulders.

Stepping close to Ivanka, Halibarda said, "There is no doubt. We knew from the start that place has connections with Dracula. I don't know how yet, but I was expecting it."

"Dracula is evil personified. He is the most evil man of history. I am warning all of you, we are going to have problems," Chlorinda advised.

"Dracula is/was good," Paul insisted.

The people in the room started to whisper. Their whispers started to become quite loud.

"I hate him. He committed so many crimes," Chlorinda said vehemently.

Paul continued, "I love him. He protected Romania. If I was in that time, in his place I would have been worse."

Chlorinda said emphatically, "No doubt about it. I know you." Chlorinda stalked to the center of the room. "None of you know how bloody this man can be," and with her finger she pointed to Paul. A terrifying silence filled the room.

Paul simply stayed in his chair. "And I know you too, Chlorinda. You with your green eyes like a poison. You are a poison. Out of here, all of you!"

Ivanka, Halibarda and Chlorinda stepped aside and Paul came in the front of the group.

"We are sorcerers. We are complicated and complex personalities. Easily each one of us can become dangerous. But we are a club. And the members of this club are good friends. Chlorinda I suggest you to make an effort if you wish to remain a member of the club." All eyes present in the room were gazing at Chlorinda.

Paul walked back to his chair. Everyone turned their eyes from Chlorinda to Paul.

Paul was turned toward me. I felt overwhelmed by emotion. It was like I had a fire in my brain. God, he is going to ask me to speak in the front of these people. But what can I tell them . . .

"Raluka," Paul said simply, "we need your opinion."

With polite gestures Raluka smiled at Paul, me and the people around her. She walked in front of the group as all of the speakers had.

Vlad came close to me, ready to translate Raluka's words for me.

"For a thousand years Romanian sorcerers were defending themselves from malefic forces. They did a good job and no one else was able to do it better. What we are doing now is a dangerous thing. That entity, according to Ivanka's observation, is connected with Dracula and that entity was able to interact with some of you."

"Is that entity Dracula's vampire or a sprit?" Paul asked.

"It is connected with Dracula. I don't know exactly what it is," Raluka replied.

Chlorinda broke in, "Don't be ridiculous Raluka, we know another . . . ."

"Silence!" Paul screamed in an unbelievably loud voice.

"Silence or what?!?" Chlorinda screamed back at Paul.

With an incredibly fast move, Halibarda caught Chlorinda and began to throttle her. Choking, Chlorinda was unable to breath and gasping for air.

"Or I will kill you," Halibarda snarled, "here in front of those people. I am not one of your snakes, you stupid woman." Halibarda said in a deep voice.

I could see no one in the room was intending to interfere.

"Chlorinda, we are tired of you. Do you want to remain in this club?" Paul demanded.

The woman was trying to say something. But she was not able even to breathe and Halibarda was still choking her. In a low voice Paul said, "Halibarda, don't kill her . . ."

With preternatural force, Halibarda pushed Chlorinda onto the floor in the middle of the circle.

"You venomous snake, next time I will kill you!" Halibarda shrieked.

Like a drowning victim, Chlorinda's face was pale and she was hardly breathing. She gasped as she tried to catch her breath and she looked at Halibarda. Halibarda bent down to Chlorinda and demanded, "Somebody in this room was just asking you a question. Would you please answer?"

Vlad's voice was shaking as he relayed this to me. I thought if I was in his place to translate, I probably would not be able to speak.

Finally, Chlorinda stood up. Simply she answered, "Yes. Actually I am interested in Raluka's analysis."

Paul was smiling, which became a chuckle and then turned into a laugh almost demonic in nature. It was chilling and disturbed and upset me greatly. It grew in volume until it echoed throughout the room. I wanted to put my hands over my ears but I stayed still.

After awhile he calmed down and said, "Good girl. I still love you Chlorinda." In the blink of an eye, his face turned to stone and he said in a flinty voice, "Now I invite you to be quiet. Speak only if I invite you to do so. Raluka, can you continue please?"

"Of course," Raluka said. Raluka was not impressed at all by the scene in the room. In fact, I think Vlad and I were the only surprised ones. It was like all of them hated Chlorinda. Hated her so much they would enjoy seeing her die.

"Last night was a beginning. There was an entity present in a dormant form. We woke it up. Now we have *only one way*. To challenge the entity. If it betrays itself as dangerous then our only way is to seek, locate and destroy it."

"Comments?" Paul looked around the room.

"How we can challenge this entity if we don't know what she is?" Drina asked.

"By doing the same things we did last night, again and again until we gain sufficient knowledge," Raluka replied.

Raluka paused, waiting for further comments as she looked around the room.

"Comments?" Paul queried again.

"It is not enough. We must accelerate this process. We need to gain knowledge in a short period of time," Halibarda insisted.

"I totally agree. I hope I am not asking too much when I ask you to change the time line," Raluka suggested.

"Yes, we have to do it," Ivanka agreed.

"Tell everyone what you mean by changing the time," Paul said to Raluka.

"I am certain this entity is connected with the moon's phases. It appears it is weak when the moon is full. I conclude from that when it is a new moon, or no moon in the sky it will be strong. However, I would expect it to still be weak as it was until now in a dormant form. There is no significant danger for now and Laura or even I can attend the next spelling," Raluka explained.

"Comments?" Paul asked the group yet again.

"Some of us are weak when it is a new moon. Our practice until now was to increase our energies according with the increase of the moon. What Raluka is asking us is a . . . dangerous thing," Drina looked very worried.

"Whoever is weak at that moment will not participate," Paul decided. "I recommend that all of you practice increasing your powers in both directions from this point forward. Try to manage your powers also on new moon nights. Danger . . . even if you cross the street it is dangerous. Hmm . . . Halibarda?"

"It will be a good drill for me. I will start to practice increasing my powers for the next new moon night," Halibarda said.

Paul turned again. "Chlorinda?"

The room was shocked that he was asking Chlorinda for her opinion. There was a general rumbling in the room. Seizing the advantage, Chlorinda stepped near Raluka. Everyone was watching her.

"I am strong whether it is a full moon or a new moon," she declared. "I will participate in the next group spelling, and regardless of what this entity is I will defend against it."

Chapter 11

Using the power of the four elements I created the magical circle. It is capable of defending me against the dangers which come from all four cardinal points.

-Incantations by Drina

I accepted the invitation of the two sisters Gina and Geta. They were always very friendly with me and I hope I will have a good time as a guest in their house. After we returned from the mountain, I stayed a couple of days in Bucharest.

Paul was quite sad. He told me that from his point of view, the group incantation was totally unsuccessful and all the things related that occurred in the meeting afterwards was based on the imagination of a couple of people. He said he felt nothing special, neither did Halibarda. Chlorinda and the others said that they felt it. They are always ready to believe what they wished to be exciting. Paul encouraged me to go to the sisters house and to learn all that they are capable of. He told me they are very proficient in foreseeing the future and I could learn some stuff from them. He told me that once I was there I would come across some . . . surprises. Also he told me that if I need something, I should call him or Halibarda immediately.

After my morning coffee and banana, Vlad offered to give me a ride to the sisters' house. I checked on the goggle map, and it said that their village was a small one located near Alexandria.

"From Bucharest to Alexandria will take us approximately two hours." Vlad informed me. As we drove I saw a big lake at the exit from Bucharest.

"It is quite nice how they are maintaining the edges of the lake." I said.

"Oh no, Laura. In fact it is an artificial lake."

"Really? But is quite large, and I see almost no activity on it's surface."

"Yes, it is an unfinished construction. Ceausescu, our former communist president, intended to transform Bucharest into a port by this lake. His plan was to build a canal to connect this artificial lake to Danube."

"Do you think it was a good idea?"

"Oh . . . yes, think about how many of manufacturing industries are in Bucharest. It was very easy for all this heavy stuff to be transported by water way to the sea and so on."

"If it was a good idea why is the construction not finished?"

"Laura, unfortunately either the economy was not strong enough to support this project or there were not enough funds available to finish it." I felt a kind of sadness about this story.

On our way Vlad stopped the car and he bought some kind of pretzel from the people who were selling them at the edge of the road. He started to eat one with an unbelievable appetite. It tried one too. It was quite hard, but I found it to be quite good. As I was eating a new one, Vlad ate four.

"In around 20 minutes we will be in Alexandria. It is a nice day so we can walk in downtown of this small town."

Vlad was right. I found the downtown quite nice. But the towers were quite low, the tallest one was only 10 levels.

"That is mainly because in our country we have a big earthquake potential. If the towers are lower, they will be more resistant to earthquakes. That's what Paul told me."

I noticed that Vlad always mentioned Paul's name as if Paul was his boss.

"I have to tell you Vlad that I am quite surprised about the name of this town Alexandria. I know Alexandria is a big city in Egypt in fact it was Cleopatra's home."

"That's right. I think it is connected with Alexander the Great."

"Do you mean Alexander Macedon was passing by here, and he made this town?"

"It might be . . . sorry Laura, I am not very good with the history . . . ."

Also the town has a small but pretty park. We walked for a while in this park. After that we visited a couple markets. I saw that there was nice handmade Romanian traditional stuff. I was not able to stop myself from buying a picture with Vlad the Impaler.

"Do you think he was a nice looking guy," I asked my Vlad about the Vlad the Impaler.

"Maybe . . . he was acceptable and handsome. But Paul and I . . ."

"My question was only for you Vlad."

"Okay, I think he was quite attractive." He paused somehow disturbed by my observation. I felt like he was a sensitive man and I had to protect him as much as I could. Until now he made no mistakes in front of me.

"From here to the sisters village is less than 30 minutes. Maybe you can call them to say that we will be there soon."

"But they were calling me a couple of times until now."

"Oh.. yes, you right Laura." Almost in the same moment my cell phone rung and of course it was the sisters.

"Hi Laura, I hope you are hungry because we have a huge lunch prepared in your honor," Gina said to me on the phone.

"Oh . . . I am hungry and I appreciate it so very much, you guys are so kind."

Coming close to my face Vlad said on the phone, "Hi girls, do you have some lamb for me?"

"For sure we do have some," and I heard the crystalline laughing of the sisters.

"Okay I will rush to come there as soon as possible with Laura. Do you need me to buy something from the market?"

"No we have everything here, but can you guys please hurry as fast as you can?" We decided to go straight to the sisters village. While we were driving I observed that this town had a big farmers market. I mentioned this observation to Vlad.

"Oh yes, I know that this is not usual in Canada, but here farmers markets are very normal."

On our way back I asked Vlad why he specifically asked if they have some lamb for him.

"Oh . . . oh . . . Laura. We have a specific method to cook the lamb, and the sisters are very good on it. You will see." Shortly afterwards, we reached the village and I was quite impressed. This entire village is composed of eclectic gypsy mansions with pagoda-like roofs. It was the first time in my life that I saw something like this. Each mansion was quite large, as though there was a competition between them.

"Actually it is a competition." Vlad said. "I have heard that the house that is the tallest will be the one that is supposed to be respected, and the second criteria will be the exterior of the house."

"God, it is like what we do in Calgary. There is a competition between the oil companies, as to which one has the tallest tower."

"What a comparison . . ." Vlad said laughing at me.

I was totally impressed by the particular style of architecture. It was quite unique and quite impressive. In my mind I thought of the Asian pagodas as they are a similar style of roof of these villas. Each of the villas also had very large balconies.

"We call these 'gypsy palaces' or 'palate tiganesti' in Romanian," Vlad explained to me.

As it was a lovely day outside I saw lots of people and I was able to observe that the majority were gypsies. I was so impressed by the dimensions of these villas that I was starting to respect these people. In the front of their houses were nice cars, lots of luxury cars and in one yard I think I saw an antique collectors car. We driving down the main street, it was paved with asphalt. I observed that the roads in the village were parallel and perpendicular just the same as our street and avenues in the big towns. Also, I noticed that not all of the streets were paved. However, it was a small thing to notice as I was totally focusing on the mansions around me.

Vlad was turning the car in one inlet road and after couple turns, he parked the car in the front of a big mansion.

"Here is the house where the twins live."

I had no time to analyze the architecture of the house as the twins Gina and Geta were running to my car. I quickly stepped out and they gave me a hug.

"Laura, it is an honor to have you as our guest," said Gina.

"I am so happy you were able to make it." said Geta. Their faces were radiating with happiness.

"As you can see we are not the richest girls in the town, but all what we have here is made using only our money, and we attained it in the right way."

"I can see that and I am totally impressed with your house and this village. Is it unique in Romania?"

"Oh no there are couple like this, I think you can search in Wikipedia about it, but please let's go inside."

Around us, I saw the other houses, the neighbors were coming out in the front of their gates and watching us with interest. Geta was making signs to them saying something in Romanian. Gina said to me "she is explaining to our neighbors that you are Laura and you come from Canada. But please let's go inside . . ."

When we where on the street I told myself that I would like to see how a house like this looks inside. I observed that the twins' villa was quite nice and very close to the architecture and dimensions as all the houses of the village. The sisters took me between them and started to ask me how the drive was. They were talking so much, they barely even heard my answers. From the main door of the house, we went directly into the living room. The living room was quite large in comparison to the dimensions of the house. In the middle was a huge table with lots of chairs around and lots of food on the table.

"This is only the appetizer," Gina said.

'Gosh . . . only the appetizer, and there is food for an entire army' . . . I said in my mind. "Oh girls . . . you are more than kind . . ."

"Laura, please let us to introduce you to our friends, this is Raul and this is George."

"Nice meeting you guys, I am Laura." They were shaking my hand one by one. I noticed that it is mostly the custom here. The two guys were quite nice looking. Or, maybe not so handsome as Vlad. I saw their skin color and I decided that they belonged to gypsy kind, or maybe from this village.

"Unfortunately none of them can speak English. We have to translate for them. And she is our niece Ramona."

"Hello Laura," she said, and with a nice gesture she shook my hand." She was trying to say something to me, but unfortunately her English was bad, and I was not able to understand. Also I observed that she seemed to be emotional and maybe she was not able to focus on the English words.

"Please take a seat Laura," Gina said.

"Or maybe you would like to see the house first?" Geta asked.

"Yes, if you can show me your house that will be wonderful. You know .. from outside I was asking myself how a house like this looks like from inside. Thank you again for inviting me to your home," I smiled to the two sisters. Vlad was taking a chair at the table and he start chatting with Raul and George.

"In the village are some houses with the living room larger than ours."

"Your is quite large too," I said.

"It is definitely large enough for our needs."

And while speaking with me the sisters showed me the main floor of the house, there was a very modern kitchen, a service bathroom and a spare room. The house had three levels. There were three bathrooms, a bonus room and several bedrooms on each level. I noticed that here it was not a custom for the master bedroom to have it's own bathroom. So all the bedrooms have to share the same bathroom. The furniture in the bedrooms, and in fact in the entire house is very nice. It is not at all like IKEA furniture. It is more of a classic style of furniture. I saw each bedroom had a minimum of one icon and each bonus room had an icon. The sisters were so proud showing me their house.

"Did you buy the house like this?" I asked the sisters.

"No, we built it."

"And we are proud to say we did all this with our money. Nobody helped us."

"Our parents live quite close, and they have a smaller house compared to ours."

"But . . . . may I ask, how you had so much money? " I asked the sisters.

"We did magic stuff for people, it is our job now. We are quite good especially to read the future and the people pay us accordingly."

"However we were loaned money too, but we will be very soon free of debts."

"Good business," I said, "congratulations girls."

"Thank you!"

"Thank you, now let's go downstairs for our lunch."

"Okay, I would like to use the washroom first . . ."

"Of course try this one, you have here hand liquid soap, bar soap and . . . ."

"Thanks, I am sure I can manage."

When I went in the living room the people were very happy, loudly chatting in their language.

"Let's have a toast," and Geta gave me a shot glass. According to the odor of the drink I understood that it is Vlad Tzuica.

"Let's toast to you Laura."

"Noroc,"

"Noroc,"

And all of us, except their niece Ramona, emptied the glass.

"One more, this time for Gina and Geta and their nice home."

We empted the shot glasses again. Vlad took the tzuica bottle and he filled our glasses.

"Yes, and this is for Vlad. Thanks for giving Laura a ride." And again the shot glasses had been emptied.

"Good , good . . . and now let's have something to eat." Geta said. I looked to the big plates. There was a considerable variety of salami, other plates with various kinds of cheese or other things which I believed was some kind of traditional Romanian food. All was nicely dressed with lettuce leaves or finely sliced tomatoes, olives green or black, or garlic olives.

"All of this looks very nice and I don't believe that you said it is only the appetizer . . ."

"Yes, our niece Ramona is so good to arrange the plates. It is her passion, she is good in our house."

"Thanks Ramona," I said. The face of the young girl became quite red. I think she easily can understand English but it is still hard for her to speak. Of course she needs a lot of practice but the beginning is done and that is important. I tried to get my plate full of everything; first to taste almost every piece of salami or cheese. Also, I saw there was stew in a large bowl. I saw Vlad having this stew on the top of a piece of bread. I did the same and its tasted unbelievable good.

"Oh.. what is this?"

"We call it 'Zacusca', Gina said. "It is homemade by my mother."

"Homemade?"

"Yes, still here in Romania it is a custom to can a lot of vegetables for the winter. We can this Zacusca too."

"So . . . this consists only of vegetables?"

"Yes it contains barbequed eggplants, tomatoes, paprika all mixed with onions and oil."

"Oh Gosh, I have to try more . . ."

"Please try also the eggplant salad, we have it in two versions, with mayonnaise or with onion, try it on the top of your bread with cheese or slices tomatoes." I did as they encouraged me, and it was all so unbelievable tasty.

"So this one has eggplant, onions you said, maybe some oil and?"

"And that's all," Vlad answered.

"Oh . . . shut up Vlad, I am very interested to have the recipe."

"But Laura . . . this is the recipe, " Gina said in a low voice.

"Only?" I was totally wondering. "Oh Gosh . . . I can just take a spoon and eat all this bowl."

"Of course you can have more, but please don't forget this is only the appetizer."

Vlad took a seat near me. "Do you want more tzuica Laura?"

I felt like with so much food I need some more to drink.

"I think Paul explained to you Laura, we prefer to have the strong drinks like tzuica before or together with the appetizer, and other like vine beer and so on with roast," Geta said. We were comfortable standing around the big table and chatting.

"And who are these two gentlemen?" I asked

"They are very good friends with us. Who knows . . . maybe more."

"They live in this village too?"

"Yes."

We where chatting like this for more than one hour. The two sisters told me about their family, mother, father and also their brother that I would meet tomorrow. They told me that it is usual to invite all of them to these kinds of party, but Paul suggested that it would be better first to be a small party and to introduce other members of the family gradually. Gina and Geta mentioned a couple of times that it is a pleasure for them to have me as a guest. After these long chats, at their insistence we decided that is the time to move on to the next phase of our lunch. The sisters helped their niece Ramona to clean the table and to arrange the roast. There were lots of roasted meat and of course the 'mititei', and lots of salad too.

"We will be happy if you could, please test all the foods and tell us your opinion."

"Well . . . this will be a quite difficult task." I said. The sisters were laughing. I saw that the 'mititei' was maybe better quality then the one I usually ate in Bucharest.

"That is because they are homemade. Our mother is very good to prepare them. Now you have to test our red wine."

George brought the wine in a large decanter. I was very impressed with the wine glasses they used. Then we toasted, and I observed that they are made from crystal.

"It is crystal from Ukraine. We have here quite good crystals but we have a very good friend in Ukraine and she sent us these crystals," Gina explained me.

"I fell like when I drink wine from these crystals glass, the wine tastes much better."

The other guy Raul started to speak with me in Romanian language.

"Da , da . . ." Vlad translated for me.

"Raul told you that the red wine has wonderful qualities against the human body. And maybe the best one is it extends life. Raul is a medical student. He always asked himself why lots of people in the village live a long time. And he believes it is because the red wine."

"But where are the people buying so much red wine? From Market?"

"No . . ."

"No?" I was wondering. These people are full with surprises.

"Almost each family has its own land to cultivate red grape vines. They store the red wine in wood barrels."

"And how many liters of wine does a family make yearly? 20 liters? 30 liters?" I asked curiously.

"Laura . . . they are making hundreds of liters. A part of the wine they keep over the winter in the basement of the house and another part is packed in bottles and sealed very well."

"And the bottles are deposited in the basement of the house?"

"No . . ."

"No? Vlad what are you talking about?"

"Well.. he is right," Geta said. "The usual method is to dig a hole in the land and to keep the bottles there. Of course this is supposed to be under 30 centimeters as it is considered to be freezing if you don't go deeper."

"But why is this?"

"Because . . . the underground will work like a thermostat, and it will keep the wine at a constant temperature and without any vibrations that may disturb the wine," Gina said.

"Except when we have an earthquake . . ." completed Geta.

"Do you have strong earthquakes here?" curiously I asked.

"Yes, quite big and quite often. Of course not like in Japan but sometimes it is worse here. For this reason we try to build our houses quite safe, taking in the possibility of the earthquakes."

The wine is very tasty and more alcoholic then the ones I have tried in Canada. I can feel it as I am becoming a big wine drinker. Raul filled the glasses again with wine from another decanter. I noticed that this wine had a different taste.

"Even if it is almost the same grape planted all over the village, because it is homemade the concentration of alcohol will vary, also there will be different wood used for the construction of the barrels, different ways to clean the barrels from one year to another and like this the bacteria types and content will be different. And not on the list they will use various plants to give a flavor of the wine."

"I like very much the wine made with the bitters plants," Vlad said.

"Around this village is the significant wine production of Romania?"

"Oh no . . ." Vlad said. Here the people are doing wine only for themselves to consume or to sell it between houses. At the hills zone of Romania, there are big wine businesses. I just read in a newspaper yesterday that the Romanian wine is appreciated very much in Europe, and it is cheaper than French wine for example. The French wine is the most famous in Europe. As a result some farmers from France decided to stop their business because Romanian competition." We were chatting more about this subject. They explained to me a lot about this process of wine making, decanting the wine and so on.

"Lets go in the back yard we have a surprise for you." As the evening was arriving it was wonderful to stay outside. The backyard of the sisters is considerably large. It has paving stones near the house and nice patio couches and tables. Near the paving area was a quite old gentleman and he was starting the fire in a pit.

"Laura, please meet our father." The old gentleman was smiling to me and with a finger he pointed to himself.

"Ion," And I understood that his name is Ion.

I found the shape of the pit to be quite interesting or . . . strange and I asked the sisters.

"Dear that is not exactly a fire pit that you would normally see. He is making the fire here to heat the pit, and there he will prepare for us the lamb. Our father has a special recipe. The lamb is placed in the pit with wool and skin and it is covered with coals. Like this the wool and skin will be easy burned, and the lamb meat will be cooked easily and nicely. Actually it is Vlad's favorite food."

"Trrrrue!" Vlad said. I looked the twin's father preparing the lamb in this strange way.

"It is a Romanian way to cook the lamb." they started to tell me this recipe looks like it belonged to Dracula's time. I was quite shocked they are speaking about Dracula like it happened yesterday. Also they explained to me when the covered lamb will be ready it will explode underground. The explosion is the sign that it is ready. We continued chatting until we heard the explosion. I have to tell you the lamb cooked like this is just a delicacy and especially when you have red wine near. And we had a lot.

*   *   *

I spend my next day walking with the sisters in the village. The gypsies were looking at me with considerable curiosity. As the sisters knew all the people from the village they were chatting with almost all of them. The people were trying to chat with me even if they knew that I don't understand the Romanian language they were trying to talk to me.

I visited the twins family, they lived in a big house too. Also the sisters have a younger brother. He speaks an acceptable level of English. He told me that he is going to visit Canada soon. I told him that if he comes to Canada he will be welcome to visit me too. He thanked me, but Paul already invited him and he knows that Paul has a large house.

The sisters are very good at reading the future using tarot cards. As a gift they gave me a pair of tarot cards. I was really happy. They started to teach me about the tarot cards. As I did with Raluka, I recorded all our lessons to my camcorder. Also, I took lots of notes on my iPad. Over time the sisters developed their own method to foresee the future. The tarot cards contain 36 cards, they are very nice colored and illustrated. Also they are able to use normal cards. But they have their own particulars signs which helps them in their forecasting. I spend lots of time with my new tarot cards. I tried to memorize the significance of each card. I decided for the beginning to make small notes on each card. It took me a while. After that I have been told about combinations between cards. I have been quite impressed about the number of possible combinations and the number of interpretations.

"It is very important to focus on what you have to answer."

"It is important to focus on the person you need to foresee the future for."

One by one the sisters gave me instructions. They explained to me that this art needs lots of attention, dedication, and lots of intuition. I have been very interested about the supposed mechanism about using tarot cards to read the future. And I found the knowledge I have from Raluka quite useful. The sisters supposedly are attracting good and superior spirits from another world. These spirits guide them to foresee the future.

"However this guidance is not complete. Please think about yourself. You have to do something; already you see on your behalf lots of possibilities. Finally you will chose for you only one. Only one . . . Think now that you have to foresee the future for a person. In the future there will be lots of possibilities and . . . lots of interaction."

"From the spirits you will receive information. These are translated for you in the significance of tarot cards and the resulting combinations. Pay attention to the details. Try to use the most possible lines of future. Finally with your own intuition chose the correct one."

The sisters were passing to me their valuable knowledge.

"Unfortunately . . . . You cannot tell someone everything you see. It might be too much for him or . . . too bad . . . ."

"Once a young and rich girl was coming to me. I started to foresee the future for her. It was very clear for me she will die in three."

"What does that mean?"

"Well . . . in our work we can have numerical information. In this particular case it was very clear for me that she will die in three. That means it can happen in three minutes, or three hours, or three days, or three weeks, or months or years . . . I decided to hide that from her. I told her only she will be in grave danger in three . . . What I mean by this, you cannot tell to someone for example she is going to die soon . . ."

"Even if this fact is so evident in your tarot cards . . ."

"And what happened with that girl?"

"She died in . . . exactly three weeks."

I felt quite disturbed by this story. I was quite shocked about this new possibility open in front of me. I could see the future to other people, and in the same time I cannot help them too much . . . when they are close to death.

"We strongly believe that Paul is right. You will be a very talented witch, but you have to learn to pay attention to details."

"At the same time don't be frustrated. It will come in time."

"And it comes with the practice."

"Think about someone who will come to you to foresee the future. This someone could be a young girl or boy or an old woman or a man. You have to choose for him a card and place his card in the middle of the other cards. Focus on being in touch with your guiding spirits, and then start to mix the cards."

"It is like sending this person in the middle of the world and in this situation the equivalent of real word is the appeal of tarot cards. They will be able to show you the future interaction between him or her and other people, or things."

"Interpreting these interactions, showed to you by the cards combination, you can know his future."

"Each card has its capital role and each one will give you capital information. But be mainly careful with these two."

"This one is the card of life."

"And this one is the card of death. Unfortunately, when it appears . . . . try to understand some number significance too."

"We can do our work only in the day because the spirits we are working with are evolutes and good spirits. Their powers are limited over the night."

"Unfortunately . . . in our club we have someone who is doing this over the night too . . . ." Gina stopped as she was not able to tell the name of that person. I thought she was maybe referring to Paul. I can see him being able to use the dark night spirits.

But Geta clarified the mystery, "Chlorinda".

I can see this woman has a very bad reputation in the Club. Paul and Halibarda were completely right about her.

"But," and the sisters were trying to make a happy atmosphere, "how about if we will try to foresee your future using our tarot cards?"

I was quite scared to say "yes", especially when I have such gifted people such as these twin sisters sitting right in front of me. At the same time I have a very curious mind and I accepted. They were doing the work together but using only one set of tarots. Firstly, they saw that I had a long life ahead of me. Also they foresaw that very interesting things were going to happen to me. I also have to make important decisions very soon. They also told me that I have to be very careful as terrible danger is always near me. They saw this danger as huge and black.

"I can see this is related to Romania. Remember if the intensity of this danger increases terribly, you go back to Canada."

"Unfortunately, this danger is connected with your past. It is something that comes from your past . . . ."

I could see the sisters sweating, and somehow being scared about what the combination the cards showed them. I felt like they knew more, but they could not share it all with me.

"But . . . I have been a quiet person all my life. I made no mistakes, no . . ."

"Sorry Laura, what we are seeing here . . . is not connected with your present life . . . . ."

Their words were totally shocking to me. What could be so terrible? And it is all from my point of view, an ill fantasy. Trying to escape from this dark moment Gina said, "Now if you could, please practice by yourself . . . try to foresee our future."

"But it will be quite difficult for me. I don't know all the technique and as you said I have to practice."

"Okay, how about an easy method? Just make the cards and spread them on the table in front of you. After that, move your hand up to them. When you feel your hand go heavy, pick that card."

"It will be easy as you noted down the card's significance."

"The method, even if it seems simple, it is very efficient. We use it when we have to answer to someone's quick question like, 'Will I live long? Will I be rich? Will my wish become reality?"

"We will be back soon with some tea. If you not tired please try."

"And let us know how your first look into the future was." I admitted that was an easy method. And if all the theory with the good, white and evolved spirit is correct . . . it might work. I started to mix the cards. I tried to eliminate other things from my mind. I was focusing only on the cards. I kept in my mind that it was very important to determine the future of the twin sisters. I spread the cards on the table in front of me. And I was waving my hand over the cards. I was not sure if I felt something particular when my hands were over a particular card but I decided to pick one. I closed my eyes. I was excited about trying it for the first time. In fact what can be dark? These girls are young, nice, beautiful . . . for sure they will have a nice future. I don't need the tarot cards to see this. I turned the card. I looked the card. It was the card that indicated someone was going to die. I started to see as the sisters did earlier . . . I become upset about this stupid thing could occur. I decided to try again, and this time I will tell exactly to the sisters what card it was and about it's significance. I mixed again the cards, I spread them again. This time it was like I felt a difference, I felt my hand heavy on top of a particular card. I picked up that card and I turned. I was going to scream. It was again the same death card. Even if I was emotional I had remembered the sisters advice 'now you have to search details about a number'. And I did. It was easy to interpret the next card. It suggested me the number one. As I heard steps outside I was mixing back the cards.

"Are you ready dear Laura?"

"Not yet . . . . I was waiting for you guys."

"Let's do it now."

I mixed the cards and I spread them on the table. Disturbed I turned one over. I hope the sisters believe my emotion is connected with the fact that I did it for the first time. I looked at the card but immediately I mixed it back in the cards package. I cannot believe that it was the death card again. I did an unnatural effort to smile to sisters.

"And look it is easy to know the significance of that card. You girls will be rich."

The sisters laughing.

"We are already rich Laura."

"But if that is true, it would be possible to be little bit more rich . . . . It will be perfect." They were laughing. Gina gave me a cup tea. For a moment it was silence in the room.

"Dear Laura, you have to practice the cards by yourself. But starting with tomorrow we will start to work on other magic stuff which Paul asked us to have ready within one week."

"But . . . but it was supposed to be done in . . . one week?"

The sisters smiled nicely at me. "The next group spells *near Dracula's castle*"

*   *   *

"One thing which Paul wants us to do is to change the experience between the club's members. It is like the sorceresses which are very proficient in a domain to share with other who are good but not so proficient." Gina said.

"We will have somebody here for the rest of the week. She will share with us her experience," Geta said. When they were done with these explanations Vlad opened the living room door. Halibarda was standing at the front of the living room. She was flanked by two women who I assumed were her assistants. With theatric gestures, Halibarda stepped into the living room.

"Thanks Vlad, you may leave us for now. We will be busy for a couple of hours. We will call you when we are done."

She was smiling at me, "I am so happy to be your teacher for this week. One week is not enough for the things we will discuss and practice. But you will have some knowledge to start with and more beyond Raluka, we will do lots of practice. We will have the help of my two assistants Gena and Geneva."

She made some gestures like she was in a theatre show. She seemed to enjoy this.

"Let's start first with some theoretical knowledge." We were taking seats around the large coffee table.

"My assistants don't speak English. As I have to speak in English for you I will ask Geta to translate for them."

"Sure!" Geta said. Around the coffee table were couches and a big chair. Geta took the seat between Gena and Geneva. I stay on the couch with two seats with Gina. Halibarda was seated in a big chair as she was of upmost importance right now.

"I agree with Paul's method. I will speak first. Please hold your questions until the end of the speech. If the time allows me to answer them, I will."

She was moving her eyes around to each one of us. She seemed satisfied about the theatre show that she was the main actor; she continued.

"In our club we admit that there are four elements: Air, water, earth and fire. However, in his book called 'The Spatial Magic', Paul uses only one powerful element. He is considering plasma to be the powerful element. But, as all humanity exists for now on only one planet we will agree with the four elements. Already we know about couple entities like spirits. They might be elementary or evolutional and they can be good or bad. There might be ghosts, stigoys, vampires, vircolaci and so on. All of these entities are associated with the four elements. When we invoke an element all the associated entities of that element will come with it to obey our commands."

She paused, gazing one by one at each one of us. She was enjoying her role enormously.

"When we are doing something magical we have to ensure that we are very well protected. "

"Why?" I did not resist asking her. She was long looking at me as if she was saying 'I said the questions after'.

"Because there are forces which might be hostile to us, hostile with what we are doing or . . . in the last case challenged by what we are doing."

She paused again this time watching the two sisters one by one. "There are only two kind of attacks. Attack from the entities who are around us or an attack from another sorceress."

We were watching each other.

"It is very probable an entity or sorceress who dares to attack you might be very strong. For this reason we are considering in our club to be able to create a strong protection using the magic circle is a capital importance. But before proceeding to the next explanation I would like to take some questions about this section. Laura?"

"Yes . . . , I do have a question. Do you know one example of an attack from another sorceress?"

"Of course, many of us had been attacked by Chlorinda. We know that she is very powerful. Our club is mostly orientated to white magic, to a good magic. Usually what she is doing is quite black. Somehow she can be in touch with what an individual is making and she feels an imperious need to interact. It is as though she is saying, 'hey I am Chlorinda, I see you'. Sometime she completely destroys the work that another witch took months to create. And, she did that in only a blink of the eye."

"Is she so dangerous?"

"Right now she is a member of our club. We are supposed to treat her as a colleague and vice versa. But I will suggest to all of you into taking lots of precautions. Especially you Laura, when she is your teacher."

"If she is so . . . unstable, why she supposed to be my teacher?"

"Sorry Laura, if this matter concerns you I suggest you discuss it with Paul. More questions?"

"One more observation," Gina said. "Drina lives a couple of villages away from us. Sometimes she is interacting in our business too."

"How?" Halibarda asked in a deep voice.

"She has remarkable kinesthetic powers. She touches our cards when we are mixing them. That could be translated into a considerable error when we are all looking into the future of one individual."

"Report her to Paul. If you won't do it, I will." simply said Halibarda. Gena was asking a question in Romanian and I had it translated by Geta.

"What kind of entity might attack? "

Halibarda hesitated to answer. She put her eyes on the ceiling of the room.

"Mainly bad spirits. I don't want to scare any one of you, but what we are doing with these group spells might be very dangerous."

"Sorry Halibarda," Gina interrupted her, "I don't agree with you." And Gina was looking to her sister Geta and asked for her support. Geta made some gestures as she was approving her sister. Somehow encouraged Gina continued.

"If we disturbed it and it is supposed to attack. It is there all the time. My sister and I we observed it once but . . . it is weak."

"If there is an entity, because we are so close with the Dracula castle, it is said that this entity is connected with Dracula. Raluka . . ."

Geta: "Raluka is an analyst. We cannot explain to her everything that we felt in that time. It is impossible to be explained in words. As she has no significant powers she is somehow isolated."

Halibarda: "If it is only like this, why does Paul trust her?"

Gina: "Paul trusts her up to a point, not totally."

Halibarda: "Okay. This is not my subject today, but we only to have to make a conclusion here, especially for this particular case. There looks to be an entity connected somehow with Dracula. If it is strong or not we will see in one week at our next group meeting."

One, one, one . . . . this number was screaming in my head. How can I politely tell the sisters . . . . 'it is very possible in one week you will die! . . . ?"

"Laura? . . . ." Halibarda was looking at me with interest.

"Yes, Halibarda." The woman was gazing me.

"Are you with us dear?"

"Y . . . yes."

"Dear . . . do you have something to share with us?" Her voice was low and she was saying her words by pausing between words.

"If you able to read my mind, why can you not tell? "

"Dear . . . . Laura, I can feel something but I am not able to read it."

All the women in the room were looking at me. I was smiling at them.

"Girls . . . it is nothing. I am not a witch. Or . . . not yet anyway." I saw that they did not believe a word that I said and they were continuing to look at me with interest.

"Well maybe I need to talk to Paul about . . . . something."

"Please do." Halibarda said. "Now, as it was a bad idea to take questions I will take the next set of questions only when I am done. Otherwise we will run out of time and even a week might be not enough . . . We associate a color with each element: air—blue, water—green, earth—black and fire—red."

She started to laugh, "Green like Chlorinda's eyes, like a poison . . . . please . . . for now associate green with water, not with Chlorinda's eyes. Here I have four candles, as I said, for colors blue, green, black and red. We will light them one by one. When we light each one we have to focus about what element the color of the candle represents. I will associate the four elements also with the cardinal points. Air to east, water to west, fire to south and earth to north. Look . . ."

And Halibarda was setting the candles on the large square coffee table. Each one at the correspondent cardinal point.

"Think about each candle being connected with the other nearby two and in a circle arch. Now use your imagination to create that circle. The candles will be the extremities of the circle and you will be in the middle. Don't create any confusion between colors, or cardinal points or associated entities. If you create the circle by yourself you have to place the candles at a comfortable distance for you. Once you are standing in the middle of the circle, that distance is supposed to be good for you to light each candle. If we create a collective circle, the people will stay in the middle of the circle and the candle will be placed at a good distance so each person can reach the candles only a few small steps away. Now let's proceed . . ."

"Blue, air, wind and spirits. Here we have a Romanian word 'vintoase'. It represents the entities like some transparent girls who are able to control the winds. Opposite to a calm wind is a storm. The storms are able to create great destructions on the earth. When you light the blue candle imagine that starting with this point of blue candle is a glass wall. Near the glass wall are these entities called to me by vintoase. They are there to obey your commands. At the same time outside a storm is starting. The storm is increasing in intensity. The vitoases are there, and they are obeying your commands. You are commanding them to protect you against the storm. Even if the storm is strong the vitoases are able to break the wind and to direct it an another direction. With your mental power, gradually you will increase the intensity of the storm. The storm is terrible by now. Nothing on the earth can resist it. But the vitoases are able to defend the storm for you. Secondary, you have the glass wall. If somebody from outside attacks you from east using the air elements your guardians called vintoases will be defending you; also he can not

penetrate your glass wall. Both will protect you against the attack.
As you are now ready you light the blue candle and say the following
spell:

*I call the elements of air. You vintoases able to control the wind
defend the outside storm for the power of my magical circle. With my
mental power I raised this glass wall and it is indestructible from any
storm on the earth. You vintoase and you glass wall . . . protect me
against the dangers that come from the east.*

Think about the power of the terrible storm which is the front
of the lighted blue candle. At the same time feel yourself getting
comfortable having the vitoases and glass wall protection. Even if
outside there is a storm, inside you are protected and safe. Focus
on this concentration for a couple of minutes or extend it until you
become comfortable with this concentration.

At the opposite cardinal point you have the green candle; water.
Inside the water we have the water elements we call fays. They are
able to control the water. The uncontrolled water is able to create
great destructions by flooding. Try a visualization of the fays. Think
of them as clever and nice entities. Ask them to obey your commands.
At the same time in the front of the green candle, with your mental
powers, you start to build a barrage. Each piece of the barrage has
origin in your concentration. When you build the energy barrage the
waters start to agitate. There are big waves. Ask the fays to control
them and to defend them on the front of your green candle, and for
the power of your magical circle. Increase the intensity of the waves.
Watch the fays and how they work for you to defend the huge waves.
When it is all done, light the green candle and say this spell:

*I call the elements of water. Your fays are able to control the water
and defend the outside waves from the power of my magical circle. With
my mental power, I raised this barrage; it is indestructible to any waves
on the earth. You fays and you barrage protect me against the dangers
that come from the west.'*

Think about the huge waves, about the fays who are calming
them down in front of your green candle. Also you have the barrage
which is protecting you. Beyond the barrage is a terrible sea battle,

but inside of your magical circle it is dry and good. Feel the calm from inside circle. Spend a couple of minutes on this concentration. At this moment you have air and water raised up.

Next is the black candle. It is the symbol of the earth. According to the Romanian tradition we have the hobs. They are very hard workers. They can dig out tunnels in the earth. They can build caverns on the middle of the earth they can enforce the cavern to resist an earthquake, and they are there to obey your commands. Try to visualize a huge hill, think about the danger it can create by sliding against you. Also think about how ugly creatures such as vampires may come from the earth. The hobs will be able to defend the vampires. But at the same time think that you are in a stone igloo. The earth cannot touch you because the stone igloo is protecting you and at your command the hobs will dig out for you. Now you light the black candle and say the following spell:

I call the elements of earth. You hobs are able to control the earth and defend the outside earth for the power of my magical circle. With my mental power I raised this stone igloo; it is indestructible to the earth. You hobs and you stone igloo protect me against the dangers that come from the north.

Spend a couple of minutes on this concentration. Now you have the air, water and earth. Try to focus at the same time on these three different directions. You can practice for example that the waves are continuing to increase and you have to intensify your mental power on that direction.

The last one is the red candle. Red is associated with the fire. The fire creatures are devils. There can be male devils and female devils. I would recommend that you focus on the female devils as they are dominant compared to the male devils and they are very susceptible to obey your command. Think about the middle of the earth as melting metal. It is fire and is moving inside. This is the one who is creating a magnetic field too. Think there are the devils and they are able to control the fire. Think about the devils the women who are working there create and they can master this fire. If this fire is coming out, it is possible that its destruction will be terrifying. But what you created around you and starting with red candle a cube made from fire resistive material. As long as the fire power increases the power of the protective cube is increasing too and it is able to protect you. Moreover, the devils are working and they are acting at your commands. Even if outside it is hot, inside it is nice and cold in temperature. Focusing on all this now you light the red candle and say the following spell:

I call the elements of fire. You devil women are able to control the fire, defend the fire and protect my magical circle. With my mental power I raised this fire protected cube. Your devil women and your fire protected cube, protect me against the dangers that come from the south.

We practiced together these concentrations again and again and again.

* * *

I walked with Halibarda in the village or 'comuna' which is what they call it here. She is so familiar with the people here, it looks like all the people know her, and there is no exception if we are speaking about young or old, men or women. However, it seems that the women are talking with her longer. Halibarda is able to talk the two languages—Romanian and Gypsy. I observed that according to the accent they are using, they seem to mostly speak Gypsy in this village. Halibarda told me that for me it might be tricky because the gypsies are using mostly their tribe language when they are speaking Romanian even if they are using the same accent as when they are using Romanian words.

She is quite able to manipulate the discussions. I saw that she can stop the discussions with other person when she observes that I am going to be bored. I found the walking in this comuna to be quite interesting.

Halibarda told me there are very good musicians and also very good metal makers. As I needed a knife, she walked me to the workshop situated the behind one of the gorgeous houses. After a quite long chat between Halibarda and the guys who were the metal workers, they invited me to see some knifes and swords. I was quite impressed by their work. I liked these knives and swords but . . . I told Halibarda that I need a special form and I need it to be by a very good metal.

"It will be by a very good metal, but what kind of shape do you like?" I made a drawing for Halibarda. She was looking at the drawing with a great interest and finally she passed the drawing to the guys.

The next day I had the knife exactly as I asked. It is somewhere between the dimensions of a knife and a sword and with a big curve like a boomerang. As I looked at the sword, I can see it is a very good metal alloy. Finally having it in my hands, I declared myself being quite happy. I was so happy I asked them to have another one made for me exactly like this one.

For the last three days we did the magical circle. First one of us was responsible for an element and for the adjacent concentrations. We changed roles and we kept practicing. I tried to feel all the elements. I tried to do as Halibarda said. It was a good idea to do it element by element. I might be able to concentrate better if I don't think so much about the possibility of death of the two sisters . . . .

"Starting tomorrow you have to do the concentrations by yourself," Halibarda said. Try to equally distribute your mental power to all the four elements. It is important to have some standby resources if something happens to an element."

I found it quite difficult to focus on these concentrations in the first day when I made the magical circle by myself. It is like dividing myself into four pieces, and more than that to keep some reserves for unforeseen stuff.

"This is not all Laura. The magical circle is only the beginning. From the inside of the circle we have to do our work. The magical circle will stay on all this time. That is . . . . you have to double your energies for the next steps. But all will come in time."

*   *   *

I spoke with Halibarda about my problem. I told her that I agree with her. The best thing might be to speak with Paul. It might be nothing, and I don't like to alarm other people unnecessarily. It is better for Paul to take the adequate actions. As the result, after three days of concentrations of doing the magical circle, we started our trip to the Romanian mountains.

We met with Paul at a small restaurant on the edge of the route to the montains. We were sitting there for a lunch of mititei and beer. All the people were quite happy. There were the sisters, Halibarda and the two assistants, Paul and Raluka, Vlad and I. The sisters told Paul about my progress. Halibarda assured him that I am doing a very good job. Also she suggested that we rearrange the cars as a chat between myself and Paul might be welcome. She insisted that Paul had to give me a direction.

As a result, I stayed in the same car with Paul and we continued our trip to the Romanian mountains, to that place . . . . *Near Dracula's Castle*.

"Maybe we have to speak a little bit about this concentration called the magical circle. How do find these concentrations?" Paul asked.

"Well it is not an easy job . . . . what do you think?"

"I do some different kinds of concentration. I wrote it all in my book. Actually a lot of people bought my book; they are normal people interested in doing magic stuff or sorceress' or non members of the club. They don't totally agree with my methods. They are kind of . . . traditional, they like the four elements better. My idea was looking at all of the universe with the major element being plasma. I said that these magical circles supposedly get replaced by a sphere of plasma around you. You can build it with your mental energy and that will stay around you, protecting you from the magical attacks. You can try it. Another way; think about the knives you just bought. Think with your mind that you are able to manipulate them around you. Gradually increase their speed until all space around you is covered by their blooming. No one is able to penetrate inside to catch you. This concentration might work well for you too."

I was quite impressed by this suggestion as it was more . . . my style.

"But why are you intending to change these things? As you said, they are old as many thousand years?" I asked Paul.

"Because, there might be a critical situation and you need to rebuild the magical circle again . . . . or a defensive magic similar to the magical circle. You might need to do it in a very quick time and . . . sometime we don't have enough time to invoke all these four elements. It requires more experience and a huge quantity of metal energy to be directed. Sometimes, it is hard to be accomplished even by the most experienced sorceresses, in such a short time and under the pressure of a big and eminent danger."

On a very gorgeous place on the mountain, he stopped the car. We were looking around us, contemplating the gorgeous mountains. I decided this was the right place and moment to tell him about my visions . . . . .

Chapter 12

"Don't check these laws.
You become foul if you understand them."
-George Cojbuc – Romanian poet

The old woman stepped into in the room.

Either she was not here last time; or I did not remember seeing her. I looked her over with interest. She was simply dressed. I could see that even though her body was now bent with age; in her youth this woman was tall. She is definitely the oldest one in the group. Her face was lined with wrinkles; however, I suspect that at her age she should have more. Her face exudes kindness and is attractive. Based solely on gazing upon her face I felt this woman is a good person. She was carrying a wicker basket covered with a white cotton cloth and we were not able to see the contents. As we all stopped and inspected her, she did the same to us. Her gaze wandered slowly over each one of us in turn.

"Buna ziua," (good afternoon in Romanian) Paul said to her. As if disturbed from taking the measure of the people in the room she turned her eyes to Paul. Immediately, her face lit up with an immense smile. I saw Paul smiling at her too.

Chlorinda went over to the old woman. As Vlad was near me, he translated what they were saying for me.

"Hey, this is a private meeting. What is your business here?" Chlorinda demanded.

The old woman merely ignored Chlorinda.

Raluka interjected, "Paul said 'Buna ziua' to you. Do you not have a reply?"

The woman continued to look at Paul. She bent her head, while continuing to smile. She performed this gesture as if she was saying 'Buna ziua' to all people in the room.

Near Raluka, Paul was looking at her iPad. I was sure they were looking in the data base to identify who this woman was. Paul became quite nervous.

"Who is this woman?" he asked Raluka.

"I don't know . . . she is not in my data base . . . I am sorry Paul."

"I thought your data base was complete . . . Raluka you are disappointing me . . ."

Raluka was extremely embarrassed that Paul said this to her in front of everyone.

As if trying to save the moment and becoming nervous at the same time, Chlorinda stepped close to the old woman. "Are you going to answer my question? What is your business here?"

The old woman continued to ignore Chlorinda even though she was standing very close to her.

Suddenly, the old woman was looking toward me, staring hard at me. I felt like she was penetrating my mind . . . I had never had this feeling before. It was extremely painful for me. Chlorinda took the elbow of the old woman and shook her. As soon as Chlorinda did that, my piercing headache dissipated immediately.

"Hey, do you like me pushing you? We can call the police to eject you from here, but I actually prefer to do it myself."

With a dismissive gesture, the old woman took Chlorinda's hands from her elbow. She was once again looking toward me. I started to think about what Paul suggested to me in the car. I imagined my two knives flowing around me, thinking 'I will not allow this woman to do that again.' She began walking in my direction.

"Stop!" Chlorinda screamed from behind her.

I stood there, stock still and terrified as the old woman walked toward me.

Ignoring everyone else in the room, the old woman continued to come to me. Finally, she was standing in front of me. She reached out and tried to touch me.

"Don't touch her!" Paul said loudly. Her hand froze in the air momentarily as if she was unsure whether to listen to Paul or not . . . then she decided to ignore Paul and tried to touch my face with her hand.

I saw Paul making a quick gesture to Drina.

Immediately, Drina's pupils constricted as she intensified her kinesthetic powers to stop the old woman. The woman's hand stilled in the air as she tested Drina's power. After a moment, however, she continued the movement of her hand to touch my face. Drina's hands flew to her chest as if as she suddenly had problems with her heart and she collapsed to the floor.

Unbelievably quickly, Paul was at my side. He caught the hand of the old woman and threw it down.

"I said don't touch her! Do you understand me?"

The old woman was nodding her head. She looked at Paul then again back to me. She checked for something in her basket and brought out a small bouquet of dried basil and some dried flowers. She gave it to Paul, making signs and it became clear that the bouquet was for me. Paul inspected the small bouquet gave it to me saying, "She wants you to accept this gift. These flowers will protect you; they were watered with holy water."

I took the bouquet reluctantly. I felt somehow obligated to tell her 'thank you' even if she previously gave me a headache, even though I was terrified by her. The old woman smiled at me.

Paul took the old woman firmly by her elbow saying, "Please, come with me." He guided the old woman to the corner of the room where the food table food was, "You must be hungry. Please eat."

The woman looked at the table then again to Paul.

Paul took a glass and filled it with water; he gave it to the old woman. She drank the entire glass almost without taking a breath. She was thirstier than I had ever seen in my life. Paul refilled the glass.

He smiled at her and said, "I know, these concentrations make me very thirsty too. Now, drink and eat something. Afterward I want you ready for some discussions." Saying that, he turned his back on the old woman and walked over to Raluka. After just a couple of steps he stopped and turned back to the old woman.

"One more thing: Don't try any tricks again. If you do, then you will have problems with me. And they will be serious problems for you."

With lethargic movements, the old woman began to eat. It was as if she took no enjoyment from the food but as if she ate to live, nothing more.

Paul signaled to us and we moved near him. He spoke in a low voice, "Who is this woman? Does anyone know her?"

"She doesn't appear in my database. She must not be a very strong witch," Raluka replied.

Paul looked at Raluka, "Or just not known by us."

Drina joined in, "She is a strong witch. She almost damaged my heart. She tried first to resist my kinesthetic power and I intensified the force, but at that level it was a danger to my heart . . ."

"She was . . . in my mind," I said.

"Describe it," Paul demanded.

"It felt like an intense headache when she was gazing me. But as Chlorinda shook the old woman, the headache suddenly disappeared."

"High level telepathy," Chlorinda said. "I heard about an old woman in a village near the Danube with strong powers. She might be that woman. What do you think, Paul?"

"Why you did not report this until now?"

Chlorinda lowered her head. Feeling the tension, everyone in the room remained silent.

"I know who she is," Paul said. "Hey you, come here," Paul commanded the old woman. Docile, she obeyed his command and moved to stand in front of him with us all around.

"Open your mouth," Paul commanded. With an embarrassed expression on her face, the old woman turned her face down.

Chlorinda stepped near her. "If you don't open your mouth, I will force you to do it . . ."

The old woman made a sign that she would do it herself. She moved close to Paul and opened her mouth.

Near Paul, Raluka was aghast. "Oh God . . . someone cut off this poor woman's tongue . . ."

A cold fear ran through everyone present in the room. Maybe Paul himself was in awe about this, even if he only guessed it or . . . perhaps he had known it.

"I understand," he said, "you cannot speak as you have no tongue. I am going to ask you a few questions. Please answer with 'yes' or 'no' by making signs with your head. First question; is the person who removed your tongue here in this room?"

The woman shook her head 'no'.

"Do you know him or her?"

She nodded her head 'yes'.

"Is he or she alive?"

She made a 'no' sign.

"Do you have any enemies here in this room?"

Again, the woman made a 'no' sign.

"Do you know . . . me?"

She nodded 'yes'.

"Do you know Laura?"

Again, a 'yes' sign, but then immediately she began making desperate 'no' signs. It was becoming clear to me that there was something very strange about this woman. It was also clear that Paul had used the answers to his first questions to study the woman's reaction for the last and most important question. It struck me as a powerful technique that would be useful for me to learn and apply.

She knows me . . . but from where? I thought to myself.

A short distance away, Chlorinda's face was bitter and she seemed lost in thought.

*   *   *

"Grave things have been brought to my attention. I am afraid I have to make you aware of them," Paul began.

I thought he would begin with the problem I had brought up to him but I was quite surprised to hear mine was not the first one.

"This woman," and Paul pointed at the old woman, "I would have her join our club. Objections?" he was looking at our faces. Silence reigned for a few moments.

"Yes," Raluka said. "With all due respect Paul, we have clear rules here. I asked her and she was not able to provide me with her identity data."

"This is not an issue. Call her 'The Old Woman' in your statistics. I know her name, but if she does not want to share it with us I will respect her wishes," Paul said powerfully.

"O . . . okay . . . but where does she live? What emergency phone number should I add for her? She is an old woman. If something bad happens to her, where should we call? Who would take care of . . . her funeral?" Raluka asked, lowering her voice.

"The answer to your questions is this: emergency number—put my number. The second question was 'who will take care of her funeral', the answer is *I will.*"

We were all terribly surprised. 'What's going on here?' I asked myself.

"Any more objections?" Paul asked in a normal voice.

Drina raised her hand. "If she becomes a member of our club, she must share her knowledge with us."

"She will." Paul answered simply.

"May I speak Paul?" Chlorinda asked.

Paul smiled widely at Chlorinda. He did not answer immediately, but eventually said, "Yes, Chlorinda."

"Raluka said she has no identity. I don't remember exactly which village is hers. How will we find her for . . . knowledge sharing?"

"That will be my task," Halibarda said.

"Good. Thank you, Halibarda." But I saw that Chlorinda was still confused.

"I hope all of you are happy. She is a strong witch, and we need people like her in our club. Also she is old . . . I see no reason for her to refuse to share her knowledge with us," Paul was looking at her, and he spoke to her, "Old Woman welcome into our club. You can help us and we can help you. Now, you have a paper to sign, please. Raluka will help you with it."

We applauded. In fact she had given us a good demonstration of her powers and abilities. I saw Raluka putting some ink on her finger and the old woman pressed her finger in the space where the signature was requested.

"Good. Next, Gina come to the front," Paul's voice was very stern like he is going to accuse Gina of something. Docile and surprised, Gina stepped to the front.

"Geta, to the front." Joining her sister, she stepped to the front.

"All of you, I need you to applaud for these girls."

We all applauded but I was totally confused . . . thinking, what ways Paul has . . .

"But . . . for what Paul?" Gina asked.

"Because we helped Laura," Geta said, and then turned to Paul. "It was our pleasure to help."

"Not only for this. I would like to take this opportunity to thank you for your contribution to our club."

"Thanks Paul. We are hoping to increase our contribution . . ."

"I am afraid you have no time left." His words were icy. It was as if everyone in the room stopping breathing.

"P . . . p . . . pardon me?" Gina stuttered.

"I don't understand," Geta added.

Smiling bitterly, Paul said, "Girls, it is very easy to predict obvious events. When Jesus Christ was born the three mages predicted exactly the time and place of his birth. Unfortunately . . . I predict the end of your lives."

"Oh . . . No," everyone in the room was protesting vociferously.

"Tonight," Paul added.

The room transformed into total chaos. Everyone looked dreadfully surprised but I was not, and near me I saw the old woman was not surprised either.

The sisters fell to the floor. They began to cry and embraced each other. Also crying, Halibarda went over to them and embraced them. Sitting on his chair, Paul had a smile on his face. He appeared to be enjoying himself and did nothing to stop it. He said nothing as if he was happy for this moment to last longer.

"I am sorry Paul, but . . . may I speak?" the young, slim white guy asked Paul.

"Speak."

"I tried to foresee the future. It appeared that tonight's meeting will be just like the last one. Some of us might feel an entity; there will be interpretation but, nothing more . . ."

Somehow losing her equilibrium with what was going on in the room Chlorinda said shakily, "Paul we need more details. Maybe we can save these two poor girls."

"All right," Paul said. "How about if you ask the questions?"

With a terrible grimace, Chlorinda said, "I knew it. When difficult situations arise you always force me to handle them. Okay. How about if I take your chair and you stand in front of us all?"

Surprised, Paul rose from his chair and moved to the front. With visible satisfaction Chlorinda took his place on the chair. Halibarda held the two sisters who continued to cry.

"Gina and Geta," Chlorinda started, "the questions I have will be for your benefit. I would like to save you girls. At times I have been unkind to you but please remember I don't wish your death." She paused, "Now try to focus, try to use all the powers you have and inform us when you have questions or observations."

Chlorinda looked angrily at Paul. "Paul, you said that you foresee these two girls will die tonight."

"That is correct."

"Why are you so sure?"

"Someone saw it in the tarot cards three times in a row. It is impossible to be a coincidence at this level. But, I don't want to tell the name of the person who foresaw it."

"Paul. This is a necessary information right now. Who was the person who foresaw this?"

"I did." I said the words strongly and clearly. I felt it was time to jump in with both feet. As Chlorinda said, we might be able to save the twin sisters.

It was clear that for Chlorinda it was difficult to manage this moment herself. She was obviously performing some mental concentrations to calm herself down.

"Laura, come to the front," Chlorinda commanded. I stood together with Paul in front of everyone in the room.

"Laura and Paul. You have shown no abilities to foresee the future. I will consider that Nelu is more qualified than you are. If he has foreseen such a thing I will believe it, but I don't trust either of you. And this is my final conclu . . ."

"Or maybe he will die too and for this reason he is not able to see the near future," Paul said.

"You bastard!" Chlorinda screamed with an unbelievable force, "Speak only when I allow you to do so!"

In a quiet voice Paul said, "I am sorry Chlorinda." He let Chlorinda savor her unexpected victory. However, she was smart enough to understand the evil was done and she had to investigate a new issue.

"Nelu," Chlorinda said, looking at the tall, slim fellow, "would you like to comment here?"

Nelu was not able to speak for moment. He was still impacted by Paul's words. Chlorinda waited a few moments, watching him. After several seconds he began to speak. "Technically, Paul is right. I cannot foresee my own future. It is a rule, and almost all of us know it. If I am going to die, either I can foresee nothing or I would see only that all will be like at the previous incantation, which I have to admit would be a grossly erroneous vision." I could hear the immense emotion in his voice.

"Paul and Laura, I need more details from you. They will die at tonight's incantation?"

"My vision was only that they will die; unfortunately I don't know how," Paul said. "If they go home it might be a car accident, if they stay here in this small mountain town and only in this villa, they could fall on the stairs, it could be almost anything."

"I have no intentions of going home," Gina said.

"Nor do I," Geta added. "If we are to die tonight we don't want to die in a stupid accident."

"But," Nelu said, "this might be a way to see how accurate the predictions are; how deep they go. I will go home. I have no objections if I have to die in a car accident."

"Laura how do you know the sisters will die tonight?" Chlorinda asked me.

"I saw it in the tarot cards."

"But I know you just began to use the tarot cards. How can you be so sure?"

"I am not sure; I only wanted to warn the sisters about my findings."

"Why you did not tell us first?" Gina asked.

"Because, according to the teachings, this is a thing we are supposed to . . . hide."

"As Paul had the same visions regarding the sisters . . . I understand now the thing is quite obvious. But, I am still not completely convinced it will really happen," Chlorinda said. "Is there anything more to talk about?" Chlorinda asked. "In approximately five hours we are supposed to be at the place for the group spelling. *Near Dracula's Castle.*"

"Yes," Raluka added. "All of you know that I have dedicated my entire life to studying these phenomena, called paranormal, or unnatural. I would like to participate in the group incantation tonight." She looked toward Chlorinda.

"I agree as long as you sign your own waiver form. That way, if you die we have a cover. I always believed you were a smart woman. I am sure you are aware of the danger," Chlorinda said.

Raluka turned toward Paul for his approval. And he said, "Yes. If you wish it so much, why not? You can come with us to observe the phenomena for yourself. Good," she continued, "now Laura, I would like you to try to foresee whether I will die tonight. Please use the same method as you did for the sisters. All of you, independent of what Laura predicts I will participate." All the people in the room were fixated on me. I was extremely confused.

"Okay. Raluka please stay at that table." I sat on a chair by Raluka. I shuffled the cards and spread the cards on the table in front of her and ran my hand across the table and up to the cards. At a particular point, I felt my hand grow heavy. I took the card and turned it over. A general 'OHH . . . ' came from the entire room. The card I extracted was the card of Death. I tried to calm myself.

"Now I will look for a number." The card I extracted showed the number seven.

"Well?" Raluka asked me. She was looking at me challengingly. "What do you foresee for me? Suppose I am not Raluka, I am a woman who comes to you and I don't know the significance of the tarot cards." She was looking at me like she was saying 'do your job Laura. I admire you and expect you to do your job professionally'.

I tried to control my voice. "Raluka tonight you will attend the club group incantations. In five hours we will be *near Dracula's castle*, and we will begin the spelling, the incantations. Two hours later you will die."

∗   ∗   ∗

On Raluka's table 27 signatures had been collected, the number of participants at tonight's incantations *near Dracula's castle*. It was taking us some time to drive there. After that we took our "tools" and started walking to the top of the mountain.

Various bags were used to carry tools. I used a backpack since I did not have too many tools yet—just a few candles, my tarot cards and my two big knives. However just in case, I carefully arranged the two knives so as to be able to easily remove them if I needed without taking off the backpack. I was not familiar with the Romanian mountains and I had been told a large variety of wild animals live there. My knives might be useful, especially as I could see no one carrying bear spray. I thought these people are irresponsible to go to the mountains like this, without suitable hiking equipment.

Only Paul and a few of the women had backpacks. Otherwise, I could see shoulder bags were widely used. The old woman carried her basket. I thought it impractical for this type of hiking. She was making an enormous effort to hike with us into the mountains. Paul and Halibarda were helping her. It appeared she had the main attention of the entire group. I felt myself being a little jealous as I was usually the one who was the center of the attention.

The slope of the mountain was quite steep. I thought it was a bad idea to climb the mountain without suitable hiking equipment. After we had been hiking for about 40 minutes, I was not sure how much longer I could go on.

Then suddenly, we reached the top of the slope and arrived at a very large plateau. It was as if someone had cut the top of the mountain off with a huge laser and we were now at the apex.

All of us were tired. We took a few minutes to catch our breath and relax. The old woman in particular was exhausted from scaling the mountain. It was difficult to see around as there was no moon in the sky. But I could tell that the mountain plateau was huge.

Raluka was standing near me and she said that it is believed here in this place Dracula in his human, natural life killed many victims. It is the most conducive place for someone with magical abilities to perform an incantation to touch Dracula's spirit. This idea struck me as being brilliant as if he is now a vampire, a strigoy or a ghost he would be attracted to these types of places.

"The ruin of his castle is not far away from here," Raluka finished her explanations. "The way we chose to arrive here is the only accessible way. Anywhere else on this mountain is an abyss. If someone fell, his body would be never found."

Even with a moonless sky, I am certain this place is amazing. This is the reason for my trip to Romania; to be in this place, *near Dracula's castle*.

Not far away from me, Paul and Halibarda were speaking to the old woman. The two sisters had formed a small group with Chlorinda and Drina. They were making a defensive plan if someone dared to attack the group with the intention of killing the sisters. Ivanka and the rest of the group remained quiet. I thought they were all nervous about the dark predictions and were thinking about the upcoming incantations.

"We're almost ready," Paul announced. "Let's make some estimates about the circumference of this area. I want our magical circle to be placed in the exact center of the plateau."

The group picked up their torches and began to move around, checking the dimensions. From time to time we heard movements and rustling in the bushes, as if wild animals were around.

"They are only curious," Chlorinda said. "Don't worry, they are small animals and will not dare to attack us."

Raluka was performing calculations on her iPad to approximate the circumference as Paul had asked. In fact I saw she has a 3D picture of this place with all the dimensions included. She counted off steps to determine where the center of the plateau was. After that, she calculated multiples of 27, the number people present for the group incantations to determine the corresponding perimeter of the magical circle.

"Our magical circle will have exactly the same center as the mountain. It will focus the natural energies and be easily understood by the elements that are occupying this place. Good, now mark the cardinal points Raluka," Paul said.

Raluka used a dagger to determine North, and then the other cardinal points. All of us had brought candles colored black, red, blue and green. There were also many white candles among us. We arranged the black candles on the north side and the other colored candles at their corresponding cardinal points. The distance between cardinal points was filled by white candles along the arch of the circle, along with some torches. We piled all our equipment in the middle of the circle.

Preparations were almost complete; the ritual was almost ready to begin. I thought that when the candles were lit that it would be a nice view if seen from above. I thought maybe next time I would have to devise a way to place my camcorders at a higher level. Right now my camcorder together with others camcorders were arranged in various places to be able to take videos from various angles. A terrible thought came to my mind, 'maybe Dracula's spirit is here now and he is watching us'.

Paul also suggested we all practice before doing some relaxation concentrations. "Arrange all your things near you. Be very careful with your knives. You can place the knives near the candles or if you decide to keep them with you, be responsible. I don't want anyone to be cut by accident. Be a team: if someone near you needs help, please help him."

The wild animals we heard earlier were now completely quiet; it was like the silence before the storm . . .

"We are ready," Raluka reported to Paul.

"Proceed with the ritual," Paul commanded.

*   *   *

"We call the elements of air. You, the vintoases able to control the wind defend with the storm the power of our magical circle. With our mental power we raise this invisible wall; it is indestructible to any storm on the earth. The vintoases and wall protect us against the dangers which come from the east."

It was like hearing 27 voices, each one with its own particular accent. There were lots of discrepancies; it was not at all like a harmonized choir. One by one we lit the 27 blue candles.

"What an embarrassment," Paul said near my ear. "These women . . . they are not able to even speak in unison . . ." After that he continued in a loud voice, "Guys I want some harmony here. Be in touch and harmonize with your neighbor and let's do a good job."

Everyone focused their concentration for a few minutes. I was trying to focus to see the storm outside of the circle, an invisible wall which was protecting us and those entities called vintoases working to defend against the storm on the east side of the magical circle.

At the opposite cardinal point, to the west were the green candles. I noticed the distance between the blue and green groups of candles and realized how large the magical circle we had to create had to be.

"We call the elements of water. You, the fays able to control the water will defend outside water's waves for the power of our magical circle. With our mental power we raised this barrier; it is indestructible to any waves on earth. The fays and the barrier protect us from the dangers which come from the west."

This time our voices were much more uniform than before. I listened to the intonation of my neighbors and I spoke as they spoke. I lit my green candle and I focused on the fays, barrier, waves and the silence inside the circle.

"We call the elements of earth. You, the hobs able to control the earth defend it for the power of my magical circle. With our mental power, we raised this stone igloo; it is indestructible to the earth. The hobs and the earth igloo protect us from the dangers which come from the north."

Lighting my black candle, I focused on the earth and the hobs which at my command are able to fight with the earth's power and creatures. I felt like I am inside a stone igloo and it protected me from all danger. At the same time I maintained my concentration for the air and water elements on the other sides of the magical circle.

Finally we were ready to light the red candles.

"We call the elements of fire. You, the devil women able to control the fire defend it and protect our magical circle. With our mental power we raised this fire proof cube. The devil women and their fire proof cube, protect us from the dangers which come from the south."

I felt the terrible fire outside of the magical circle and the silence and coolness inside the magical circle. I saw the devil women working for me, for us, to protect the magical circle.

"Now light the white candles that connect the cardinal points," Paul commanded.

The women around me hurried to light the candles. I thought again how beautiful the circle would be if seen by *someone* outside it, in the sky.

"Now ... the dangerous moment comes," Paul announced. "Some of us will call dangerous spirits who . . ." suddenly he screamed. At the same time, I felt a brutal undulation throughout the energies of the magical circle.

"What the heck is this?" Paul was screaming.

In the woods we heard a terrifying noise. It was echoing throughout the woods and scaring all the small creatures. We could hear the sound of some poor wild animals being killed by the mysterious animal.

Desperately, Paul was looking around at us. "There is something wrong! Report, tell me what do you feel?" he shouted.

"Paul!" Raluka shrieked, "This stupid old woman was humming bad spirit incantations among us. A terrifying demon comes at her call!"

"You stupid woman!" Paul yelled at her, "What did you do? We were supposed to raise this evil demon gradually so that we could control it . . ." He was stopped by a terrible screech outside of the circle. It was like the sound a predatory bird makes as it swoops for the kill. But even amplified, it was far too strong to be a bird. Or if was a bird . . . it was humongous.

"All of you stay in the circle. Don't let the fear overwhelm you. Stay inside the circle and you live, go outside the circle and you die."

Some of the women whose names I had not learned became very scared. They disobeyed Paul's order and ran out trying to find in the darkness the path we used to come here. They disappeared into the night. But shortly we heard noises like great wings beating and the women's anguished screams. I had never understood the phrase 'death scream' before, but I did now.

"Somebody must go help them!" I was shaking and sobbing in my terror.

"Nobody can go there," Paul replied to me in both Romanian and English. "Anyone who goes there will die."

A few of the women came back running as fast as they could; when they came close to our circle we were able to see a dark shape behind them in the candlelight. The last one started to scream terribly. Chlorinda took a torch and moved the light in that direction. All we could see was a huge pair of talons grabbing the poor woman by her shoulders and lifting her into the sky. She was screaming desperately. After a few moments her noises stopped abruptly and then . . . silence. The other women were back in the circle. The members in the circle tried to calm them. They where extremely agitated. Regaining her voice for a moment one of them said, "Three of us are dead."

"Tell us what is there? What did you see?" Paul demanded.

"It was like a giant bird, black, huge . . . and it tried to kill us. It will kill all of us! There is no escape."

"Silence!" Paul commanded, trying to regain control of the group. But behind him, the terrifying bird appeared. It was flying in Paul's direction.

"Halibarda," Paul yelled as he jumped in the air. His jump was unusually high, so high it didn't seem possible to be done by a human being. At the same time, Halibarda threw a sword to Paul. Leaping into the air, Paul was wielding the sword to attack the terrifying creature. With a loud cry, the terrible creature disappeared into the dark. Paul fell to the earth inside the magical circle. He checked the sword. There was blood.

"Good. You hurt it," Chlorinda said.

"It is coming again . . ." Halibarda screamed. We felt the wind from the creature's wings as it approached us.

"All of you get behind me," Drina yelled. She was running in the direction of the creature coming toward us. She raised her arm. I realized she was trying to stop the creature with her kinesthetic power. We heard a screech and a noise like a big body crashing to earth. Chlorinda and the other women were trying to shine light in that direction with their torches. Each grabbing a sword, I saw Halibarda's two assistants running to the monster's body, still lying where Drina had forced it to crash. They tried to impale its body, but nothing was there—the body was melting in the night.

"Gena, Geneva," Halibarda screamed their names, "get back in the circle!" The two women began to run back to the circle but the creature was once again appearing from the dark, right over top of them. It was like a piece of night fell over the two women. They each screamed and fell to the earth, dead.

"Five now," I heard Raluka counting, "this is a kind of malefic spirit able to materialize itsel . . . ." She began shrieking desperately. The horrific creature came over top and extracted Raluka. We heard Raluka's scream coming from the sky and then nothing, only the noise of a body crashing to earth.

"Raluka! Raluka!" Halibarda was shouting her name.

"All of you listen to my command!" Paul said loudly. "Each one of you arm yourself with knives and swords. I will focus and I will feel the direction that creature is trying to attack us from. I will indicate to you the direction. We will raise the knives in that direction. Chlorinda you try to feel the creature too."

I grabbed both of my huge knives. It was as if the creature was hanging back and studying us. For many long moments there was silence.

"I feel it close to us," Chlorinda said.

"All of you; face to the north. Watch the sky from the northerly direction," Paul commanded.

Suddenly, the creature tried to attack us from the north. We could see it swooping down towards us and we all ran to that end of the circle with knives raised. With a louder screech than ever before, the creature backed down and disappeared. I suddenly remembered the premonition I had regarding the twin sisters. It was beyond the middle of the night and they were still alive. I tried to stay close to them. We were listening, focusing. Chlorinda stood up with her arms wide open like she was trying to feel any vibration in the air. She stood like this for awhile, focusing. Finally, agitated, she started to scream.

"It's coming . . ."

"From underground," Paul yelled. "In the direction of the green candles!" Immediately all of us started to stab our knives in the earth.

"It is going underground to the east! Blue candles!"

Oh dear God! The twin sisters had been there a few moments ago! There was a terrible scream, which then became two. I recognized the desperate death screams of the twin sisters. The creature was able to grab both of them and drag them underground. The old woman ran in the direction the twin sisters had disappeared. She began to bang her rod on the earth, while humming some Romanian words. With a terrible screech, the creature appeared from the earth. It had a snake's body but then immediately sprouted wings and was able to fly.

From the underground hole we heard the twin sisters groaning. With some effort, we were able to extract them. We rushed to give them some water, but they were unable to drink. I was sure they had many broken bones and they were barely breathing.

"Leave them there!" Paul screamed. "We have a new attack . . . from the south!" We were ready to run to the south. But the old woman was already there and making strange signs with her rod. The creature was again screeching and retreated into the night.

Silence again.

"I think the creature is afraid now," Halibarda said. "It will not dare to return."

"But we have to finish it," Chlorinda said loudly and ran outside of the circle. "Whoever you are, come here and attack me!" We heard nothing, only Chlorinda's words. "Whoever you are, come here to . . ." sharply, Chlorinda screamed. She continued to scream, but at the same time the terrible creature was screeching also. We heard a big crash. It had to be the creature's body as the noise was too loud to be Chlorinda. I heard Chlorinda yelling, "I will kill you! I will kill you! Using the power of the four elements, I take your power!"

Drina ran outside of the circle too, toward the noise of Chlorinda's shrieking. The terrible creature was groaning as the two women were destroying it.

Chlorinda and Drina were shouting as they tried to take control of the situation and demanding the creature die. But shortly their yells of aggression turned into victims' screams.

"Halibarda," Paul commanded. Halibarda took a candle and began to say an incantation as she advanced in the direction of the two women. Paul ran there too. He quickly returned with the two women. Behind him Halibarda retreated as she continued to say the strange spell. Chlorinda and Drina returned to the circle.

"It is coming again." I heard a voice full of emotion. It was Ivanka.

The creature was attacking Ivanka now. Unexpectedly, Ivanka uncapped a small bottle and threw liquid in the direction of the creature. The creature retreated in fear. A few drops of liquid from Ivanka's bottle touched the creature and I saw smoke rising.

"I know who you are," Ivanka said, like an incantation, "and I defeat you with holy water. Don't dare to come back, the holy water will burn you."

We stayed in the magical circle until the sun rose. The creature had disappeared. We were horrified by the scene around us. Eight of us had died. Even with all the warnings we were able to give to the twin sisters, they died too.

Chapter 13

"So sad bird . . . .
She is flying, flying without any target.
When she sees a clean fountain she runs like crazy,
When she sees a bad fountain she makes it muddy, and she drinks
that water.
When she sees a hunter she is running to his front.
Sir, please shoot me, I want to die!"

-Romanian folk poem

"*In the name of Father, Filis and Spiritum sanctity, amen.*"

Paul was breaking leaves from a tree branch and throwing them around in an ironic gesture. After that he took my hand and said "let's go."

"Where the heck do you think you are going?" Chlorinda was screaming at Paul.

Paul turned towards her.

"Be careful with whom and how you speak woman!" Paul said looking meanly at Chlorinda.

"I am speaking with you, and you will go nowhere!" Chlorinda screamed without being intimidated.

As if changing his mind, Paul smiled to Chlorinda.

"Chlorinda, I thought you were a competent woman and you could manage this without me, but I see you cannot." His eyes moved to Halibarda, "Halibarda call the emergency services."

Halibarda immediately dialed the emergency number from her cell phone. It took her quite long time to explain. When she was done she said to me, "Good Lord, these guys are crazy! So many explanations . . ."

"Well it is quite unusual to have eight deaths at once," Drina said. "We are going to have a looong morning."

We were all lying down on the ground, tired and horrified by the things that happened last night. Could there be an explanation for all this? I was so confused. Everyone looked tired, except Paul and Halibarda. A little away from the group Halibarda and Paul were chatting in hushed voices. They seemed to be planning something. I saw Chlorinda staring at them with her disapproving green eyes. She spoke to me, "They need a good plan. I don't know how they will explain all this to the police."

I felt so tired; my brain was like lead, so heavy. Finally Paul and Halibarda came towards me. They said nothing; it was a long hard silence. I was waiting. The silence was broken by Paul's cell ringing. He was chatting in Romanian in a normal voice. I could see the others listening to his conversation and wondering about it. Ivanka was nervously tapping the ground with her fist.

"What's wrong?" I asked Halibarda who was near me. "What can be much worse than what has already happened?"

Halibarda looked at me for a long time; I saw that she was also tired. Through her emotion she said to me. "It was the ambulance service. They informed Paul that his friend Nelu died in a car accident."

I was terrified by this news too. So, Paul was right; this was going to happen to the sisters also, if they did not come with us. I remembered Raluka's teachings about fate or 'ursita' as they call it here. Even with all the drama, I took some time to myself to remember a couple happy moments. *I am able to foresee the future. I have witches powers. Paul was right; I will be a strong witch! Even though these people died here, I am excited about my new powers.*

Shortly, we could hear ambulance and police sirens. It would still take them some time to drive up the hill and arrive here. We all tried to stay relaxed. I thought about the questions they might ask me. What was a Canadian citizen doing here in Romania participating in these satanic kinds of incantations? I was supposed to be embarrassed, but the truth was that I was not embarrassed at all. This stuff intrigued me; there were so many unanswered questions, and now I feel like I have to find the answers.

Finally the emergency crews arrived. There was also police and news crews. I remembered my camcorder and I checked for it. Disappointed I saw that it was smashed. During her flight the creature was smashed along with my camcorder. It was like she knew that these instruments will be a proof of . . . something, and so she smashed all of them.

"What a heck happened here?" a cop asked us.

With a natural voice and calm demeanor Halibarda answered, "My name is Halibarda,' the people with TV cameras were recording the surroundings, but they started to record what Halibarda was saying. With theatric gestures Halibarda continued, "And I am a witch. We tried to complete a night incantation here until something unexpected showed up."

"Sir," said a lady who was looked to be in charge of the ambulance crew, "we have eight deaths."

"Good Lord! How can you people explain this?"

"We don't know exactly what happened, we cannot explain . . . maybe in the middle of the incantations they became so exited and . . ."

Drina was translating the discussions for me, but Halibarda was explaining for a long time. She started to argue with the cops and with the TV reporters. Their discussion became very excited. A reporter touched her; he tried to calm her down. Halibarda, started to scream like crazy, she came to Paul and me screaming, "that guy tried to push me . . . he tried to violate me . . ."

"Okay guys,' Paul said, "I have been patient enough. It is clear to me that you cannot handle this matter properly. None of our group killed these people, and this poor woman is scared. She may die of fright and you will have nine deaths. I'm certain you don't want this to happen. We can go to the villa I rented and we can hold a press conference." They appeared to approve Paul's proposal.

*   *   *

I had a couple of minutes for a quick shower. When I went down to the living room I saw a lot of reporters with their cameras and also some police. Almost all of us were there. Chlorinda helped by Vlad appeared to be keeping things in order. She made a line in the middle of the living room and she did not allow the reporters to pass.

The reporters were taking pictures, making videos and they were quite talkative.

Our people were standing in the other half of the living room; Paul was stood in the middle between Halibarda and Drina. I took a place near Drina because she was going to translate for me.

"Okay gentlemen," Paul started, "my name is Paul Negru. Unfortunately we have not slept. My apologies but this press conference will be no longer than 30 minutes. We need to get some rest. I hope you understand." Paul looked around the room at the TV reporters and police. "What I have to say to you is this: we were here last night, all twenty-seven of us, trying to light some candles and perform spells. Unfortunately we were attacked. We don't know by whom or why. This attack tragically ended with eight deaths. I have to say that my people are emotional after last night events, and I will not tolerate more of the behavior like one reporter who was quite, 'impolite' with Halibarda, one of the members of our group. Now I am ready for your questions, because you don't have much time I suggest you stay on topic."

There was a raucous as all the reporters tried to speak at once, but Paul raised his hand. "Okay, Vlad will allow you to ask questions one by one."

Vlad was happy to do this job; he allowed the first reporter to begin. A young reporter started, "I am Christian for . . . ."

Immediately Paul interrupted him. "One moment, I am not interested at all who you are or what channel you represent. As our time is so limited, only ask your question."

"Okay," the reporter was conforming to the rule, "you might be not interested in who I am but I am interested who you are."

"I am afraid a don't understand the question. Vlad next question please."

A young lady was next. "I understood your name is Paul and you are the VP of the magic club who organized the group incantations last night. Is that correct?"

"Yes."

Vlad started to assign turns to the reporters presented in the room.

Reporter: "What was the subject of the incantations from last night?"

Paul: "To perform what we call, the magical circle. Usually it is done by one or two individuals. We decided to perform it in group."

Reporter: "Is this the first time?"

Paul: "No, it is the second time. The first time there was no incidents."

Reporter: "Do you have an explanation for this?"

Paul: "There are theories but, I am sorry I cannot be sure . . . for now."

Reporter: "It will be the last group incantation?"

Paul: "Possibly, as it seems to be becoming extremely dangerous."

Reporter: "Are there fees for your club?"

Paul: "There are no fees. If someone wants to organize an event he can sponsor it himself or he can ask for volunteers. The members of the club are wealthy, money is not an issue.

Reporter: "Can I become a member of the club?"

Paul: "You will have to prove that in the community where you live, you are recognized as a wizard, you have to prove some aptitude, if you can do that, then 'yes'. If not well . . ."

Reporter: "Do you feel that you are responsible for the deaths of these eights people?"

Paul: "Before this group action each participant had signed a waiver that they are in good health, are participating without outside force, and are aware there might be a danger; as a result each one had an emergency number to be called in case of a situation. After this press conference, please leave your business cards with Vlad and we will have this waiver scanned and emailed to you. You will find in the signatures of the eight dead people in addition to the rest of the group. I am not guilty for their deaths nor is any member of my club."

Reporter: "What is the reason for the deaths?"

Paul: "As I said, we had been attacked. It might be a wild animal; some of the group believes that it is a yet unknown entity. I am sure there will be a police investigation. The group and I will be very cooperative with the police. I believe for now all eight deaths were an accident. It's like when you go camping with a group and a wild animal attacks the campsite. This is an unhappy accident. If you have another opinion please share."

Reporter: "Why is Laura, the famous singer, here? Did she participate in these group incantations?"

Paul: "Laura is a friend of mine. We live in the same town in Canada. She is interested in Romanian magic; she hopes to find these rituals a source of inspiration for her new album."

Reporter: "Why did you choose this particular place?"

Paul: "Because it is close to Dracula's castle."

Reporter: "Your group incanting has an objective to wake up Dracula or its spirits?"

Paul: "Possibly . . . ."

Reporter: "Please answer with yes or no."

Paul paused and he fixed his gaze on the young reporter. "What's your name?"

"My name is Dan. Could you please answer my question?"

"Dan, sometimes it is not possible to answer 'yes' or 'no' definitively to a question. This is especially true in regards to magical stuff, but I like your direct style. After this press conference I will have exclusive contact with you. You will be the press representative in this matter. However, the answer at your question is YES!"

A chaos started in the room. Vlad was unable to keep the people silent. Paul looked at Vlad with disapproval; he made a sign to Chlorinda. She was slamming his fist on the table trying to regain order.

"Silence! We need silence here; we have not slept all night long and we are tired. Please leave! The press conference is finished. Thank you for your questions."

The reporters were unhappy, they had more questions and they were ready to protest. They began shouting questions all at once. I was not sure that my Romanian friends were able to catch what they were saying.

"Chlorinda, please I would like to take one last question, as a bonus, from Dan," Paul said.

With strong emotion in his voice Dan said, "Paul, ladies, if that is true and you woke up an entity connected with Dracula or Dracula itself; we are in grave danger. Will you be able to help us?"

Paul looked around the room. A silence flooded the room. Paul enjoys these moment of suspense. I might have to introduce into my music some pauses at certain moments; they could make my music more interesting.

"If, indeed what you say is true . . . Our club is the only force in the world able to handle the situation."

*   *   *

Seven days passed since the terrifying night. The Romanian TV channels were still debating the subject. We were often interrogated by the police, finally we were trusted. Not one of us killed the others; all of it was totally voluntary according to the waiver signatures. It was determined an accident.

In order to have some peace and quiet immediately after the police interrogation Paul decided to take me to one of his proprieties in the south of Romania. It was a wonderful idea. His house had four bedrooms on the upper floor as well as a very nice and large living room on main floor. I understood Paul's preference was for medium sized houses that are very well organized, not at all like the gypsy castles I saw. The property has a huge yard and it was very close to the river. Around the river was a dam. It seemed that there was no flooding danger, but Paul told me that the danger still exists especially in the spring when the snow is melting or there is lots of rain.

"The danger is not from the river. The danger is from the accumulated water which of course is not able to skip the dam. There are pumps stations that are supposed to pump the water; unfortunately they are not well maintained." Paul told me.

I observed the village did not have running water, gas pipeline or sewage. Paul explained to me that he has a well in the yard and a pump that will bring the water to the house. There was a septic tank for sewage, and for gas he used big propane tank. The propane would be enough to last a year.

This village was so quiet. I was surprised to see that the village was a mixture between old and new. Never before had I seen such a mixture between very old and very new. I had been told that almost all the families who have children have internet, but I was quite surprised to see these same people still use horses or other animals for transport or to work the land.

The days were about recovery for me after the terrible night and a chance to explore the village. I recorded a lot with my camcorder;

I think my friends back home will find it interesting. I was happy to meet the little girl who lived couple houses down from Paul's with his brother and family. She was always a very welcome guest. Always happy, always ready to talk with me indefinitely; it was amazing for me to see how nicely she used both languages, Romanian and English.

These days I didn't dare ask Paul what was happening, but maybe today is the right time.

Vlad was lazy this morning. I was eating my banana and watching the news with Paul. They are still talking about the event, there was video from the funerals of the eight people. As Raluka had no relatives, Paul assigned Halibarda to take care of Raluka's funeral.

Halibarda was quite busy, she was also present at almost each day's news cycle talking about the incident. She seemed happy to be such a news star.

After we were done with morning coffee we decided to walk around the river. It is a medium sized river and I had a good time walking around. I took caution to only go out in day light, and always with Vlad close by. On the other side of the river was a forest. Whenever I looked into the forest I had the feeling that a terrible animal might attack me. We walked around the river from almost thirty minutes watching the river birds, and people fishing. It is quite relaxing. It definitely was a wonderful idea to come here. Paul stopped to say, "you know Laura, I am afraid that things are now beyond control. You might be in danger."

I was surprised by his observation, I could feel the danger. I was not sleeping well at night but with him and Vlad near me, I felt quite safe.

"What are you saying Paul?"

"You might want to consider going back to Canada. I will be going myself soon."

"But, something has started, and . . . we started it together. I think we should finish it together."

"Yes," he said after coming to a small beach, the sand was fine and clean. "But you don't have enough experience with this stuff, and you saw how dangerous it is."

He was silent for a period.

"I will feel much better if you were not here . . ."

"Please, Paul. Please, don't insist. I have decided to stay. You told me I can learn more and I am ready to learn more. I was impressed by my talent of seeing the future . . . even if it was seeing the deaths of people. Please tell me how do you foresee the future?"

He was looking at me, "Well, I don't do it with tarot cards, or a crystal globe. I have a special talent, a gift. For some things, I am personally involved . . . and so I can see the future. It's like this; when we think about doing something, like the next group incantations, there are a couple possibilities. I call them lines of future. For example there might be no group incantation, or it is only me there by myself, or it might be you and me, or you, me and Chlorinda and so on. I call this the method of active thinking about the future 'extrapolation'. But from all the future lines, from their extrapolation and a careful analysis only a couple of them will be logically possible. And, from all of possibilities only one will happen. To foresee the future using the extrapolation method you must be a very good analyst of human personalities, interaction between life events and so on. Or you could just be lucky. First I use the extrapolation method; but after that it is all premonitions. I can see quite clearly what's next, especially if I am involved in what's next. Other people can see the future in tarot cards, crystal globe, clean water, corn beans, and so on."

"Your method sounds like it is quite different, and convenient for you. Other people are not able to see their own future, and you are. "

"You are correct." We walked along the river couple of moments in silence.

"And, using your premonition powers . . . do you think I am in danger if I stay here?"

"I have had no premonition yet regarding your participation at the next group incantation. Or I would tell you, I am on the extrapolation stage. But right now, I think you are taking a risk. You can't just end your magical training, and we can continue it next year or another time, when the things will be much clearer and much safer."

"But, Paul . . . it looks like there is an entity, and we have woken it. It was in a dormant form and now she is active because of us! I think it is my duty to help stop it."

"Don't feel guilty, you did nothing wrong. Therefore you don't have any duty."

"I am sorry Paul, but I have decided to continue, please help me with more magical training."

He looked at me with no emotion.

"If it is what you wish . . . . I will do my best to help you."

I smiled at him to soften his resolve. "Thanks Paul!"

*   *   *

I was not paying attention to the route, but we passed Alexandria almost an hour ago. I thought we were going to Bucharest, but Paul was driving country roads. It was an unpaved, deserted route. We took this road for almost 30 minutes. All around us were corn crops. I had to admit the corn crops here looks very good. I saw the crossroads, and there were three cars waiting. I recognized Halibarda, Chlorinda and Drina waiting for us. Their cars were left a couple meters off to the side. We began our meeting at the crossroads, nobody to witness but the corn.

It was turning out to be an interesting meeting.

As if they were all able to understand it, the conversation began in English. "Thanks for coming girls." Paul said.

Halibarda smiled at me.

"How are you Laura?"

"I am good Halibarda, thanks for asking. It has been nine days since that terrible night and . . . I missed all of you." The other women were also smiling at me.

"She has decided to continue . . . what we started, " Paul said.

Drina was surprised, "but, Laura it looks dangerous, we already have eight deaths."

"Nine.' Paul corrected her. "First, I hope you have nothing electronic for recording this conversation," said Paul looking at Chlorinda. She did not answer; but blushed at Paul. Paul ignored her and signaled to Halibarda. Halibarda started to check Chlorinda for hidden devices, she found nothing.

"Happy now?" asked Chlorinda looking as cold as stone at Paul.

"Yes." Paul simply answered. "You have become mature Chlorinda."

"What has happened has made me focus as much as I can. I'd like to stay alive!"

Halibarda checked Drina too. She also found no recording devices.

"Thanks Drina!"

"Now, I need a report regarding the situation of the entity." Paul said.

"The entity is not strong enough. There were couple dead wild animals found. Lots of people think it is the work of a strange animal. I suggest doing our work at the next new moon," Drina proposed.

"No." Paul simply answered.

"Look Paul," Drina said, "I am tired of your attitude, orders and bullying like this."

"Drina! That will be last time you address me like this!"

"If not?" She asked gazing Paul, challenging him.

"I will punish you," Paul said stepping towards her.

"I might be able to defend myself."

"Okay, Okay" Chlorinda said in disgust. "Paul, would you like to explain to us why you don't want to have the ritual at the next new moon?"

"The entity is not strong; therefore she cannot create much damage. The police are monitoring us. After a time they will become tired of that. I think it is better to wait one more full moon's time."

"So, you are suggesting doing the incantation at the second new moon?"

"At this moment it looks like it will work better," Paul said, "also Laura will have some more time to learn and practice. This is her wish. So? Second new moon; are we agreed?"

All of us agreed.

"The place has to be the same. Because it is in the mountains it is quite hard to be monitored. But . . . ." And suddenly Paul stopped.

"But what?" Chlorinda asked upset by Paul observation.

As if trying to gain time for Paul, Halibarda started to talk,

"We are five participants here, Dina do you think Ivanka will come?"

"Yes she will," Drina approved.

"Good we will be six members for the second new moon night incantation."

"Seven," Paul said.

The women were quite surprised.

"Who is the seventh mysterious participant?" Chlorinda asked with a grin in the corner of her mouth.

"The old woman."

"Who is she?" Asked Dina.

"What is she?" Asked Chlorinda.

Paul was pausing as if to analyze the questions, then he simply answered,

"She is a witch, a strong one. Maybe, she is Ivanka's type, not very interested in the money or not very interested even to pass her knowledge to someone."

"If that is so, how you can be sure she will come?' Drina asked "you had a premonition about it?"

"No," Paul said looking at Drina, "for this intuition is enough." There was a moment of silence.

"Okay," Halibarda said, "it looks like we are seven participants. All good? We can go home and we will be in touch for the next two months."

"One moment Halibarda," Paul asked and then he paused for a long time. "Unfortunately, I have to make you aware of ... something." He paused again. "I would like to avoid the problems with police, mass media and so on."

"We want this too," Chlorinda said, "I think all of us want this except Halibarda." Chlorinda was looking harshly at Halibarda.

Halibarda just ignored her.

Drina raised her hand as if forbidding Chlorinda to speak further.

"And how do you propose to avoid it?"

With a bitter smile Paul said "If there are deaths . . . the bodies has to be . . . lost."

As if waking from a dream Drina said "Lost? You mean if I die . . . wait, how do you intend to lose my body?"

"By throwing it into the existing crevasse near the incantation place, they will be unable to track your body. You will all announce to your relatives that you intend to go on a long trip before to coming to the incantation."

Drina was faint; her legs were not able to hold her. She felt down on the ground. She was trying to say something but she did not have enough energy.

"I agree." Chlorinda said in a grave voice.

"I agree," Halibarda also approved.

"After we die our body is an empty cover and it needs no treat."

"You . . . you mean my trip in this world is over, and my body deserves no respect?" Drina asked with a sinking voice.

I tried to calm her, "I am sorry Drina; you are tired. Tomorrow you might think differently."

With an empty face she looked at me.

"You agree with this Laura?"

"Well . . ." I said with some confusion; "I cannot think about failing."

"But if you fail . . ." Drina was persisting.

"If I fail . . . I think it is a story which must be forgotten," I said very convinced, "and my body deserves no respect."

"I am sorry, but if I fail, I would like my body to be sent to my children to be buried . . ."

"Stop," Paul screamed at her, "Here we need no drama. What you are doing now is a cheap melodrama. And it is disgusting!"

"How dare you speak to me like that! " Drina stood and moved toward Paul. "You are worse than that entity."

Unexpectedly, Paul slapped her so hard that Drina had blood on the corner of her mouth.

She looked at him with sadness and anger, "You are a monster, and I don't follow you anymore."

"It is too late Drina," Halibarda said, "There is no way back, and you know it. It is not like you to be a weak woman."

"No. I am out of it. This is my way out." Drina said simply.

With violent gestures she turned her back and she walked to the car. We looked her as the distance between us grew. When she was nearly seven steps away, she turned back with a quick movement and sent a strong kinetic force to smash Paul. As I was very close to Paul the force knocked me down. But with an inhuman speed Paul was near Drina and he grabbed her throat with a hand. With an unimaginable force he threw the small woman on the top of her car. I was shocked by this, but Halibarda and Chlorinda were passively looking on.

Drina lost consciousness because of the force! Finally she awoke, and she climbed down off the car, trying to open the door.

"Tomorrow I will bring Laura to you. Starting with tomorrow it is your duty to train her."

Without saying anything Drina stepped in the car and drove off. Her car disappeared on the coming evening.

Chapter 14

The people are often speaking about good and bad witch, about white and black magic. To all of you I tell you this, the line between life and death, good and bad, day and night is deadly sharp and always confusing in magic.

-Raluka – magical analyst

I am somehow scared, and embarrassed about the idea. Today I have to go to Drina. She did not say if she wanted to have me as a student or not. Also her departure after the last meeting was . . . violent. Maybe she hates me, as she hates Paul now. And as she said she is 'out of the business'. Her village is around two hours away from Paul's house according to what Vlad said.

"On our way we will visit Ivanka. Her village is almost 30 minutes from Drina's village." The village was quite nice, but she lives at the edge of the village and the houses there are quite poor. I observed that the people there are mostly gypsies. Vlad was driving the car on a poor part of the road. When he stopped the car lots of people were coming around our car curiously looking at us. Paul lowered down the window of his car and he addressed to a young gypsy girl.

"How are you Yolanda?"

"I am good, Paul" the girl answered in English.

"Did you continue to study English language?"

She was not very sure she understood everything or maybe she was little bit intimidated by Paul's personality.

"Yes, Paul."

"Good," Paul said, "now can you call Ivanka?"

She was not very sure what Paul said in English but when she heard the name Ivanka, she immediately said "Yes, of course."

After a couple of minutes she came with Ivanka. Ivanka had a smiling face, she was happy to see us.

"Buna seara Ivanka" that is "good evening Ivanka." And I tried to repeat his words.

"Buna seara Ivanka"

"Buna seara, buna seara . . ." she said. After that she started to speak unbelievably quick. I understood that she was speaking in Romanian but her accent was like she was speaking in Spanish. I asked Vlad, and he told me that because usually they speak in the gypsy language.

"Okay, Okay," Paul said to Ivanka, "now let's go to have a look Laura."

Vlad decided it was better to stay at the car. Already a couple of young gypsy ladies came, and they start quickly chatting with him. I was quite impressed to see that almost all of them knew Vlad, and he knew them too as he was calling all of them by name.

"That is because quite frequently I send him here to pick up Ivanka for various issues I have."

We were walking around and I saw again that poor houses with very small yards. I thought about Paul's huge yard, it was half of the size of this part of the village. We were walking little a bit and I found the smell was not very pleasant.

"This is her house," Paul showed me a small house. I observed that in the yards these people are somehow close like our north Indians. Some of the yards also have horses.

"What they are doing with these tents?" I asked Paul.

"Some of they live there, or they meet there for fun. Ivanka keeps her tent to do magic. Let's go inside."

Inside of her tent was a small place to make a fire in the center, a small table as it was possible for us to sit directly on the floor around the small table.

"Here we receive people who are coming for magic from Ivanka. However, I don't like the smell here. .."

Paul started chatting in Romanian with Ivanka. After a couple of minutes, I understood that they were arguing, and Paul was talking to me.

"She is trying to explain me that she prepared some herbs for a magic purpose and this smell is where the smell is coming from . . ."

In the corner of the tent I saw a basket with a knife, a goblet, a pair of tarot cards, and a wand. A quite large vessel was also close, I decided that it was the vessel used to foresee the future in the new water.

"Yes, you are right," Paul said as though he understood what I thought. "These are the usually magical tools used by the ancient witches. I like her. She reminds me somehow about a rude tradition, quite archaic and quite . . . forgotten somehow."

He was smiling to Ivanka, and he continued his chat with her. The things they were saying were also in a high voice, as though they were arguing. Finally Paul was taking money from his wallet. I think there were a couple thousand Euros all together and he gave them to Ivanka. After a moment, as though he was changing his mind he said something and he took 500 Euros back from Ivanka. Ivanka was increasing her voice, and Paul was making disgusting gestures. Ivanka went sprayed the air in the tent.

"I don't think it is the herbs that smell, she is sweating terribly and here she does not have running water. However, even if she had it, I don't think she loves water that much . . . ."

"But . . . Paul, it was like she was arguing with you; what's the matter?"

"She has a couple of kids, sons and daughters. But with a particular one she is having problems. From time to time he steals things from people. He is afraid of me usually I am coming here because I try to correct him . . ."

A young man was stepping in the tent followed by Ivanka.

"Marian." Paul told me his name. He was a quite attractive man, poorly dressed and on top of his hygiene I realized.

Paul told Marian my name as well.

After that Paul started to explain to me a short story, yesterday Marian stole a chicken from the yard of some neighbors. Even if they did not catch him they still believed that he did it. Even though there was not much value, we are speaking about a chicken, this was not good for the relations between the gypsies and the Romanian neighborhood.

Patrick Vaitus

Under Paul's observation Marian was studying me. I was studying him too. He was quite attractive. His skin was quite dark and the muscles of his body were nicely developed. Paul was starting to talk with him using a high voice, but Marian observed me and ignored what Paul was saying.

At an unexpected moment Paul started to slap Marian. The guy stood up, very furious. With a gesture he attempted to run to the corner to catch Ivanka's knife. Using this quick movement, Paul put him down almost at the same time. Paul calmly returned to his place. I was impressed with how he can move so quick. Marian was laying down. Ivanka was arguing near Paul in high voice. Paul was screaming to her. I realized that it was the Romanian word for 'silence'. She became quiet almost immediately.

Paul was starting his discussions with Marian again. He was quite cooperative this time. Marian was speaking in a low voice, as though he had regretted what he had done. Paul took some Romanian money from his pocket and put it in front of Marian. Lazily, Marian took the money that Paul put down. When he collected all of them, he looked to Paul and he said "thank you." Paul smiled to him and said to me, "I told him to go back to that family and give them the equivalent money for two chicken and apologies for what he did. Also he has to pledge to me that he never will do this again."

Paul was looking again at them, and he was talking in a normal tone.

"Let's go Laura, I don't want to be very dark when we reach Drina's house. There we have another spectacle." And he laughed strangely.

*   *   *

Drina lives quite close to Ivanka. I had been told that the twin sister's village was under one hour away. The two, Gina and Geta . . . I miss them so much . . .

Here is a quite normal Romanian village and in a corner, separate, are a couple of castles that are very similar in architecture as I saw in the two sister's village near Alexandria. Outside it was a nice evening. The dark was starting to settle in the village, and there was a quite silence. It was almost like a painted picture.

206

Vlad was driving the car quite close to the big houses, as there was no paved road. He stopped the car in the front of a man who was standing directly in the middle of the road. Vlad let the engine run. A couple steps behind and on the other side of the man we saw other two people. I was quite scared when I saw that they were armed with metal bars.

"Paul they are many more men on the other side of the road too!" said Vlad.

"I know Vlad," after that he turned to me, "they are Drina's men. It looks like we are not very welcome here . . . ."

"Well . . . let's go back!" I said scared about the people.

"I am afraid that they will cut off our way back too." Vlad announced with the same voice.

"Very well," Paul said satisfied, "by all means there is only one way to solve this matter. I have to tell you that, they are quite good fighters, one strike with that metal bar and they can kill a man. Also, they have knifes, which in fact are quite deadly too. You guys stay here in the car. Their problem is with me, not with you. They will not attack you."

After saying that Paul opened car's door to go outside. I tried to stop him and I caught his hand.

"Paul, it's dangerous. They can kill you!"

Paul was looking at my hand that had grabbed his. Then he looked at me.

"They might kill me . . . if they can." And sadly he smiled to me, "actually I am thinking of the opposite about how I can deal with them without hurting them too much." He laughed in a scary kind of way. He was walking outside of the car laughing. As he mentioned the other guys that were there had no issues with us. All of them were creating a circle around Paul. The circle was quite large at the beginning, but with small steps they started to close in on Paul. In the middle of their circle Paul was continuing with that disgusting laugh. I saw that they have metal chains, big knifes, and metal bars. In the middle Paul stopped laughing and he said.

"Okay guys, I know that you are Drina's boys, you know she has kinesthetic powers. Now answer a question. Except Drina who else can grab your tools from your hands using the kinesthetic powers?"

At the exact same time all their guns were thrown from out their hands. The guys were quite disturbed about the new perspective, being so close with Paul and unarmed. Paul was starting laughing again.

"I can."

Close by them, Drina showed up.

"Guys, you are so many and he is only one. Still you can defeat him."

"Or they can go for you," Paul said, "you have a nice dress Drina."

"Kill him!" Drina screamed the order.

All the guys were running to Paul. With a gigantic jump he flew outside of their circle, and landed close to Drina.

"How abut a new arrangement guys, you can try a new attack." Paul said and he starts making a disgusting sign with his tongue to the small woman.

"I still like you Drina." He said. "You can fight too, think that I am here to violate you," and again he made the disgusted sign.

The first three guys attacked him. With his extremely quick movements he swiped them. Shortly afterwards they were down in the soil almost unconscious. Until the others were able to react, Paul jumped in the middle and practicing a couple of karate swipes towards them. Another four guys went down on the ground. They were trying to quickly get up. At this time, he used his leg plant to swipe another guy in stomach. That guy stopped briefly and he remained down on the soil. As other one was on his back, Paul turned rapidly and with the edge of his hand he pushed the guy roughly, he felt immediately. The other one was coming as quick as he was able to and tried to immobilize Paul. But Paul was much too quick for him, and with the edge of his hand he punched the stomach of the next one. The guy fell first to his knees and after that he fell to the soil. Retreating a couple of steps from the four guys who were still able to attack him, Paul said:

"Okay guys I will be quite patient with you. Go on and pick up the sword if you want. I will wait."

The four guys immediately ran and they picked up some weapons. Three of them picked up swords, and another one grabbed the metal chain. They made a circle around Paul.

Quite relaxed he said, "A small rule here, each one will feel his own knife or the knife of his fellow man," he was sadistically laughing again, "quite fair I think."

The guys were playing with the swords quite experimentally, almost like professionals and so was the guy with the chain. Two of them were at opposite sides of Paul, screaming and attacking him with their swords. With a quick move Paul caught the armed hand of one man and placed him in the front of another one. As the second was fast, he almost stabbed the first man, but Paul was attacking him back, and this helped him to avoid a deathly blow to his fellow attacker. However, the first attacker was stabbed in the leg by the second. The second guy was attacking again and screaming at Paul. Paul was fending them off, and with an upward sweeping movement caught the arm of the attack with his knee, immobilizing the man's arm between his thigh and calf.

"This is called 'snake immobilization' in karate." Paul said.

As the guy with the chain was trying to punch him, Paul released the hand of guy with the sword and he crouched low down. The guy with the chain was unable to stop the chain, and then the chain hit the second guy and bloodied his fellow attacker. With a terrible pain, the guy screamed and fell down.

Without losing time Paul challenged the remaining guy with a sword. It was easy for Paul to catch the armed hand of the guy and hold it in a painful position.

"I have made an exception, and I will break your arm." Paul said.

"Nu. Nu . . ." Screaming the guy begged Paul.

At the same time the guy with the chain was trying to attack again but Paul put the guy with the immobilized hand in front of him.

Quickly, walking in the same direction, Drina said, "Okay, Paul game over. You won. Now release the boy."

Paul started laughing in that unnatural way. "Drina, you are not the one who commands here. Don't try to stop me with your meager powers." Saying this he started pushing in the hand of the boy, and his arm started to pop. The guy screamed desperately.

"I like this sound Drina." When the guys hand broke, Paul released him.

"As your participation in this fighting camp is poor, I suggest you liberate the field; it's a no woman show," and Paul started laughing again.

He moves his eyes to the last guy, the one with the chain.

"You know I always told my fellow karate mates that the metal chain is a very good weapon . . . if they know how to use it. Do you know how?"

The guy was confidently playing with the chain and moved closer to Paul.

"Okay, you don't know too much about the metal chain. But I will show you."

Paul twisted his body in the front of the guy with the metal chain and with a precise movement he caught the chain. After that with a quick and strong move he was able to disarm the guy. As he lost his equilibrium, the guy stumbled a couple steps backwards. Armed now with the chain, Paul started to play with the chain. Even in the Kung Fu movies, I have never seen somebody playing like this with a chain. He was totally confident in his movement, and at the same time he jumped in the air. The spectacle was quite amazing. Finally Paul stopped and gave the chain to the guy.

"Your turn now, try the same moves as I did."

The guy was unable to speak as he was completely impressed by Paul's chain demonstration. He feels on his knees to beg Paul with an apology.

"Sorry man, but you dared to attack me," Paul said, "According to the rule, I have to put you in pain. I challenge you to fight."

I was so distressed, it seemed like enough and I wanted to stop the bloody spectacle, I ran in front of Paul and said "that's enough Paul." It was clear he was winning and no one else needed to be hurt.

He was looking at me disappointed. He was ready to badly hurt the guy and I had to interrupt him.

"I thought I said no women here."

Ignoring me, he went towards the guy who was slouching from fear. Paul forced him to rise up and he immobilized him. I was quite shocked how evil Paul could be. Chlorinda was right, he is so cruel. Without saying anything, near me Drina was looking at Paul who was holding the other guy.

Paul called Drina's name, "Driiina . . . . !"

Paul was opening his mouth wide, as though he was going to bite the guys neck. Or . . . like a vampire he was going to suck the guy's blood.

Sadly Dina smiled. She came to me and she took my hand.

"Welcome to my village Laura. I will be your teacher for a couple of weeks."

*   *   *

Drina lives in a nice big house. I cannot compare it to the twin sister's house. Maybe Drina's house is little bit smaller. However, it is medium sized for the village she lives in. "I live alone. I don't need a bigger house."

She showed me around the room, and to the bathroom.

She asked me if I was hungry. But I was not hungry at all, especially after watching the fighting with Paul. All I wanted was to go to my room . . . and to hide until tomorrow.

I had a good sleep, and in the morning I felt quite lazy. I was awoken by the birds chirping. Downstairs was Drina waiting for me.

"I know that you like bananas in the morning," she said, "please have one, and I would like to invite you to join me for a walk in the woods."

"How about a coffee?" I asked Drina.

"Yes, I have that type of coffee you guys use so much in Canada. Paul gave me some for my birthday . . . ." she was like dreaming couple seconds, "I always take a cup of coffee and go in the morning for a walk in the woods."

The coffee was very good. These guys know that I like dark coffee; no sugar or cream.

Drina's house is quite close to the woods. In less than fifteen minutes we reach the woods, it was a nice morning for a walk.

"I found it very relaxing to go walking in the woods in the morning," Drina said, "I hope you will like this too."

"Yes," I said, "I love the woods. In Canada there is a large section of woods around my cabin."

"With the dream catchers made by your wizard, Paul told me that he is a strong one . . . ."

"Yes, he might be. Maybe one time I will invite him here, or look . . . how about you come to visit me there? We can go and walk in the woods there too."

"I would like that very much Laura. I think you are feeling like me, a strong attraction to the woods. A strong attraction to . . . the dark places."

"Yes. That is true."

"I hear Laura that your area of woods is quite large and so is your property. I think that is wonderful." Drina was looking with admiration around the woods. "Here in this woods, lots of people come to me. Sometimes I start to dream, I am not too old and I like to dream, or to do some concentration exercises and people can come around. They disturb me . . . . I felt this a couple of years ago, after my husband died and my kids were gone. In that time I was not comfortable meeting people in the woods; there I looked to find some silence. Now, I am starting to be comfortable accidentally meeting people and saying 'hello'. Other things like concentrations and day dreaming, I do this only inside my house."

"You are not afraid to walk alone in the woods?" I asked Drina.

"No, it is not a big danger. It might be in the winter when the wild animals can be hungry and they can attack. Other people walk through here quite often and the wild animals avoid them."

"How about you, Laura?"

"Well, in my woods there might be some danger. There are lots of wolves, and they can attack. In fact they attacked me once . . . I always have a gun with me. I am able to defend myself."

"You are a strong woman Laura."

We walked for a while, admiring the scenery. The grass was growing in some places quite tall. I felt myself very relaxed.

"Drina what do you think about all this? All the stuff that was happening at the last incantation?"

"Well, as Paul said we all miss Raluka. She was doing so great an analysis for us . . . . there is an entity which we woke up."

"Do you think it is . . . Dracula?"

"Even Paul is not sure. We can admit it is connected with Dracula . . . but how much? Is it his spirit? Can it become a vampire again?" She was shaking her head. "Nobody knows yet."

I watch Drina. She still looks nice, her hair is long and still blond. She was almost always dressed in the gypsy dress. It is unbelievable how much power her small body can hide.

"How about fate Drina? If you guys are so good at seeing the future, in the premonitions you can see who it is or what will be next."

"Maybe or maybe it is recommended that we have just to do what we have to do . . . . I don't need you for example to foresee my future . . . as you did for the twins."

"But they taught me how to do it . . . ."

"There is something diabolic. Maybe much more complicated than the entity . . . ."

"I don't understand you Drina."

"I am still shocked about Nelu's fate," Drina said. "Paul premonitions were so exact. If Nelu was coming to the group incantations he was going to die too. Just to test all this he decided not to participate and he died. I think that even if the sisters decided not to participate they were going to die in the night." She paused. We found a fallen log and we sat down there. We still had some coffee in our cups.

"I don't know what fear is since I was a child. Now I have fear. I have a sensation like we are like some chess pieces on a chess table. It is like there is someone smiling and he is playing with our lives."

I saw on her face that she was sad.

"Our lives . . ."

She paused, again quite sad.

"And do you know what? Paul is somehow involved in this."

"Oh Drina . . . we all are involved in this. When we decided to do the group incantation, when we signed the table, when we started to light the first candle of the circle we . . . are involved."

"I mean he looks like he is able to influence the future events."

"But this is not possible. You now that is from millennia even in your tradition, we can call it 'Ursita', or fate; but it cannot be influenced."

"How you can be so sure?" Drina asked watching me with interest.

"I don't know . . . look Drina I am so sorry about your guys. I am so sorry for what happened yesterday."

Drina was put up her hand in a disapproving gesture.

"I am guilty too. I paid these guys to fight against Paul."

"So . . . did you intend to kill him?"

"No. I was hoping I would hurt him, and after I could force him to tell me all that he knows." She said somehow forcing the words. "I did not realize he was so strong . . . and did you see the way he was moving . . . It is too quick for a human being . . ."

I was quite confused. I thought maybe the best thing was to change the subject.

"Drina I have to tell you that I admire you very much. How did you gain your kinesthetic powers?"

Drina was smiling and I saw that it is a favorite subject for her.

"I think that I was born with these powers."

"How did you discover that?"

"I was in these woods. I had just a couple of years. I was enjoying to walk in the woods by myself. My parents were insisting that I not go alone in the woods but I always found a way to hide and to go anyway. Finally they accepted that I was going. One day, I was running around this place. I was lying down trying to relax after the run. After a couple of minutes I heard a snarl; it was a wolf. I saw that he was coming towards me. I remember my people taught me that if a dog tries to attack you, don't run. You have a better chance to escape by staying down on the ground. So I did. But that wolf continued to snarl and to come towards me. I was so desperate and I felt I had to do something to defend myself. But even with a gun, as I was a child I don't think I was able to defend myself. I remembered when my people were sacrificing a pig or a lamb. I was always curious to see the heart of the animal. I looked the wolf directly in the eyes. I raised my hands in its direction, and I tried to imagine that I could see its heart inside of its body. Once I saw its heart I tried to control it. I thought if I am able to smash it, then the animal will die, and I can save myself. Otherwise the wolf will kill me; one way, or another."

"And?" I asked the small woman.

Smiling at me she simply answered. "I was successful."

*　　*　　*

Drina was relating to me stories about her life, her family and so on. Her husband died four years ago from cancer. She has three sons and all of them live in Spain. She visits them quite often. Also from time to time, they visit her. However, a couple times per week they chat over the phone or over the Internet. She is quite connected with her sons. All three of them are married and she has two nieces and a nephew.

She was quite proud when she was telling me about her family. I really like Drina. She is a sweet lady. Even if we had only two days together we were very attracted to each other. We just had our coffee in the woods. And we were standing near the cut log where Drina said it was the first time that she observed her kinesthetic powers. We were sitting back to back each one of us watching the other half of the woods.

"I think around you right now is a strong question. " Drina said.

"What do you mean?" I asked her.

"We were admiring your abilities to read the future, now everyone is waiting for me to see if you have kinesthetic powers."

"Do . . . do you think I have them?"

"It is a gift. I have to check to see if you have it. Even if you have some abilities I can help you to improve them. I hope you have these . . . abilities."

I was very excited about the possibility of having kinesthetic powers. It was a possibility which can open lots of doors . . .

"Why you don't start to test me Drina? I am so excited to see what was inside me . . . . What I can do with my latent energies . . . ."

She did not answer. I thought I would have to turn to her but there was an equilibrium already established between us and between us and the woods, between us and the wind; between us and spirits or other entities which were here, at this moment of time and space.

As though in a dream Drina started to speak:

"The woods . . . . think about how many trees are in these woods, think about how many lives are in these woods . . . we will choose a leaf, and we will try our kinesthetic powers on it. It can give you today a strong happiness or . . . a strong disappointment . . . But, remember, one way or another I will be with you."

She paused. I thought about her words. Sometimes in our life we are unable to choose one way or another. We took a coin and according to what side we flipped we will choose the first or the second way. Starting with that time our lives might be so different. And now a leaf . . . . trying my powers on it. I will know soon if I do or don't have kinesthetic powers. Soon the world will be so different for me. And all this will start from a leaf, from a tree, from the woods. It was like I was staying for a couple of moments on this stage . . . on this unsure, undefined stage.

In my life I am always in a big rush, always in a hurry. If the speed limit was 110, I would push it up to 150. Always in my life I tended to push the accelerator. Now I want to stay here with my back to Drina, contemplating the woods together. Thinking to ourselves, about our friends who have died, thinking about the future and the next things that are going to happen to us.

We were sitting for a while . . . in a good harmony. Finally we decided that was time to move on to the next stage of our life.

"Yes its time." Drina said understanding my impatience. "You can go to choose a leaf."

I was walking around a bit. There were a lot of leaves, I was quite undecided about which one to choose . . . and which one would show me my future. Finally I chose one. It was a big leaf, full with life. I was praying to the leaf 'please show me that I am powerful. Please show me that I have kinesthetic powers.'

"Now, set the leaf on top of the log." Drina told me. I did as she told me.

We were standing up watching the log with the leaf on top. Drina was a small woman and I was a quite tall in comparison. Both of use had long hair, but hers was blond mine and mine is very dark and curly. Usually she holds her hair in a braid at the back, but now it is long down her back. A calm wind was easily blowing on our hair. I thought we looked like two sorceresses.

"One way or another I would let you know . . . I will be with you," Drina said. Saying this she raised her arm and the leaf was rising up from the log under the effect of the kinesthetic power that Drina applied.

"Now it is your turn," Drina said. "Lets try it without any training and we will see what happens."

* * *

Three days have passed since I came by myself into the woods to try and hold the same leaf. Despite my concentration the leaf is still there on the top of the log. I am very frustrated about all this trying in vain. Today I stood up for more than four hours in front of the log. I felt quite exhausted, and so disappointed that I fell on my knees. I almost started to cry, and I fell forwards on my elbow.

Drina came up to me, and in a friendly voice she told me,"Lets try it together."

She put her palm on the top of mine. It was like her magnetism penetrated my hand, and the kinesthetic force was transmitted to the leaf. The leaf was standing in the air. We tried this couple times. I was quite embarrassed, when she was took off her hand the leaf simply fell down.

"We can try it a different way. I will try to send some energy to your brain and you will try to send it to the leaf."

I felt something hot in my brain. I tried to be comfortable with it. Afterwards I rose my hand upwards and I was focused on the leaf. And . . . the leave stood up in the air. We practiced like this for the rest of the day.

At night I was not able to sleep until late. Her house was quite large and I was aware that it was only the two of us. I stepped into her room and because her bed was quite large there was room for me to sleep too.

*   *   *

"It is also my job to teach you magical attacks from outside of the magical circle."

We were in the upper level of her house, it is a large and dark room. Exactly in the middle of the room, Drina decided that we have to create the magical circle exactly in the middle of that room. We started to light the candles saying the associated incantations and making the concentrations.

"Here we are, according to our powers and the intensity of the opposite forces from outside we are supposed to be protected now. Hold on to all your energies. You will create a balance with your powers. Soon it will feel like all is natural, you will be very confident being held by this concentration. As you have new reserves you can go on doing some work."

I focused on Drina's words.

"For example we can fly to that incantation place *near Dracula's castle*. Or if someone caused some upset for us we can attack him now or . . ."

"Let's go *near Dracula's castle*," I proposed to Drina.

"Okay," Drina said, "Sit down in a comfortable position. Think about your body becoming lighter, and lighter until it is light like a feather. It might take you some time."

She became silent as she was concentrating on it.

"Now together let's ask the wind elements, vintoases to come over and to help us to fly. Say, the following spell: '*my body is light as a feather. You vintoase take the feather and hold it above the house.*'"

We started to say the spelling together. We did it a couple of times. I felt the wind elements taking my soft body. They were rising up around my body in the room and they were taking it out of the house by the open window. Like a light wind the vintoases were rising my body above the house. I saw Drina's village, almost all the people were sleeping. In a corner of the street, a guy and a girl were kissing. I was quite impressed about the capacity of this magic.

"Please focus on what you are doing." I heard Drina's voice near me. "Now think about how to control the vintoases. Have a look when you are above the village, but don't let the small things penetrate you. "

I started to do some circles around the house. I observed that I had become quite familiar with this magic.

"Now," Drina said, "we are in the south here, the Dracula's castle is in the north. We always have to give the vintoase a direction. Also be careful they are strong elements. When you ready follow me."

After a short time I heard Drina saying "*You vintoase, with the power of the wind bring me in North, near Dracula's castle*".

I took a couple of moments and afterwards I said the same words as Drina, "You vintoase, with the power of the wind bring me in North, near Dracula's castle."

Instantly, I felt an unbelievable acceleration on my body. It was like I was staying in the same place and the land below me was racing towards me. It was quite scary in that moment. It was only a moment later and I felt my body go soft. From the air I was able to see the ruins of Dracula's castle.

I looked around to our incantation place. Our place *near Dracula's castle.*

I saw the abyss at one edge of this place. I saw the small path we used to walk up to the place. I was admiring the silence of the night. It was so beautiful, so silent, and so magical. Until suddenly I heard a terrible scream. It was quite familiar to me now . . . it was the scream of that strange creature or entity, which dared to attack us in the incantation night.

I heard Drina's voices. She was speaking quite quickly:

"Say with me and focus on what you are saying, '*You vintoase, with the power of the wind bring me back at the south where my body is*'."

It was brutal this time. It was like the wind elements were perturbed by something . . . . It was like a crash over Drina's house, through the window and back to my body. Near me I heard Drina breathing quite agitatedly. We shut off the magical circle and we decided to go bed. I felt myself feeling quite good having Drina's small and soft body near me.

*   *   *

"How could that be possible?" Chlorinda asked.

It was almost afternoon when we woke up. We decided to have our coffee in Drina's living room. Drina asked Paul, Halibarda and Chlorinda for a web conference. In her huge living room she had a video projector, so we were quite comfortable staying in our chairs and seeing the web participants. Also, our webcam was properly adjusted and they were able to see us too.

"How might this be even possible?" Chlorinda was obviously nervous about her question.

"Don't be ridiculous Chlorinda!" Paul replied. "They were flying around Dracula's castle and they were going to be attacked by . . . that entity. It was quite predictable. Oh God . . . I miss Raluka . . ."

Near Paul, Halibarda was lighting a cigarette. "And why is this thing so impossible for you Chlorinda?" Paul was looking at Halibarda. Her cigarette smoke was disturbing him. "I know my cigarette smoke is disturbing you but . . ." Halibarda tried to defend herself.

"Not only is the smoke disturbing me Halibarda, so is your question." Paul said quite nervously.

As though she was successfully making Paul and Halibarda feud, Chlorinda started laughing.

"Okay, tell her you were there too Chlorinda." Paul said in a harsh voice. Chlorinda laugh was cold.

"How do you know I was there?" she curiously asked.

"You are very predictable Chlorinda. I told you that you wouldn't succeed especially with me. I hope you will deeply reflect on this. I am monitoring you, and you will not do crazy stuff. It is not the time for that." Paul said raising his voice.

"Okay, Okay . . ." Chlorinda tried to make peace, "I was at that *place near Dracula's castle* last night."

"Maybe you were there at a different time Chlorinda," I tried to clarify the situation.

"I had been there all night." Chlorinda said looking ironically at me.

"Oh . . ." I was reflecting, and looking at Drina. "I did not know that . . ."

Paul was starting to speak on the phone. He was stepping away from the web cam for a couple of moments. Finally he came back with her cell on the speaker.

"We have a new member at this conference, she will speak on the phone so we can hear and she can hear us. We are listening to you Ivanka."

"Just a question Drina, what time was it when you was *near Dracula's castle?*"

"Maybe around two at night."

"That is interesting." Ivanka said. "At that time I had a vision, a bad man with his month full of blood was running around that place . . ."

"So what?" Halibarda asked.

"That is the . . . how do you say it . . . ." Ivanka was looking for the word.

"Entity." Chlorinda was showing her disapproval with Ivanka's intervention.

"That was the entity that bothered you last night." Ivanka concluded.

"But this is not the first time that I have done this . . ." Drina tried to protest.

"I am not addressing you Drina. I am speaking to Laura!"

*   *   *

We decide for the next day and night not to do any magic. It was time for us to recover our powers. We were cooking together and we had a gorgeous meal. Like most Romanian ladies I have met, Drina is a very good cook. She made meatball soup, it was quite sour but very tasty. Like the roast we had the gorgeous 'mititei' and lots of salad with veggies from Drina's garden. I found it to be very organic. As it was a warm summer day we decided to drink beer. It was a gorgeous day, no wind blowing. We were staying on Drina's patio in the backyard under the shade of an old tree. The nice meal and gorgeous day helped me to relax from the terrible things that happened last night.

It was more than an hour since we were chatting about us, about our life. I found that Drina was very interested in my cabin. She likes the idea of living alone in the middle of the woods. Actually she told me that she was quite confident in her kinesthetic powers, she was feeling quite a bit stronger . . . until a couple days ago with Paul's demonstration.

"Sometimes . . . I feel that something is wrong with that guy." Drina said taking a huge sip from her beer.

"I don't know what I can say. Maybe he is an example for us, he looks to like he is quite strong and . . ." I tried to calm down Drina.

"Laura . . . he tried to bite the neck of one of the guys . . . like a vampire . . . ." Drina said looking deeply at me, imploring me. "Please understand the gravity of the situation."

I took both her hands, and I looked at her. She has nice black eyes almost like the twin sisters Gina and Geta.

"He was joking, his intention was to scare you, but don't let him to frighten you."

"I am sorry Laura but I am afraid that things are quite complicated . . . . the twin sisters predicted that there is a connection between him and Dracula."

"In what way?"

"We don't know."

"I saw that around me people believe that there is a connection between me and Dracula too . . . but Drina . . ." I touched her long blonde hair, "please lets focus on this gorgeous day for now."

We paused a couple of long moments of silence to enjoy the day. It was quite hot.

"I think it is around 38 C." Drina said, "in the middle of the day like this the people stop their land work. It is recommended to work only in the early morning and late evening."

"I saw that the people are doing a very good job on their gardens."

"Yes," Drina approved, "their vegetables will be organic. However for some of them it is a source of income . . . . Sometimes the only source of income." She bitterly smiled to me. "Paul told me that in your town you have street people or homeless people?" She was looking at me.

"Yes, but they are somehow different from what I saw here . . ." I said, and I thought it was better not to give any examples.

"Can you give me an example?"

I took a deep sip from my beer. After I looked at my beer glass I decided to empty it.

"Would you like another beer?" I asked Drina.

"Yes please." she answered me sweetly smiling.

I come back with beers. I filled up my glass and Drina's glass and I took another deep sip.

"Well . . . regarding your question. I once saw a homeless man collecting empty bottles, he had a lot, and he was talking on his cell phone. You know, having a cell phone is quite expensive in Canada. Look here, I took a picture of him." And I showed her on my cell the picture I took. She started to laugh; a very crystalline laugh. And I laughed too. Finally, I asked Drina:

"Drina, I need to know more about the magical stuff."

"Like what?" She was looking at me surprised.

"If yesterday that entity was able to catch me . . . . What was going to happen?"

She was looking outside, avoiding answering my question.

"To understand better let's think about what was going to happen, think about if he broke your hand; you would feel the pain. A terrible pain, as your bones broke. No doctor will be able to cure you. Even if you take pain killers they would not help you. And that is because this time the pain comes from directly in your brain."

This possibility created a big fear. I will have to take more cautions in the future.

"But how about if he caught me and kept me with him?"

"Then your body will be like a vegetable; possibly for the rest of your life." She gave me a bitter look.

*   *   *

The next day we were walking in the woods very early in the morning. We came up to our cut log. We somehow recovered after the relaxing day yesterday.

"You said, I will be a vegetable if he caught me . . ."

"Yes, suppose that evil entity caught you. That means your spirit is not with your body, you are flying. It is called 'the etheric stage' in our club terminology. As the entity is keeping your soul from going back to your body you will be a vegetable"

"Does this happen in these situations?"

"Yes, here in Romania we have many of these situations. A similar thing might happen when a witch is working up an entity, and that entity affects her, or it will start to posses her . . . she will look crazy."

"For this reason I have to take cautions," I added.

"That's right," Drina said. "It is a dangerous situation for a beginner like you. "

"How about an experienced sorceress?"

"The first thing I have to tell you is that an experienced sorceress will know first the limits. He is more aware about the forces that he is dealing with and he will act with caution."

She was looking at me, "now can we start to practice with the leaf as you learn this exercise? Or the kinesthetic abilities, which is how it is correctly called."

"Yes Drina. We can start to practice the leaf. But . . . how can it be possible that Chlorinda claims that she was there and she saw nothing. Instead, Ivanka who was not there, felt . . . something," I tried to debate the subject.

"Unfortunately I don't know the answer . . . yet," Drina said, looking down embarrassed. "Chlorinda is a very strong witch. But sometimes she makes mistakes. Ivanka has a terrible sensibility. I think Paul is considering that she is stronger than Chlorinda."

"But, you know Drina . . . that woman hates me."

"No. She is quite rude, I know that. But she doesn't hate you."

"At our first lesson she had a terrible reaction."

"We know that . . . She was quite shocked about a possible connection between you and Dracula."

"But . . . you said Paul had this connection too . . . why doesn't she have this reaction with him and she is experiencing this kind of reaction with me?"

"Because there might be different kinds of connections. You might be connected in one way and with Paul in another way." Drina was looking at me.

"You mean my way; my connection with Dracula is bad?"

"Not necessarily."

"I am sorry Drina but I don't understand."

"Okay, stop a man in the street, in any town of Romanian and ask him about Dracula or Vlad the Impaler. He will tell you that, he was a good man; they will tell you that it would be very useful and welcome if he comes back. He was a gorgeous king; even if he killed thousands of his own people. We would consider that he did it to serve justice."

She paused giving me some time to think. "For example, if Ivanka felt there was a connection between you and the one called 'Radu the Handsome' you will be bad connection for Ivanka."

"I am sorry Drina . . . who was this Radu the handsome?"

"He was Dracula's younger brother. He was the one who betrayed his brother. For this reason, Ivanka, Paul, Chlorinda and all Romanians hate him."

"And . . . do you hate him to?"

Drina was taking a huge breath and after that she strongly answered:

"YES"

* * *

Still we have not a clear conclusion regarding my kinesthetic powers. Or it might be that Drina doesn't like to tell me that I have no kinesthetic powers.

"I have a question for you Drina."

"Please Laura, ask me."

"If there is a connection between me and . . . Radu the Handsome . . ."

"Yes . . ."

"And . . . . if you guys hate me so much, are you are going to punish me?

"Oh . . . don't be ridiculous Laura. Firstly, it is not clear whether or not you are an incarnation of Radu the Handsome. But let's assume it is true. In another life you were him, and you accepted the sultan favors . . . ."

"What?" I reacted.

"Laura . . . we are speaking about things happening a hundred years ago . . . . But we know that he had a relationship with the sultan. He was strongly motivated because this relationship made him fight against his brother and against his country."

"Unbelievable . . . this thing is not written in history."

"It is," Drina answered calmly to me, " . . . betraying your brother, created an unbelievable order in his country, because you are in a relationship with the sultan . . . ."

"But what kind of relationship are you talking about?"

"Well, think about how the sultan was calling him 'Radu the Handsome' . . . . It is said that he enjoys having relations with guys."

"Was he gay?"

"However, if you were weak in another life, now as a reincarnation you are aware about your old mistakes and you try to correct them. We do believe in evolution."

"It looks like a complicate situation."

Drina was nicely smiling to me.

"It might be a complicated situation. But I am here to help you."

I smiled at her too.

"Also . . . I would like to please ask you for something Laura."

"Yes?"

"If it happens, and I die at the next facing of the entity . . . I would like you to be the one who throws my body into the abyss."

"Drina . . . I . . ."

"Please . . . just say 'yes'. It might not happen of course. But just in case, I need YOU to do it."

"Okay . . . Yes."

I tried to change this subject dramatically.

"What do we have to practice today?"

"We will try to fly little bit."

"Okay, but . . . let's not fly very close to that place *near Dracula's castle.*"

"That's okay."

*   *   *

We started the night training again. It is difficult to do magic during the day. All the human beings are awake, and the animals too;

so much life, energy, and activity around. We try to do something, and it is easy to interfere with their energy. Or their energy might disturb us and we might disturb them.

Drina arranged the room, and put tables close to the corners of the room. Each table has been filled with empty bottles.

"We will start practicing the attack today." Drina said.

"I saw that you are quite good in manipulating the wind elements. And that is good. Soon you will be able to command other elements. Practice today is quite easy. We will raise the magical circle and we will think those bottles are the enemies. We will try to break them using the wind elements. Of course we can break them using for example the fire elements, but I don't want my house burning." And she was laughing with her crystalline laugh.

"Don't forget that your mental power is involved." She smiled to me, "Do you have any questions?"

"Yes. I thought all that we are doing here is quite passive, the only exception is your kinesthetic powers."

"Well you're quite right. But now it is the time to do some active stuff. Let's try it."

We were standing again on Drina's upper living room. At the north a dark candle, a red candle at the south, at the east the blue candle and the green candle at the west. We lighted them saying the corresponding incantations and making the right concentrations. I looked around me as I was focusing on the all possible attacks from the east, south, north or west. I was also aware of all the bottles on each table. I started my concentration on the wind elements. I was increasing their strength. Near me I felt Drina using her kinesthetic powers to smash the first bottle. I was taking a wind element and I sent it to the next bottle. With a loud noise the bottle fell down from the table and broke.

"You might tend to break more bottles when they are together but I would like that in this exercise we do it one by one." Drina told me. In less than one hour all the bottles were broken. We continued the practice during the next few days.

In the woods, we went near a small lake. We placed targets that looked like torches with inflammable materials; they were placed almost 10 meters distance from the center of the magical circle. The exercise was to light them. On the second night we lit them, and after that using the water elements we put them out. Usually we practiced in the morning.

"I think you are quite good Laura," Drina said. "Maybe you have to go on to the next teaching to be ready for the next group incantations."

"Next teaching? Do you have any idea who will be my next teacher?"

"You have to be extremely careful with the next teacher." We heard Paul's voice. Good Lord, this guy was here all night long watching and observing us. We were not aware of it. Drina was also surprised to find this out.

"That's right," We heard another voice, and I realize that was Halibarda's voice. She came close to us making theatric gestures with her. "Good evening girls, and good practice by the way. However, don't let yourself be turned off by your new teacher."

"Especially by her green eyes." Paul said.

"She has such green eyes . . ." Halibarda completed Paul statement.

"Like poison."

"She is poison."

"She is Chlorinda"

*   *   *

Later on in the afternoon we were on the main floor of Drina's living room having coffee together. Vlad has joined us, he was their driver. He was so happy to see me again, and I was happy as well.

"You are good guys," I said, "I did not observe you last night"

"We are very thankful about your progress Laura." Paul said.

"Your progresses are remarkable." Halibarda added.

"She was working very hard. I would suggest that she keep practicing by herself." Drina was looking at me with a protective gaze.

"Thanks Drina. You are a very good teacher." I said.

"Your report Drina," Paul asked without any kind of introduction.

'Well . . . as I said, she was working hard and . . ."

"Are you drunk Drina?" Brutally, Paul interrupted her. "What I am wanting from you are only a couple of words. In fact the answer, does she have or not have kinesthetic abilities?"

Drina looked a little bit confused.

"Paul, until now she did not prove kinesthetic abilities . . . . Sorry if I disappointed you guys."

It was a cold moment. Paul gazed at the coffee cup in front of him. Suddenly the cup exploded. Vlad reacted by standing up.

"For god sakes Paul, control yourself . . ." Nobody moved, and he brought napkins from the kitchen. He cleaned the mess from the broken cup. Then he looked at Paul. "If you pledge to me that you will not break your cup again, I can give you another one."

Paul was laughing as though this was a joke. "Okay, you again Vlad, I like your humor on this matter. I would appreciate if you can give me a cup of coffee."

"Well, speaking about teacher, as we mentioned last night it might be a good idea to have Chlorinda as a teacher." Halibarda said.

"Are you sure guys?" Drina asked, she intended to say more but Paul was gazing at her, she decided it was better to be quiet.

Vlad was back with a new cup of coffee for Paul. Paul was smiling to Vlad.

"So . . . your new teacher is Chlorinda. She is not a pleasant person and also not thrilled to have you as a student." Paul said.

"If she thinks like this, I would rather pass." I tried to defend myself.

"But it will be good for you to have training with her." Halibarda said

"And we would like you to spy on her." Paul was smiling sweetly to me.

"W . . . what?" I was quite confused.

"Paul!" Halibarda said warning him, "Well . . . Laura things are not like they seem. She always has been a rebel. Of course as you will be in her house you can see what she is doing, the way she is doing her magic and we would appreciate if you could share it with us."

Paul was smiling

"Yes, we will appreciate if you can share with us what you observe while you are there." Paul was quite amused about this situation.

"Well . . . I don't know . . . . As long as she will tell me that is not a secret . . ."

I saw all of them including Vlad watching each other.

"Laura," Drina said in a low voice, "she will try to turn you against us." Drina's words were full of fear.

"But . . . why?'

"As I said Chlorinda has always been a rebel in our club and in all her life. This is her style." Halibarda was consistent.

"Because she is poison!" Paul screamed in the room. "And let's make this short. I brought you here from Canada. You are supposed to be on my side not with that bitch."

* * *

Halibarda decided to stay a couple of days with Drina. So in the car it was only Paul, Vlad and I; Vlad was driving the car.

Paul was tired and he decided to have a nap. I understood the terms of the spying they wanted from me. Paul is mostly interested in seeing what Chlorinda's feelings are regarding the remaining members of the group. Halibarda was mostly interested to knowing what Chlorinda was doing with her magical stuff. Even Drina . . . she was interested in how you can act to hypnotize a human being when he shows opposition. I can see that they don't know the limits to Chlorinda's powers. Finally Paul woke up.

'So . . . what do you think about Drina?" He said being disturbed by the day light.

"What more do you want to know about her? I already told you she is a good teacher, she . . . . ."

"Is she a lesbian?" Paul interrupted me.

"W . . . what?' I asked shocked about his observation.

"Dear we are from Canada and we are quite permissive on these kinds of matter. Raluka put a question mark on Drina's profile regarding this matter. I would like to complete Raluka's data base with the right information."

I decided not to answer Paul's challenge. I was also quite embarrassed by Vlad. Maybe he will think the same thing about me . . .

"Don't be afraid Laura," Paul continued, "Vlad is bisexual too."

Immediately Vlad pulled the car on the right side of the road and started to scream Paul.

"Hey! Have you completely lost your mind with your fucking magical stuff?"

Paul was looking at Vlad. Immediately Vlad covered his eyes and tried to defend himself from being hypnotized by Paul.

In a normal voice Paul said. "I did not try anything bad towards you Vlad. How could I? Instead, I am doing a normal thing. You have to understand that is Chlorinda, and she might say bad stuff about you, and Laura has to be advised."

"Okay, Okay . . ." Vlad said holding his head with his arms. He looked straight at me. "Look Laura, maybe I did some fun stuff when I was younger, but . . . I am a different person now."

"I believe you Vlad." I said almost immediately. After that I asked Paul.

"If Chlorinda is such a . . . bitch, why am I supposed to visit her?"

Smiling to me Paul said, "Because . . . you need to know how the other side is." After a short pause he said "ah . . . one more thing . . . . Sometimes when you are with Chlorinda, it will be very possible for you to face fear. In this situation you need to have your own fear litany. Or . . . I have one and I can teach you if you want."

He was fixing his gaze on me. As I said nothing he continued.

"I would recommend you to say something like this:

I am in the evil valley. The danger surrounds me from front and behind, from laterals, from above and below. I am in the death's valley; but I will not fear by the evil."

I said it a couple of times in my mind, and I found that it helped me. I found it was so nice to hear it from Paul, and have him tell me the prayer.

"Thanks Paul, it really helps me. When I focus on its words I feel like I find energies to recover myself."

I rehearsed it again and again in my mind. Also I reanalyzed its words . . .

"But, why did you say that when I am with Chlorinda I might need this fear litany?"

He was smiling at me,

"Take it as though you might be very fearful and might need to recover yourself. You might be in danger and you can recover yourself by saying this fear litany. I think it is essential to show strength on these moments."

"But what kind of danger can I can face from Chlorinda? In what kind of situations would I need the fear litany?"

He continued to smile cruelly at me,

"Maybe like being in a room with very venomous snakes"

Chapter 15

The nature likes entropy.
-Laura

I could see that Chlorinda's house was quite similar to Paul's, maybe a little bigger; but near a river and isolated. All of the other houses in the village were in rows except for hers. Actually it is the same river that flows by Paul's house. He explained me that his house is downstream from the river by Chlorinda's.

"It is a big advantage for me," Paul said to me once, "when we are doing lots of magical stuff using the river. What she sends, I can see downstream."

Vlad explained me that Chlorinda used to have a house nearby in the same village as the lovely twice sisters, but she was in conflict with her neighbors, and always in conflict with someone in the village. The reaction of her gypsy neighbors was quite violent. She was never afraid of them, but because she decided to do some personal business which was going to disturb the village she decided to sell her villa and to build a house similar to Paul's. Paul recommended his architect and as she had all the necessary money her new villa was ready in a couple of months.

The road to her house is not paved. As I looked around I saw a couple of dogs running nervously around our car. Vlad stopped the car near her house.

"I don't want to go inside." Vlad declared. "May I ask you, please, Paul be as quick as you can?"

"You will not stay with me?" I asked Vlad.

"No, I hate this woman," Vlad said disgusted.

"Okay, I will do it as quickly as I can."

Paul and I walked towards her house. Behind us the dogs were running and barking, by now they had reached the car. They were running around the car, continuing to bark.

"Crazy dogs," I said.

"Yes, they are a still problem in various parts of the country as they have no owner. These strays breed and breed, they grow in numbers. If one of them gets nervous, the others will do the same. I know cases where people were gravely bitten and they died shortly after in hospital."

"But, Paul these dogs look quite bad . . . ."

"Yes, they don't have an owner, so they are almost always hungry. However now they are, for some reason, more under control compared to a couple of years ago . . ."

"Paul, Vlad looks like he is having problems. Look there . . ."

I saw another dogs running; now they were almost ten dogs around his car. The dogs looked terrible. Because they were nervous the drool was flowing from their mouths. It was a terrific spectacle. I thought if I was in the car, isolated, like Vlad and I would be very scared.

From around the river at least seven more dogs were running in our direction. We turned back to the car; the dogs around the car reacted to the new dogs that were arriving from the river. The dogs were disturbed by our approach to Chlorinda's house. It was really scary when I saw nearly twenty big dogs agitated and running in our direction. I thought they could kill us!

"Paul, Paul! What we can do?" I was so afraid. The dogs were approaching so quickly I barely had time to register the depth of my fear. Still I had time to observe that Paul was not scared at all. The dogs were just a couple of steps from us, their barking so very loud. I was terrorized!

"Laura, lay down!" Paul commanded me with a relaxed voice.

The first dog jumped into the air, trying to catch Paul's neck, but with a quick move Paul caught the dog from air and he twisted the dog's neck. He threw the dog on the next group of arrivers. For a moment the dogs slowed and they made a circle around us, they continued their ferocious barking as the circle closed in around us. Paul started to laugh; the same evil laugh from hell. His laugh was louder than the barking of the dogs that were so extremely close now. Intimidated by Paul's laughing they began to decrease the intensity of their barking. They were still very agitated, but I saw that they started calm. One dog, it looked like the biggest one of the group, stepped up to Paul, barking and moving with the intent to bite. He did not dare attack but he was very angry. I have never in my life seen such anger in a dog. Without a care for the dog's ferocity or danger Paul began patting the dog's head with his palm.

"You are a little Chihuahua," Paul said, and immediately the dog was silent. The other dogs also became nearly silent, but I saw in their eyes the agitation remained.

"It's all okay. You can stand up now Laura. Now, let's go to see what Chlorinda is doing." Without ringing the bell Paul opened Chlorinda's gate and went into the house. I was still afraid of the dogs and stayed close to Paul.

Chlorinda was at her kitchen table staring at us, smoking from a long cigarette and drinking from a large glass. From the smell, I thought she was drinking tzuica.

"I hope this is the last time you play with me like this. And say 'thank you' because I did not react as I could have in this kind of situation!" Paul said angrily.

"Thank you," Chlorinda said simply. She did not offer us a chair or a drink.

"Look, try for once in your life to be a nice person. Try with Laura."

She was analyzing me with her green eyes.

"I will try," she simply answered Paul.

Paul looked at me, and was smiling as if he was saying 'courage Laura', without saying any more he walked out. I was left standing, watching Chlorinda. She was watching me too. There was a long moment of terrible silence; I thought it would be a good idea to break this pushing silence.

"Oh! Chlorinda those dogs, they were so agitated. Never in my life have I seen such angry dogs and . . ."

"Dear girl," she brutally interrupted me, "hypnotizing animals is an easy trick. I would like you learn it quickly and move to the next one."

Accentuating the words she said "to hypnotize humans!"

*   *   *

I was so intimidated in the morning by this woman. I woke up early, and I decided not to leave my room because I might disturb her. I saw that it was 8:30 when she left her bedroom. I quickly went to bathroom and got dressed. I finally got up the nerve to go downstairs. She was in the kitchen and I could smell the nice fresh coffee. Chlorinda was filling her can with coffee and without turning her head she said:

"I know you like having bananas in the morning, but I hate them. As result you will have no bananas during your stay here."

I saw in the back yard a woman coming close to the window. In that moment Chlorinda began screaming like crazy at her in Romanian. My gosh, Chlorinda has extremely strong lung. Very scared the woman took off almost running into a warehouse which Chlorinda had in her backyard. She took a seat at the kitchen table fixing her green eyes on me. I decided to stay calm for now and not let her see my anger. I thought about all the things I knew about psychology to find a way to deal with Chlorinda.

I wanted to go and take some coffee, because it seemed she did not want to have to serve me, but this might make her angry . . . I decided I'd better ask,

"Chlorinda, may I have some coffee please?"

Snorting, she walked to the counter and poured some coffee in a very small can. She brought me the can on a plate. With a deliberate gesture she turned the plate and spilled the coffee down my front. It was a brutal gesture and the coffee spread all over the table.

This is too much for me, I thought.

"What kind of manners are these?" I asked Chlorinda aloud. "Now I understand why all the people hate you."

"I don't care what the people of this world think or say about me!" She raised her voice and stared at me defiantly.

"Look, my name is Laura, and . . ."

"And?" she interrupted me again.

"I am a great person. I don't allow anybody to treat me like this."

"You are my student and I will treat you as I wish." she retorted.

Good, I thought to myself, *this is the first step; she admitted that I am her student.* I have to speculate this.

"That's correct, but I will only accept abuse in relation to the magic lessons."

"Hmmm," she made a strange gesture, looking at me but at the same time she appeared to calm herself.

"You have to accept a couple of other small things too."

I decided to keep her in suspense. I walked to kitchen counter and a chose a can bigger than hers, I filled it to the brim with coffee. She was watching me closely. Then I took a kitchen towel and a cleaned the coffee she spilled from the table. I tried to calm myself; I took long sip of coffee. I felt like the coffee helping me immediately. It was like I was gaining some energy to confront this terrible woman.

"What are these small things I'm supposed to accept?" I asked looking directly in her green eyes. I think everyone was right to be afraid of this woman; there was something strange in her eyes. In the back of my mind I was hearing Paul and Halibarda's favorite joke.

"Green, like a poison; she is a poison; she is Chlorinda."

"Some work, not connected with the magic. I have some small animals and you can help me feed them."

"Oh, that would be Okay. I like small animals. What kind of . . . ?"

"Rats!" She said almost screaming the word.

I was going to say, *'Are you crazy Chlorinda?'* But I reluctantly stopped myself. After that there was long period of silence.

Finally she started.

"So, we already have eight deaths in this story." She said studying me.

Taking a deep breath I answered her.

"The media in your country has said, and I will say the same 'it was an accident'."

"You have a role in their deaths, do you know that?" she continued like she did not hear my answer.

This woman is a poison. She was making me totally angry this time.

"Like me, you have a role too."

"But mine is minor compared to yours." She spat back at me.

"Don't be ridiculous Chlorinda . . ."

"Don't start with me about the ridiculous hypotheses of the accident! What we woke up there . . . . ." and she suddenly stopped. I understood that she stopped because nobody sure yet exactly what the entity is.

"Yes?" I tried to challenge her.

"We stared this project two years ago."

"If you started this project so early why it is not complete?"

She looked changing her defensive attitude with one more acceptable.

"Because you were not here."

I smiled to Chlorinda, "I didn't notice my role was so . . . important."

"Oh! But it is . . ." she was smiling at me also.

"Why?"

"You are a . . ."

"A reincarnation . . . I know, I know. According to this theory we are all reincarnations."

"True," she said, "but you are a special one, in a previous life you were connected with Dracula." She was looking at me so seriously.

"Well . . . I had been told that I might be Radu the Handsome in the . . ."

She snorted, "I don't believe that. You know nothing? No. You were not Radu the Handsome."

"No?" Now I was confused. She was so serious that I started to think about the possibility the group had lied to me and Chlorinda might be right.

She saw my confusion and with certainty in her voice she continued.

"In a previous life, you were the woman he loved."

I was shocked by this possibility. She waited a moment for me to regain composure and continued.

"We did incantations and spells two years ago, but the entity didn't come when we asked her. She did not respond to any of our methods. We thought that the legend might be true. Dracula was killed a second time, but in an irreversible way and . . . he was gone. Paul came forward; he told us we have a new chance as the reincarnation of his love lives in our time. Because it was not working until now, we started to believe that if you joined us when we complete the spells that the entity connected with Dracula will be attracted to you. We thought it might be a really good chance to wake up the entity."

I was dumbfounded by this new development; Chlorinda was very serious, and what she said was logical.

"And how in the world did he find me? Does Paul have such abilities?" I asked Chlorinda curiously.

"No." She simply answered. She mad a long pause.

"We believe he has a contact person. She did it. We don't know who she is, what she looks like, where she lives or what she wants. But she was able to find you."

Chlorinda paused, and she studied me with her green eyes. Her voice lowered as if she was telling me an interesting story.

"Because you were in the same town as Paul, it was his duty to bring you here."

"What are you talking about? I came here because I wanted it, not because you or anyone else made me."

"Oh . . . poor girl!" Chlorinda looked at me with surprise. "However I didn't understand why it took him two years to bring you here . . . ."

I was surprised this time. *God . . . if this was going to be her mission, what was this woman able to do with me? She was able to use her hypnotic powers and kidnapping me was a joke for her. But, Paul was able to use hypnosis proficiently also; yesterday, when the dogs attacked us they where under Chlorinda's hypnosis and he was able to break her powers and to calm them! But Chlorinda's question was right, why did Paul choose to wait so long?*

"But it is done now, how did he convince you to come here . . . .?" Chlorinda was analyzing me now.

"As you know he told me about what you were all doing here, magic, incantations, etc. and I was curious. I am attracted to magical stuff."

"Oh . . . She looked at me with compassion, 'poor girl'! You are a victim; he was hiding the truth from you. He has always been hiding the truth. We were the ones who needed you here. How he did he do it? Did something strange happen to you before you came?"

"Hmmm, I had a dream . . . a little girl; I dreamt of her a couple times before . . ."

"Laura . . ." she was looking at me with sympathy. "It is impossible to dream an unknown person more than once!"

"But, I did! I know what I dreamed. I dreamed of his niece."

"That is . . ." she became excited. "That image was introduced into your mind by Paul."

I had never thought of this possibility. *Yes! God! She is right . . . again!*

"But is he able to do this?"

Chlorinda was looking at me, ungrateful.

"He is hiding himself; always he comes to us with new abilities. Drina realized only lately that he has kinesthetic powers stronger than her . . . I was quite surprised yesterday to see his hypnotic powers are so strong."

She became nervous and took some time to calm herself.

"But let's recount the entire story. What did the little girl tell you in these dreams?"

"Actually she was singing to me, she became a best friend of mine first. It was like I just wanted to sleep, praying to meet her."

"Oh . . . I see . . . what a technique," Chlorinda said with a low voice thinking deeply. "And . . . what did she sing to you?"

"Actually her songs were inspiring to me, and I created my new album, which was a worldwide success."

"It looks like you'll have to pay copyright; these songs in fact belong to Paul! He introduced you to the image of his niece and he was the one who suggested these songs to you."

"Why he has done this? The quantity of money I gained was enormous. If he is so talented he could have had this money for himself."

"Because he needs you, He had been sent there to bring you here. And he chose this way."

"But Chlorinda, he could have come to me, given me the songs and had half of the money, now he can prove nothing."

"Here we don't think about money. We are beyond those living options. We have examples in Romania of the old witches who could be very rich but they were and sometimes still are searching for something more than money. For us, being strong in magic is the equivalent of being rich. I think he believed that once you were rich and when you saw his niece you will want to do everything that he suggests to you without using any tricks this time."

"And he was right! I love his niece, in my mind she was a friend of mine and she made me rich. In fact I had no inspiration one year after, and nothing important or interesting to do. Coming to Romania was an escape from a boring period in my life."

Chlorinda was apprising me; she stood watching me for a long time. Then with a consoling voice she said, "And here we are, eight deaths . . . ."

"But, it was an accident. In regards to my stay in Romania, I had an interesting time. It doesn't matter to me what I was in another life, in this one I am a witch. I want to be a strong one, like you! And I've met an interesting man, Vlad; my Vlad is a gorgeous guy . . . ."

Astonished, Chlorinda interrupted me, she covered her month. "Oh . . . Laura! Poor you! Poor girl . . . ."

"I know, I know he did some sexual stuff before . . . ."

"Do you mean he is changed now?"

"Yes. He loves me."

"Are you sure?"

"Look Chlorinda, please don't play with me!"

I was now angry with this woman but at the same time I felt she knew something, a new truth and I needed to know what she knew.

"Vlad is a prostitute. We've known him from a long time. He will have sex for money and in the past we have paid him to do so . . . "

"Don't be disgusting Chlorinda!"

Without saying anything Chlorinda turned on her huge TV, and she popped in a DVD that was waiting there for me where she was making love with Vlad. I saw the date of the recording; it was almost 2 weeks ago. When I was taking magic lessons from Drina he was having sex with Chlorinda! I felt like I couldn't breathe. Chlorinda is more than fifty years old and Vlad is less than thirty! It was disgusting seeing her having sex with Vlad. I think Vlad must have a strong stomach! It was awful and all I could see was blackness. I heard Chlorinda at my ear saying, "I know Paul is paying Vlad to stay with you. For Vlad everything is money. He is unable to love. Oh . . . poor you, poor girl, so sorry Laura . . . ."

* * *

Yesterday I stayed in my room all day. I thought about the things Chlorinda had said. I was furious with Vlad, and Paul, all of them!

239

Why did they hide these things from me? I thought about what I have to do next, the next the morning I went to Chlorinda's living room. Without asking I took my can of coffee and then I saw in the kitchen a couple bananas. Without thinking I took one. Chlorinda was sitting on a chair at the table between the kitchen and living room. She seemed friendly today, or as friendly as she is able to be and she even smiled at me.

"I decided to get some bananas for you. In fact you are a poor girl, all the people you call friends betrayed you."

I smiled at her too. "Good morning Chlorinda. Today I am very sad, but I think I lived the most wonderful love story of my life. He might have done it all for money but now he is only a memory for me. However, you brought in my attention some interesting things."

"I made you face the reality! These people have been lying to you."

"Okay, you're right; and as a result . . . I see no reason that you and I don't become good friends and allies."

Chlorinda jumped up from her seat and hugged me!

*   *   *

I thought this woman was crazy, but she definitely wasn't joking! She is indeed raising rats. Near the house she has a special cellar which is quite large; on the ground floor she has a storage room for cereals, storage for the rat food. Off to the side was another room, she did not show me what was inside. I couldn't even guess what's in there and she always keeps the room locked. I could tell that she was quite organized. The rat food is arranged by type, she explained to me that the cereal which is mainly used for the rat's food is quite cheap and easily purchased in the village or nearby villages.

"We will go into the basements where I keep the rats. I have a ventilation system but I have to advise you that the smell is strong."

We went down into the basement and I saw a lot of cages. There were mostly terrariums with glass walls and inside I saw the rats! I saw that she kept the rats sorted by age, she had an impressive collection. All she had to do is to fill the feeder for each cage, which she did that except for a couple of cages. The ones she skipped totaled about one. Hundred rats.

She showed me the baby rats from a particular cage.

"Their end has come. I don't like to feed them anymore. Why I should waste money on food if they will die today?" she said smiling hugely at me.

The cages were connected to an automatic water line and each one had a valve automated by a level sensor.

"This way my rats will have always water, they don't need much else." she laughed. Her laugh reminded me of Paul's evil laughing, the type of cackle than the evil sorceress always has in the movies. It took one hour to fill all the cages with food, I helped her. She liked to do the things slowly and take caution.

"Laura, like most witches you must come to love rats. They are quite useful in magic." She said and she happily continued to work looking at me with worry.

"I . . . I don't like them much Chlorinda. Sorry . . . ."

"That's Okay. I don't like them much either." She said. "Actually my favorite ones are in the level below. Let's go."

I was first down the stairs, they were so narrow. I am a tall girl and I needed to bend to make it through the corridor. Chlorinda did the same; I was wondered why she didn't build the stairs larger since she goes here often.

"I pay a woman from village to do this for me. I pay her very little, but this business is quite . . . large."

I thought she was crazy, who can make money with rats? Who would buy rats and for what price? But I decided to not ask or contradict her. Finally we reached the end of the stairs and I was happy to be at the second level of the basement.

But down there . . . I was taken aback; I almost recited the fear litany. The room was filled with venomous snakes!

Noticing my reaction Chlorinda started to laugh, she was really enjoying herself now! She was a large lady with substantial breasts, which were bouncing out of control with each laughter filled breath.

"They . . . are my favorites," and she continued to laugh.

I looked around the room. The snakes were all in cages; some of them were quite large. Their bodies were curled and their eyes were fixed on us. I thought to myself that hopefully none had escaped and were slinking about on the floor. Chlorinda assured me that everything was okay. She installed movement sensors for the floor, if by chance one escaped an alarm would sound in her house. Also the stairs were specially constructed so they would not be able to escape from the basement. It looked like she had a couple hundred mature snakes! Extremely happy now she started to put baby rats in the snake's cages.

The spectacle was quite horrifying! The small animals squeaked in fear and agony and the snakes devoured them, becoming quite happy. Once the rat has entered its cage the snake bent its body, becoming excited and then with a precise move he catches the poor animal. I wanted to run away from this horrifying spectacle, but instead I said the fear litany a couple times and defeated my fear. Paul was right; actually he had said exactly, *I might need it if I found myself in a room with venomous snakes!*

I thought it might be a good time to try a conversation with Chlorinda. She was quite happy and it might help me get over the stress. At least I didn't need to be afraid of escaped snakes because of the movement sensors on the floor, if one got out Chlorinda would know.

"I see that you have some video cameras too Chlorinda."

"Yes! My daughter helped me with the video surveillance system. I can even watch them over the Internet when I am away from home. It is also equipped with sound. I watch the woman when I am away so I can give her immediate instructions." Chlorinda smiled to me "she is quite stupid. I told her once a viper will bite her." As she said it, she made a biting gesture towards me and started laugh again.

"So, these snakes are vipers?"

"Yes," she said proudly.

"But I see a kind of . . . corn on their nose?" I was too intimidated to get close to the glass.

"Yes," she whispered as if sharing a secret. "They are corn vipers. More dangerous than normal ones and, they are my favorites!"

Without hesitation she opened terrarium.

"Chlorinda! What are you doing? It is a very venomous snake!" I screamed at her.

Nicely smiling at me she took a viper. *Oh God!* I was panicking now. Her snake could kill both of us. She was playing with the snake as if it were a pet and not a very venomous corn viper.

"Soon I would like you to be able to do this Laura."

"I . . . I am not sure I want this Chlorinda."

"To put your mind at ease, I have two things to tell you. One, the captive vipers are not as agile as the ones who live free in their natural habitat and second my abilities to hypnotize them are strong." She smiled at me. "I thought about sending a couple of them to Paul's car. But if I had I might lose my license for this business and of course I don't want this. However, who knows . . . maybe in a day, I might have a surprise for him!" Then she was laughing again.

After that she became serious. She returned the corn viper to its cage. I tried to relax after the terrible tension with this crazy woman and her venomous corn vipers.

"Chlorinda, why are you raising these corn vipers?"

"For their venom, it is the most poisonous natural substance known in nature and . . . . it is very expensive. Come with me." She almost ran upstairs and she unlocked the door in the main floor room. "Here is the laboratory,' she said 'and this is what I am selling." She showed me a vial filled with a white powder.

"Why is it powder Chlorinda? Their venom is a liquid, why don't you just put it into the fridge?"

"You are quite correct, their venom is liquid, but as it contains 70% water I transform the venom into the white powder which is easier to store and sell. A gram of this may sell for at least one thousand Euros!" She was very proud about what she was doing. "It is used in pharmaceuticals and cosmetics." She added with a large smile.

The next day from the video surveillance I saw her collecting and preparing the venom from her 'babies' as she called the vipers.

*   *   *

Finally we also started doing some magical training. I could tell that she was a real expert! She told me that she does the magical circle almost daily; we did it together a couple of times. She liked to fly a lot. She usually went close to houses where she knows there are sorceresses.

"I am a curious person by nature," she told me, "and I always like to know what others are doing . . ."

We saw Drina by herself making some magical stuff or walking in the morning in the woods. We also went near Ivanka's tent, not too close as we noticed that she is quite sensitive. Also Chlorinda watched another sorceress, as they are strong but don't belong to the club. Everything we did together in the first days was what she called 'harmony'. She was studying me, my energies, and my abilities. Finally she decided we could practice some attacks.

"Make sure to always in life search for the easy and understandable explanations. Also here, speaking of attacks. Do the magical circle and where you feel my attack defend yourself by increasing the intensity of the attacked zone. To an attacker you oppose the correspondent energy barrier."

Each one of us did her own magical circle. In a couple minutes, I raised up my magical circle by the power of the four elements. All was ready and balanced; everything was in a good harmony. My mind was equally controlling the elements of wind, earth, water and fire until . . . . I felt something going wrong in the earth side. I increased my mental energy on that side, but there it needed more and more power. It was like the earth was increasing its pressure there, smacking against my earth elements and trying to smash my rock igloo. I could hear my rock igloo cracking under the fabulous earth pressure. I continued to increase my mental power to the earth side. I recovered my goblins and I reinforced my rock igloo. Everything was almost under control, until I felt the waves increasing in the water side. I immediately commanded the fays to stand their ground and to calm the waves down. I fought like this for almost half a day with Chlorinda.

"You're good," said Chlorinda. And we decided to stop. I smiled at her. I was totally exhausted.

"You have to remember,' Chlorinda said, 'sometimes you might be attacked on two sides, three or all around. You have to be prepared for this. Not all the sorceresses can do this,' she smiled to me, 'but I can. Also the intensity of the attack on one side can increase dramatically in a blink of the eye, not easily as we did today. To defend yourself you have to act quickly. Be prepared for this."

We spent almost a week fighting like this, and almost all day long flying. In the couple hours when I was allowed to sleep I slept deeply.

"I am sorry dear girl to tell you . . . but if you choose to become a sorceress, you have no right to sleep."

"Why?" I asked Chlorinda confused.

"Because, if another sorceress would like to attack you the best time is when you sleep. Your brain is quite relaxed in that time and you are out of the magical circle."

"What can I do to correct it?"

"When you start sleeping you have to concentrate and to hold your concentration over your sleep. Then if someone dares to attack you, you will feel him and defend immediately. It might be hard at the beginning but it will become second nature for you in time by practicing."

She explained to me that for her it is very easy now. When she is sleeping normally and she just feels if something is going wrong.

"When you are proficient like me you will not need at all the dream catchers made by your North Indian wizard. You will be able to fight by yourself with the bad spirits of the wood."

I also discussed with Chlorinda a lot about the moon phases. The cycle of the moon is always influencing magic. She explained me that some magical stuff takes quite a long time and all is done in accordance with the moon phases. Usually it begins at the new moon. After that the magic is done night by night and the biggest steps will be completed when there is the full moon.

"However, at Raluka's suggestion Paul has asked us to do it in the opposite way that is we start our steps when the moon is full and we increase the concentrations each night according to the decreasing of the moon. Our final and biggest magic concentration has to be done when there is no moon on the sky."

"What it exactly does that mean?"

"It means from white magic makers we become black magic makers," and she stared to laugh hysterically.

*   *   *

I think all the witches of Romania love nature.

"In fact the earth's nature helps us by challenging us." Chlorinda said.

She likes very much to walk along the river. The river is the same one which flows by Paul's house, a couple villages away in the safety of the river.

"This was a bit inconvenient for me," Chlorinda announced to me. "First when I decided to sell my old house, the one in the gypsy's

245

village, I saw Paul's house and I really enjoyed the location. He recommended his architect; the building company and I started to build my new house. When I was done, I saw the great disadvantage is that he lives in the safety of the river and not I."

"Why?" I asked without understanding.

"I will tell you, at the right time." And she refused to talk further.

"Chlorinda, I saw that the magical circle is a quite strong magic. I don't understand how that Dracula's entity was able to pass the circle."

"It is a strong entity. Think about when we practiced our attack between magical circles. If I will be enough strong I will suddenly attack you with a huge energy, and I will break a small portion of your circle. This is what it is doing. In that moment it can catch us one by one . . . ." She moved her eyes to the river. At a curve were couple noisy birds.

"Maybe it is a good idea you to go home Laura. You might get hurt. And none of us wants this. We have our differences, but I really love you Laura. "

I was watching that noisy group of birds too.

"I don't know exactly what I was in a previous life, but for now I want to be a strong witch. I would appreciate if you can teach me some strong tricks."

*   *   *

"Starting today I will teach you a new kind of strong magic."

Chlorinda was dressed in her typical style, a sleeveless dress tight to her body, even though she was a large woman. I didn't understand why she called these dresses, kimono dress; they looked nothing like a kimono.

The night was about to begin, it was a hot day and the night was welcome as it would bring some coldness.

"If somebody came in contact with this type of magic it would be 'nashpa' for him." I remembered the word 'nashpa' was Romanian word for bad.

"It is called '*the magical tough goblin*'." Chlorinda said in a low, secretive voice. "Be very careful with it. It is quite a strong magic, and not all of the sorceresses know how to do it or even about it."

She was continued to speak in the low voice, "Sometimes, we need somebody to do something on our behalf. This magic will create an entity, it will be able to exist by himself and it is quite rational. It can think and can take the adequate actions. All the actions the goblin takes will be in order to accomplish the task you gave him."

"That is brilliant!" I said quite excited.

She smiled happily at me.

"What we need for this is an egg, but the kind of egg which is able to generate an embryo. In other countries it may be difficult to find, I will show you how you can determine from a bulk of eggs which is a good one." She had ten eggs with her. Chlorinda told me that that only one is good. In fact the test was quite simple. What I had to do is to place the egg in the front of a strong source of light and if I see something dark inside that is the embryo. To be successful this test has to be done in a dark room.

"If you fail to find a good egg all your magic will fail." She looked at me waiting to see if I understood this important point.

"Also we need a covered box for this magic. Make sure the cover is very tight so that it closes completely and no light can go into. You need enough black cotton or cloth to cover the egg and fill the inside of the box. When everything is ready you can start your magic on the first night of the new moon. You will hold the egg with the both hands, fixate on the egg and focus your mind energy towards the egg. When you ready say the spell:

From this egg I create the goblin. Goblin, I create you with my magical power. You will be born in 23 days. I create you to . . .

And you say the task you give to the goblin. After that carefully pack the egg in the black cotton and place it in the box. Put the box in a room where nobody lives and no one enters. You can't place it in your bedroom or living room, failing to do this means the spell will fail. You have to calculate when the moon will be in full size and start your magic 23 days before that. Each night repeat the spell and be careful to say the exact number of remaining days. If you make a mistake counting, the magic will fail. Also, you cannot change your mind. You cannot give to the goblin a task and then after a couple days change it. If you need to change the task, you have to destroy the egg and start to calculate again 23 days to the next full moon. On the last day you say the following spell:

> *From this egg I create the goblin. Goblin, I created you with my*
> *magical power.*
> *You are born tonight.*
> *I created you to . . . (Say the task)*
> *You will have no rest until you accomplish . . . (Say the task)*
> *You will have no rest until you accomplish . . . (Say the task)*
> *You will have no rest until you accomplish . . . (Say the task)'*

After that you will pack the egg as in the previous nights. You don't touch the egg for three days after. After three days when you check the egg, if it is still intact the goblin accomplished his duty. You can destroy the egg."

"How can another wizard defend against this magic?"

"This is a strong magic and very few can defend against it. They usually start to fight with the goblin. But it is an invincible entity, and they will begin to lose their powers. Finally the goblin will gain power. Let's say I do something against Drina. If she is able to see my goblin before it starts to attack she has to think where I keep the egg that I used to generate the goblin and use her kinesthetic powers to break the egg. If she breaks the egg the magic is destroyed and the goblin will die. If she fails the goblin has very good chance to accomplish its mission."

I was impressed by this particular method of magic. I will definitely have to try it! "Can we use it against that entity which killed our people?"

"Of course we can. But, the other method to defeat the goblin is fighting with him. As the goblin is quite strong a normal wizard cannot resist him. But the Dracula entity looks very strong. I would not expect a goblin to be able to defeat her. However it might be a help. Also remember, the goblin will not recognize you. He has a mission. If he has to fight with the opposite entity and you are in his way the goblin can destroy you."

"I understand." I said starting to analyze all the possibilities open to me by this magic technique.

*   *   *

Chlorinda also explained to me the possibility of doing magic with Voodoo dolls. The Romanians witches have something quite similar to Voodoo magic. Chlorinda explained me that to do this I need to build a doll and I need to put inside some DNA from the person who I want to interact with, the doll is the equivalent of the person. I can do actions on the doll and the actions will be reflected to the person. I was always attracted to this magic of Voodoo dolls.

"Can you kill a man with this magic?"

"Not typically." Chlorinda said convincingly. "Remember about fate, karma or *Ursita* like we call it here. If the *Ursita* of the one you are making magic on is to live longer you cannot kill him. With this magic I can give him grave injuries, for example he can remain like a vegetable but he will live as long as *Ursita* settled him to."

"And another wizard can help him?"

"Usually yes. If that other witch, for example is Halibarda, I would expect her to understand what kind of magic has been done. And she might be able to undo what I have done. If she is stronger than me, she can be successful and the man can return to life and live long as per his *Ursita*."

I was quite impressed with these possibilities.

"Do things like this still happen?"

"Yes and quite often."

"Why?"

"Well because people will always love money and power. Suppose somebody has a problem with another person. He will come to me, and ask me to act against that person. After that the relatives of the punished person may think someone did magic and they will hire another witch. Of course she will be well paid, and she will try to defeat my magic."

"Then you will be in conflict with that which?"

"Yes somewhat. I understand that I took money, I did a job. Also she took money and she has to do her job too. And so she must use her magical powers against my magical powers. And here is the challenge." She paused and looked as if to ask '*Isn't it?*'

"For this reason if you stay in the world of the magic I would recommend you understand your powers, and try to form alliances with the wizards who are stronger than you."

"Chlorinda, are you scared about the next group incantations?"

"I am more excited than scared." She said fixing her green eyes on me. "Why should I be afraid?"

"Well . . . last time eight people died."

"Look, you have to think like this, if you or I succeed the victory will be a light in our life. If we lose, it doesn't matter much." She tried to look convincing.

"And what about . . . the unfriendly treatment of our bodies?"

"As I said at our last meeting, without a soul our body is nothing more than an empty cover."

* * *

It was quite early in the morning; I was not able to sleep. I saw from my window the woman who works in Chlorinda's viper farm. She always comes early in the morning and feeds Chlorinda's 'animals' or 'babies'. She is a quiet woman. Actually, I never took to her. Chlorinda told me that *her job is to work, nothing more.*

I saw an old man was also coming to Chlorinda's property. I knew she was still sleeping. The man rang the doorbell, when he saw nobody answered; he held the bell for a long ring, after that he started to pound the door with his fist. I thought he seemed quite desperate. I thought about going to open the door, but Chlorinda was faster than me. I heard her, speaking to herself in Romanian on the way down the stairs. I thought that the man made her angry. She would punish him for sure! But once she opened the door her voice became kind. The man was telling her something which I could not understand as they were speaking in Romanian. She invited him into the kitchen and offered him a chamomile tea. He only took one sip from the tea before he started crying. I saw the tears in his eyes, he was very sad. I understood that he was hoping Chlorinda could help him. From the tone of Chlorinda voice I could tell that she was trying to calm him. For a long time she explained something to him, finally, he stood up and on the verge of tears of happiness he left the house. As if it was a bad dream, Chlorinda watched as he walked away without saying anything. It was like she was not aware of my presence in the room.

After a long moment of silence she spoke to me.

"He is John, a very good friend of mine. He is very good jeweler. He has his own small business, he is a successful man and he is making good money. Unfortunately, someone stole all of his business possessions together with all the jewelry he made and the unprocessed gold. For him this is a huge lose, almost the end of his business. Of course he is very sad, and he asked me for help. I asked him who he is suspected. He told me that he is suspecting a couple of friends."

"But, did he call the police?"

"Yes. But unfortunately they were not able to solve the case. The thieves were quite professional."

"And do you think you can help him?"

"Of course I can. Please remember, when the police, medicine, or science are not able to solve the case we sorceresses are *always* able. Where their area of expertise ends, *ours begins*." She was very convincing with what she said.

"I told him to go to all the suspected people and tell them to return what they stolen, otherwise I, Chlorinda, will make a terrible magic against them. They will become very ill and will stay ill as long as they refuse to return what they stole."

"And do you think that will be scared and they will return the stolen stuff?"

"Not at all, or not for now. But when he returns to tell me they refuse, they will become very ill they will be really scared," and Chlorinda smiled. A huge smile.

"Come with me." As she said this she took a large vessel from the magic room and her knife for magic. I guessed from with my previous magic lessons that might be the vessel for reading the future in water.

"Take your knife too." She commanded me. "I have a spring well in my yard."

We walked to where the spring was in her yard. Chlorinda kept that corner of her yard quite wild. The spring was like a small lake with a tiny river as wide as finger flowing away from it. With a great care she filled the large silver vessel with water. Then with careful steps she carried it to an open part of her yard. She put the vessel on the soil and waited until the water was calm.

Looking at me she said, "Here we have to do something different than usual. I usually use this method to read the future. But now, because of the situation I have to go *back in time* and to see what was happened there, to find some indication of who was responsible for the theft.' Saying this she took her knife and cut the air above the vessel of water.

"You have to do the same, and the spell is:

With this sharp knife I am banishing the bad spirits from around my water vessel. Good spirits I call upon you. Stay around my water vessel to help me to see what I wish. Bad spirits go away from here; if you come back I will cut you with this sharp knife."

She asked me to do the same. After that she closed her eyes and she was placed her hands above the vessel. Chlorinda started to slowly to move her hands above the water vessel. She did this for a couple of minutes. I observed that she was focusing deeply, like she was in a trance. After that she opened her eyes and concentrating, she started to look at the water in the vessel. I did the same; I saw couple reflections from the sun. I did not think I saw something to help conclude who the thief was. Maybe I was supposes to see there a face, or faces, or couple guys going into the home of the poor man and stealing his stuff. Finally Chlorinda raised her face from the water vessel and looked at me; she seemed to still be in a trance. It took a minute until she started to blink her eyes.

"Clear," she said.

After that she took the vessel of water and spread the water at the roots of some plants.

"Tonight we have work to do," she announced to me.

*   *   *

It was a nice night.

I wondered how the sky seemed so clear from here; from Romania I could see so many stars. It is not like this if I watch it from Canada. When I have this kind of sky so full with stars I always enjoy watching it from my cabin. Quite warm and silent.

I am with Chlorinda at the river. I was curious and I touched the water of the river, it was very warm as the day had been a very hot summer day. I thought it probably was over 40 degrees Celsius previous day. With the humidity in the air it was quite hard to support these kinds of summer days here in Romania.

"I thought that it is a big advantage having the house near the river. Our magic involves the usage of the river, and not only as a water element. In our tradition if you put something in the river it might flow forever. It is like you can transform an ordinary item into something that will live forever. And we use this to strengthen our magic. If I say an incantation over the river, the water of the river will bring it to the next big river which is for us 'Dunarea', and after that into the sea and then the ocean. And like this the magic I performed will never die." She was looking around the river as far as we could see.

"You will witness today me making a strong magic. The action of this magic is rapid. I would like to help that poor man as quickly as I can. And I can!" She said settling her green eyes on me. Chlorinda had a cartoon box, a candle, and two dolls hand made by her from straw.

"These two dolls represent the two thieves I saw in the morning in my silver vessel. I will put them in the bottom of this box. Usually I use a special kind of pot made from a particular pumpkin that has a very tiny shell and it is ideal for floating on the water. I will use this cartoon box to show you that the magic also works with this item when you don't have that special pumpkin. I will put the candle between them. It is very important the candle to be fixed well. The candle has to be able to burn by itself until it reaches the bottom of the box. When it reaches the bottom of the box where the dolls are touching the candle they will start on fire. The entire box will burn. In that moment our magic will be activated. If you want do this magic it is best to postpone your work for a night without wind. We have to light the candle, to say the spell, and to push the box to the middle of the river. We have to make sure that it has a good chance of floating the river forever. If the river permits we can walk close to the middle of the river." And we did as the level of the water was low.

She was focusing on the two dolls, she lit the candle and she said the spell:

"I call the supreme powers to punish the thieves. I ask the supreme power to make them ill and the illness to not pass until they return all the stolen things. I call the supreme powers to punish the thieves.

Let's repeat this spell together please."

We said the spell three times and Chlorinda launched the box on the river's water. We watched it float away until we couldn't see it anymore.

"Even if you are not in the magical circle you have to try to use your mental power to coordinate the air and water elements to give a good direction to the floating box."

"I hope the magic will work."

"Yes, like this I can punish people I want."

"And how can they be released?"

"They can pay another witch and she can do the same magic to try and reverse what I have done," she smiled at me. "I told you that it was a big disadvantage Paul having the house down river. Lots of stuff I did he was able to stop . . . ."

"This will work. He is in Bucharest right now.

She paused, "even if he was around, he will allow this magic. It is done to correct an evil action, where the police were incompetent."

* * *

Chlorinda was right, the next morning we heard about two friends of the jeweler were very ill. They went to the doctor but even though took the prescribed medicine the illness was persisting. They a terrible headache and they were unable to eat, after one week they looked really bad. At the end of the week John, the jeweler came to Chlorinda. He gave her a heavy golden chain and he was happy to drink his chamomile tea with us.

"He can't speak English; I told him you helped me when I did this magic and he wants to offer you something. Do you have any preferences?" Chlorinda asked me, John was gazing at me with his eyes as if trying to understand my wish.

"Look . . . I have lots of gold given to me at my first meeting with you guys. I would like some of it to be melted and something made for Vlad and . . . Paul."

Chlorinda's face was suddenly lit with a huge smile, "it would be a good idea to make two crosses with chains for them. John does wonders with gold and who doesn't love the cross?" she said enigmatically. I decided to have the crosses made but my intention was still to pay the man. Chlorinda assured me that it was absolutely John's pleasure.

The next day he came back and I saw that how talented he was in his goldsmith work, I really like the way he manufactured the crosses. I decided to give the small one to Vlad and the big one to Paul. I told Chlorinda she seemed extremely satisfied with my choice, '*maybe she loves Paul?*' I thought.

The next few days and nights we were spent continuing to practice the magic of the magical circle, attack and defense. Chlorinda also started to explain to me how she focuses when she is applying hypnosis. She suggested starting with small animals. I tried to do it with a couple of rats, I was not very successful. I was amazed to see her powers against the small animals.

She told me that she can feel a power from me.

"You have to keep practicing. Soon I am sure you will be very successful. But it requires a lot of practice."

"May I suggest that she can start with a break?' I heard Halibarda's voice, Chlorinda was surprised too. We had no idea how she came into the room so near to us, watching and listening, without us being able to see her.

"I think Chlorinda was teaching you lots of good stuff and lots of bad stuff." Halibarda said making some theatrical gestures with her hands and smiling with satisfaction.

"Let's say I offered Laura a better point of view towards reality." Chlorinda said trying to have the same look of satisfaction on her face as Halibarda.

"Speaking about reality" Halibarda said "a couple of vipers were escaping from their aquarium cages, and they are quite agitated. It will be your task to put them back into their cages." Halibarda stopped smiling.

"Bullshit, if one of them escaped then the alarm . . ."

Halibarda closed her eyes and stood back, concentrating, at the same time the alarm stared to sound in the living room. Automatically the TV turned on, and we saw a couple of aquariums were broken. Some of the vipers were looking quite nervous because were hurt by the broken glass.

Chlorinda gnashed her teeth, "bitch!" With an enormous effort she tried to calm herself "I am sure I can manage."

Halibarda smiled at Chlorinda again,

"Good luck! And remember, it was not Paul's idea. It is my gift to you."

Chapter 16

All gypsies love me,
Romanians love me too . . . .
They know I am a magic creature.
-Gipsy folk song

H alibarda was a terrible driver and received four tickets along the way. I was very frightened to drive with her. My intention had been to start a discussion with her regarding the lies they told me but I decided to do it when we arrived in Bucharest if . . . we ever reached the city alive.

Whenever the police stopped her she tried to flirt with them and be sexy, or as sexy as she could be with her pudgy body and pot belly. Her dress was skin tight and short, ending just above her knees. She tried to seduce the police each time but so far had been unsuccessful. Finally, we parked at a restaurant which had a lovely patio. She decided to take a break and have some mititei for lunch.

The wait to receive our order was extremely long and Halibarda got frustrated and went to argue with our server. As this was taking a long time, I decided to make a call to Chlorinda as I was concerned about the escaped vipers . . ."Hello . . . Chlorinda?"

"Yes, Laura," she answered me but I could hear pain in her voice.

"You okay, Chlorinda?"

"I hope so; yes . . . a viper bit me."

"W . . . what? But their venom is very poisonous!"

"Yes, yes . . . I did have the antidote with me. It was very painful but has started to improve. I appreciate your concern for me."

"Why you did not wear a rubber coverall to protect yourself?"

"I have one but I never wear it."

"Oh, Chlorinda . . . you must wear it next time."

"Okay, Okay . . . how are things there?"

"Oh, all right . . . but Halibarda is such a terrible driver and . . ."

"What? What are you talking about?"

"Chlorinda, I don't understand you . . . maybe it is effect of the venom . . ."

"No! Listen to me! Halibarda is an excellent driver. She told me once it is as if she was born in her car . . . there is something going on . . . let me think about this for a moment . . . oh yes. She was distracting you because she does not want to have a discussion with you about the things I made you aware of."

"But . . . why?"

"Paul probably ordered it. Halibarda might be his lieutenant, but he still likes these discussions to occur under his direct supervision, and . . ."

"Okay then, Chlorinda. She is coming; talk to you later," and I quickly closed my cell.

Halibarda made her way to the table, followed by an attractive waiter with hands full of plates. The waiter seemed stressed by Halibarda and appeared quite embarrassed by the scene Halibarda had made.

"They are very unprofessional . . . it is so frustrating . . . and all this is because of Chlorinda. Whenever I meet her my day goes badly. I hope a viper bit her."

"Do you want her to die?"

Suddenly Halibarda was looking at me. "No. What kind of a question is that? She is a member of our club: we are like a family . . ."

"Strange family, Halibarda . . ."

"Yes," she grinned, "like the Adams Family."

I laughed, Halibarda was very sarcastic and her jokes were always good. "Still I don't understand . . . if you are a family why did you put her in such a dangerous situation?"

"Because she needs to learn a lesson."

"But she could die! The bite of a viper is deadly."

Halibarda started to laugh, "We have a saying here 'you will never see hell, so die'."

"And you need some more driving lessons."

She smiled at me. "Oh Laura, Laura . . . all that is important for us right now is to focus on this wonderful meal. I went into the kitchen and watched; it all looks very good. I would like to have a beer, but . . . you know I am driving. However, feel free to have one yourself and maybe I will have a sip from yours."

*   *   *

Paul and Vlad were waiting for me in the living room. "Hello Paul, Hello Vlad," I saluted them.

"Hello Laura," Paul said, and he offered me a chair. "Would you like to speak first?"

"Yes," I answered. I took out a small wrapped box with the golden cross for Vlad. "Vlad, I have a gift for you."

His nice face lit up with a gorgeous smile.

"Oh . . . thanks Laura," he took the small box and prepared to open it but I stopped him.

"And our relationship is over. I would like you to leave the house now."

"But . . . Laura, please . . ."

"Now!" I said.

With a desperate gesture, he looked toward Paul. Paul gazed at him with compassion. In a low voice Paul said, "Vlad, we have important things to discuss here. If we need your services again we will call you."

Vlad was very distressed. He looked back at me and finally, with head bowed and shoulders slumped, he went slowly to the door.

"One last question Vlad," I stopped him. "Were you paid enough?"

"I am sorry?"

"I can give you more money if you need."

"No Laura, but thanks," he answered me. "I don't need your money. I . . ."

"Vlad, this is all for now. It was not my intention for things to end like this," Paul said. "Please accept my apologies."

Vlad smiled bitterly at Paul then with a final glance at me and Halibarda he left the room.

We remained silent for a few moments. In a way, we all regretted how it had ended and each missed this gorgeous man.

"It was not your intention to end it like this?" I repeated Paul's words angrily. "How long was it your intention to persist in this lie?" I was extremely upset.

Instead of answering my question, Paul looked toward Halibarda as if saying 'now it is your turn'.

"In fact it was my idea. The evening before your arrival I had a drink with Vlad and I got the idea that it would be for your benefit as he is a gorgeous guy and a wonderful lover," Halibarda said, trying to convince me.

"But still you had to tell me . . ."

"That was my intention," she said, "but the morning you woke up and he was not there you told me, 'Halibarda today I am disappointed, but I think I just lived the most amazing love story of my life.' How could I break your heart? And after that . . . things just evolved and . . ."

"And Chlorinda!" Paul almost screamed. "With that poison! She always has to be in the opposite direction. Next time it will cost her more than a viper bite."

The room was silent again. I was surprised by Paul's unexpected vehemence. I thought to myself, *he is trying to intimidate me.*

"However, Vlad was not the biggest lie. That was the dream . . ." Halibarda lowered her head as if she felt very guilty. Paul fixed me with an icy glare. "I thought if we knew more about each other you could trust me . . . us . . . more."

"But . . . how did you do it?"

"It is one of my abilities. I can induce images in your brain. I chose to put the image of my niece in your brain."

Chlorinda had told me in detail about these abilities, but I had still wondered about the truth of this. Hearing this now, I found it shocking.

As if proud about what he had done, Paul continued, "After that I wanted to give you a gift. I always enjoyed your music. I thought of some songs which are very close to your style and which you could be successful with. I added to your songs the color you always missed, which would push you over the top to become a star. Otherwise you were going to swim in mediocrity forever."

"Should I thank you for that? Or are you going to accuse me of copyright violation?"

"No. As I said, it was a gift. I am happy that you have been so successful with these songs."

"But even with all your magic talent and everything else, I am wealthier than all of you now. You keep all that for you and come to me for a musical collaboration?"

"Don't be stupid Laura. I am a sorcerer not a singer."

"Still I don't agree with your methods. You manipulated me; you invited me and my friends to one of your parties . . ."

"I needed you here in Romania, not there in Canada. I was not sure you would accept my invitation . . ."

"But you could have tried."

"Were you going to accept my request in those circumstances?" He and Halibarda were fixing me in their stares. I preferred not to answer.

"If you would have said yes, we apologize," Paul said. "However, the next candidate to bring you here was Chlorinda as she travels quite often in Canada. Her daughter lives there. I can guarantee you that she would not have been as gentle as I was. Think about that."

Halibarda intervened enthusiastically into our discussion, "But you must focus on the good things Laura. You have beautiful albums with wonderful songs, you have success and celebrity, you visited Romania and you had a good time here. You . . ."

"Why did you need me here so desperately?"

"Here we go . . ." Paul said smiling. "If you think we all lied, it is time to tell you that Chlorinda lied too. We tried many incantations to wake Dracula's entity and nothing was working. Until I discovered the reincarnation of somebody very emotionally close to Dracula was alive. We believed if that person was with us in the magical circle we would have better chances of succeeding."

"And that was right." Halibarda completed his thought.

"The meeting was in fact a big theatrical event, it was not real. Everyone was excited about your presence. That is the reason they gave you so much gold. Even Chlorinda was acting. She did not tell you why we needed you."

"Okay, how about if tomorrow I get on an airplane and go to Canada?"

"You can go," Paul answered simply. "We no longer need your help."

"Why?"

"The entity is awake and comes now at our call. Now it is our business. It killed nine of our people . . . I don't allow anyone to act like this. Even if that someone is a strange entity . . ."

"And if I want to stay?"

"I suggest you would prefer to live. Things have become dangerous."

"Look, I don't know who I was in a previous life, but now I am a witch and I want to defend against that entity too."

"This is not your war Laura," Halibarda observed.

"I will stay for now. I will attend the next incantation."

"There is a deadly danger. Are you aware of that?" Halibarda asked.

"Yes."

"Are you aware that if you die we will just throw your body into the abyss?" Paul inquired.

"As I will do with your body," I replied.

"That's right," he nodded acceptance.

"Now tell me who I am."

"How should I know?" Paul asked back.

"I . . . I don't know . . . you are smart, you are talented and you have your methods. Am I the reincarnation of Dracula's wife?"

"I don't know. What can I tell you exactly? I cannot be sure."

I tried to calm myself.

"Even when I die," Paul said, "I have no guarantee about what comes next. Do you want to hear another lie? What was quite clear was your strong connection in a previous life with Dracula and . . . your talent for magic in this life."

We were at the point where I had to decide whether to make peace or leave. "Okay, maybe you manipulated me and I find it extremely embarrassing. I accept for now the situation as it is. I . . . am ready to proceed with this." I looked at both of them.

Halibarda was happy as she came and hugged me. "I love you, Laura . . ."

"Paul," I said, "I have a gift for you too."

"Really?" he smiled at me.

I gave him the wrapped box with the other golden cross. He continued to smile and look at me even as he was opening the box. Finally, he held the chain and the cross in his hands and he looked down at the cross. With a terrible cry he threw down the cross and with preternatural speed he ran to the opposite corner of the room and covered his eyes.

Rapidly, Halibarda took the cross and covered it with a black cloth. Then she looked angrily at me. "Laura, there are so many symbols in the world; you could have chosen a star, a pentagram, the Greek life spiral . . . why did you choose a cross?"

I was absolutely shocked by Paul's gestures. As if hypnotized, I answered Halibarda's question. "Chlorinda suggested it to me."

"Oh that bitch . . ." Halibarda started speak invectives about Chlorinda. But I did not listen to her, I looked at Paul. He was still in the corner of the room shaking like he had a terrible scare.

"Who are you? What are you?" I asked him.

*   *   *

Chlorinda was looking at her vipers with immense love. "It might be the last time I see you my Children . . ."

She was feeling nostalgic. She had put much work into the business and now it was running nicely . . . *maybe I should stop performing magic and stay with my babies.* She understood she could be rich enough with only the business. Perhaps she could still keep magic as a hobby, nothing more.

Magic, magic . . . it is going to kill me. She deeply regretted that she had no premonition powers like Paul. *That bastard! He knows what will be next, he and that bitch.*

Suddenly, she became nervous. She took a few deep breaths to calm herself. *It is so ridiculous . . . I can read the future for the people who come to me for this, but my own future is a mystery.* She looked one by one at each mature viper. *They are remarkable creatures.* She knew she would miss them. She said *goodbye* to each one of them in turn. Finally with slow steps she began to go to the exit of the viper farm room. *Maybe it is better to stop now.* She turned back and sat on the stairs, looking back in the room. *The price is so dear . . . but I must continue on. I don't want that bastard to gain everything for himself.*

With decisive steps she walked up the stairs, spending no time in the rat room. She walked directly into the house, into the living room.

She began packing a carry-on bag. She put her magical tools, an extra sweater and the cell phone charger. *Just a few things, it appears to be a short journey but . . .* she smiled to herself *. . . dear Chlorinda, what is certain is that nothing is certain.*

The woman who worked for Chlorinda on the viper farm was just arriving and waited in the yard. Chlorinda never invited her inside. She spoke to her rarely and only regarding the things connected with the work on the viper farm.

"I collected the venom of the vipers yesterday. All you have to do is to feed the rats and feed the vipers. I am going to visit my daughter in Toronto. I will return in one month."

The woman tried to say something but Chlorinda interrupted her. "I don't have time for you and your asinine questions. Go to work," saying this, Chlorinda turned her back to the woman and she went inside. She took a deep sip from her now cold coffee. It was as if a voice inside her was telling her *. . . don't go, it is too dangerous . . .* but she fought with the voice, *I am powerful enough to go on. I am sure that I will be successful.*

Finally John arrived. She had asked her friend to give her a ride to the airport. "Laura called me yesterday," Chlorinda said. "She really liked the crosses you made. Especially the big one," and she smiled widely at John.

They chatted for awhile about the gold, vipers and the long flight Chlorida would have until she reached Toronto. Then they decided it was time to go to the car and drive to the airport as it would take more than three hours.

John wondered why Chlorinda was going with only one piece of carry-on luggage.

"Why do I need more? I have clothes at my daughter's house, and I enjoy shopping in Toronto. I will come back with this carry-on and a large suitcase," she smiled. "I will bring a gift for you John."

In the car he tried to keep chatting but Chlorinda was quiet and eventually John realized he was talking to himself. He decided to turn on the radio as the news is always interesting in Romania; he never got bored listening to Romanian news.

"I am sorry John, I would like to sleep," Chlorinda said to him. "You know it is night time there right now and I am trying to get acclimatized."

The ride was long and silent. John found it extremely tedious. He tried to capture the images of the people along the way and to analyze their faces, necks, and hands to think what kind of jewelry he could create especially for each one of them. When they reached Bucharest they took a beltline through town which allowed them to drive straight to the international airport. Idly, he wondered why they changed the name of the airport. Previously, it had been known as Otopeni, everyone knew the name Otopeni. Now it was called Henry Coanda. *That will generate a lot of confusion*, John thought to himself. The drive from Bucharest to the airport is not very long. Normally it takes less than one hour but that day the road was very busy so it took closer to one hour. Finally they arrived.

John suggested to Chlorinda it was time she woke up. In reality, behind her closed eyes she was not sleeping at all. She was thinking about the immense power she could gain if she attended this new incantation. It was imperative that she succeeds despite the immense danger.

With a courtly bow, John opened the car's door for Chlorinda. He took her carry-on and guided her inside. Chlorinda was elegantly dressed in comparison to her usual attire. Seeing her in these new clothes John thought that she was still a beautiful woman.

"We have time for coffee, John," she said.

"But . . . you know it costs so much here, Chlorinda. Everything is unbelievably expensive . . ."

"I agree with you John. My daughter also complained about this. But it would be my pleasure to buy you a coffee." They stayed there with their coffee between them. Chlorinda was quiet. Other times he drove her to the airport she had been very open to chatting but when he attempted to buy a coffee or a drink at the airport she had refused.

"John, I would appreciate it if you would look in on my house from time to time. That woman is quite stupid and . . ."

"I will, Chlorida. Don't worry. Just concentrate on having a good time with your daughter."

She smiled at him. "You are a wonderful friend, John. Thank you for everything."

They decided to go to the check-in point. John always found these types of things complicated. He was always confused about the timetables and schedules; he was never able to understand them . . .

"It is okay, John," Chlorinda said. "I can manage from here. You don't have to stay with me. You had better retrieve your car. I don't want you paying more money for unnecessary parking time." Saying that, with a masculine gesture she shook John's hand.

John was confused. After Chlorinda's husband died, he had been attracted to Chlorinda. But she had a strong personality and he knew there was no point in arguing. The only thing he could do was to shake Chlorinda's hand and say, "Have a good trip Chlorinda."

She smiled at him. "Thank you, dear friend." With this, she turned her back to John and proceeded to the check-in area with her carry-on.

John followed her for a little way then returned to the car. He still had a long drive back to the village.

Instead of going into the check-in area, Chlorinda walked to the end of the corridor. After making a huge arc she turned back. *John is gone now for sure* she said in her mind. *I respected Paul's instructions. Now I have to look for* . . . but she couldn't complete her thought because she saw Drina near her. Also elegantly dressed with a carry-on, Drina had done the same thing, suggesting that she would go to visit her sons in Spain for a few weeks.

They were happy to see each other again and chatted about escaping from the village for a short period of time as they moved toward the exit. Chlorinda was quite tall and Drina a small woman, to a casual observer they made an interesting couple. "Now we must travel incognito to our place *near Dracula's castle.*"

*   *   *

Paul had slept a little longer in the morning. I decided to take a short walk in the park with Halibarda. The morning was nice, but it was apparent it was going to be a very hot day. I was enjoying this pleasant morning in this beautiful park. We had been walking for several minutes without talking. Like me, Halibarda seemed to enjoy the park and the nice morning.

I couldn't stop thinking about what was going to happen tonight, about who I am, who I was, what was wrong with Paul ..."Halibarda, I was very ... surprised by Paul's reaction yesterday."

Halibarda stopped walking and looked surprised by my question. "Laura, think about when you hate something. You hate it with every fiber of your being and somebody is offering this thing to you ..."

"Halibarda, you guys have done nothing but tell me lies until now. Let's stop lying ..."

Halibarda maintained her surprised air. "But ... Laura ... I know that he does not like the cross. He is very ... superstitious, if I can use this word for people such as ourselves. He noticed that he is unlucky when he wears a cross ..."

"Halibarda, he was shaking and terrified, like a ... vampire."

"Don't be ridiculous Laura. Vampires don't walk during the day; Paul is with us during the day. Vampires don't go into churches, we been with Paul in church."

"His leap at the last incantation ... it was unnatural, impossible for a human being ..."

Halibarda took my hands. "Laura, in stressful situations we find unbelievable resources within us. Things we cannot do under normal circumstances are possible when we are under great stress. He was under that effect. You were also extremely scared when all that occurred and you may have lost your sense of proportion."

I paused for a moment. Her explanations appeared to be logical. But I was there and I was quite sure about what I saw. "His speed is also supernatural. I saw him moving preternaturally fast many times, and I was not under stress in all of those moments."

"I noticed that too. He is very rapid in his movements. He told me that it is a consequence of an accelerated metabolism. After he does that he needs a considerable quantity of food." She paused again looking at me, "Laura, the people you met here are not normal people. Each one possesses special powers as do you. Think about that you foresaw with unbelievable accuracy—the deaths of the twin sisters." With a theatric gesture she continued walking.

I was still quite confused. "That ... entity is Dracula?"

"We are sure it is connected with Dracula."

"As I am connected too."

"Yes, we know that you are a reincarnation of someone very close to Dracula. He is attracted to you."

"I am the woman he loved."

"Who can swear? Who can guarantee this? No one. But it is very clear that he is attracted to you. Look, tonight stay between me and Paul and we will protect you."

I gazed at the lake. There was no wind and the lake was completely still, the surface like glass. A few birds were flying and touching the lake surface, creating small ripples. "In his natural life Dracula was an evil man?"

"Oh I can show you a collection of the movies I have called *The Most Evil Man in History*. He was indeed the most evil man in human history. Even Paul was impressed when he discovered that Dracula meted out capital punishment to the pope for a few minor errors. In that time there were no TV or similar devices and he enjoyed taking his lunch and watching the executions for entertainment. The impaling. For this, we call him Vlad the Impaler or in the Romanian language Vlad Tepes."

"Did he become a vampire after he died?"

Halibarda paused as she tried to avoid answering my question. "Possibly, yes. He took an abnormal enjoyment from seeing blood. It is said his servants collected blood from his victims and he ate it with bread. It is also said that when he was born the icon of the Virgin Maria cried bloody tears. The Orthodox Church excommunicated him."

I watched Halibarda, "These things are so far in the past. Maybe . . . nothing is sure."

"One thing more," Halibarda said, "in the communist regime his tomb was exhumed. They found only animal bones there."

I thought about all the possibilities. "Thank you Halibarda. As I said to you, I don't know what I was in my previous lives, but in this life I am very attracted by magical things, even more than my music. I enjoy being a witch and I want to be a powerful one."

Halibarda nodded her approval. "Yes. I totally understand you. After the . . . confrontation with the entity you might gain powers. It is like energies which laid dormant inside you until now may awaken. But . . . the danger is . . . very severe."

*   *   *

Evening was drawing near. Paul drove the car. I was in the back seat and Halibarda in the front beside Paul. He drove the car with very good ability. I was able to recognize that we were close to Dracula's castle. Paul searched for a place to hide the car. He went onto a small side path. It was not at all suitable for a car, it was quite impractical. He drove more than a hundred meters on this path. Finally he parked the car in a place where the trees opened up just enough to accommodate the car on the right side.

"Okay girls," Paul said. "Please take your stuff and let's hurry."

We retrieved our backpacks, this time we also each had a rod. We thought it would be useful when we hiked up the mountain and as well as to perform magic. Without speaking much, we began our hike up the mountain. This time we took only a few very short breaks, we all felt the urgency of the situation. The day was hot and the arrival of the evening was a blessing. We hiked for almost 20 minutes up the mountain. Waiting for us at a big log were Chlorinda, Drina and Ivanka. Drina . . . my lovely Drina. I was so happy to see her again and we hugged each other while I enjoyed the sensation. I felt like I was as powerful as she was. I felt like together we could fight any entity from this or another world.

I also hugged Chlorinda. I noticed that Chlorinda and Drina were elegantly dressed. I wondered why. I thought they needed some comfortable hiking clothes and nothing more.

I then said *hello* to Ivanka and gave her a formal hug. Paul and Halibarda hugged them as well.

"So . . . of all the brave and powerful sorcerers of our club only six of us remain," Chlorinda said sarcastically.

"Seven," Paul corrected her.

"Maybe seven if you include the entity we are fighting," Chlorinda added, maintaining her mocking air.

"Then we are eight," Paul said, more calmly than usual. "Now let's hurry up."

We began hiking. The evening was beautiful and I was having strange thoughts such as *I would like to die on a beautiful evening like this* . . . I became momentarily afraid by this. As if she were waking me up from a bad dream, I felt Drina's small hand touching my hand. She smiled nicely at me. It was a kind of revelation about who is able to bring you back from thoughts of death. Drina . . . my lovely Drina. I answered her back with a smile.

In almost thirty minutes we were at the top of the mountain plateau. I was still wondering about this plateau. I also had the odd sensation that the mountain continued up and did not end at the plateau. It was very level, too precise to be a mountain plateau; it was like the top of the mountain was somehow . . . cut by someone. I was beginning to think that maybe it was artificially made. Maybe Dracula made it, he commanded his people to work and they were so terrified by him they worked hard to make this plateau completely flat. After that, perhaps this was his favorite place to sacrifice his victims, taking enjoyment from the macabre spectacle.

I began asking myself what was going on with me. I wondered if this was just a stray thought, a rebellious idea in a corner of my brain or . . . if it was a memory from a previous life resurfacing.

When we reached the plateau I saw that Paul was right. There was a seventh person waiting for us. The old woman was there.

"Who is she?" Chlorinda asked.

"What is she?" Ivanka echoed Chlorida's question.

The old woman stayed crouched down on the earth. With small gestures she was eating bread. She looked at us. She made a sign with her head as if she was saying 'hello' to us. I made a polite sign to her with my hand.

Paul walked near her and removed his bag. Checking inside his bag he removed a sandwich. I saw that the sandwich had plenty of meat inside and some lettuce leaves. He gave the sandwich to the old woman. With both hands she took the sandwich from Paul's hand. She took a long look at Paul, as if she was enjoying watching him. She smiled at him quickly began to eat the sandwich, clearly savoring it even though she didn't have a tongue.

Chlorida took a small sip of water from a plastic bottle.

"Okay everyone," Paul said. "We are seven. We are here to battle the entity which is supposed to be connected with Dracula. Immediately we will set the magical circle and that will be a challenge to it. I expect it will be stronger than last time. Now that it is fully awake, it is not confused and will use its entire power to try to defeat us." He looked at our faces as if making a final analysis of each one of us.

"I don't wish that. But it is possible tonight one or some of us will die," he paused again. "The protocol is: the ones who remain alive in the morning will push the dead bodies into the abyss over there and go home. If I die tonight my body will have the same destination. Don't forget that we are sorcerers. Even dead some of us might find the way back." He showed us his strange grin, his crazy grin.

"Why are we, I mean our souls, supposed to stay in such boring places as hell or heaven? We have work to do here." He laughed for a moment. "We have Laura with us. She is at the beginning of her experience. Halibarda and I will protect her. If possible, please do your best to protect her but don't forget about your own protection. No one needs to be brave alone; I need us to be a team. I need the team to defend against the entity. When we feel it is attacking at a specific point we must defend it. It is very animalistic. It is powerful but not clever enough and we have to use all its flaws against it, especially that one," he paused and looked again at each one of us.

"Last but not least... thank you to everyone for your perseverance. You guys are amazing sorcerers."

*   *   *

We lit the candles. At each cardinal point were also knives buried in the soil. It was a sharp barrier against the entity penetrating our magical circle. The night was silent; there was virtually no wind.

Suddenly a wind started to bloom. It was enough strong to blow out our candles. Ivanka hurried to light them again. Everyone tried to do the same. If the candles were not lit our magic would become less, like our magical circle's power was decreasing in intensity.

"There is something around us," Ivanka declared. "Something is trying to undo what we are doing here." She appeared to be focusing on something that was trying to destroy her inside. She moved her head in uneasy circles.

"Let it show up, Ivanka. Don't fight with it by yourself," Paul commanded.

Ivanka fell down, her body extended. At that moment in one corner of the plateau an enormous, strange animal appeared. From a distance, I thought its body was massive like a bear's. It was galloping toward us with incredible speed. I was mesmerized by the animal's red eyes. As it came toward us rapidly, I saw that it was not a bear at all. Its ears were like a wolf's but about six times larger. Its tongue was hanging out from its mouth and saliva was hanging in ropy strands beneath its jaw. It was so horrific I almost forgot my fear and I felt my stomach heave.

"I am first!" Paul said in a loud voice. He was standing in the direction the animal was trying to attack us from. As the animal loped toward him, Paul stood in front of it as if he was an easy target. But as the animal came close to him, Paul put his rod in front of it. Seeing the strange animal was trying to come to a sudden stop, Paul thrust and tried to use his rod to penetrate its body to reach the heart, if it indeed had a heart . . .

The animal tried to stop but its momentum was so forceful it was able only to change direction. But it passed close enough to our circle that Paul was able to badly skewer the strange animal with his rod. The animal made a terrible scream of pain, a sharp sound I had never heard an animal make before.

"As I said the entity is quite animalistic," Paul said.

Closing her eyes, Chlorinda was trying to catch the strange animal in her hypnotic wave. As if feeling it, the animal ran to the edge of the plateau. We could still hear it screaming. It sounded like the animal was running down the mountain. Suddenly all was silent again. In some far trees we heard some birds crying, scared by the strange noise.

I attempted to calm myself, saying in my mind the fear litany:

I am in the evil valley. The danger surrounds me from the front, from behind, laterally, from above and below. I am in valley of death; but I will fear no evil.

"It is afraid of me," Chlorinda declared. "I was just about to capture it and it realized that. It recognized its inferiority and decided to run."

"For now. Let's focus Chlorinda," Paul said. "The night is not over yet."

"I will go to see where it is," I said. Closing my eyes, I used the wind elements to take my astral spirit up above the woods. By now I was proficient in using this magic. My body became light as a feather. I was above the plateau and I could see the circle created

272

by the candles. I saw the seven people in the middle of the circle.
I was excited to see the other six people and my own human body
too. Without losing time I flew around the plateau. The strange
animal was not there. I flew around the mountain but I could not
see the animal anywhere. Suddenly I felt somebody calling me back
by shaking my human body.

"Laura, Laura . . . come back, come back," Drina was shaking
my body. With incredible speed I was back in my body. Drina was
scared . . . afraid for me. I saw tears in her eyes.

"I am good, I am good," I said immediately.

"You stopped communicating with us and we were anxious,"
Paul added.

"Are you Okay Laura?" Drina asked. With a delicate gesture I
touched her face.

"I am Okay."

"Report," demanded Chlorinda, "did you see the entity?"

"No, it is not around. I did not see it."

Suddenly Ivanka became agitated. She started speaking quickly
in Romanian. Near me almost instantly Halibarda started to translate
her words. "It is not gone. It is searching for us. Before morning it
will execute all of us," and she began to tremble uncontrollably.

"Shut up woman!" Paul screamed at her. "Chlorinda calm her
down."

Chlorinda caught Ivanka's face with her hands and moved close
to her face. With her green eyes she looked directly into Ivanka's eyes.
Ivanka was calming down and lowering her voice gradually until she
became silent. With a dismissive gesture Chlorinda pushed her over.
As if the woman was a vegetable she fell down to the earth.

"The wound I created to its physical body caused pain, but it
is around watching for us . . ." Paul intended to say more but all of
us were surprised by an unexpected movement by Ivanka. She had
recovered a few moments after Chlorinda's hypnosis and now with
her powers regained she began to run to the edge of the plateau
toward the path we had used to come here.

"I thought you were watching her . . ." Paul said angrily to
Chlorinda.

"She tricked me . . ."

Halibarda screamed something to Ivanka in Romanian. I
thought she was asking her to come back.

273

Ivanka was not able to reach the edge of the plateau because the strange animal appeared again. Screaming, the animal was running with supernatural speed toward the woman. Ivanka stopped and turned to the animal. Holding a large knife in her hand, the woman waited for the animal's approach.

The night was dark; we were not able to see the scene clearly.

Halibarda continued to shout verbal instructions at Ivanka.

"Okay," Paul said, "each one of you take a candle."

Halibarda took the north candle, Chlorinda the south candle, Drina the west candle and the old woman the east candle. Paul and I stood in the center of the circle.

"Let's move the circle in Ivanka's direction. No one leave the circle. Don't increase the speed enough to blow out the candles. The candles must remain lit," Paul commanded.

As we approached Ivanka we were finally able to distinguish her agonized face in the dark. To calm myself I again said in my mind the fear litany:

I am in the evil valley. The danger surrounds me from front, from behind, laterally, from above and below. I am in valley of death, but I will fear no evil.

As if sensing it was surrounded, the entity moved to another side of the woman.

"Let's take her in the circle. We might save her," Paul barked.

As she held her knife, I heard Ivanka screaming in her language to the entity. Crazily, she began to attack the entity with her huge knife. The entity ran around her with supernatural speed. As we drew very close the entity realized it didn't have much time. It attacked the woman's legs. I saw blood gushing out. Screaming, Ivanka fell down. Without losing time, the entity began to bite the woman's face. Desperately, Ivanka tried to use her knife. But to no avail . . . soon her body was headless; the strange animal had decapitated her. Shrieking loudly, the animal disappeared again into the woods.

"It is gone," Drina said.

"Let's go back to the middle of the plateau," Paul commanded.

"Tonight I will destroy the entity!" Chlorinda screamed.

"Let's stay together. All of you: control yourselves. I need you alive," Paul said.

We arrived in the center of the plateau.

Suddenly a wind came up. It was strong enough to blow out our candles.

"We cannot relight the candles. The wind is too strong this time. Each one of you pretend the candles are lit. Try to control the protective elements around us. The entity had a taste of human blood. Now it has the same ability to control the elements we do."

The night was unbelievably dark. I could feel the entity around me. It was if it was flying around us. "It is in the air."

"I feel it too!" Halibarda screamed.

"Chlorinda, use your hypnotic power to bring it down," Paul commanded.

"I have it," Drina screamed. "I caught you, bitch!"

We heard a loud noise like a huge body was plummeting down to the earth. As it became close to us the entity was making sharp piercing screams.

The old woman was holding her rod. Raising it like a javelin she threw it in the direction the sounds were coming from.

"Let's do the same," Paul commanded.

With quick movements we took our rods and threw them in the entity's direction. Its screams were increasing in intensity. Finally we heard a long howl and after that . . . silence.

"We killed it, we killed it!" Drina screamed triumphantly.

"Drina calm down." Paul commanded sharply.

"Paul, it is down." Drina said. "I have to go there to destroy it completely."

"No!" Paul screamed.

"Let's go together," Chlorida asked. Without waiting, the two of them went in front of us. As we approached we saw an enormous body with our rods implanted in it. Suddenly, the body started to move. In an instant, the huge animal was between us and Chlorinda and Drina.

The two women moved back to back to protect themselves. With a precise movement Drina threw her knife into the animal. Even though the knife was deeply planted in its leg the animal did not scream this time.

Instead of doing the same, Chlorinda threw her knife down. "I don't need this knife to destroy you," she said.

In the dark night I began to sense forces increasing their intensity to terrible levels. I saw the red eyes of the entity beginning to glow; but then Chlorida's green eyes did also. Both red and green began increasing dramatically in intensity as they did battle. Helping Chlorinda, Drina extended her hands toward the entity. She applied amazing kinesthetic force against the creature's body. The remaining four of us were trying to use the wind elements to push the entity to the earth.

I could feel a strong storm surrounding the entity. It was not able to move from its place as it was totally enclosed. But it was resisting with a supernatural force. In a fraction of moment it pushed us back several steps like it was using the wind or a kinesthetic power. We began to lose our forces. Then suddenly it leaped toward Chlorinda and Drina. What I heard in the dark night was only Drina's death scream . . .

I felt my heart breaking. "Drina . . ." I shouted into the black night.

"Get a grip on your emotions and let's go closer," Paul commanded.

We saw the animal's immense body and Chlorinda on its back. Frantically, she was repeatedly stabbing her knife into the animal's huge body. The animal was running away with Chlorinda on its back. Even though the animal was in agony it was gaining on us. After that it shook itself strongly, trying to dislodge Chlorinda. As strong as she was, she fell off its back. We felt the thud from the impact in our feet and Chlorinda appeared about to lose consciousness. The animal ran over top of her, screeching and trying to bite Chlorinda's face. But as it came near it was unable to move. In a final effort Chlorinda was focusing her strong hypnotic power. I raised my hand in the direction of the animal. I felt like I now had kinesthetic powers like Drina had. It was as if she died and transferred her kinesthetic powers like a gift. The animal fell off Chlorinda. As soon as she was free she tried to stand up but it she had been badly injured when the animal threw her down. She was not able to move into an upright position. Immediately, the animal jumped back on top of her and I saw . . . fountains of blood. The animal was eating from Chlorinda's body and drinking her blood. It appeared to be regaining power, and again it disappeared into the woods.

"Now we are four. Each one of you hold a cardinal point. We will move according to the entity's attack," Paul said, taking control. I took the west side, the wind side. Without giving us any more time the entity appeared in front of me. This time it had taken the form of an almost human body with bat wings. As it was too dark I was unable to distinguish its face but I could see its eyes. Red eyes. Demonic eyes. It hovered in front of me trying to break the energy barrier I had created. I gazed directly into its glowing red eyes. It was intensifying its energetic attack. I felt a surge as the forces increased dramatically. I was reminded of the exercises I practiced with Chlorinda. I increased my energies at the same rate.

It was not able to penetrate my direction. I had the sensation it was trying to communicate with me. It was trying to say something to me. I tried to focus to understand its words. It sounded like . . ."*Welcome back.*"

With terrifying speed it moved in the front of the old woman. I thought for a moment the end of the old woman had arrived, that she would not be able to resist the entity's power. The old woman stood up straight and made some strange signs with her hands. At the same time she was trying to articulate a spell with her missing tongue. Screaming like it was injured; the entity sped away from us.

We had a long break which was quite welcome. I thought to myself this old woman is full of surprises; the magic she knows is very effective.

But again the entity returned and tried to attack from Paul's side, then Halibarda's. After that she tried to come at me again.

We battled like this all night long, the entity constantly attacking and retreating, searching for weakness, until the morning when the sun rose and it finally disappeared.

*   *   *

When the sun was further up in the sky, I took Drina's small body and threw what was left of it into the abyss near the plateaus. Halibarda did the same with Chlorinda's body and Paul with Ivanka's.

"Let's hurry up to the car and get the hell out of here," Paul said. "You," he pointed to the old woman. "You come with us for now."

We hurried to the small path. We went down the mountain as quickly as we could and made our way to the place where Paul had hidden the car. All the way back I felt a chill deep in my soul as I heard the entity's words resonating in my head:

"*Welcome back!*"

Chapter 17

I was walking on a small path
And I was so sad . . . . .
On my way I met three women.
They were wonderful women.
The first two gave me good advice
The third one did not.
She was only looking and me and intensely studying me . . . .
And she said me that,
She is in the same situation as I am
She said to me that she is sad like me and for this reason she
totally understands me.

-Romanian folk song

I was very depressed.

We spent the day in the town of Risnov, just Paul and I. Halibarda offered to give and the old woman a ride back to a town, which was close to her home. Paul and I rented a room over night. He told the people who would believe it that we were married. We slept over night in the same bed. I had the chance to see him naked; I think it is customary for him to sleep naked. He is an attractive man. Even though we slept in the same bed we did not make love. We were too tired for this.

The events prior to this were devastating to us. I saw that he was sleeping quite well at the beginning. I was up for at least an hour. It was frustrating because he was sleeping so deep and I was not able to sleep at all. Until now there were eight people who had died at the first incantation, one death was connected with the first incantation and three with the second incantation. Until now twelve people had died. I was quite horrified by these events. How could Paul so well after all this?

I tried to close my eyes . . . blackness was all around me. I am afraid about blackness and Paul was afraid of the cross . . . So strange. Who is afraid of the cross, the evil, the devil, the vampire . . . . who is this man? What is he?

I made a painful effort to sleep, none of my concentrations were useful. The disturbance was too high. There was blackness all around me. It was like the black was becoming a type of darkness. Dark as Ivanka skin and . . . I could not sleep. I opened my eyes and I saw that Ivanka was near me. She was looking at me with interest and curiosity. I had always been curiosity about her, starting with the first magic lesson.

She continued to study me. I thought that I had to ask her something, but she started to speak first.

"I warned Paul that you were dangerous . . . . . he did not listen me. I told him this danger has to be manipulated with immense caution. He did not listen to me . . . and look now . . . look where we are. Look where . . . I am . . . ."

"Ivanka . . . . I am so sorry . . . ."

Her face was looking little bit different. She was quite relaxed, not in the same tension like before. Like reading my mind she said:

"Always I had been tense. Paul was right when he told me that I have to pass the ordinary stuff and to focus to the superior things and, ideas. I was so preoccupied by my ordinary existence . . . and this was a regrettable mistake."

She bent down towards me. She was looking at me with intense curiosity. Without saying anything, she tried to touch me. Suddenly she became scared like she always did when she tried to touch me. She started to scream, her scream made me wake up. I saw so much, it made me all sweaty.

Nearby Paul felt me.

"Hey. You ok?"

"I . . . I need to drink some water. I will be ok."

I took a huge sip from the water glass from the small table near the bed.

"A dream?" Paul asked me.

"It . . . it was . . . it was so real. She was near me. Watching me . . . ."

"Hey! You first have to learn to control yourself even when you sleep. Calm down. Breath. Control your breathing until you can fix it to a normal rate and keep it like this."

He was touching my brow. "You have a fever . . . or maybe it is too hot in this room. I will open the window."

He walked naked through the room and he opened the window. I felt the cold mountain air. He was right. The cold mountain air helped me, it was cooling me down and relaxing me.

"Better now?" he asked "Ok lets go back to sleep. Try to focus now on sleeping. Think about how it is the only important thing in the world."

He smiled to encourage me.

I was quite relaxed now. My breath was normal. I turned my back to him and even if I was little embarrassed with my body I touched his body anyway. The sensation of a human body gave me more confidence. It allowed me to fall asleep.

I think I slept for a long time. I would have slept longer but a noise made me wake up. Two women were talking in a quiet voice. One was a tall and solid woman and the other was quite small, with very long, blond hair. Chlorinda and Drina. They observed that I was there and watching them. They stopped their chat. Both of them were studying me in silence for a while.

"You are so nice Laura . . ." Drina said.

"You are a poor girl Laura . . ." Chlorinda said. They were looking at me, and at each other.

"Now do you have kinesthetic powers?" Drina asked me.

"Now do you have hypnotic abilities?" Chlorinda asked me.

I was feeling all these new powers inside me and I was ready to tell them *yes*. But I was busy thinking to another direction.

"Girls . . . . I am so sorry . . . ."

They were quite surprised about my answer.

"Why are you sorry Laura?" Drina asked me with a crystalline voice.

"I feel like I am guilty for your death."

"Death . . . ? . . ." Chlorinda was repeating like an echo. They were watching each other and they melted under my eyes.

I woke up. I fixed my eyes on the glass of water. I became so angry, and I applied all my anger to that glass. Immediately I saw and heard the glass exploding in a thousand of small pieces and the rest of the water flowed down to the floor. Paul almost jumped from the bed.

"Laura, what the heck is this? . . ."

I was looking in his eyes. He watched my eyes for a moment, then he covered his eyes.

"For god sakes Laura! Do not try to hypnotize me. I can react and you will regret it."

After that he was looking in my eyes to threaten to me that he was ready if I wanted to try and hypnotize him. He was ready to defend himself.

"What is all this mess here Laura? How did you break the glass . . ." but he stopped himself. It was like he was receiving new information. He came close with his head close by mine. After that he looked deeply to me "they were here . . . . I see . . . ."

He was thinking for a moment.

"Laura we are tired, lets sleep. We need to sleep to refresh our energies. Please forget about other things. Try auto hypnosis as you try to sleep. This will be useful and relaxing."

He convinced me, and I put my head on the pillow and tried to focus on my sleep. The concentrating was working, and I was really tired too. I felt myself relax. All around me was quite calm. I felt like the morning would come soon. The light of the sun will wake up the day creatures of the earth. The light of the sun will throw out the night demons.

This is good. I am at least not lost in time. But where I am? I was looking around me. It was like I was in a country village very similar to Paul's village. I was walking on an unpaved route inside of the village. Behind me was one or two people, I was not focusing at all to the couple who followed me. I felt like one of them was Paul and maybe in a behind him was an old woman; she was trying with her weak body to catch us. I was excited to walk quite quickly to reach the end of the street. It was like I was sure that at the cross roads I would find something dangerous. It was dark. I was not able to clearly see the road intersection. For this reason I hurried up. I was curious about reaching the intersection of the roads and to see what was there. The people behind me were walking quite slowly and I advanced faster and faster. I looked back to make sure that they did not lose me. And . . . it was like suddenly I closed in on the cross roads. I was able clearly to see now . . .

Exactly in the middle of the cross road was a terrible kind of animal like the one which attacked us. Its body was massive, more massive than a bear's body. Its tail was quite long and its hair was like a wolf's hair. Its head was like a huge wolf, but it stood on its hind legs. Its mouth was open wide, as the massive tongue came out from his mouth. The drool was dripping out from his mouth, like it was a rabid animal. His eyes were red, like fire. It was looking around, scanning each one of the four roads. Finally he was looking to the road where we were.

The terrible creature was saying an incantation in human voice. I heard his words: *"night amen, night amen, dark night amen . . . ."*

He was gazing at me with his red eyes. I felt like my legs would not listen to me. I was going to tumble down, but Paul was near me. He caught my falling body. I was like a vegetable, unable to move. From the behind the old woman was coming close. She was stepping between us and the terrible devil animal. She was saying a kind of incantation with her mouth and cut tongue.

I heard Paul's words, "we have to cross the road. We will walk easily near this devil and he will let us pass. He will let us pass only if we do not show fear. Laura, Laura do you hear me?! Stay with me. The old woman will help us. Let's stay together the fear litany. He started first and I said the fear litany with him:

I am in the evil valley. The danger surrounds me from front, behind, from laterals, from above and below. I am in the death's valley; but I will not fear by the evil."

I heard Paul's voice,

"Let's walk slowly. It will be easy for you to avoid looking at him. Laura, do not be afraid. The old woman is with us. She is a strong witch, she will help us. She will protect us against the evil."

We were starting to walk with small steps towards the cross roads. It was like I felt the evil of the devil animal. It was increasing in intensity with each step we made. Also I felt a fire burning and with a human voice the devil called my name.

"Laura, Laura, . . . come here. Laura . . ."

His words were like a hypnosis. I regained my legs and I went towards the animal.

"No Laura! No!" Paul was saying in low voice, as he did not intend to upset the devil animal. "Laura, stay with me. Stay with us."

It was like I intended to go the animal. It was like my body did not listen to my commands. The batting of the old woman's rod on the ground helped me to regain the control of my body.

But, it was also like the animal was increasing its hypnosis "Come to me . . ."

I was very certain that I wanted to go to him. I felt an irresistible attraction to him. But Paul was holding me. I observed that he made a sign to the old woman to increase her magic against the devil. This time Paul was screaming my name.

" Laura! Laura! . . . ."

I woke up. Paul was strongly shaking my body. I woke up and I looked around the room like I been in a strange place. The morning was just beginning. Paul was quite preoccupied by me.

He said "We have to analyze in detail this . . . dream."

*　　*　　*

I found an enjoyable way up to the old feudal city. It was a nice morning and the cold mountain air gave me a nice feeling. We were staying to look around at the nice view from the walls of the old city. I think Paul really loves this place.

"I am quite sad after all this . . ." Paul was trying to start a conversation with me.

"Yes? . . . finally you have one less enemy."

He was bitterly smiling.

"You are referring to Chlorinda. She was not my enemy. She was a rebel. Always a rebel, but never an enemy. Now with her dead I miss her. I miss her arguing. She was always arguing, but always quit predictable. I used her arguing to make my speech in front of the people. I am gonna to miss her. She was strong, her powers were strong. She was a remarkable woman . . . ."

"And Drina was a remarkable woman too," I added.

"Yes. All three of them were remarkable woman. So sad that they are dead."

There were lots of tourists around us. I think this place is almost always busy with tourists. They took pictures, making videos with their cameras. The reality is that this place is beautiful.

"But . . . what are your conclusions Paul? What are we fighting with? What is exactly this . . . . entity?"

"We know that he is . . . connected with Dracula's soul. It is a lost spirit, but a potent one. His personality was very powerful. It was quite clear that after his death he will be converted to . . . something."

"Maybe a vampire?

"It was possible. But we are speaking even after. Usually in Romania we always found ways to eliminate the vampires. The problem is what is still happening with these lost souls after they are . . . . defeated."

He paused like taking a break to think.

"I think a strong personality will never chase that easily. Think about it, a vampire needs a physical body; over the day he is sitting in his grave. Over the night he is chasing. But he cannot chase during the day because he is sensitive to the light. After he is killed again . . . for some of them, it looks to be possible to pass into a superior phase. They do not need a body which in fact is mindless."

He looked for a while at the wonderful view.

"How about me? Who am I?"

"You seem to be someone who he loved very much . . . . A reincarnation of that woman."

"His wife?"

"Or maybe he had somebody else for love. This story goes deep into history. You seem to be that woman whoever she was." He turned his face towards me.

"I have to warn you again. It is dangerous game. You might consider going home."

"Why?"

"The entity is now quite connected with these places. If you continue to be around the entity will . . . maybe, start following you.
"

He paused to let me to realize the gravity of his words.

"You told me details from your dream from last night. It is clear that the entity is trying to possess you."

I was very shocked. Paul is able to tell very grave things in such a normal voice. It was though he was asking for sugar for this coffee and . . . . by the way do you know that you will die tomorrow?

"It is my life. As you said about your strong personalities they can not chase easily, so neither can I. How can stop him from possessing me?"

"Da . . ." He said, "da, da . . . that is the right question. Think about after a "dream" like that you had if you go to the doctor, the doctor will give you medicine. Or he will recommend some rest. If you go to the priest he will try to help you but he has no magical power. The reality is that my club is the only institution in the world that can help you."

Near us a couple of tourists who understood our discussion almost run away scared. He was smiling at me, like he was telling me *here we are.*

"Even if we lost valuable members we can help you."

"How?"

"There might be painful ways but I will suggest an easy way to you. Usually if we are speaking about any entity who will try to possess a girl, the entity will chase if the girl is always with a guy but will not be as powerful."

"Ok. I will always stay with you Paul."

"Do not be ridiculous Laura. I have my personal stuff to do."

"That is why you brought me here, and you let me die now? And, all because you have stupid personal stuff to do?"

"There is a better possibility."

I was kind of unsure what he was suggesting me. He has a big smile on his face.

"Vlad"

"But . . . Paul here we are playing with a dangerous entity. Do you think he will be safe?"

Paul started laughing. Some of the tourists were looking disturbed in our direction.

"He is good. There is almost no magic. If that entity will try to posses you and you will have sex with Vlad, the entity cannot take your mind. And, you know Vlad is good."

I felt that Paul was playing with things that he should not play with.

"How do you know so much about . . . Vlad?"

"Because I commanded him to help me with other cases too . . ." He smiled at me. "And those cases was not only girl cases."

Joyfully smiling, he left me alone and went into the yard of the feudal city becoming very occupied by studying an old torture device exposed there. I was quite shocked about all this stuff. These were crazy guys. I decided that I have much time. I dialed a number on my cell phone.

"Hello Vlad. How are you . . . . ?"

*   *   *

We had our lunch at a gorgeous restaurant close to Risnov. After that Paul asked some guys to give us a ride to Bucharest. We had no car as our car is with Halibarda. Finally he asked the guys to let us off at a small village. The evening was near. The village looked quite small. The roads were not paved but because it was close with the mountain there were lots of rocks on the roads so they looked almost paved. The roads are narrow. It is difficult to fit two cars on at the same time.

I thought that Paul was looking for a room for tonight. He appeared to be very familiar with the village. We walked for more than twenty minutes on the roads of this village. I found the village to be quite backward but somehow . . . romantic. From place to place people were in the front of their gates chatting. Paul showed me a house that was in bad shape. It was in the middle of the village. The other houses had fences and gates. From each house's gate you can walk into a small yard and after that into each of the houses. The house Paul showed me was different. It did not have an external fence as it was build directly from the road.

"That is my property," Paul said. "I bought it almost for nothing. It was extremely cheap. That was because no one from the village wanted to buy it."

"Why was that? What was so wrong with this house?"

"Well a man committed suicide inside . . ."

"What? . . . and you want us to sleep there?"

As though he had not considered my words, he continued to speak.

"After he died the problem was his ghost remained in the house. It was what we are called an eerie house."

I was gonna to ask him if we could sleep somewhere else. But he was ignoring me again.

"After he died his ghost was quite active. The neighbors were hearing noises inside. Some of them were seeing objects moving in the house. There were enough things happening that no one wanted to buy such a house. It was quite easy for me with very little money to buy the house from his brother. After that I promised to the neighbors I would quiet the ghost."

"So . . . now the ghost is gone?"

He was looking at me.

"Why am I supposed to eliminate it totally? The ghost will be there and she will always protect my house. Nobody will dare go inside to steal something. However, I do not have valuable things."

I was not totally sure, with the problems already I had, if I wanted to sleep in a eerie house.

Some neighbors were looking at us with interest. I saw their eyes showing some fear. Paul was made a hello sign to them. They answered almost the same but were not very excited about seeing us and especially when they observed that we are going into that house. Paul found a big key in his bag and opened the door. The door made a terrible creaking noise.

"I am hooome!" Paul sung in a high voice. He was going to put on the light but suddenly the bulb exploded. I was quite calm. *What can I expect in an eerie house?* Especially in one like this with an active ghost.

"Laura . . ." Paul screamed to me, "We are in danger." I felt fear in his voice. "Stay close with me, behind me."

"W . . . what's wrong you said the ghost is active . . ."

"Now it is something more dangerous. Somebody made us goblin magic. This goblin looks quite strong."

Suddenly lots of objects were thrown down in the room. Paul was rotating quickly trying to locate the goblin. I was trying to stay behind him. I felt something dangerous too. I had the sensation that I could see a midget with a terribly ugly face. It was sometimes just a shade, sometimes quite well materialized. He was trying to attack Paul. But Paul was always focusing and the goblin was rejected after each unsuccessful attack. The goblin made strange and sharp sounds.

Paul was bending his hand like he was sending an immense energy. For the moment the terrible creature was not able to move. It was making terrible sharp noises. I was unable to look in the

287

direction of the goblin because he ugly and especially now when Paul was immobilizing him. The spectacle was disgusting.

"Who sent you here?"

Ignoring Paul's question the goblin continued to scream and making sharp noises.

"I will punish you like you have never been punished. Your only alternative is to let me know who sent you." and saying this Paul was appeared to intensify the energy to punish the goblin. For a moment, it seemed like the goblin was saying something.

"Oh . . . Chlorinda . . . . That bitch. She created a weapon to attack me after, in the event . . . she would die."

I understood that we were in grave danger. Now Paul has to divide his energies in two. One side to keep the goblin immobilized and other to check around Chlorinda's house to see where the egg that Chlorinda used to create the goblin was.

I decided to help Paul. I quickly made up my mind in the magical circle. Speedily I made the incantations and the requested concentrations. After that, I used the wind elements to fly and check inside Chlorinda's house. It felt like Paul was there too. We were looking in all the corners but there was no black box and no egg. I continued to hear the goblin trying to escape from Paul. Suddenly an idea came to my mind.

"On the river Paul, the egg must be in a box on the river." Immediately Paul and I were flying along the river.

"Try to feel the energy that connects the egg with this goblin," Paul said. I was able to find the connection. And I tried to apply a kinetic energy to the egg. But it was as though I was a second late. Paul smashed the egg. With a terrible noise the goblin was exploding, transforming into a very dark and gross smoke and then disappeared.

The effort was quite huge for me. As a result I fell down on the floor.

"Good job Laura!" Paul said looking at me. "Thank you for your help."

*   *   *

The rain outside woke me up. It was quite late in the morning. I opened the window wide. The bedroom window looked into the yard. I was quite surprised that the garden looked so good. The flowers and the plants were growing up quite wild but in nice harmony. I remembered a calm dialog I overheard the night with the ghost of the house. The ghost of the man explained to me that he was enjoying working in the garden and the neighbors considered him to be crazy because he didn't use his yard for vegetables and he was using it for flowers. *But do you see Laura? Even if I am dead my flowers will live. And they always will.* The ghost was quite silent. He encouraged me to sleep. He told me that Paul asked him if another entity will come by if he will watch and wake up Paul and me in time.

It was a welcome sleep. And now this morning rain was a blessing. Paul made instant coffee with cold water. I found it very good, and we enjoyed almost 30 minutes of watching the rain.

"So . . . . did you see what a bitch . . ."

"Who? . . ." I asked. I did not understand the meaning of his word.

"Chlorinda of course. Remember in your life do not be predictable in front of your enemy. She knew my custom to come from time to time to this house and she sent the goblin here. She created the goblin before she left her house because she thought she would be dead and would need to get revenge . . . what a bitch. And at this exact moment I was ready to excuse all her mistakes forever . . . ."

The rain stopped outside. I could see that the flowers in this garden were able to survive by themselves. They had only the water from the rain to live off of, and no fertilizer. In the autumn they will die and their stems would become fertilizer for the plants for the next year. They were very beautiful, the flowers offer so much and they are asking for nothing.

"Do you like my garden?" Paul asked me. He was watching the rain with me, and admiring the flowers.

"Yes. The flowers are . . . remarkable."

"Thanks Laura," he said. "I like the flowers very much. It is said that my grandmother was a very strong witch. She developed very strong magic using flowers. Her defense was very strong as no one dared to attack her."

"She taught you magic?" I was curious and also I tried to be polite with him. But instead to be thankful he was addressing me with a disdainful look.

"She . . . Listen. Never believe a witch."

And he refused to speak with me for a couple of minutes. I felt like I made a mistake; felt like I was guilty, and all I did was to try to be polite. I noticed that sometimes we try to be polite and instead we get the opposite result. Instead of creating a comfort for the person, we end up upsetting them. But I am quite intrigued, this seems like it will be an interesting story.

"Would you like to tell me about this?" I dared to ask him.

He invited me to the garden. There was a small table and a nice bench. Using a cloth he cleaned the bench and the table with the rain water. We were sat on the bench. I felt the strong smell from the picotees. These picotees look very nice and their smell is so strong, unbelievable strong. He was collecting a bucket and he offered it to me. His gesture impressed me. This smell was so strong and so comforting. I closed my eyes and smelled the flowers and after that I could dream, dream, and dream. We spent a couple moments contemplating the delicate garden. It was a unique picture to see a garden after rain.

"Some flowers were already here in the garden. You already know that. He is a talkative ghost. I am sure he told you. But a couple of flowers like these picotees, I brought myself from the garden of my grandmother. "

"Do you keep that garden too?"

"No. I sold the house, the garden, and her magic stuff. All of it. I don't want any memories of that woman."

"But what was so wrong there? I hope you can share with me"

"Of course I can share with you Laura. In fact there is nothing much to share, or nothing very interesting. She was a strong witch. But she always refused to teach me magic."

He moved his eyes to a bush of dark lilies.

"Why?"

"Because she was not smart like Dracula or other people. She was a traditionalist. The tradition in Romania was to pass your knowledge to a daughter or niece. Her daughter totally hated magic. She has three nieces, and only one was potentially gifted with some abilities. She was quite poor. My grandmother observed that I was the gifted one and instead of teaching me . . . . she hated me."

I became emotional especially now that I knew his abilities. When somebody like he got upset, the results could be a disaster. I hoped he was not fighting with his grandmother.

"If you can imagine I was almost always sleeping in bed with her, we were walking in the night in the cemetery to see if someone was transformed into vampire and to stop him. We were always together and she was refusing to accept that I was the gifted one. Also, there was no love, except when she was caring for me, even though she did not even clean my clothes. She was almost always saying it is my mistake because I am not careful and I would get my clothes dirty."

"Oh . . . Paul. It sounds like a sad story."

"Yes. I started to observe her. I started to steal all the magical practices from her until she started to respect me."

He took a sip from the cold coffee.

"Once we were sleeping and I felt an attack. I woke her up. First she did not believe me. Afterwards she felt something. She brought me in the middle of our flower garden and started making concentrations as there was not enough time for the magical circle. I saw that in her magic she was using the flowers power. She used each piece of the volatile pollen of the flower which was floating in the air. It allowed her to create an impenetrable defense. She was so focused. She asked me to stay near her. I was thinking it was time to show her who I was. So I stepped from her making the same magic with the flower. Shortly afterwards the attack that came from another witch ceased.

She had a bad personality, and as a result she had lots of enemies. This time the attack was strong. I understood that I was able to wake her up and that was an advantage for her. Otherwise she would be destroyed."

"There was someone who was going to kill her?"

"Laura I told you the fate called Ursita, here in Romania cannot be changed. Maybe that someone was not able to kill her but chose to transform her into a vegetable. She was going to stay like this almost fifteen years until she finally died.

"She was quite tired after all this. I used the same magic against her. The smell of the flowers was concentrated around her and he was not able to breath. I let her be with this for a minute. I felt I was able to kill her. I felt so powerful like I was able to change the ursita. Finally, I decided to not to kill her. Even though she was mean to me, I decided the best punishment will be to sit with her and undo all that magic she has created."

"How did she react?"

"Well . . . the next day she tried to fight with me. It was custom for her to physically punish me, to privy me by liberty; sometimes for days. I was a strong boy and she an old woman. She tried to bat me with her rod. But I was able to defend myself and to disarm her. I told her never to physically fight with me, and if she tried again I will hurt her badly. Starting with that night, I decided that I could have my own room. She was quite scared that another witch will attack her again. Her powers started to decrease with her age. I told her it was not my problem if she was able only to create enemies and no friends."

"Do you now who was trying to attack her?"

"Of course I know. It was Chlorinda's mother. In fact Chlorinda was the one who was permanently attacking her as her mother died couple years after."

"But what was the reason?"

"They were both recalcitrant woman. Also they were complex witches."

"Did she try to attack you again?"

"Yes, but not physically. For me it was like training to increase my abilities. I was focusing on what she was doing. I tried to touch her mind to understand when she would be intensifying her energies to attack me. Three days after she came in the night, she came in with a some embers and magical herbs. That is strong magic, if you are close enough with another wizard you can make him to lose his magical abilities. Immediately when she entered into the room I broke her can even if it was a metal one. I was going to kill her. I was holding her for a couple minutes. I think a normal human being would have died as I applied this strong force to her throat. After that she pledged to me that she will never attack me. And she never did. She understood that I could kill her with my kinesthetic powers and it could look like an accident because she was very old."

"What happened after that with your grandmother?"

"She fell into decline under my eyes. Age, losing her magical power, nobody loving her . . . however she was living quite longer. I was still wondered about how much she was able to do all by herself. At the end we were friends. I was spending my vacation with her. She was encouraging me to ask her about magic. She was ready to pass me all her knowledge."

"And . . . you accepted?"

He was snorting.

"Accepted? Laura, there was nothing she was able to teach me. I was much stronger than her. And my best revenge was to create her the feeling that she will die and she has no one to pass her knowledge. For a Romanian, a witch that is worse than the death.

*   *   *

In the afternoon we went back to Bucharest. Vlad was waiting for me. We had a nice dinner at the restaurant by the park. We were happy to have a nice table near the lake. The evening was cool after the hot day. Halibarda joined us. She was unhappy because she was not able to follow the old woman. She gave her a ride to Giurgiu; this is a Romanian town port at Danube.

For now this woman is still a mystery to all of us. We decided to have some vodka shots. And Halibarda explained to me that it is custom to do this in the memory of the dead. And up to now we have 12 dead . . . .

Halibarda told me that in this situation it is not normal to toast the glasses. We shared an appetizer and after that we decided to have some roast with veggies. They chose a nice Romanian wine for the roast. After couple drinks we became relaxed and happy.

"Tomorrow I will leave Bucharest a friend of mine invited me in Alexandria," Paul said. "Laura you will stay with Halibarda and Vlad. Guys I think both of you know that Laura is going to be possessed. Hey," he asked, "can we have another bottle of wine?"

I was shocked about this *combination Laura is going to be possessed, can we have another bottle of wine?* Whatever is going to happen to me can be crucial and he is placing these things together with a bottle of wine.

"But . . . Paul, I was guessing you will help me out with this . . . . I might have serious problems . . . the process can be irreversible . . . ."

"Laura don't worry. I can help you," Halibarda said.

"Yes, we are the most competent and qualified people in the entire world to save you."

"But all of you know that we are dealing with a strong entity. I am in danger and I might need you Paul here."

"Vlad will stay permanently with you and he will monitor you. I will be in touch with Halibarda and if the situation requires I will be back here. But Halibarda is very good with this stuff. She is able to handle this situation."

It was silent around the table for couple of minutes. I am so scared.

"Laura," Halibarda said. Please calm down. In couple of days I will fix the problem."

I was very nervous, and I tried to calm myself. Vlad and Halibarda were watching me. Paul was somehow absent from the table. Like in a dream I heard his words *"and now after so long this old woman came . . ."*

*   *   *

The new arrangement was for me to sleep with Vlad and Halibarda will sleep in another bedroom. If there was some need Vlad had he would be able to call Halibarda in our bedroom. The night was already here, and I was afraid to sleep. I felt like I was so weak. I decided to try to sleep; I immediately closed my eyes and saw the terrible devil animal. Its enormous body, its red eyes . . . . Vlad was trying to come tight with his body but . . . . I was not able to focus on what he was doing. He decided to call Halibarda.

She came into the room. I explained to her that I was not able to close my eyes because I could see that animal, a devil. She calmed me down. It was taking a couple of minutes.

"Now close your eyes."

I did and she was right. The animal was gone, I was tired. But the animal was gone and I was much calmer now. I was able also to feel Vlad's touching and to enjoy it. I slept very well until morning. In the morning I tried to stay close to Vlad's body. I tried to touch his hand and I felt like he had very long hair. But . . . there was something wrong . . . my Vlad did not have long hair. He has a very short hair. I opened my eyes and indeed near me was guy with long hair sleeping. I closed my eyes and I opened them again. The guy with the long hair was still there in my bed. I tried to call Vlad's name

"Vlad, Vlad . . ."

"Yes Laura," the guy with long hair answered me and he was turning his face to me. I stared to scream. How come this strange guy is in my bed . . . . ? I felt someone shaking me.

"Laura, Laura, it is me Vlad. Laura calm down . . . ."

The shaking woke me up. I saw all was an illusion. Vlad was in my bed and everything was my imagination. In a house coat, Halibarda was running in our bedroom. Without asking anything she started to massage my temples and repeated her complicated spell.

The next day was quite normal and we spent the day walking in the park. We also had tea in the afternoon, and watched TV. Halibarda mentioned to me that she was sending out information to Paul about the event. She and Vlad encouraged me to try to fight with that man whoever he was.

After that, I slept I dreamt that I was in an old castle and I was quite shocked to recognize from the window of the castle, the place where we did the magical incantations. I decided I was inside of Dracula's castle, but the castle was not a human place. I saw blood around me, and a man with long hair was walking towards me. From the corner of his month blood was dripping.

"Welcome back," He said. I started to become agitated and near me in bed Vlad was waking me up.

"Hey Laura, wake up. It was all a dream. Please! Let it go . . ."

"But, it was so real . . . ."

"Try to focus when you feel something strange, these strange dreams will move your hands and it will wake you up. It is supposed to be easy for you."

I am so scared. The idea of going to sleep is scaring me now. All night I was fighting sleep and I had the image of the old castle and that man who wanted me there with him. I hated what he is doing, I could not be with him. I tried to fight by myself. I said the litany of the fear couple times:

I am in the evil valley. The danger surrounds me from front, behind, from laterals, from above and below. I am in the death's valley; but I will not fear by the evil.

In my dreams I tried to create an imaginary magical circle. It helped for a while. I was able to stay calm inside of the coldest of the caste and kept the evil man away from me. But it was like I was fighting with his negative energies. He became stronger and stronger . . . . . so strong I could not resist. I felt like I needed to go back to my bedroom near Vlad. He felt my movements and he woke me up.

Then next day I related in detail to Halibarda about all this.

"Halibarda, I am very concerned about Laura." Vlad said. "Did you report all this to Paul?"

"Yes, but . . . I do not think he read his emails, and he doesn't answer his phone. the entity is trying to posses you Laura. Tonight I will not sleep. I will be with you."

She said her spells over the entire day. When the night arrived she stayed in the living room and decided not to sleep. Immediately after I fell asleep I felt myself inside of the castle.

He appeared again with his mouth full with blood, as though he just ate his victim. I told him that he was an evil man but he looked like he was not listening to me. He was looking out from the window of the castle. I did the same and saw that he was looking at the place where we did the magical incantations. I saw Halibarda sitting alone and watching the castle.

He became nervous, and in a blink of an eye he was near Halibarda. I saw that he was trying to attack her but it was like she had a magical circle around her that he was not able to penetrate. He was trying again and again and again until he became exhausted. He fell down and Halibarda walked towards him. As she got closer to him he tried to retract himself. It was as though her approaching him burnt him. At a moment Halibarda was looking at me.

"Soon I would like you to be able to do the same."

*　　*　　*

Halibarda's report to Paul:

"The situation is critical. I can see that he is learning from us. He is learning and adapts quickly. We are dealing with a superior entity. We need to manipulate it with an immense caution. In the mean time I would like to save Laura. She is quite exhausted after all these attacks. At this time I request strong actions to surprise him. I have to go in with a heavy attack. I ask your permission to proceed."

*   *   *

I did not see Halibarda almost all day. I had a long walk in the park with Vlad. I was relaxed.

"It is clear that I am the reincarnation of Dracula's wife," I said to Vlad. "What is known about that woman?"

"Not too much . . . our history is focusing mostly on him and his brother. In some literature it said that he loved her very much. But I do not believe that. He was a crude man. I do not think love was occupying much place in his soul."

"I remember I saw a movie with Raluka about this. His wife committed suicide. She was a very sensitive woman. She was affected by his strong personality. She was very religious but the methods he used were not religious at all . . . . she had the sensation and she heard the voices of the people he killed . . ."

"Yes I saw that movie too. However, Paul observed there were a lot of discordances. For example they are using a name that is totally Italian. We do not have a name like that in Romania. But what is important is that, he was excommunicated from the Orthodox Church. His customs were very bloody, and there is a strong possibility that he was becoming a vampire. Do not worry . . . . Halibarda will help you."

Late in the evening we went back home. When I opened the door of the apartment I smelled something very strange. Halibarda was waiting for us in the living room. She was holding her goblet with both hands. She gave me the goblet and asked me to drink from it. I did as she said. The contents of the goblet tasted awful. Immediately I lost my consciousness and I fell to the floor.

*   *   *

I felt like I was back at the castle. I was looking for him and he was not there. I thought he is outside, and I spent a long time searching for him. I went to our magic place. He was not there either. I decided to start the concentrations for the magical circle. When I was all done I used the air elements to fly around. I was very focused on finding him. I had a feeling like I did not fear him. I flew quickly and was easily able to find him. He was silent this time, and sad.

"Welcome back!" he said again without looking at me.

"I am not here to judge your human life," I said. "But I am here to stop you in from evil things you are going to do. I want to stop you forever."

Finally he turned his face to me. I was wondering if he was able to change his face easily like he was able to change his body into an animal or a bird.

"Laura, please stay with me," he asked.

"The answer is no." I said in a deep voice. "You are giving me bad energy."

"Why have they manipulated you like this against me?" he asked, and I observed a kind of sadness in his voice.

"Nobody manipulated me. Maybe we had a relationship in another life but now, at this moment in time and space you are an evil entity and I am a witch. I am a strong one. So strong that I will destroy you."

"I have to warn you there will be a terrible fight, and there will be irreversible consequences for you."

"I have to warn you that, there will be a terrible fight and you will be destroyed." I said.

He was sitting on a big rock looking down at the river. I stood up looking down at him. It was an abyss down there. The small river was cutting its own valley in the rock of the mountain.

"This is the place where you committed suicide . . . ."

I controlled myself and decided not to let any human emotion effect me. I wanted to defeat him. Even if I feared him, the antidote of fear is desire. And I have a strong desire to defeat him.

"I do not care about the past. But in this life you tried to possess me, you tried to harm me, so I have to defend myself. Until the final fight stop harassing me or trying to possess me."

"They used you to bring me back . . . . You have to be with me, not with them . . . ."

"You stay away from me. Never come for me."

"Or what?"

"Or I will destroy you!"

"Are you so sure?"

I bent my body until my face came close to his face and I said in his native language:

"Da"

Chapter 18

Grow up flowers.
Grow up bigger and stronger.
Grow up and bloom,
And protect me against the dark magic
-Romanian spell

They were a poor family.

The husband worked for the wealthy families in the village to earn money. It was hard, back-breaking work for very little money. On 'lucky days' when he found some work he returned home extremely tired. The people who hired him for the work day ensured he worked to the point of exhaustion. She could hardly find a job even for a day or two. There was barely enough money to buy food for their family. They had two sons, aged three and five years. They were polite and clever kids. The husband worried about when the kids would go to school and where they would find money for books, clothes . . .

The kids were playing in the yard.

She dreamed of having a washing machine like some of their neighbors. She always washed the family's clothes by hand. Right now she was in the front yard washing the clothes. The two kids played near her. She warned them from time to time to stay close and not to leave the yard.

"But we like to play in the grass," complained the eldest son. She always tried to be good to her sons. Her mother had not been good to her . . . she swore that she would love her kids.

"Okay, you can play outside the gate. But stay close to the fence. Don't go far from it. The cattle from the village are out there and some of them might be aggressive." The boys were happy they could play in the grass.

Their house was at the very edge of the village. A road in front connected their village with the next one. Immediately adjacent to the village and their house was a large meadow. It was owned by the village, and used for the village's cattle. The meadow was large and the grass was lush and tall.

It was pleasurable to watch her sons playing and she found a few moments of happiness, temporarily easing her constant stress and anxiety. Across the street were other houses and the neighbors were not always nice, she barely spoke to them. She had only one friend: Maritza. She thought to herself that it was such a shame Maritza couldn't speak. She was happy living in the furthest house in the village. But sometimes she wished her house was the middle of the village and that they had good neighbors .... *oh ... no ... Maritza is happy here. If we lived in the middle of the village the people might not accept her because of what she is doing ...*

She emptied the dirty water from the laundry, refilled the large tub with hot water and added the next articles of dirty clothing. She pushed the clothes down into the washing tub with her hands to wet them. She had forgotten how hot the water was and she felt her hands burning. She tried to quickly wave her hands in the air to cool them off, then took some cold water from a nearby vessel and poured it into the washing tub while putting first one hand then the other under the stream of cool water. The cold sensation helped to soothe the earlier burn of the scalding water as she continued to wash clothes. She realized she had lost track of the playing children and decided it might be a good idea to go to the fence to see what they were doing. She walked softly so that they didn't hear her coming and she saw the kids were playing nicely together in the grass. She watched them and thought they were such good sons. They didn't seem to have a care in the world and had not yet realized they were a poor family. She told them again to remain near the fence and they agreed they wouldn't stray far away.

It was late in the morning during the hottest days of summer; she decided she would let the kids play for an hour then ask the kids to stay in the shade or their exposed skin would become sunburned. She returned to washing tub and began to work harder so as to finish as early as possible.

She was thinking it was a blessing they had a second hand television. Last night they watched an American movie about a poor family, like their family. But the family in the movie had money to buy pizza for their children. She smiled to herself and thought *I can't even imagine having money to buy pizza for my kids. I think the poor families in America are still rich compared to us.*

As she concentrated on washing the clothes she forgot about the time. Her husband arrived home. He said he had an argument with the man who hired him for work that day. "There was too much work for only one day . . . I asked him to pay me for half the day and I quit. I had a difficult time getting him to pay me. He refused to pay me for half the day but I decided to take what he gave me. Some of the men in our village are far too demanding. I will never work for that family again . . ."

"I agree with you. Let me stop washing clothes and prepare lunch. I made a wonderful chicken soup for lunch."

"That is good Maria, I always wonder how you manage make such delicious soup from just a few ingredients."

She smiled and said, "That is my secret."

"Where are the children?"

"Oh, they asked permission to play over there in the grass."

"But . . . Maria . . . I heard yesterday they are going to put a bull in with the cows, and it is very dangerous . . ."

"Oh . . ." the woman was pierced by an apprehensive thought. "I just checked them. They were right near the fence . . . I asked them to stay close to the gate. I had better go back!"

"I'll come with you," the man said. They ran outside the yard and . . . the kids were nowhere to be seen.

"Where are they? Maria . . . woman . . . where are they?"

The woman looked desperate but tried to hide her anxiety. "They were over there. They were in the meadow right by the fence."

"If they start to run the bull will become agitated and . . ."

Maria started shaking from fear. "Go now and call Maritza. I will walk calmly over there to save them. I will tell them not to run, and to wait for me there. Now go, and call Maritza. She will be able to help us."

Immediately the man ran from the yard, desperate to call their neighbor Maritza.

Fighting her fear, but moving slowly and gently, Maria started to walk in the kids' direction. She decided not to call them and thought when she reached them she would warn them to be silent, stay calm and not to move quickly. This would give them the opportunity to escape alive and not catch the attention of the fearsome bull.

She walked quietly for half the distance. Until now everything had been okay. A large group of cattle could be seen in the distance. Some were peacefully grazing while others were wandering slowly looking for fresh grass to eat.

The kids continued to play, oblivious to the great distance they had moved away from the fence and the danger they were in. Eventually the younger son saw his mother approaching and became excited and with childish glee he began laughing and running toward her.

"No!!! Stay there. Don't run. A bull is in with the cows!!! If you run you will attract his attention!!" she tried to shout the words to the children but they were excited and both enjoying running back to their mum.

Suddenly a big animal moved away from the herd, initially walking in their direction but abruptly it began to run with awe inspiring speed. It was a fierce bull; it saw a potential target and decided instantly to attack.

Now the kids saw the terrifying animal too, and became frightened. They ran faster toward their mother, thinking she would save them. The woman was desperate now. She was convinced she and her sons were living the last moments of their lives. They could hear its hooves hammering on the earth and snorts of rage as the heavy animal thundered toward them.

Near the fence the man had returned with their neighbor as his wife asked him. He was certain he would witness the death of his family. The animal was so furious no force in the world seemed able to stop it.

The old woman walked into the meadow leaning on her rod to stand upright. After a few steps she stopped, pounded her rod three times into the soil and let it fall over. She held her head with both hands as she began to focus all her energy in the direction of the bull.

The bull continued to stampede in the kids' direction. The kids had only a short distance before they reached their mother. She decided to run to them and they would die together . . .

The husband also started to run toward them.

The old woman continued to hold her head with her hands. Her intense concentration made her fall to her knees. Almost at the same instant as she fell, the animal seemed to trying to come to a sudden stop but its momentum was so great it wasn't able to and it crashed to the earth with a thunderous noise.

The kids were now near their mother. She took her youngest son in her arms and the other one by his hand. She started to run frantically in the direction of her husband. The animal tried to stand up but remained in its place as if being kept down by a stronger force. It appeared it had broken its leg during the fall.

The family sprinted back to the old woman. A thin thread of blood was trickling from her nose and she lay on the ground, disturbingly still.

Putting her son down the woman started to shake the old woman's body. "Maritza, Maritza . . . wake up. Wake up!"

The old woman slowly opened her eyes and looked at the children. She wiped the blood from her face and held her arms out widely to the two boys. They rushed in for a hug. Maria wrapped her arms around them together with the old woman. Maria's husband watched his precious family saved by . . . a miracle.

*   *   *

Halibarda had hidden herself in the yard. It was guarded by a big dog; instantly the dog felt her presence. Barking ferociously, the dog came in her direction intending to bite her.

"Who's there?" Maria's husband shouted into the night. It was too expensive to have an electric light in the yard even though it would be useful in times such as this.

Halibarda sent out a hypnotic wave and the dog calmed down immediately. Maria's husband relaxed as he knew if someone entered the yard uninvited the dog would not allow him in; the person would receive a vicious bite.

Sitting in a bush near the house, Halibarda played with the family's dog.

"Who was there?" Maria asked.

"No one . . ."

"But . . . I know our dog," Maria said. "When he is barking like that someone is around the house. He will not let any one inside. No one, except Maritza."

"Yes, at first I did not trust what you said about her; but now after that happening . . . I am convinced."

"You'd better be."

Suddenly, Halibarda entered the room and they looked fearfully at her. She had been able to pass by their dog and come into the house and they felt no presence whatsoever.

"What are you doing here? Who are you?" the man asked her.

Halibarda smiled widely at them and showed them four 500 Euro bills.

"What . . . what are those . . . ?" Maria asked.

"They are Euros Maria. This could be a nice amount of money for your family; it is yours now," saying that, Halibarda put the bills in Maria's hand.

"They are just paper Maria, counterfeit money," her husband said. "Who are you?"

Halibarda continued to smile at him.

"I wish to be a fay, but I am too black," she laughed. Her laugh somehow made the atmosphere seem darker.

"Maria, give her back the money. It is just paper, not real money."

"But you know Maria it might be real money; and I assure you it is. With it you can make good purchases for your family."

"You lie!" the man accused Halibarda.

"Look at me . . . these rings are gold. This massive bracelet is gold. This chain is gold. I am a rich woman. Why would I lie to a poor man like you?"

The man was about to say something, but he stopped.

"What do I have to do for this money?" Maria asked. Her voice was full of emotion. She was sure it was real money and not fake. They had never had so much money. She would be able to buy nice clothes for her kids, some good food; they could make some repairs to the house.

"Nothing bad or illegal. I am looking for some information."

"What kind of information?" the man asked.

"You cannot give me this information," Halibarda said calmly, "but Maria can. Maria, three friends of mine are waiting me at the nearest pub. They would like to ask you some questions. After you answer we can give you more money. What I just gave you is only half."

Maria stared at the black woman in front of her. "Will you or your friends hurt me?"

"No, we will give you money. It will be an enormous help to your family."

"Maria . . ." her husband tried to break in.

But Maria raised her arm to stop him. She continued to look at Halibarda for a few moments then turned to her husband. "My duty is to do all I can for my family. Until now I had no way to contribute financially. But this is a good opportunity. She knows we are poor and she can steal nothing from us. It won't hurt if I answer some questions. Take this money. I know she does not lie. I will come back to you soon with the other half of the money. You always told me if you had a motorized saw you could do your work more easily. Tomorrow we will have money for it and for things to buy for our sons."

Maria turned to Halibarda, "Let's go."

*   *   *

I did not like this bar very much. It was quite . . . offensive and the people appeared to be quite rude as well. They were all drunk; they were all watching us. We decided to have beers directly from the bottles as there was no guarantee the glasses were clean enough.

Finally Halibarda arrived with Maria, the woman who could give us some information about the old and mysterious woman.

Paul was quite anxious to hear information about her. It was obvious that she was a powerful witch and perhaps we could learn things from her . . . if she would share them with us.

Halibarda entered the pub dramatically followed by a poor looking woman. The woman was quite embarrassed to enter the pub.

Some drunken guys were watching Halibarda. She grinned at them. One of them stepped in front of her. Instantly, Vlad translated his words for me, "Hi beautiful woman, where are you from?" he asked Halibarda.

"I think you are beautiful too," Halibarda said back sassily, "but unfortunately we are busy. No time to speak with you." She came to our table with the poor woman.

"Hello guys, this is Maria." After that she spoke privately to the woman. She pronounced our names and I understood she had introduced us to Maria.

"Please Maria, take a seat," Paul said in Romanian to the woman as Vlad translated for me. "Would you like something to drink?"

"Nu," the woman answered. Vlad did not have to translate easy words like this any more as I already knew it means no.

"Two glasses with coke and two vodka," Halibarda commanded the bartender.

Maria watched me, fascinated. She was not a part of the small dialogues around her. As she became more comfortable she started to talk to me. Vlad translated for me, "I know you . . . you are Laura, the famous singer. My sons enjoy your songs very much."

I smiled at her. I was amazed. One of my videos was playing in the room and no one had recognized me except this poor woman . . . she inspired within me great empathy.

"Maria, Laura is our friend," Paul started. "If you thought we intended to steal something from or hurt you it is not true. We want only to ask you some questions and I would like you to focus on the answers."

"I will do my best," Maria said, taking a sip from her coke.

"Three days ago you and your sons and were in grave danger. Who saved you?"

"Maritza, our neighbor."

"Maria, I don't understand," Paul said. "How could an old woman prevent a fearsome bull from attacking you?"

"In our village is known that some people don't fear any animal and have powers to control the animals. I think she is the strongest in our area and is known as the village witch . . . if you believe such things . . ." Maria's eyes were downcast as if she was little embarrassed for saying stupid things.

"We kind of . . . believe," Paul said. "Do you fear Maritza?"

"Not at all. She is a good woman."

"But you said she is a witch."

"Yes, but she is a good witch."

"How do you know that?"

"She never hurts anyone, she always helps people. The people give her money. Sometimes she gives me some of her money . . ." Maria looked down.

"What kind of magic is she performing, do you know?" Paul asked.

The discussion continued like that for more than an hour. Afterward Halibarda gave Maria the rest of the Euros she had promised. I noticed she was doing it surreptitiously so the people in the bar did not see her doing it.

"Maria," I called her and gave her a gold ring with the same furtive gestures. She looked into my eyes and I heard Vlad translating her words.

"Thank you Laura, but instead of giving me this ring it would be nice if you could meet my sons. They enjoy your music so much . . ."

"I will come to meet them tomorrow," I said and I saw Maria's eyes were filled with tears.

*   *   *

Halibarda knocked on the window. As if pushed by a kinesthetic power, the door opened and Halibarda entered the small house. There were only two rooms; one was a kitchen area and the other a combined living room and bedroom.

Maritza, the old mysterious woman, invited Halibarda to take a seat with a gesture. With a flourish, Halibarda sat. Her eyes wandered around the room. The room showed its occupant was far from wealthy. Many items such as the blanket and some pictures were hand made and there was no clutter at all, no unnecessary items only a bed, table, two chairs and a terracotta furnace. Halibarda was sure in the winter it provided enjoyable warmth in the room.

"You know Maritza . . . you remember me from my grandmother." Since she moved to a condo in Bucharest to live closer to Paul, Halibarda missed the comforting warmth exuded by a terracotta furnace. The condos in Bucharest had central heating and her only option was to keep it that way. She had many fond childhood memories of eating hot delicious soup beside a terracotta furnace during the long cold days of winter.

The old woman watched Halibarda with interest.

"You can use sign language to speak to me," Halibarda said. "I am familiar with this type of communication. A relative of mine was deaf and I communicated with her using signs."

The old woman asked her with signs if her mother was dead. Halibarda nodded *yes* with her head rather than signing. For a moment the room was silent. The two women watched each other.

"You were close to your mother?" the old woman asked.

"Yes," Halibarda answered, "she taught me magic. She was a powerful witch."

"I heard about her," Maritza said with signs.

"If you like I can help you clean up a little here, rearrange your things. I can see you are an old woman and need some help. I would be happy to help you."

Maritza made signs and Halibarda understood that the house was small and even if she was old she could manage. Maritza invited her into the nearest room which served as a kitchen and magic room. There she had a propane stove. She showed Halibarda the soup ready on the top of the stove.

"Oh, bean soup," Halibarda said, "my favorite. I would like to have some. Thank you for inviting me. Can I serve you some? Let's have some soup together."

Humming a happy song, Halibarda ladled soup into two bowls. She also saw in the corner a big pickle jar. Maritza looked in the same direction and Halibarda understood that she wanted some pickles too so she took some out. Shortly, the small room was full of the pleasant aromas of the bean soup and dill pickles. Halibarda then arranged some chilled peppers on a small plate. It was obvious the vegetables were from Maritza's garden.

"We have soup, we have pickles," Halibarda said and she looked philosophically at Maritza. "We need some *tzuica* to truly be festive." Saying that, Halibarda took a bottle of tzuica from her purse. With grand gestures, she poured two shots. Since the room was dim Halibarda lit two big candles.

"That's better. We may be witches but we still enjoy a romantic atmosphere."

Maritza laughed and picked up her tzuica shot. The two women lifted their shot glasses, looked into each other's eyes and toasted each other "Noroc". The tzuica was extremely potent and both of them shook their heads vigorously and laughed.

Without wasting another moment Halibarda filled the two shot glasses with tzuica again and they drank. Then they turned to the food. First they ate a little chilled pepper then with great appetite began to eat the bean soup. Each one tried a pickle as well.

The old woman looked at her tzuica shot glass and Halibarda smiled. "You are welcome to have as much as you want. I brought the entire bottle for you." They had a few more shots during lunch.

After lunch, they went into the garden with their tzuica glasses. Maritza had a wild pear tree and they sat on a blanket in the shade of the tree for awhile.

"It is growing late," Halibarda said. "I'd better leave. It was nice seeing you again Maritza."

Maritza made signs that she would like Halibarda to remain there over night.

"Well . . . I don't want to disturb you."

Maritza signed that she was lonely and would like having Halibarda over the night. With a big smile Halibarda accepted.

Maritza's bed was fairly large and there was enough room for both of them. They had planned to sleep late the next morning since they stayed up late into the night discussing magic and telling funny stories. But a knocking on the window woke them up. A woman about 35 years old was standing outside holding a baby girl. Maritza invited her inside.

The woman was speaking very worriedly about her daughter. She said she had consulted a few doctors who prescribed various medicines but none of them had any effect. The baby girl was always complaining about a bad headache. The woman believed that Maritza could help her.

"I can help you," Halibarda said. "I am a witch also."

The woman regarded the black lady in front of her who claimed to be a witch and said, "Thanks. But Maritza is from our village and we trust her." Halibarda said nothing, merely moving her chair closer to the window and gazing outside with interest.

Maritza held the baby girl in her arms and appeared to enjoy holding the baby. At first the baby was frightened by being held by someone other her mother, but after awhile she began to watch the old woman's face in fascination. She tried to touch the old woman's face with her tiny hands and soon she fell asleep.

"That is amazing," the baby's mother said, "she has not slept this soundly for many days."

Maritza showed her three fingers and made signs.

"I am sorry Maritza . . . but I don't understand . . ." the woman said, embarrassed.

"She is telling you that you have to visit her three more times if you want your daughter to be completely cured."

"When?" The woman asked, looking toward Maritza but she could not understand Maritza's signs and looked back at Halibarda for assistance.

"She said at your convenience."

"Okay, I will come again tomorrow morning," the woman said. "Is that good for you Maritza?"

Maritza made a yes sign.

"Okay, now . . . here," the woman said as she gave Maritza some paper bills. Maritza divided the bills and tried to return the other half to the woman.

"No, no . . . ," the woman protested, "Maritza, money is not a concern for me but the health of my baby girl is. Please accept the money for this and I will give you the same amount at each visit. Please help me cure my daughter."

Maritza made emphatic *yes* signs with her head.

After the woman left, Halibarda prepared some coffee and they moved their chairs outside. "Maritza, we are concerned about you," Halibarda said.

Maritza look like she did not understand Halibarda.

"Please don't attend the next incantation. We don't want you to die. It will be much more complicated than hypnotizing a baby or an animal," Halibarda paused, taking a large sip from her coffee.

The old woman made some signs.

"Yes, we are in grave danger too. But Paul and I can handle this. We don't require help from anyone any more."

Maritza made a sign that she didn't care about putting herself at risk.

"Maritza you are a powerful witch but you are old and your body is weak. The considerable amount of concentration we need to perform the next incantation may cause your . . . death. Please stay home." Halibarda turned her face toward Maritza and Maritza saw tears in Halibarda's eyes.

*   *   *

Maritza had not seen someone crying from concern for her for a very long time. Halibarda's tears impressed her but she had work to do, plans to finalize. She couldn't sleep so she went to the cemetery to visit her sister's grave, as she often did. Even though they only had a few years together they loved each other dearly. She knelt down and touched the stone cross atop her sister's grave.

As yesterday Halibarda had tears in her eyes for Maritza, now she had tears in her eyes for her sister. They had been together almost five years, but were then separated and spent more than 60 years apart. She loved so dearly that child who was her sister and she knew her sister loved her very much too.

She always felt so peaceful . . . alone in the cemetery at night. The cool silence, the darkness wrapped around her like a blanket and . . . the spirits of the dead people helped to calm her.

She tried to relax tonight but she felt there was something strange around. She was able to feel ghosts and vampires but this was a different feeling. There was . . . a man watching her. He was rather tall and she was not able to see his face but she could see his eyes . . . his red eyes. Hastily she invoked the four elements around her as she set a magical circle into place. The man with the red eyes merely watched her without attacking. She wondered about that and became a little scared, which was odd because she hadn't felt frightened for a very long time. Suddenly she heard a voice behind her. There were two? Why had she not felt the second presence?

"Good evening, Maritza." She immediately recognized Paul's voice. The red eyed man continued to watch them with interest.

Paul came near Maritza and reached out to touch the stone cross, then looked at the man with red eyes.

"Leave us!" Paul commanded in an icy voice. "You have no business with us until the next incantation."

Obediently following Paul's command, the red eyed man immediately transformed into a dark smoke which instantly vanished.

Maritza wondered why she had not felt Paul's presence. This was one of her strongest abilities: sensing people approaching her, even from long distances.

"If we don't take firm control of him we may experience immense troubles."

The woman showed her approval by making a gesture.

"I would like to thank you for everything you have done, Maritza. We are concerned about you. I sent Halibarda to you to let you know you don't need to come to the next incantation. He will fight with us like a rabid beast. We have already had several deaths. We care deeply for you. Please don't come."

The woman watched him, probing deeply and did not answer *yes* or *no*. She refused to make any sign. Paul was an excellent mind reader but he was not able to read anything in this woman's mind. *Maybe she can read my mind . . .* this thought arose in Paul's mind. *I hope not . . . no, I would have felt it. She was surprised when I came; she cannot feel me.* Paul became confident again about what he was doing.

He respected this woman's courage. His grandmother had told him a lot about her. She had always known Maritza was alive but was never able to determine her location. All she could feel was that her sister was deeply unhappy. His grandmother had always admired her. *As my grandmother said, she is a remarkable woman. I was always tempted to find her, to meet her.*

Now he was standing with her beside his grandmother's grave, gazing at her headstone together.

That bitch . . . Paul felt like spitting on her tombstone. He made an enormous effort to calm himself in front of the old woman. *She is a respectable woman and her life story is so . . . unbelievable.*

The old woman made gestures to tell him that his grandmother loved him. Paul tried hard to control his facial muscles and attempted to smile nicely at her.

Continuing to use sign language the old woman said, "She is dead now. But I am here to watch you. To protect you. I am your aunt and I love you."

"Oh . . . no. Listen to me, you shouldn't do anything. The forces we are creating now are very, very dangerous. I don't want you to die for me."

"If the situation is so dangerous you might die too," she said with signs, "and my duty is to protect you."

*   *   *

I had noticed Paul arrived home late the previous night. We were all staying at his house in the village. Normally we slept late into the morning but today we found it impossible to sleep because there was a terrible thunderstorm. For hours, the lightning flashes and deafening booms continued. I had never heard anything like it in all my life. It was as if a fierce war was being fought in the sky and the entire house was vibrating because of the thunderclaps.

I found Halibarda in the kitchen making coffee. I took a banana.

"Good morning Halibarda, what a storm . . ."

"Good morning dear Laura," Halibarda answered. I saw that she was tired too. "The rain is welcome but this noise . . . I really wanted to sleep awhile longer."

"Too many sorcerers in Romania," Vlad said, trying to make a joke. "Maybe the sky doesn't support you."

"I don't think that is funny, Vlad," Paul said as he descended the stairs.

"Why not? I know you like dark humor. Maybe it is your poor influence on me," Vlad kept on with his attempt at comedy.

Paul looked at Halibarda as if he was speaking only to her, "What do you think about these crazy kids? We are their teachers, we teach them and they try to replace us."

Halibarda and I were wondering about these stupid jokes.

Vlad was laughing uproariously. Paul smiled at him.

"I like your optimism Vlad."

"I am always an optimistic person in the morning. You just never notice because you are busy with . . . your dark magic."

"Lovely. I will do my best to change it," and Paul smiled again at Vlad.

We each poured ourselves a cup of coffee and sat together at the round table. I noticed the intricate pattern and beauty of the table cloth. Paul saw me looking at it and said, "It was hand made by Drina."

"Really?" I asked and could not resist touching it as I said again in my mind . . . *my dear Drina* . . .

"Maybe I will give it to you. You were a good friend to Drina, even better than I was."

"But Drina gave it to you."

"I can make one similar to this," Halibarda said, "and I will make one for you Laura."

"Oh . . . Halibarda, that is an enormous amount of work. I can't believe it is hand made . . . it will take you a long time to make it . . . I don't dare ask you for this . . ." Halibarda silenced me, making a dramatic gesture as if to say "it is my pleasure."

"Paul, did you meet Maritza last night?" Vlad inquired.

"Yes."

"You never told us the whole story."

"Last night I went to the cemetery and met her there. She was at my grandmother's grave who is in fact her sister. My grandmother always told me about her sister. They were together almost six years until the young one, Maritza, was stolen by gypsies."

"What?" I was absolutely stunned.

"Yes, it was long time ago . . . I remember during my childhood my grandmother tried to scare me by saying *the gypsies will steal you*. A few days after her sister was stolen my grandmother felt a terrible pain, which she understood was a telepathic pain. The gypsies' cat had eaten a piece of her little sister's tongue."

"Oh . . . how terrible," I said.

"Actually my grandmother was happy when she felt that . . ."

"How could you be happy at all about that?" I was shocked by the horrible story.

"Well . . . she realized the gypsies had decided to keep her alive and not kill her. After a few years she became aware that a witch from the gypsies' tribe felt the little girl had remarkable talent as a witch and since she was not blessed with any children she decided to keep the girl for her own. The gypsy witch cut out a part of Maritza's tongue after giving an anesthetic. They were afraid she would escape and tell her story. Because they wanted to keep her, the surgery was done cleanly and she was well taken care of afterwards. Because of the care the wound was not mortal."

Like me, Vlad was impressed by the story. Halibarda listened to Paul with great interest. She was so focused she did not even blink her eyes.

"From time to time she had telepathic communications with her sister. The gypsies were afraid she would escape and talk to other Romanians and that would get them into trouble because they had stolen her. But that was the only bad thing they did to the girl. When that happened the old gypsy witch gave her strong painkillers made from plants and stopped the bleeding. She worked hard to care for the girl so she would be healed quickly. Soon, the little girl began to be happy with them. They treated her well and she quickly learned how to prepare medicine from plants. It became clear she possessed strong magical powers, exactly as the old gypsy witch had said. She lived with them for a long time, until the communists forced the gypsies to remain in a village and not travel from place to place as they had before."

Paul paused like he was not prepared to relate to us the entire story in great detail. "To make a long story short, she never met her sister again while she was alive. But when my grandmother died, Maritza felt a terrible pain. She became aware her sister had died and was actually able to locate the place. Last night I realized she has a great need to protect me. I asked her not to come to the next incantation. She is so old . . . it is very possible she could die."

"We can visit her at her house for a few days to make sure she is okay," Vlad proposed.

"She has incredible kinesthetic powers," Paul said looking at Vlad. "I don't want to have an intervention like this. I hope she understood the danger I was trying to convey, and my request." It appeared Paul was going to relate more but we were interrupted by the doorbell ringing. Paul sent Vlad to answer.

"Two . . . two priests are at the door Paul," Vlad said, his voice trembling.

Paul appeared surprised. "What the heck are priests doing at my house . . ."

"We need to talk to you."

We all turned, surprised. The two priests had entered the living room uninvited. Maybe Vlad had left the door open and they took advantage of it. One was old and one young, both of them looked fairly ordinary.

"You are a smart man, Paul," the old priest said in English.

"A small discussion won't hurt," the young one said. "Please allow us to have a short conversation."

Before Paul could answer, Halibarda said, "Yes, please come in. It is always an honor for us to have priests in the house."

Paul made a face as if he was not totally in agreement with Halibarda.

"Would you like some coffee?" Halibarda asked, watching the two priests and smiling politely at them.

"No, thank you . . . ma'am. Some herbal tea would be nice though," the young one said. Their English had a strong Romanian accent but was perfectly understandable.

"Oh . . . my name is Halibarda, that is Laura and over there is Vlad. I think you already know Paul."

"Yes. I have been watching him since he was a child," the old priest said.

"You were watching me?" Paul repeated his words, and then added, "If I remember correctly, you are Father Anton . . ."

"Yes," the old priest agreed.

"I am Father Ion, or because we are speaking English here," and the young priest fixed me in his gaze, "you may call me Father John."

Halibarda returned to the room with two mugs of tea, sugar, milk and lemon wedges. The priests each added lemon and sugar to their tea.

"Father Anton, I noticed you have been watching me since I was a child, but I thought I knew the reason why. I thought you were a pedophile," Paul said, smiling cynically at the old priest.

"Paul, you are being extremely impolite," Halibarda said sharply.

"Did I ever hurt you?" the old priest asked in a courteous voice.

"No . . . you were kind to me . . . even though I did not come to church very often."

"Why did you not attend church?" the young priest asked.

"Because the communists insisted we not to go to church—this was part of a communist education."

"Paul . . ." the old priest said with immense kindness in his voice, "you were a rebel. I asked myself why. I watched you because your grandmother was a witch and I realized she would teach you her ways. I always wondered why you refused to go into the church, because she always came to our services. She told me you always refused to come with her."

"I already told you, because of the communists. You know very well I was not the only one, I was in the majority. They kept lists of students who attended church events and the next day the teachers would criticize them in front of the other students."

"All right, to summarize," the young priest said, "you were raised by a witch and you did not attend church because of the communist regime."

Paul moved his gaze to the young priest. "What exactly are you accusing me of?"

"There may be a conclusion to be made. You might be a powerful wizard because you don't like religion very much . . . and you are a dark wizard. It is important for you to understand when you doing good or evil," the young priest said calmly as he took a long sip from his tea.

"And . . . do you think you are on the positive side? Listen to me, even if it is that way, the positive can generate the negative. Unfortunately, you cannot punish me," Paul said beginning to lose control.

"It is not our intention to punish you," the young one said. "We are here to ask you something."

"Please Father," Halibarda interjected.

"*Near Dracula's castle,* over the last several months people have found dead animals. Then the bodies of two dead tourists were also discovered. It appeared someone had sucked their blood," the old priest said.

"It might be wild animals," Vlad said to the priests.

"It might be," the young one said. "But we think there may be another possibility."

"Which is?" Paul asked.

"By performing magic you awakened a vampire."

Paul began laughing. Vlad looked frightened. Halibarda gazed at the floor. I looked at Paul.

"Fathers," Paul said, "realistic people will believe the first version."

"But the phenomena of dead animals drained of blood began after your group incantation. It is a huge coincidence." The young priest said, fixing Paul with his hazel eyes.

Paul maintained his version. "That is a depressing conclusion. You are implying even if there is a wild animal, the church will accuse us because of this coincidence. You always opposed my club. Why don't you ask the village to come here and burn down my house? It is an opportune time for you to accuse me; it is what you know best," Paul was almost screaming at the two priests.

"This is like an earthquake reaching nine on the Richter scale. It will kill all of us. Please do something for our protection," the old priest added in calm voice, "we are here to ask for your help."

"And if I refuse you? What you will do? Will you go to the media? Will you send the police to arrest me? You have no power. I, we," and Paul gestured toward our group, "we will be able to defend you, but . . ." Paul raised a finger, "if you start a war with me, you will indeed have a war."

"Paul," the old priest said, "remember when you were a child, even if you did not come to church, whenever I met you around the village I stopped you and I spoke to you kindly. I always understood your angst."

Paul gazed bitterly at the two priests.

"I realized you were an extremely clever child," the priest continued. "I always appreciated you. We are concerned about these phenomena. If you did something, if you started something, I am sure you can stop it. We need the truth. Don't be afraid of the truth. It is wrong for people to be murdered," he looked toward Paul, who appeared angry.

"Thank you for the tea Halibarda," said the young priest. Smiling at me he handed me a small vial, "this is holy water Laura, you might need it." They each made eye contact with all of us in turn and then left the room.

Halibarda hurried to the window to ensure the priests were gone. Returning to the room she said, "They are right."

"Oh . . . shut up Halibarda!" Paul screamed as he hurled a coffee mug at the wall. The mug broke into many shards and made a dent in the wall.

I saw that Vlad was terrified; strangely, I felt no fear.

Ignoring Paul, Halibarda said, "They are right. In one way or another we must finish this."

"We will finish it in a couple of days," I said. They all looked at me, surprised.

"Laura . . . after my conversation with her, even the old woman . . . my aunt, will not come . . ." Paul said quietly.

318

"I thought she would come," I said.

"Laura, we are dealing here with a malevolent entity. This is not your business. You had better return to Canada."

"I will decide for myself when I will go back. We are a team. We started this together. Let's finish it together."

"Yes," Halibarda said, "we started it together, but Paul and I can finish it. You might be a powerful witch, but we have not had enough time for adequate training. You don't know even a fraction of our knowledge. You are not confident yet in your powers. We are concerned that the entity could . . . kill you."

"Laura, you don't have to show us how brave you are. Please go back to Canada. The entity is watching us. Last night he was in the cemetery studying me and my aunt."

"Really?" Halibarda said, surprised. "We are unsure of the extent of his powers and he is already learning about us."

"Please Laura," Paul said quietly and pleasantly as he came very close to my face. His face was very relaxed.

"Paul. He tried to possess me. This is personal now. I will be there with you and . . ." I was not able to finish my words as his expression became very harsh.

"Okay, let's try this a different way. Your body will be thrown out into the abyss. No one will find it there. You deserve that at the very least."

"I am warning you to watch your words," I said angrily as I stood in front of Paul.

He sneered at me.

"You are a disposable piece in this puzzle now. We needed you before to wake up the entity because of your connection to Dracula and no other magic was working. At that time you were indispensable, I waited for years to make you comfortable and coerce you into doing what we wanted."

Paul's face was livid as I stood face to face with him but I was just as angry. I said, "Vlad, take my luggage to the car and wait for me there. Can you also please make a reservation for a hotel in Bucharest."

"Yes, Laura," Vlad answered meekly.

"I will pay him now. He will do what I ask him to do and I will do what I want. "

"This is a terrible mistake Laura," Halibarda said, "please don't go there. We must fight the entity. We might not be able to protect you. We don't want you to die."

Paul broke in, "I will not give the least amount of help to you . . . do you know why? In a previous life you were a Hungarian spy. He loved you and you betrayed him. He had no support from his brother or from you. When the Turkish army attacked and he needed support, you committed suicide and made him weak. You are an inferior soul. I hate you. You deserve to die again in that abyss in mountain. I will not lift a finger to help you."

His words took me by surprise. I was speechless. I decided to remain silent. I turned my back to Paul and walked to the door. There, I turned to Paul and said quietly but forcefully, "If I have the opportunity to help you Paul . . . I will move more than one finger."

I was ready to leave, but I saw Vlad coming back.

"The keys are in the car Laura. I am sorry but I cannot go with you."

"Why? The money I gave you is not enough?"

"Laura," Vlad said, "there are things more important than money and sex."

"Such as?"

"Such as fidelity," he said and turned to Paul. "Paul, what do you want me do?"

As this occurred, Paul watched me calmly. Without saying anything he made a sign with his hand to Vlad as if to tell him he could go with me.

I felt like slapping Vlad . . . but I still decided to take him.

* * *

Back in the room, Paul and Halibarda remained silent for awhile.

"She will die if she comes," Halibarda said, "I hope Vlad will convince her not to come."

When Paul did not reply, she continued.

"I am concerned about the old woman, Maritza, your aunt . . . she is too old for a fight like this. Her heart will not support the . . ."

"I am concerned about you Halibarda," Paul said.

"Don't be ridiculous Paul. Surely you don't imagine you can defeat the entity by yourself."

"I can," Paul accentuated the words.

"Well, I will be there, just in case."

"You will not. That is an order."

"You know what? I am tired of so many orders," Halibarda said. "I live in this house too and you are obviously in a miserable mood. I will see you in three days at our place *near Dracula's castle* when the new moon occurs."

"As I said to Laura, I will not lift a finger for you. I have more important things to do than to protect you. Battling the entity will require all my concentration."

"As Laura said to you, I will do my best to protect you," Halibarda replied.

"If you are able," Paul said contemptuously. "Am I supposed to be flattered being protected by three witches? Not one of you is good enough to fight the entity. If you try, you will die. Starting now each one is by himself."

Saying nothing in reply, Halibarda left the house, slamming the door behind her.

Paul was now alone in the house. He looked for long moments at the door banged shut by Halibarda and said to himself,

"Here I am."

Chapter 19

Try to control your human emotions when you deal with difficult situations. You cannot totally eliminate some of them, like fear for example, but you can reduce it to a manageable level.
-Paul—Teaching the club

Vlad is giving me a ride. This afternoon we stared our trip from Bucharest to that place *near Dracula's castle.*

Tonight will be the last confrontation.

All the days and nights I was practicing all the magical stuff my teachers taught me. I observed that now I have kinesthetic powers too. But not as strong as Drina. I can move small objects but the level of concentration required is quite high and I feel me very tired afterwards. Halibarda and Paul were right to be afraid for the life of the old woman; these concentrations require a high level of energies. For sure her heart is quite week . . . And she could die.

Also I discovered my hypnotic powers. In a night I went with Vlad on a dark street and couple street dogs attacked us. Here in Bucharest Vlad told me these feral dogs are a real problem and they always were. He remembers cases when the people died being bit by stray dogs. That night we went on the street and some very ugly dogs attacked us. We were going to have problems but, I felt Chlorinda near me encouraging me to use my hypnotic powers against them. I saw that is not very hard for me. And I remember her words "*dear girl, hypnotizing animals is a easy trick. I would like you to learn this quickly and to try the next step . . . hypnotizing human beings.*"

I spent a couple days living with Vlad at a quite nice and modern hotel called the Intercontinental Hotel. I was happy having a room with window looking out to Magheru Boulevard. The view is unbelievable nice. I saw that lots of buildings here are like Paris's architecture. I remember that Paul mentioned once that Bucharest was called the little Paris of Europe.

However, now I checked out of the hotel. I loaded my luggage in Vlad's car. My appointment with Vlad was to leave me near the mountain where the path is to the place *near Dracula's castle*. I will find the path by myself, and I will get on the plateau of the mountain. Maybe Paul will be surprised. I have not called him in many days. Vlad told me that they tried to reach him but he did not answer. Once I will be there, on the top of the mountain I will spread my tools and I will wait for the entity to show up. There will be a fight. There will be a terrible fight. I took into consideration the possibility that I might die. For this reason Vlad will have a small video of me. I say in it that I decided to spend one night on the mountain by myself. It is not the first time I have done this, I do this in Canada too. With this video he will be protected; so he cannot be accused of my death because of all the people that saw us together. Still I believe my chances of success are 50%. I do not why . . . but I feel strong tonight. Maybe I have 60% to succeed. *For God, I am not ready at all to die tonight. I will succeed.*

We are so close. In couple of minutes Vlad will stop the car and I will go by myself to the mountain. I can see that Vlad has a lot of feelings for me. I would like to succeed and to meet him again tomorrow morning. I will want to stay connected with him. This guy has so much to offer.

Finally he stopped the car. In silence I took my heavy back bag with tools. I arranged on my belt the big knives made for me by the gypsy. I kissed my Vlad for *good luck and goodbye*, and I arranged the heavy bag on my back. I took the rod with easy steps I started to hike the small path up the mountain. It is a wonderful evening. So wonderful compared with the terrible things which are going to happen. The path is so tiny. The mountain wood is so quiet. I always have been attracted to dark places, by humid places.

According to Paul it is not something which comes from the previous life. Or however, not from that previous life. There I was a very religious woman. So religious as I was not able to accept the things which my husband did. He was using fear to fight with his enemy. He was using capital punishment to punish his people even for minor mistakes, because there was huge disorder. As result he got order. He was remarkable fighting with the Turkish enemy. But he had no real support. I, his wife, was not even in the church in the name of which he was fighting. I was a catholic and he was orthodox. Even today these churches are not unified even if they believe in Jesus Christ together.

I stopped my hiking for a couple moments. I drink some water from my bottle. What kind of things in my mind . . . who can swear that I was his wife? All my teachers mentioned to me that the magic is not an exact art. There might be some . . . evidence that I was, in one of my previous lives, his wife but . . . what is sure is that, nothing is sure.

I started to ascend the top of the mountain again using the small and narrow path. The lighten the mood I started singing a silly children's song:

"Don't be sad, don't be blue.
Frankenstein is ugly too."

I was thinking again about the church. They missed the point that he is fighting to defend Christianity and they excommunicated him instead of protecting him, as he was fighting to stop the Islam from spreading. He felt because he was excommunicated by his church and his soul cannot go to heaven . . . or even to hell. But also he was a superior soul, and a strong spirit after . . . maybe he became a vampire . . . As Paul said there were signs at his birth that he might become a vampire. That was a possible *way to eternity*. I know people who are very interested by this possibility. It is like it doesn't matter if you will hurt another person as long as you gain the eternity.

I do not agree with this; in fact it matters. It matters very much!

I am quite close. The plateau is near. It was quite hard to head here as tonight the sky is dark without the moon.

I was thinking about his recent actions. He tried to possess me. Halibarda was able to stop him. I am asking myself if it is possible he was successful? Now I was going to be a fool, and I have to punish him for this.

Finally I was here on the plateau!

It is dark but I can see that I am not alone on the plateau. There is the old woman, now we know her name Maritza, and we know her life story. She is Paul's aunt and she had a terrible life. Also Halibarda is here. Their locations are distant from each other. I remember very well that Paul warned us that we are alone in our actions tonight.

Halibarda is doing something around a small fire. She is boiling something in a small and strange shape vessel on the top of the fire. What she is doing there is so gross. The terrible and bad small is covering the entire mountain . . . .

*   *   *

Fingerless gloves, tarot cards, candles, my two big knives, two curved Chinese swords, a magical wand, two pistols and an automatic gun, silver bullets, light generating bullets, a venomous viper, a goblet, holy water, magical stones, army boots and army uniform, three amulets, a magical rod, four wind resistant lighters, four kerosene troches, two flashlights, a magical bell used against bad spirits, one double ax, and a couple other small things considered by me potentially useful in the next confrontation.

I bought the guns from the Romanian black market, Vlad helped me. They cost me lots of money but this is not a problem at all. As the entity is manifested itself in a physical form from time to time they will be quite useful. Somehow, I miss my cabin rifle. I still feel the blood of the wolves I shouted when they attacked me. I arranged the guns to be handy inside the magical circle.

Vlad was proving a real talent when he was sharpening the knives and swords for me. They are now razor sharp. I had a hard time when I practiced with them. Because they are so sharp, a second of lost focus and I can get badly hurt. I was always sleeping with them near me. It was like I charged them with my energy, they will help me. I am now their master. If in front of me will be a vampire or any evil, my knives and swords will cut them. No one can face them. When I have them I am powerful, I am invincible. With the fingerless gloves I can easily hold them and I have a really good grip on their handle.

Carefully I rearranged all the stuff around me as all of them to be handy for me according to the situation. I screwed the kerosene torches into the soil by their stake, each one in the front of the cardinal candle. Between them I closed the arches of the circle with white candles. Near each one I placed a lighter. My intention was to use only one but if the situation will require I decided that it would be handy having a lighter near each one.

I kept closest to me the magical rod and the magical wand. All the other stuff close enough to reach and very handily arranged.

With everything arranged, I closed my eyes and I repeated in my mind the position of each item.

Soon I have to start the concentrations for raising the magical circle which will be my shield against the entity. I know he is stronger and he can penetrate it. But it will be a first barrier in his way. After that I will have other surprises for him.

Before starting my concentrations, I looked around me at the two women.

Halibarda was totally focusing to the nepenthe which she was boiling and which was spreading such a bad smell. I wonder how she can stay there. I am at an acceptable distance and the bad smell is still almost is making me vomit. She has a small metal vessel in the top of a small fire. She is continuing to say in a low voice a spell. She is burning in the fire an extremity of her rod too. Now it looks like a sharp flaming lance. She will use for sure it against the entity it is now a good weapon against any physical manifestation. With her fingers she is creating strange energies around the vessel. From time to time she is mixing the vessel contents with her magical wand. With her rod she started to scratch a circle around her, because she used the flaming end of the rod it left embers and made a circle of fire. It looks to easily increase in intensity. It is magic . . . . We are sorceresses. Now I can do this too.

Maritza, the old woman was doing nothing.

She was just staying alone looking hypnotized into her basket. I do not know what she has in her basket. It is covered and I cannot see inside. I was thinking she have some sharp tools too. However this woman was for me a big surprise. Her old body hides such powerful energies. Her rod was near her. It was exactly the rod I dreamt she had with her when she helped me to pass by the devil entity.

I was thinking it would be better if we will try to create a group circle of power as we tried last time . . . But Paul told us *each one by himself.* I already started to think it is a terrible mistake. But there looks be no choice.

I saw the flames of Halibarda's magical circle rising up, and that made me to think that it is the time for me to start my concentrations too.

*   *   *

From the direction of the path Paul appeared.

He was covered with a back gown. I saw that he is caring in his hand only the straight Chinese sword which I admired in his house. I always enjoyed watching the dragon sculptures of the sword holder.

With decided steps he was walking directly towards the old woman as he if did not see me or Halibarda.

He knelt in front of the old woman. Then he assumed a lotus type position. I remember from my karate training calling it "seize". He lay down his sword, and looked to the old woman.

"Hey! I am here," he said to the old woman.

As if waking from a dream she looked to his face, it was like she was under a hypnosis. She smiled to him. And she touched his face with her hand. Like he was enjoying her touch Paul stayed like this a couple moments. After that he took her hand and kissed it.

"I am so thankful you are here. Thank you for trying to protect me", Paul said.

He was looking directly into the eyes of the old woman, his eyes were working to wake her up from the hypnosis.

"You are a brave woman Maritza. Very few people have your courage. I wish you to be strong enough to be alive after this night."

He kissed the old woman's hand again and he stood up.

He walked to Halibarda. I wondered how he could get so close with that bad smell. He was walking around flames of the magical circle.

And I heard him say to Halibarda:

"You crazy woman, my instructions were for you to stay home tonight."

Halibarda was only focusing on the nepenthe she was boiling and murmuring her strange incantation making strange signs by her fingers around the vessel with the nepenthe.

"This is the first time when you disobeyed my order. Unfortunately it will be the last time too."

Saying that he turned his back to Halibarda.

But at the same time I heard Halibarda saying: "I am afraid it is the first time since I met you when you are wrong."

Paul was ignoring her words and he started to come to me.

Soon he will be near me. With quick movements I lighted one by one the torches and cardinal candles saying the rituals and making the correct concentrations for each element water, fire, earth and air. Also I lit the white candles. When I was done Paul was near my magical circle.

He was looking inside at my tools. After that he was gazing at me.

"Laura, it was a terrible mistake for you to come here. I am afraid you will pay with your life."

With very confident movements I played with my huge sharp knifes.

"The words I was expecting from you Paul were *lets do this together Laura.*"

He bitterly smiled

"I am afraid here is not a together. The only advice I can give you is to protect your own life as much as you can . . ."

"Down Paul!!!" I screamed.

Quickly I took my gun. At the edge of the plateau a man appeared. It was very dark. But I was able distinguish that he is a tall, slim man and he has long hair. His eyes are red. They are red as the eyes of the devil women who protect my magical circle.

*   *   *

With a terrible speed Paul was distancing himself from me.

He was taking out the sword and with an immense speed he stared to swing it around. It was like he was creating a sphere around him. Suddenly he stopped but it was like the sword was still in the air and the protective sphere remained. I was sure if the entity will try to pass into that sphere he will be cut.

The strange man was waking with small steps and with a very lazy walking he was coming to me.

Closer and closer.

I focused to the items of the forth elements and held the gun in his direction.

"Do not dare to advance one step!" I warned him.

As if listening my warning, he stopped.

"Laura, you can stay with me. The others will die tonight. Please accept my offer."

"You bastard, you failed to possess me. Now is the time to fear me." I screamed to him. "I am a witch, I will defeat you, I will destroy you!"

"That gun will not help you, old tricks silver bullets and light generating bullets. Now . . . thanks to your incantations I am more than a vampire. I cannot be hurt by such things."

"If so, then touch them!" I screamed to him and I stared shooting in his direction. He quickly moved to Paul. Paul was making a quick sign with his hands. The sphere created by swords disappeared. The vampire jumped against Paul. But with great speed Paul caught one of his hands. The vampire caught Paul's other hand. Now they tried to punch each other while fixated on each one's eyes.

The vampire tried strongly to push Paul. Paul was letting him come close with his neck, after that with a terrible speed Paul bit his neck. The bite was so deep as we heard a terrible scream around Dracula's castle. Paul retracted displaying in his mouth meat from the vampire's neck. With disgust Paul spit it out and he said to the vampire.

"I can bite too."

Screaming terribly the vampire disappeared into the woods. He was running like a horrifying animal and he was running terrible distance as if the running effort will calm his pain.

"He will be back soon." Paul said to us.

Suddenly he appeared near the old woman. Quickly Maritza took her rod. Rhythmically she was pounding the soil. It was like the rhythm of her batting was so terrible to the vampire, hearing it he covered his ears.

In a blink of the eye he was near Halibarda. Halibarda was making some signs with her hands like directing the nepenthe steam to vampire direction. He started coughing. I saw him come close to me. He laid down and vomited close to me.

"Laura, help me . . . help me . . . Laura."

I was looking directly in his red eyes, so red and opposite them . . . so green. I felt like I was Chlorinda herself, I was sending to him the strongest hypnotic wave I can produce. He was continuing to look at me and he said: "I never believed that you would betray me."

Without letting him too much time to recover I sent him a strong kinetic power charge saying in my mind "this is for Drina". Firstly he was trying to resist to my kinetic power. But my wave had blown him to the trees far by us. He was screaming terribly. It was like all the universe was filled by his screaming.

I thought he was quite far away from us. But I almost had no have time to realize when he appeared near Halibarda.

"Come here you bastard. If you need my blood you have to work for it." Like gaining some courage the vampire started to approach Halibarda. He was still expecting surprises from her side and I observed that he was prudent. When he was close enough with her Halibarda threw out in his direction the contents of the vessel which she had boiled. Her intention was to throw it on the face of the vampire. But he was able to move. The liquid still touched his arm. A big slice of the flesh from the arm felt down. He was screaming again in an agonizing pain. Profiting from this moment Halibarda tossed the vessel she used for boiling the liquid onto his head. Screaming he was running close to me. I took immediately the two curved swords. I used all my skills to attack him. With extremely quickly moves he was able to avoid my deadly slices. I was continuing to fight like this with him a couple of very exhausted moments. Paul was coming close to me. With his sword he tried to apply also to the vampire deadly stabs. Applying a sweep with his leg Paul was able to knock the vampire down; after that without losing time he tried to screw his sword into the vampire's heart. But the vampire was digging under ground and he avoided Paul's sword. Paul's sword remained strongly screwed into the soil. Regretting the lost chance, Paul spat on the ground.

From underground the vampire was showed up extremely close with Maritza. As if knowing that he will appear near, Maritza was ready. She took from her basket a rope. On the wires of the rope she had knitted green garlic. With an unbelievable dexterity she was able to put the rope around the vampire's head. The vampire started to run throwing down the old woman. She was strongly keeping with her hands to other extremity of the rope. Immediately Halibarda was near the old woman trying to help her. Halibarda took the rope and the old woman removed her hands. The effort was too much for her old heart. She lay down, unable to breath.

Halibarda proved that she was able to keep the vampire in place, like a dog on a leash. Paul took the rope together with Halibarda. I took my two knifes and I ran around the vampire I tried to cut his legs. He was running in circle unable to get away, stopped by the rope held by Paul and Halibarda. After couple moments he looked like he was not able to breath and he fell down. It this moment I stabbed my knifes into his legs. I forgot for moment I did not have a sword with me to implant it in his heart and to kill him.

Paul screamed to us.

"All of you focus your powers against him and say this spell: *you never dare to show up in vampire form*"

"*You never dare to show up in vampire form*," I heard Halibarda voice.

Instantly I focused my powers on the vampire saying "*you never dare to show up in vampire form.*"

Immediately the vampire became a very dark smoke which instantly disappeared.

"Quickly," Paul said, "all three of us back to back. Lets focus to the magical circle."

I raised the magical circle as I know. I did the incantations extremely quickly and focusing. We felt a terrible storm. All of us started to increase the energy of wind elements to stop the opposing storm. I saw couple trees bowed down by the storm. In the same time I felt something attacking from the earth elements. It was like a sand trying to absorb us. I immediately was focusing to throw down solid rocks and earth to stabilize the disequilibria induced by the flowing sand. As if showing all the powers he has, the entity threw against us a big fire. It felt like being in a volcano and its lava and fire was going to burn my skin and all my body and burn me alive with my two friends. I focused to water. As I was in a big agony I called a strong rain as I saw here in Romania occurring; after that I commanded the water to increase, to increase more and more.

"*I command you to stop!*" Paul said to the entity.

"*I command you to stop!*" I heard Halibarda's voice.

I was trying with my mind to find where she is and to focus my remaining energy at her.

"*I command you to stop!*" I said too.

The storm, the sand and the fire were stopped.

"Show us in the form of smoke." Paul commanded.

"Show us in the form of smoke ." I commanded focusing all my energy against the entity.

In front of us a dark smoke was appearing.

Paul immediately took his overcoat and he covered the smoke. He used the overcoat like a bag holding inside it that kind of smoke. Initially the smoke or the manifestation of the entity was agitated inside of the bag. Paul made the entity to become silent.

In short time the entity becomes silent.

With one hand kept tight on the overcoat bag Paul sat down on the land. We did the same.

Strongly focusing on the bag Paul said:

"Now I can kill you. But I command you to stay here when I open the bag"

Saying this easily he opened the bag. The dark smoke shaped like a dark ball of smoke. The ball stayed in the air in front of us. Paul, Halibarda and I were keeping our hands with the fingers largely open around the dark sphere smoke. Each one of us was applying a kinesthetic power around the entity manifested now as a ball of dark smoke.

"Now we can destroy you totally." Paul said.

"No . . . no . . . ."

With a voice I heard in my mind the entity tried to protest.

"In my existence I did good things too . . ."

I felt Paul pushing his kinesthetic power. Halibarda and I did the same.

"The old witch is almost dead. If you free me I can send her soul back to her body."

I felt Paul hesitating.

"Staring with now you are at our command," like touching our minds we said together.

"Go and send the old woman's soul back to the body. After that come back here." Paul said.

We released the kinesthetic powers against the dark smoke sphere.

We went around the old woman's body. For now she looked totally dead. It was just a couple seconds and we felt Maritza breathing again, and the smoke ball come back to its initial place.

"Back, as you commanded," I heard the entity saying in my mind.

"Good!" Paul said, but one more thing and we applied again our magical power against the smoke sphere.

"I bind you against completing bad actions against us or any normal human being." Paul said these words and we repeated them again and again.

I was almost lost my consciousness by focusing my magical energy around the entity. When I woke up the entity was not there.

With crazy eyes Halibarda was looking deep in the night,

"My magic will keep the entity away."

Paul . . . where is Paul? For a moment I was scared , but I saw him near the old woman's body.

"Both of you here!"

Like waking from her dream Halibarda immediately walked up and we went near Paul. The old woman was hardly breathing.

"It is not enough her soul is with her body. We have to help her to survive," Paul said and he moved his eyes from the old woman to me and Halibarda. I saw tears in his eyes.

"I do no want her to die. Not now. It is not time yet for her," Paul was gazing us. "Please help me. I need your help."

We stood around the body of the old woman.

"I will help her hearth, you Laura try to rescue her breath and you Halibarda help her blood to run in her body."

I put my fingers up to the body of the old woman. As I started my concentration hardly I saw what Paul or Halibarda did, but I guessed that they did the same. I felt like in her breath was no movement. I tried to make a gentle massage by kinesthesia hoping breath will start again. I started with small and easy movements. Always I tried to feel the reactions of her old body. It was like the old woman was refusing to live, like refusing to fight for herself. Or too tired to fight for herself. But I insisted again and again. I think that focusing was taking a while when I stopped the sun was rising and the old woman was breathing almost normally.

The black smoke sphere was gone.

Chapter 20

From my left and from my right,
from front and from behind and from all over;
I am creating a plasma sphere.
It will protect me against the
dangers that arrive from everywhere.
It will also help me to attack.
-Fragment from Paul's book 'The Spatial Magic'

Vlad was driving the car in silence.

"In 20 minutes we will be at the airport," he announced.

"Thanks," I said, "I do not understand why Paul didn't come"

"He is busy. He invited Maritza to live in his village house as nobody lives there when he is in Canada," Halibarda answered.

"And Maritza accepted?"

"At first no. But I insisted together with Paul and she finally accepted. There she will have all that she needs,." Halibarda said watching the window.

"I am always having a good time when I go this way to airport, and specially in the morning. I like to watch people how they are preparing to start a new day. Always I am having surprises. If I am trying to foresee the future I can see that the life is always offering me surprises."

"May I come to visit you in Calgary?" Vlad asked.

"No" firmly Halibarda answered. "You have no business there. And I find it to be even impolite to ask about."

"I can invite you soon to Calgary my dear," I said to Vlad.

Halibarda remained silent watching the window. The way was really beautiful. Some people were chatting at the edge of the road.

Halibarda was gazing so deeply. With her powers it was like she was inside their small groups and listening to them.

"If Laura will invite you I hope you will have a very nice trip in Canada."

Vlad was looking to me with love, "Thank you Laura, I am so curious to discover Canada."

"How about you Halibarda? Do you want to visit me?"

"Yes, I can come there in any time. As I said I have already been there. Paul's house in Calgary is so nice, and I like Alberta. Maybe I will come with him. He and I are so curious to meet that Indian wizard. The one who made the dream catchers."

"It would be my pleasure to introducing you guys to him. Actually I think he is going to be my first best friend," I commented.

"I think you would have enough inspiration to create a new album now too," Halibarda suggested me.

"Yes, for sure. But . . . this time my music will be little bit weird, like . . . a magic." I smiled to Halibarda. "Actually I am thinking of writing a book also."

Shortly after we reached the airport. Vlad took my luggage and we walked inside of the elegant airport. I observe Halibarda's face very sad.

"So sorry dear, I really like you, and . . . . I will miss you . . . . ." she said.

"I will miss you too Halibarda, but I will call you almost daily."

She took my hands and she was looking in my eyes,

"Dear, you will be busy. I know that. It is impossible to not be inspirited after such a vacation. When you go home you have to release a your new album. And it will be great, and . . . . you will be busy. You do not have to call me daily. But I will appreciate if you would call me . . . sometimes."

I felt tears flooding my eyes "I will call you Halibarda. I promise you."

I took my boarding card. Vlad cuddled me and he gave me a passionate kiss. I saw some curious Romanian watching us. I didn't pay any attention to them. His kiss was so hot, but was like I was not able to focus on this kissing. My main focus was to Halibarda. She was so sad.

And I am sad too. But I will call her, as soon as I can. Maybe I will invite both of them. I really enjoy their company. I felt like to have a final look at Halibarda "My dear, please do not be sad. We will always be in touch."

She was hugging me and tried to laugh, " OK dear, you have to go. Checking in will take you some time and I'd like for you to be in time to catch the airplane."

In the waiting room two handsome guys came to me, "I am sorry to disturbing you. Are you Laura? The famous Canadian singer?"

"No," I said, "I look a lot like her. Lots of people make the same mistake. I am not Laura. Please leave me alone."

*   *   *

The flight to Amsterdam was quiet. The food they serve us was wonderful. I was wondering why in Canada the airlines do not offer us food included in the airplane ticket. It is sometimes uncomfortable to travel long distances without food.

I waited a couple of hours in Amsterdam for my connection to Calgary.

In the airplane I felt tired. Almost like the little girl who fell to sleep almost immediately when the airplane is in the air.

I think I fell asleep. A silent sleep at the beginning. And I was like seeing lots of colors, until one become dominate. A dominant color. Green. A green, so green like . . . Chlorinda eyes. And yes . . . . The green start melting forming Chlorinda eyes. Like in a movies where the image is zooming I saw her face. She was looking at me. She was studying me. Her study was so deep, so focused. Near her was Drina. So silent around. In this silence distinctly I heard some voices:

"Her eyes are so green."

"Like a poison."

"She is a poison."

"She is Chlorinda."

Even if I know it is a dream, I tried to perform a good analysis of the situation. As Raluka taught me. I know Chlorinda died. Drina died too, but . . . maybe they try to communicate to me something beyond the death . . . .

"What do you think about all this dear girl?" Chlorinda asked.

"Well we fought with . . . something. With a entity, and we won."

"Oh . . . poor girl. What a child you are. I told you always in the life search for easy and understandable explanations," Chlorinda said.

"That was the vampire spirit. You were in grave danger!" Drina added.

"But I am alive!"

"Why you did take that grave danger? It was possible to die," my lovely Drina asked.

"Because I am a strong witch. Now I am stronger even then you both were in your life time." I become arrogant as Paul taught me in my dialog with Chlorinda.

"And . . . did you win? Or he has won?"

Chlorinda is so unpredictable, even now when she is dead.

"I misunderstand your question, can you explain more Chlorinda?"

"That vampire spirit is something very dangerous and . . . very powerful. It is a difficult entity to be handled because he is destructive and chaotic, however he is like a wild animal. Now he is scared. Now he will obey the commands to the one who was controlling him. That one is his master now. And I am afraid the master is not you. His master is Paul as the other two women Maritza and Halibarda obeyed his orders too. The vampire spirit will obey Paul's commands and that simply because you are not there. For this stupid reason if you think you win you are wrong, very wrong."

"My dear Laura, I am afraid you lost in the last second," Drina added.

Suddenly I become very agitated.

"Fuck . . ." I jumped up . . ."Fuck, I have to go back to Romania."

"Too late," answered a guy next to me. "We are flying now straight to Calgary. You cannot turn the airplane back," sarcastically "even if you had magical powers."

epilogue

The smell of the dark coffee flooded the air like a dark magic.
   She was a tiny lady. Maybe too slim and maybe too short. But her face expresses a strange intelligence and power.
   He looked to the woods by the glass wall.
   "So quiet. So silent here."
   She comes close to him "yes, indeed. I cannot stop myself contemplating the wood."
   "Oh dear . . . should I remind you that I found it foolish for a lady to live alone in the heart off the woods . . ."
   She did not answer. She spent a couple of minutes in silence contemplating the wood.
   "I lived here for more than five years," finally she stared to talk. "I have electric power by wind and sun, water from my well, the sewage in a septic hole. I do not pollute nature and I live comfortably here. This kind of living is very much in accordance with my philosophy."
   "And . . . you have lot of movement sensors and video cameras. You know when somebody is close to your house and you can take defensive action if required. Of course I am referring mainly to the wild animals, as this place is far away from human beings."
   "I deactivated all of them."
   Paul's face showed big surprise.
   " Ww . . . what? . . . Why?"
   "Do you see there?" she showed him a little deer. He, looked with interest at the cute little animal.
   "Yes, why is she here?"

"A couple wolves killed and ate her mother. And this happened near my house. I saw it all in a spy camera. I was not quick enough to act. I feel so embarrassed about it. That should not happen. Not near my house. Now I feel guilty for this little animal. She will live near my house and she gets my protection."

"But with the wild animals this is happening frequently. These wolves can come in any time to attack her again, to attack you too; and especially in the winter. They are very hungry in the winter. Not enough food for them. And you know this. Please do not be ignorant to the danger."

"I have enough telepathic, hypnotic, kinesthetic powers to keep them away. Now even if I sleep I can feel any animal, human, ghost, spirit who tries to come even close with my house. Believe me this is the best defense we have, not these sensors, video cameras and alarms."

She paused looking with love at the small animal.

"I can feel the positive energy which comes from the brain of this little animal. It is so lovely to focus on it. It is like when outside is a tiny wind and you are listening a Chinese bell. It is a pleasure to focus on it."

With a quick move he turned to her.

"But even if you are so isolated here you like to control. You like to control all."

Enigmatic she smiled, "what do you think about this?"

He as making a long and repetitive sign of *yes* with this head.

"Your predictions were unbelievably accurate. I know you like to hear that, I am impressed. You were right. Laura is not his wife or a lover of that entity. But the entity has a strong affinity to Laura."

She smiled largely.

"Let's finish our coffee," she said.

It was that kind of coffee with a lot of grinds maybe it was unhealthy, but very tasty. They continued with small sips to drink their coffee.

"Yes, I wonder how your predictions can be so accurate. If you were choosing to share them with . . . Chlorinda she would be the winner now."

She was laughing, a deep belly laugh, " I told you. I chose you to be my partner in this . . . business."

"Thank you. I hope I did not disappoint you."

339

She touched his hand. She took his empty glass of coffee and she turned his coffee cup, and they remained silent for a couple moments. Both of them were focusing to the turned coffee cup.

There, in the remaining grinds from coffee she will read the future. The future, with an unbelievable accuracy. Paul said in his mind. After that he said with a normal voice, "sometimes I am afraid of your predictions."

She turns her eyes to him.

"But my predictions were helpful for you."

"They helped me, I was able to extrapolate scenarios and consequences. We are able to fight with these . . . . unknown forces."

"Yes . . . ."

There was a long silence moment. With delicate gestures she took the coffee cup.

Paul comes close to her, paying maximum attention.

Smiling she said:

"Let's see what's next . . ."